FADING
Paramour

A. L. Rose

Order this book online at www.trafford.com
or email orders@trafford.com

Most Trafford titles are also available at major online book retailers.

Printed in the United States of America.

ISBN: 978-1-4907-0508-8 (sc)
ISBN: 978-1-4907-0507-1 (e)

Trafford rev. 08/27/2013

 www.trafford.com

North America & international
toll-free: 1 888 232 4444 (USA & Canada)
fax: 812 355 4082

To Diana,
Who reads with pen in hand.

Chapter 1

David Smith woke up to the beeping sound of a bed side heart monitor. He turned his head to look at it. It was a white computer looking thing held up by a silver stand. He looked down at his arm where he saw an intervenes needle stuck into it. He was suddenly aware of the pain and the scratchy feeling in his throat. He tried to swallow but his mouth was dry and the action was excruciating. He tried to sit up but his body wouldn't let him. He tried to call out but the sound he heard was a husky growl. He could feel a hand touch his arm. He turned to look at it. The hand was that of a well-manicured man's hand. He looked up the black leather arm to the man's face. It was Mr. Alan Black, David's history teacher and supposed second best friend next to Amanda Moore. David could smell Alan's intoxicating cologne and the memory of what had happened rushed into his mind. He remembered seeing Alan for the first time on his first day of grade 11 just months ago. He remembered the intense arousal that this man had given him from just the sight of him. He remembered his mother setting up a 'Big Brother' type arrangement for David and Alan. He recalled the time they had spent together and the building of feelings David had for him. He remembered Gabe, Amanda's older brother, and the affair he had with him before he died at the hands of David's uncle Carl. He remembered how Alan had been there for him through the difficult time. He remembered the building relationship with Amanda through all of this and her confession of love as well as her brothers. He remembered playing his guitar with Alan. It had been the first time he had played since his father died. He remembered the long stares they shared and the quiet conversations with Alan's best friend Carman about them. He remembered falling in love with Alan and was thinking about telling him until he saw this man he loved kissing his mother. He remembered the pain and the anger that had pushed its way into his body. He remembered driving Gabe's big black Hearse to Look Out Point where Gabe's tree and hangman's noose had been. He remembered climbing onto the top of the car and putting the rope around his neck. He could remember seeing Alan run over the hill as he stepped from the car. The rest of the memory was a blur of fear and pain. He pulled his arm out from under Alan's hand and closed his eyes. Tears burned under his lids and Alan got up and left the room. He returned with David's mother Nancy and his girlfriend Amanda.

"David, can you hear me?" Nancy asked. David nodded but left his eyes closed.

"Can you say anything?" Amanda asked sitting down on the bed next to him. David opened his eyes and looked at her. She looked tired and scared. David shook his head and shut his eyes again. He could hear Alan clear his throat.

"I think the damage to his throat won't let him speak." He said in his quiet, seductive voice. David moaned and Amanda rubbed his arm.

"It's ok David. The Doctor said you'll be ok. You just need to stay here until they are finished treating your throat." Amanda said.

"You'll have to pass a psychological exam too, son." Nancy said. David sighed and shook his head. His suicide attempt was ridiculous and now, he would have to atone to it. Amanda rubbed his arm again and sniffed. She stood up and David could hear her leave the room. "This is so hard for her." David heard his mother whisper to Alan.

"She has been through a lot this year." Alan whispered back. David could hear them kiss before Nancy left to talk to Amanda. David growled and winced at the pain it caused his throat. He could hear Alan sit down in the chair next to him. "David, I'm so sorry." Alan whispered and David growled again. Alan let out a sigh and David could hear him sit back in his chair. "We should have told you." Alan said referring to his secret attachment with Nancy. David rolled his eyes under his lids but said nothing. "Your mother thought it would be best not to tell you until you were comfortable with the idea of her with someone else." Alan explained. David opened his eyes and glowered at Alan. He winced at the anger in David's face. "Please understand that we were just trying to ease you into the idea." Alan whispered. David shook his head and closed his eyes. He could hear Alan shift in his chair and touch his arm. David pulled away again and they both remained silent.

Why are you here? Can't you just fuck off already? I don't want you here. David thought to himself as the scent of Alan's cologne slowly found its way into David's nose and throat. He groaned and opened his eyes. Alan held his head in his hands and was looking down at the floor. His shag-like, blonde hair slightly curled around his fingers.

A nurse walked into the room and came to David's side. Both men turned to look at her.

"Shall we try sitting you up?" She asked in a slight Irish sounding accent. David nodded and the nurse tilted up the bed. David gave her a half smiled before she left. He kept his eyes on the door so he didn't have to look at Alan.

"Can I get you anything?" Alan asked quietly. David sighed and lifted his middle finger at Alan without looking at him. Alan sighed and stood up. "Do you want water?" He tried. David turned his head and looked at him. He tried to speak but even just moving the air in his throat hurt, so he gave up and turned away. Alan left the room and David sighed out a quiet, painful growl.

I hope he stays gone this time. What makes him think I want him in here? God! How could he be with my mom and not tell me? How could he be with my mom? How did I miss that? I guess what they say is right, love IS blind. Love, the first time in my life I actually really was in love and he's fucking my mom. God I hate him! David thought. He could feel tears burn his eyes again and he closed them.

As soon as I'm out of here I am taking Amanda and we're leaving. We could go to Montana where her grandmother is or Texas where her cousin is. Anywhere is better than here. We can just leave and never look back. I would never have to see my mom or Alan ever again. David thought to himself. He could hear someone come into the room. He opened his eyes to see Alan carrying a cup of ice chips. He set the ice chips on the little bed table and wheeled in in front of David. David rolled his eyes and then shut them. He could hear Alan sit back down in the chair.

"The doctor says you damaged your larynx. He said you'll talk again but it will take a while. They are keeping you in here to monitor you and watch for any infection." Alan said quietly from beside David's bed. David shook his head but never opened his eyes. "I brought you something." Alan said and set something on the bed table. David opened his eyes and looked at the table. There was a small pad of paper and a pen. David raised an eyebrow and looked at Alan. "You can write if you can't talk." He offered. David looked back at the paper and slowly moved his arm up to the table. His body was hard to move and David frowned. He managed to get the pen in his hand and write,

GO AWAY!

Alan sighed and shook his head.

"I can't. I promised your mom and Amanda I would stay with you." Alan said. David sighed and underlined the two words again. Alan sat back in his chair and shook his head. David set the pen down and dropped his arm. He closed his eyes and growled again. "I would do whatever you asked, but I can't leave." Alan said quietly. David raised his eyebrows and looked back at the table. He got the pen back into his hand and wrote,

If you won't leave, then SHUT UP!

Alan cleared his throat but said nothing. David closed his eyes again and turned his face away from the man in the chair. He could hear someone come in.

"Hey, are you ok?" Amanda asked and ran her hand through David's hair. He half nodded and looked at her. She smiled and looked passed him at the sheet of paper then at Alan. "He saved you David." Amanda said quietly. David sighed and shook his head. He didn't want to hear her defend this man. He didn't want to hear anything about him, or from him at all. Amanda held David's hand and looked into his eyes. "He wants to help you." She said. David growled and Amanda's eyes filled with tears. She wiped them away and looked at Alan. "What can I do?" She asked in a whimper.

"You can sit here with him while I go get a coffee." Alan said and got up. He smiled at Amanda and then left the room. Amanda got up and David followed her with his eyes as she went around the bed to sit on the chair that Alan had sat in. David picked up the pen and wrote,

Why can't YOU stay with me? I don't want him here.

Amanda smiled and shook her head.

"The hospital is shorthanded and needs your mom to work. I have to take care of Mike." Amanda said. Mike was Amanda's little brother who had been left with her when her parents took off to Florida and never came back.

Bring Mike with you.

Amanda laughed and shook her head.

"A three year old" Amanda paused then added, "In the hospital? He wouldn't last ten minutes before he was whining and wanting to leave. The idea is that you get better." Amanda said and rubbed his arm.

Get somebody else!

Amanda sighed and smiled at David.

"I will see what I can do, ok? Is there anyone you would like to come?" She asked. David thought for a second and shrugged. He had no idea who he wanted to spend an untold amount of time with. Amanda shook her head at his silence. "It's gonna be Alan until you think of someone else then." Amanda said. David rolled his eyes at the motherly sound in her voice.

I don't need a babysitter.

"I know you don't. But your mom and I feel better if there is someone in here with you all the time. It wasn't an accident that put you here." Amanda said. David growled and shook his head.

I won't do it again if you get him out of here.

Amanda shook her head and sighed. She rubbed his arm and looked at the door. David turned his head to see what she was looking at. It was Alan. He was standing in the doorway holding a brown cup of coffee. David rolled his eyes and looked back at Amanda. She could see the anger and pleading in his eyes. She half smiled and got up to leave. David whimpered and Amanda kissed his forehead.

"I'll be back in a few hours." Amanda said and left the room. Alan stepped aside to let her leave. David glared at him as he walked over to the chair. He read the paper in front of David and sighed.

"I can find my own replacement if that's what you want." Alan offered in his gentle, seductive voice. David looked at him and shook his head.

I don't want anything from you.

David wrote and threw the pen across the room. Alan shook his head and got up. He went over to the pen on the floor and picked it up. He looked at it in his hands and sighed.

"I would have never kept this from you if I knew how you felt. Amanda gave me your journal so I could find you. If I had known you had such strong feelings David . . ." Alan stopped mid-sentence and looked at David. David's face was riddled with anger over the confession of the journal reading. Alan sighed and set the pen back down on the table. He sat in the chair next to David's bed and looked down at the floor. "I will never repeat what I read, David." Alan said quietly, never looking up. David growled again and whimpered at the pain it caused him. Alan looked up at him, "Do you need more pain killers?" He asked. David sighed and grabbed the pen.

STOP trying to help me!

Alan sighed at the note and shook his head.

"David, I know you're angry. I would be too but, let me make it right." Alan said. David mock laughed and winced at the pain. Alan winced too. "Let me get the nurse and another shot of pain killers." Alan said. David shot him a dirty look but Alan got up and left the room to fetch a nurse. David made a fist out of each hand.

Don't you understand that I don't want any more help from you! David thought. The nurse followed Alan back into the room and administered the pain killers into David's I.V.

"There you go. Now your dad doesn't have to see you in pain." The nurse said and left the room. David's eyes shot wide open and he tried to yell but the sound was a squeaky growl that hurt terribly. He shot a look at Alan and Alan sighed.

"I don't know why she called me that." He said and sat down in his chair. David's chest heaved with his angered breathing. He looked up at the ceiling and a tear ran down his cheek. Alan gently wiped the tear from David's face. David looked at him and scowled. Alan swallowed hard and sat back down. David closed his eyes and clenched his fists.

DAD! For the love of god! I don't even look like him! Maybe if he would just FUCK OFF, people wouldn't think he was my . . . DAD! David's mind raced and he tightened his fists. Alan sighed and David looked at him.

"David, I am really sorry." Alan said in his seductive voice. David rolled his eyes and stared at the ceiling. Alan sighed again and leaned back in his chair. "Have you thought more about my replacement?" Alan asked. David sighed and shook his head. Alan nodded and leaned forward in his chair again. "I think Carman would come if you wanted him too." Alan offered. David turned his head and looked at him. He grabbed the pen and wrote,

Does he know what happened?

Alan shook his head. David nodded and tried to clear the scratchiness from his throat but it was painful.

Call him.

David wrote and Alan slowly nodded. He pulled his cell phone out of his pocket and dialed the number. David stared at him as he waited for Carman to answer.

"Hi . . . . You need to come down here . . . . David is in the hospital . . . . I'll let him tell you . . . . No . . . . no really, he can't talk . . . . I don't know . . . . Ok . . . . can I tell him your coming? . . . . ok . . . . Yea he is . . . . it's my fault . . . . No, nothing like that . . . . Ok . . . . ok . . . . thanks Carman . . . . Yea, I'll tell him . . . . ok bye-bye." Alan finished the call and put the phone back in its pocket. He looked at David and smiled. "He will be here by tomorrow morning." Alan said and sat back in his chair again. David sighed and stared up at the ceiling. He tried to breathe through his mouth so he didn't have to smell Alan's cologne but the air going down his throat stung. He sighed and closed his mouth to continue breathing through his nose. Alan ran his hand through his hair and it caught David's attention. He looked at Alan and clenched his teeth. It seemed even his intense anger couldn't stop the attraction he had for this man. Alan sighed and leaned his elbows on his knees. "If I could turn back time, I would tell you all about my first date with your mom. I wish I could do that. I wish I could have saved you from this pain." Alan said and shook his head. He looked back down at the floor and shook his head again. David turned his head to look at the table. He picked up the pen and wrote,

If you wanted to save me from this pain, you should have just left me hanging there.

Alan read the note and stared at David. He caught his gaze and held it but, it was Alan that looked away. David smirked and shook his head.

"How could I leave you there, David? After everything we have been through together. After everything you wrote down about me . . ." Alan stopped talking and cleared what sounded like a sob from his throat. "I couldn't leave you there." He whispered and looked back down at the floor. David steadied his hand and wrote,

What would you have done if you were me?

Alan read the note and shook his head. He stared into David's waiting eyes. He could see a pain that ran so deep in them that he had to look away. He had read the journal and knew that the love David felt for him was deep and obviously worth ending his own life over. Alan looked back up at him and sighed.

"I would have tried to change your mind if you were me and I was you." Alan said and looked back down at the floor. David squinted at the answer. He took the pen back in his hand and wrote,

Change your mind about what?

Alan read the note and shook his head. He looked up at the ceiling for a minute and seemed to plan what he was going to say next. It looked as though he was looking for the right words and that they would be written on the ceiling tiles for him. He finally took a deep breath and looked back down into David's eyes.

"Change my mind about being with your mom." Alan answered the question and stood up. David blinked at the answer. It came as a shock so he had to know,

Would that have made a difference?

Alan read the next question and looked into David's eyes. He sighed again and left the room. David threw the pen and pushed his head back into the pillow.

FUCK! What the hell is he talking about? Is this conversation hypothetical or what? Talk him into changing his mind about being with my mom. What the hell for? So he would have been with me? That's fucking crazy! God, I can't wait for Carman to get here. He'll know what that means. I'll ask him about it. David soothed his anger with thoughts of Carman's arrival. He opened his eyes and looked up at the ceiling. He counted the lines in the painted tiles until his eyes felt heavy. He shut them and tried to sleep. Just as sleep began to take him, someone entered the room. He looked at the door and seen his mom. He sighed and swallowed the invisible spit in his mouth. He winced at the discomfort it caused as she came to the little bed table and handed him the ice chips.

"Alan said Carman is coming down to stay with you. He said you don't want him in here with you." She said as David put some of the ice chips into his mouth. He rolled his eyes at her as she sat down on the bed next to him. The ice melted in his mouth and the cold water felt good on his burning, scratchy throat. "Why didn't you tell me you were gay?" Nancy asked quietly. David giggled through his nose and winced at the pain it caused in his throat. He grabbed his pen and wrote,

I'm not gay. I just happen to like guys as much as I like Amanda.

Nancy giggled at the statement. She ran her hand through David's hair and sighed.

"I don't care. Just so you know. I'm not your father. You are perfect no matter who you sleep with." Nancy said. David giggled again and shook his head. Nancy brought her legs up on the bed and lay next to David. She cradled his head against her shoulder and pet his hair. "I hope you're not mad at me." Nancy said. David reached for the pen and wrote,

Well, I am. Just not as mad as I am at Alan.

Nancy read the note and sighed. She continued to pet her son's hair.

"It was my idea that we didn't tell you." Nancy said. David nodded but didn't write anything else. He didn't want to hear his mother take the blame for any of this. She seemed, to him, to be an innocent bystander. Nancy hugged David and he sighed. "I wish I knew what was going on in that head of yours." She whispered. David half smiled and shook his head. Nancy giggled and hugged him again. "I don't?"

She asked. David shook his head again. "Amanda said you're in love with Alan. Is that true?" David didn't move or write anything. He didn't know how to answer his mother. This man was the same man she was currently with. He still had to wrap the idea around in his own mind before he could answer her. In addition, he was so angry at Alan that he now had no idea *how* he was feeling. Nancy sighed and handed the pen to her son. "Please talk to me." She pleaded quietly. David sighed and took the pen.

I don't want to talk about it.

Nancy read the note and sighed. She pet David's hair again and he let the weight of his body lay against his mother.

"When you're ready to talk about it, I will be ready to listen." Nancy said. David nodded and closed his eyes. Nancy stroked his hair until David started to drift off. When she stopped petting, he woke up but didn't open his eyes. He listened to her heart and lungs. He could tell she was silently crying. He heard someone come into the room but he kept his eyes closed. He heard the new person sit down in the chair and then he could smell the unmistakable sent of Mr. Alan Black.

"Is he sleeping?" Alan whispered the question. David could feel his mother nod. "I don't want to be in here when he wakes up." Alan added and Nancy sniffed.

"I was wrong Alan. I should have never thought that keeping us from him was a good idea." Nancy said. David could hear Alan move in the chair. The smell became stronger so he knew that Alan had leaned forward.

"This isn't your fault. David was hurt and felt there was only one way out. Don't blame yourself." Alan said. David could feel his mother sigh.

"I wish I paid closer attention to him. I would have seen this change in him if I was just paying attention." Nancy said. David could hear her crying steadily worsening.

"Nancy, this isn't anything that you could have changed. David's journal was the only thing he had to talk to that wouldn't talk back, wouldn't judge. He wasn't ready to talk about this stuff. Not to you, or me. Amanda was the only one who knew as far as I know. He didn't want us to know." Alan said. Nancy nodded again and Alan sighed. "This is hard now, but it will get better." Alan added. Nancy sniffed and David could feel her raise her hand to wipe her tears away.

"He was afraid because of the way his father felt about gay people. I should have made my opinion better known or something."

"From what I know of David, he isn't afraid of much Nancy. I think it was just too new a feeling to express." Alan said. Nancy sighed and gently pet David's hair again.

"I don't know what I would have done if he . . ." Nancy stopped talking and David could feel her chest lift up and down from crying.

"I know." Alan said quietly. He could feel Alan rub Nancy's shoulder. He could hear them kiss and he mock stirred in his fake sleep. He could hear Alan sit back in his chair and Nancy sniff.

"Do you think he will ever forgive us for not telling him?" Nancy asked Alan. Alan sighed.

"I am sure he will. It's the other stuff he won't be able to get over easily." Nancy held her breath for a second.

"You mean the stuff Amanda said about you?" Nancy asked. Alan must have nodded because Nancy's sigh was that of an answer that was difficult to hear.

"She was right too. His journal was explicit." Alan said.

"What did it say?" Nancy asked. David couldn't help but tighten up a little. Nancy rubbed his back and David calmed.

"I'm not going to say, Nancy. I think I have betrayed his trust enough for a life time." Alan said. David swallowed and Nancy gently pet his hair again. "This is my burden to carry Nancy, not yours or Amanda's. I know that David will never let it go either. He wanted me to leave him in that tree." Alan said. Nancy started to cry again and Alan sighed.

"How will he pass the psyche exam if he wants to die over this?" Nancy asked. Alan sighed again.

"I don't know." Alan answered. David could hear a nurse ask for Nancy.

"I have to go. Please don't leave him alone." Nancy pleaded through her tears.

"I won't." Alan said. David could feel Alan's strong arms wrap around him and lift him off of his mother. David tensed in Alan's strong arms as Nancy moved off the bed. Alan gently put him down on the pillow and slid his arms out from under him. Nancy kissed David's forehead and then Alan before leaving the room. David sighed and slit his eyes open. Alan stood at the door looking out. Even through the anger he felt, Alan's incredible looks still hit him like a freight train of lust and impeccable desire. He closed his eyes and clenched his teeth.

Why do I still feel like this? Why can't my body hate him too? I can't stand this. Carman will be here in the morning and I won't have to see him or hear him anymore. And what's with all the kissing? I wonder how often I've missed it. David tried to recall a time when Alan was around that he didn't have his eyes glued to him. He couldn't think of one. He opened his eyes and looked at Alan again. He had turned around and was looking at him.

"You're awake." Alan said and came back to his chair. "I tried to not be here when your mom left but she asked me to stay." Alan said as he sat down. David sighed and rolled his eyes. He grabbed his pen and wrote,

I don't want to hear you ok.

Alan read the note and nodded. He sat silent in his chair while David stared at him. Alan held his gaze. David could feel his body reacting as it always did to being lost in Alan's eyes. David looked away and whimpered as he did so.

"Sorry." Alan whispered and David looked at him. Alan smiled but looked away. David frowned and picked up his pen.

Are you really going to keep what you read in my journal a secret?

Alan read the note and smiled.

"Yes, I promise." Alan vowed. David nodded and turned his head to stare at the ceiling. Alan sighed and sat back in his chair. "Can I ask you something?" Alan said and David looked at him. "I know you don't want to talk to me but I promise not to say another word if you answer this question." Alan wagered. David thought about it for a second before nodding. Alan leaned forward and stared into David's eyes. David sighed and raised his eyebrows as if to say, 'well ask already'. Alan sighed and looked down at the floor. "Did you try to kill yourself because of me and your mom, or because we didn't tell you about it?" Alan asked. David sighed and picked up the pen. He stared at the paper for a few seconds before he wrote,

Neither.

Alan read the answer and frowned. David set the pen down and stared at the ceiling.

"Then why?" Alan asked quietly. David looked at him and this time, it was his turn to frown. He grabbed the pen and wrote,

Just because it's not the answer you wanted, doesn't mean you get to go back on your side of the deal. NO MORE TALKING.

David handed the note to Alan and he read it. He sighed and set
the paper back on David's little table. He sat back in the chair and
leaned his head back on it. He closed his eyes and crossed his arms
across his chest. David sighed and faced the ceiling again. He listened
to Alan's breathing and smelled his cologne. He growled and picked up
his pen. He wrote Alan a note and waved the folded paper in the air.
Alan opened his eyes and looked at the waving paper. He sat foreword
and took the paper from David. David sighed and closed his eyes. Alan
sat back in his chair and opened the note.

Alan, There are a million reasons why I did it. The biggest reason was
because you lied to me. You should have told me about you and my mom
right from the start. It would have saved you from this guilt. My mom is
a great lady and I bet you make her happy. Don't hurt her Alan, I'll kill
you if you do. Don't let her fall in love with you just so you can walk away
from her. You can do it to me, but not to her.

Alan read the note over and over again. He looked up at David
and seen that he had fallen asleep. He stood up and put the note in
his wallet. He gently pushed a stray bit of hair from David's face and
sighed. Tears filled his eyes and he bent down to David's ear.

"I am so sorry, David. I promise not to hurt her. I can do that for
you." Alan whispered. David stirred in his sleep but didn't wake up.
Alan smiled and wiped a tear from his face. "Good bye, David." Alan
said and left the room.

Chapter 2

David awoke with a dry scratchy throat. He tried to clear it but the pain made a growling sound and he winced. He could feel a straw touch his lips. He opened his eyes to see Carman. David smiled and took a small sip of the water Carman offered. Carman smiled back and set the cup on David's little bed table.

"Hi good lookin'. You're alive." Carman said quietly and sat down in Alan's chair. David nodded and grabbed his pen.

When did you get here?

David wrote. Carman read the note and sighed.

"I have been here for about half an hour. Alan just left." Carman said. David nodded and stared at Carman. "You don't look to bad. What happened?" Carman asked and leaned forward to read as David wrote,

I saw Alan and my mom kissing. I lost it and tried to hang myself. It didn't work.

Carman raised his eyebrows and looked back at David. David took another sip of his water and looked at Carman.

"Alan and Nancy? That's news to me too. He never told you?" Carman asked. David could see the shock and surprise on Carman's handsome face. He shook his head to answer no and Carman sighed. "What a fucking surprise." Carman said quietly. David sighed and shrugged. "How long has this been going on? Do you know?" Carman asked. David shook his head. Carman sighed and set his hand on David's arm. "Well, I'm going to find out." Carman said and patted David's arm. David raised his eyebrows and watched Carman pull his cell phone out of his jean jacket pocket. He dialed a number that David could only guess belonged to Alan, and sat back in his chair. "Hey . . . . How long has this thing with Nancy been going on? . . . . Uh huh . . . . What? That long? . . . . How could you not say anything? . . . . I don't care. You should have told me. You should have told him . . . . Too late for that isn't it? . . . . Yes . . . . I doubt it . . . . Would you stay? . . . . Well, I'm sorry Alan, but I'm with David on this one . . . . Yea, but that was a hundred years ago . . . . I don't care, Alan . . . . Well, he's hurting. I don't blame him . . . . Ok . . . . I'm going to stay till he asks me to leave . . . . If I have to . . . . I own the company, I can take as much time as I want . . . . Well, just better to stay away . . . . I will . . . . I know . . . . Ok, Alan . . . . Yep, bye." Carman hung up his phone and shook his head. He put the phone back in his pocket and looked at David. "So, he's on the shit list. Does that make you feel better?" Carman asked. David shook his head and picked up his pen,

Don't lose your friend because of this.

Carman smiled and shook his head.

"Alan and I are best friends David. That will never change. Being in shit with me hurts a lot worse than anything you can dish out right now." Carman said. David giggled and it hurt. He took another sip of his water and looked at Carman. "Want to know how long?" Carman asked. David sighed and thought about it for a moment. He wondered if it would make a difference knowing. He stared at Carman's gentle looking eyes and nodded. Carman leaned forward in his chair and put his hand on David's arm. "Since September. This whole time he's been with her. I guess it started the day before the fishing trip." Carman explained. David closed his eyes and shook his head. The news hit him like a dagger through the heart. Carman rubbed David's arm and seen the tears start to form in his eyes. Carman sighed and shook his head. "You really feel something for him, don't you?" Carman asked quietly. David looked into Carman's blue eyes and nodded. He knew that lying about it to Carman was counterproductive at best. Carman nodded as well and then looked at the clock. "Want a smoke?" Carman asked. David raised his eyebrows and looked at the I.V. machine. Carman followed David's eyes and smiled. "It has wheels." Carman said adding a lisp as a way to tease him. David smiled and nodded. Carman got up and went to the hallway to get a wheel chair. He helped David in to the chair and shook his head. "Was there spinal damage or anything?" Carman asked. David shook his head and pointed at the pad of paper. Carman handed it to him and David wrote,

They are keeping me drugged so I don't escape.

Carman read the note and laughed.

"I'll have to remember that." He said and winked at David. David smiled and shook his head. Carman wheeled him out of the room and out the closest door. He sat on the bench outside and pulled David in front of him. David pulled the I.V. machine with him. Carman lit a cigarette for David and then one for himself. "So, how is that?"

Carman asked as David took his first painful drag. David winced at the
hot pain and shook his head. Carman giggled and watched as David
fought down another puff. "He feels really bad." Carman said quietly.
David rolled his eyes and picked up the pen off his lap.

Don't Carman.

David wrote. He was starting to get very tired of hearing people
apologize for what Alan had done. Carman read it and sighed. He took
another drag from his cigarette and looked around. David stared at the
blue smoke circling in the air in front of him. Carman looked back
at David and smiled. "So, Alan said you asked for me. Should I feel
privileged?" Carman asked. David giggled and then winced. Carman
winced with him and watched David write,

I had to get him out of here somehow.

Carman laughed at David's sarcasm and shook his head.

"Well, I'm glad you picked me. I needed a break from work."
Carman said and winked. David giggled again and then glared at
Carman. "Sorry, no laughing." Carman said and took another drag
from his cigarette. David looked at his and sighed. "You don't have to
finish it. We can come out again." Carman offered seeing the dismay
on the younger man's face. David nodded and Carman put out David's
cigarette. He put it back in the pack and watched as David looked
around them. Carman smiled at him and tilted his head to one side.
"Are you glad you survived?" Carman asked. David sighed and looked
into Carman's eyes. He hadn't been asked anything like that yet. He
smelled the fresh air and half winced at the tickle it caused in his
sore throat. He looked at the trees and plants that made the hospital
yard look like a park. He listened to a couple of birds that seemed to
be fighting over a branch in a nearby tree. Thoughts of his mother
and Amanda filled his mind. He couldn't imagine what life would
be like for them if he had succeeded. He smiled at the last thought

and nodded. Carman giggled and shook his head. "I get why you did it, David. I thought about it once too." Carman said. David raised his eyebrows and Carman nodded. "He has that effect on people." Carman said and put out his cigarette. David shivered at the feel of the small breeze and Carman stood up. "Let's go." He said and pushed David back to his room. He helped him get back into bed and put his paper back on the little bed table. He put the chair back out in the hallway and came back to the room. He sat down in the bed side chair and sighed. David looked at him and tried to talk but sound wouldn't come out. "It will come, David. Don't force it." Carman said referring to David's voice. David nodded and grabbed his pen.

Thanks for coming.

Carman smiled and nodded. He sat back in his chair and sighed again. David looked at him with puzzled eyes. Carman smiled and shook his head.

"Don't worry about me, David. I just really hate hospitals." Carman said and shifted in his chair. David nodded in agreement and looked down at the table. "Don't feel bad, I want to be here with you. Ok?" Carman said. David looked at him and smiled. Carman smiled back and winked. David giggled and then glared at Carman again for making him laugh. Carman laughed at this and leaned forward in his chair. "Don't you get tired?" Carman asked. David nodded and smiled. Carman laughed and shook his head. "Do you need anything?" Carman asked. David sighed and looked around the room. He looked at his cup and seen that all the ice had melted. He picked up his pen and wrote,

Ice.

Carman smiled and grabbed David's cup. He went out of the room and David smiled at him as he left. A nurse came in at the same time and looked at David's I.V. machine.

"Are you in pain?" The little Irish nurse asked. David shook his head and the nurse smiled. "You need to speak to a doctor named James Kelly. He is a teen suicide counselor." David rolled his eyes and the little Irish nurse laughed. "I know it sounds stupid but it is mandatory. You get a clean bill of health from him, you can go. Ok?" The nurse said. David sighed and nodded his head. He wasn't very fond of hospitals either. The nurse smiled at him and patted his arm. "You should practice talking. The sooner you get that voice box working again, the better." She said. David nodded and she smiled at him. Carman came back in the room and she said hello as she left.

"New girlfriend?" Carman asked referring to the little round nurse and David laughed. It caused a coughing fit that brought tears to David's eyes. Carman patted his back and helped him get a sip of water out of the ice chip cup. "Sorry." Carman said. David smiled and shook his head. He lay back on his pillow and looked at Carman. Carman sat back down on the chair and smiled at David. "I saw this hot doctor out there. Is your doctor hot?" Carman asked. David giggled and shook his head. "That's too bad." Carman said and looked at the door. David giggled again and shifted in his bed. Carman looked at him and cleared his throat. "So do they have a counselor picked out yet?" David nodded and grabbed his pen.

He's called James Kelly.

Carman rolled his eyes and sighed.

"I think a first name for a last name is retarded." Carman said with his face askew. David giggled and shook his head. Carman laughed and leaned forward in his chair. "Maybe you'll get lucky and he'll be hot like that doctor I saw." Carman whispered. David found it difficult not to laugh at everything Carman said. Carman giggled and sat back in his chair. David yawned and Carman shut the lamp off. David looked at him and he smiled. "Have a nap." Carman said. David nodded and shut his eyes. He could hear Carman yawn and he smiled. "No smiling, go to sleep." Carman mock scolded. David giggled and winced at the pain. Carman fell silent and it wasn't long before David was asleep.

David awoke quite a few hours later with a new tickle in his throat. He tried to clear it and noticed he could hear his voice in the rumble. He raised his eyebrows and looked at Carman. He was asleep in his chair and David smiled. He had his legs hanging over one arm and had his head leaned back against the wall. He had his strong looking arms crossed on his chest. David was amazed at how good looking Carman really was. He had an almost perfect complexion next to a five o'clock shadow that had started on his well-cut jaw. His spiky hair seemed to never be messed up. David smiled at him and opened his mouth.

"*Carman.*" David whispered in a husky sounding voice. Carman opened his eyes and looked at David. He frowned and moved himself to sit properly in the chair. He quickly stretched and yawned.

"Did you just talk?" Carman asked in a tired sounding voice. David nodded and Carman smiled. "Do it again." Carman said and leaned forward on his chair.

"*I need a smoke.*" David whispered. Carman giggled and shook his head.

"You sound like The God Father." Carman said. David giggled and nodded. The sound that came from him was definitely not the voice his ears where use to hearing. Carman got up and went out to get the wheel chair. He helped David into it and took him out the same doors they had used earlier. He pulled David in front of him again and sat down on the bench. He lit David's saved cigarette and then lit one for himself. "Are you feeling better?" Carman asked. David sighed and nodded. He took a drag of his cigarette and winced at the burning sensation it gave him. "Will you be ready to talk to that first name last name guy?" Carman asked. David giggled and nodded again.

"James Kelly." David whispered. Carman raised his eyebrows and nodded.

"Yea, the first name last name guy." Carman said again. David laughed and took another drag from his cigarette. It hurt but he seemed to enjoy it better than the earlier one.

"When am I supposed to talk to this guy?" David asked. Carman shrugged and took another drag from his cigarette.

"I guess I'll have to find out when we go in, huh?" Carman asked. David nodded and they sat quietly and smoked. As they put out their cigarettes, Amanda came up to them.

"Hi, guys." She said and kissed David on the forehead. David smiled.

"Hi." David whispered. Amanda looked at him and smiled.

"You're talking?" She asked in her high pitched, little Amanda voice. David nodded and she giggled. "That's awesome baby." Amanda said and kissed him again.

"You guys chat, I'll find out about the first name last name guy." Carman said. David laughed and watched Carman go back into the hospital. Amanda sat down on the bench and smiled at David.

"I need to talk to you about something." Amanda said and took David's hands into hers. David looked into her eyes and waited. She suddenly looked worried and squeezed his hands.

"What is it?" David's harsh whisper asked. Amanda smiled and looked into David's bright blue eyes. David could see tears forming in hers and he frowned. She took a deep breath and said,

"Remember your birthday?" Amanda asked. David nodded. "Well, pulling out didn't work." Amanda said and waited for the news to sink into David's head. He thought about the whole evening and how it had ended in a planned 'in the car' love making session. He stared at her for a second and then raised his eyebrows.

"*Are you pregnant?*" David asked. Amanda nodded and David giggled. "*That's awesome.*" David said and Amanda laughed. "*It's awesome right?*" David asked. Amanda's tears ran down her face and she nodded.

"I was scared you would be mad." Amanda said. David giggled and shook his head.

"*Are you kidding? If anyone was gonna have my kids, I'm glad it's you.*" David said. Amanda smiled and kissed David on the mouth. He closed his eyes and enjoyed Amanda's gentle tongue massage. She finished the kiss and stared into his eyes.

"I want to keep it. Are you ok with that?" Amanda asked. David smiled and nodded. Amanda giggled and kissed him again. They heard the door open and they both looked. It was Nancy.

"Hi, I heard your talking." Nancy said and came over to the bench. She sat down next to Amanda and put her arm around her.

"*I have to talk before our kid does.*" David said. Nancy raised her eyebrows and looked at Amanda.

"You told him?" Nancy said excitedly. Amanda giggled and nodded. Nancy hugged them both and looked onto David's eyes. "I am so happy for you guys. Amanda IS a little young." She said and smiled. Amanda giggled and David smiled. "If you guys need help, I will be here for you, ok? You and Amanda could probably stay in Gabe's house and . . ." David cut her off.

"*We're gonna move.*" David said. Amanda and Nancy both looked at him with shock on their faces.

"Can we talk about this?" Amanda asked. Nancy nodded and looked into David's eyes.

"You guys should talk about this." Nancy said. David sighed and shook his head. A nurse opened the door and called Nancy. "Please talk about this. I'll come see you in your room later, ok?" Nancy asked.

David nodded and she kissed his forehead. She smiled at Amanda and went back inside.

"Move? Where?" Amanda asked. David looked at her and shrugged. "What am I supposed to do with the house?" Amanda asked with raised eyebrows.

"*Sell it, rent it out. I don't know.*" David whispered and rubbed his cold arms. Amanda sighed and pushed David back into his room in awkward silence. Carman seen them come in and helped Amanda get David back into bed.

"Can we have a minute, Carman?" Amanda asked.

"Sure." Carman said and left the room. Amanda sat down in the chair and looked at the clock. She rolled her eyes and looked at David. "I have to get Little Mike soon. Why do you want to move?" Amanda asked. David shook his head and cleared his throat.

"*You have to ask?*" David asked and looked at the little bed table. Amanda sighed and shook her head.

"David, we need to be smart about this. I have a whole house we can raise Mike and the baby in. Why would we move?" Amanda asked. David shook his head and looked at Amanda.

"*Two doors down from my mom and her BOYFRIEND.*" David said trying to raise his voice but the attempt was thwarted by pain. Amanda sarcastically smiled and nodded.

"So, you want to be selfish?" She asked. David looked at her and frowned.

"*Of all people, Amanda, I expect you would understand.*" David said. Amanda shook her head and pulled her hair out of her face.

"David, I do understand. But this is our baby, our lives. Did you just think that we can find a place and finish school and get jobs in seven months? I have a house here. We are already enrolled in school here. Why would we leave?" Amanda asked pleading her case. David shook his head and ran his hand through his hair.

"Amanda, by September, you aren't going to want to walk around a high school. I personally don't feel comfortable with going to the school that Alan works at either." David said. Amanda shook her head and stood up. David sighed and watched her walk to the door. She stopped and faced him.

"David, have you ever considered what other people might be comfortable with? I want to do this with you. I just ask that you think this through before you uproot us and take us to god knows where just because Alan didn't turn out gay." Amanda said and left the room. David shook his head and closed his eyes at her sharp words.

What the fuck does she expect? I can't stay here after all this. Gabe's murder, my poor attempt at suicide, Alan and mom! God why can't she see this from my side? David thought. He could hear someone come in. It was Carman. He walked over to the chair and sat down.

"I couldn't help but over hear." Carman said and David rolled his eyes. "So, you're having a baby and you want to move." Carman said. David nodded and stared into Carman's eyes.

"I can't stay where Alan is. He's kissing my mom and sleeping in her bed . . . Carman I HAVE to leave." David whispered in his husky sounding voice. Carman sighed and nodded.

"I get that David, but Amanda has a point. She has a house and your mom is here to help. You can't just turn a blind eye to Alan and your mom or something?" Carman asked. David sighed and looked down at the little bed table.

"These are my choices. I live in the house that Gabe had his last breaths in. The same house we had our last night together in before he died. OR, live in the house where Alan is fucking my mom. What would you do?" David asked. Carman sighed and shook his head.

"I think you need to explain it like that to Amanda." Carman said. David nodded and closed his eyes. "Are you tired?" Carman asked. David nodded again as talking was taking its toll on his damaged throat. Carman looked up at the clock. "Well, you can sleep for two hours. The first name last name guy will be here at 6:00." Carman said. David raised his eyebrows but didn't open his eyes. He fell asleep easily.

Carman woke David at 5:45.

"Sorry dude. You better knock the cobwebs out. That doctor guy is gonna be here soon." Carman said. David slowly opened his eyes and looked at Carman. He yawned and stretched and Carman giggled. "You're so cute when you first wake up." Carman kidded and David laughed. The action hurt and he glared at Carman. Carman winced and sat down in the chair.

"*So, I thought about it.*" David said and Carman raised his eyebrows.

"Ok, and?" Carman asked. David sighed and shook his head.

"*I need to leave. The thought of being so close to Alan and mom is too hard to shake. I need to get away from them.*" David whispered. Carman smiled and nodded.

"I would want to leave if Alan was fucking my mom too." David laughed and winced. Carman apologized and handed David a new cup of ice water.

"*Now I just have to convince Amanda.*" David said. He took a sip of his water and let it trickle slowly down his throat.

"She doesn't want to be alone with this baby coming." Carman said. David looked at him and frowned.

"*She's not alone.*" David said. Carman smiled and shook his head.

"I'm not talking about you. She's gonna be 17 years old when this baby is born. She's gonna want your mom around to help since hers has fucked off." Carman reasoned. David sighed and nodded. "Look, I get where you're coming from but you have to think of her too." Carman added.

"Aren't I? I mean, I will be miserable if we stay here. I don't want us to fight or there to be problems because I hate where we are." David said. Carman smiled and nodded.

"Well, you need to tell her this stuff." Carman said. David nodded and looked at the form in the door. There was a tall, good looking, African man at the door. David and Carman both raised their eye brows and the man smiled. His teeth were perfect and his smile was like a bright light in David's dim lit room.

"Planning for the future is a good sign, David." The man said and came into the room. He reached his hand out to Carman and shook his hand. Carman shook it and smiled. "I am James Kelly, You must be David's father." James said. Carman and David both laughed.

"There is so much wrong with that statement." Carman said and David laughed. "I am David's friend, Carman." James smiled and turned to David.

"And you are David right?" James said. David nodded and shook the doctor's hand. He looked passed him at Carman. Carman smiled and mouthed 'once you go black.' David giggled as Carman left the room. "So I hear your having a new baby." James said and sat down. David smiled and nodded. "How do you feel about that?" The doctor asked and took out a note book and a fancy gold pen. David sighed and shook his head.

"I think it's great." David answered. James smiled and raised his eyebrows.

"But?" James asked in a coaxing way. David raised his eyebrows and stared at James's face. James reminded David of Wesley Snipes.

"*Well, I think we should move but she doesn't want to.*" David answered. James wrote in his book and looked up at David.

"Why do you want to move?" James asked. His voice was gentle but sounded like he would be scary if he were to yell.

"*I can't stay here.*" David said and James raised his eyebrows.

"Can't or won't?" James asked. David sighed and thought about it. "David," James said and leaned forward on the chair. He crossed his hands in front of him and looked into David's eyes. "I ask that you be only as candid as you are comfortable with being. That being said, the more I know, the better my assessment can be." James said. David nodded and sighed.

"*Well, the house Amanda wants to stay in is her brother's house. He died in October.*" David explained.

"Ok, were you close?" James asked. David nodded and looked down at the little table. "What was his name?" James asked.

"*Gabe.*" David answered and cleared the lump out of his throat. James shifted in his chair and wrote in his book.

"How would you describe your relationship with Gabe?" James asked. David raised his eyebrows and shook his head. "Just answer as best you can." James said seeing David's discomfort with the question.

"*Um, we were very close.*" David said having a memory flash back of Gabe in his shower. James smiled and nodded.

"Would you say he was your best friend maybe?" James asked. David shook his head and felt tears fill his eyes.

"*He wasn't just a friend.*" David said still thinking of the water and soap on Gabe's naked body. James raised his eyebrows and wrote in his book.

"Was he your lover?" James asked. David blinked at the question but nodded. James wrote in his book again. "And he is Amanda's brother, correct?" James asked. David nodded and James wrote. "Ok, so your history with Gabe makes you feel reluctant to live in his house." James said very matter-of-fact. David nodded. "Ok, so what about staying where you are?" James asked. David sighed and clenched his teeth. James noticed his anger and wrote in his book again. "Let's talk about that, shall we?" James asked. David looked at him and James could see pain in David's eyes. "Tell me what you're thinking." James said. David sighed and looked down at the bed table.

"*The problem there is my mom's boyfriend.*" David said and closed his eyes. James nodded and wrote in his book.

"You don't get along with him?" James asked. David rolled his eyes and swallowed hard.

"*I did until I found out about them.*" David whispered. James frowned and crossed his hands on his lap again.

"Can you explain that to me a little?" James asked. David sighed and looked at James.

"*Alan was the reason I was with Gabe in the first place.*" David said.

"And, Alan is your mom's boyfriend?" James asked. David nodded and James wrote in his book. "Ok, so how did he get you with Gabe?" James asked. David sighed and scratched his head.

"*I hope you have a lot of paper.*" David said. James smiled and nodded. "*Well, Alan was my History teacher.*" David said. James wrote as David spoke. "*I was just a normal guy until I saw him. He was so sexy to me. I never saw guys like that before.*" David explained. James nodded but said nothing. "*Anyway, since my dad died back in 2002, my mom had been looking for a big brother or whatever for me. When she heard that I didn't hate this new teacher of mine, she thought he would be perfect.*" David said. James nodded and wrote in his book.

"Did she know about these sexual feeling you had for him?" James asked. David shook his head and James wrote in his book. "Ok, so you

31

start spending time with him away from school then?" James asked. David nodded and continued his story.

"*Yea, it started just fishing and coffee. Then he started an after school mid-evil project for the renaissance fair. So we spent our time together along with this project.*" James nodded and wrote in his book.

"This mid-evil stuff is an interest of yours?" James asked. David nodded and continued.

"*Anyway, Alan has this friend Carman.*" David said. James smiled and nodded.

"The man that was here?" James asked and David nodded.

"*He has a collection of mid-evil torture stuff that he said we could use. He had this Iron Maiden that Alan calls David's Lady.*" David said.

"Why does he call it that?" James asked.

"*Well, cause it's my favorite.*" David said. James smiled and wrote in his book.

"So how does Gabe come into all this?" James asked and David sighed.

"*Well, before all this other stuff happened, Amanda thought it would be a good idea for me to explore this being gay thing so she set up a date with a guy named Todd.*" David said. James nodded and wrote in his book.

"Did you think this was a good idea?" James asked.

"*Well, not at first. I actually did it because she was having trouble at home and I thought it would make her feel better to get her own way.*" David said. James smiled.

"Ok, so what happened with Todd?"

"*Well, it didn't go as well as planned. He got a little more interested in having sex with me than I would have liked.*" David said thinking back to the almost rape and fist fight with Todd. James wrote in his book.

"What happened next?" James asked.

"*Well, it turned into a fight and he broke one of my ribs.*" David explained and James nodded. David continued, "*THAT'S when Gabe comes in. He saved me from getting beaten to death by that ass hole. That's also when I found out that Gabe was gay and had hidden it from everyone his whole life.*" David said. James wrote in his book. David sighed and ran his hand through his hair.

"So, how did you end up being Gabe's lover then?" James asked.

"*Well, it was sort of an agreement at first. Gabe would answer all the questions I had and that kind of thing. Amanda was too scared to help care for me after the fight so, Gabe did. He helped me in the shower and all that kind of stuff. I would talk to him about Alan and he was very open about what I didn't understand. Soon it turned into a sexual thing.*" David said and sighed. James nodded and allowed David to continue. "*So, through all this, I was sleeping with both Amanda and Gabe and at about the same time, they both told me they loved me.*" David said. James raised his eyebrows and wrote in his book.

"How did you feel about that?" James asked.

"*Well, it was weird cause I was already in love with Alan I think.*" David said. James smiled and wrote in his book again. He looked at David and crossed his hands on his lap again.

"So, through all of this you're falling in love with Alan. So what happened when Gabe died?" James asked. David took a deep breath and closed his eyes. James waited quietly for David to answer.

"*It was Halloween night and the first day of the fair. We had our first show and it was awesome. We got all the school funding and the credits and even a full scholarship. We were celebrating in the beer gardens when I saw my dad's brother Carl there. We have had our little tosses in the past so it pissed me off to see him there. He was being mean to some lady there so I got up and confronted him.*" David stopped there and looked down at the table. James wrote in his book and looked at David.

"Then what?" James asked quietly. David remained silent for a moment remembering back to the horrible night.

"We got in a fight. Gabe came to the rescue again and Carl stabbed him." David said and closed his eyes to fight the tears that were forming. James wrote in his book and sighed.

"That is a very difficult thing to have witnessed, David. I understand your pain." James consoled in his cold, out of touch doctor voice. David took a deep, painful breath and nodded. He felt he had successfully fought back the tears. "Can you continue?" James asked. David looked at him and nodded.

"Anyway, Gabe was gone and it was just me and Amanda again. I still spent a lot of time with Alan and I talked to Carman all the time." David explained.

"At this point in your story David, would you say you were in love with Alan?" James asked. David nodded and sighed at the confession.

"I think I was. He was everything I wanted and more. He drives a hot car, he plays guitar, we like all the same stuff. He's perfect." David said and the tears formed again. James sighed and sat quietly as David composed himself.

"We can stop if you want." James said. David shook his head and cleared his throat. It hurt so he took a sip of his water.

"Anyway, Alan and I took another trip to Carman's place during spring break and that's when I told him I was interested in guys. He was cool with it but I couldn't bring myself to tell him how I felt. When we got back I thought things would just go back to normal but . . ." David stopped talking and James leaned forward on his chair.

"I get the feeling this was the turning point in your story." David nodded and looked into James's dark brown eyes.

"I walked in to the house one day to find Alan and my mom kissing. I lost it. I just thought I couldn't live with something like that. It was just

so . . . so . . ." David took another deep breath and shook his head. "*I'm nuts, aren't I doc?*" David asked. James smiled and shook his head.

"You had a very overwhelming year, David. What you experienced is called a psychotic break. For someone your age, it can manifest as suicidal thoughts. Are you still feeling like you want to die?" James asked. David sighed and swallowed hard.

"*No, I have a baby to live for. I have a life to live. This is like a second chance and I want to do it right.*" David said. James nodded and wrote one last thing in his book before he shut it.

"Well, David. I believe you will do what is right for your new family. I think a move is a good idea. There is a lot of pain here for you *and* Amanda. I think it's something to consider." James said. David smiled and nodded. "That being said, as long as the doctor says you are healthy enough physically, I am confident to give you a clean mental health assessment. I do, however, think that further counseling would be a good idea." James said. David smiled politely and nodded again. "Ok." James said and stood up. He shook David's hand and walked to the door. He turned back and looked at David, "Is Carman a good enough friend to help you through this?"

"*Yea, he's awesome.*" David said and James nodded.

"Well, you should probably try talking with him about these things." James said. "Is he also gay?" James asked. David laughed and winced at the pain.

"*Is it that obvious?*" David asked. James smiled and shook his head.

"Just a lucky guess. Good luck." James said and left the room. David sighed and closed his eyes. To his surprise, he fell asleep.

Chapter 3

David woke up in the middle of the night. He could see Carman and Amanda talking in the hallway. Carman looked in the room to see David awake. They came in and Amanda turned on the light.

"Hi." Amanda said and sat down on the bed.

"*Hi.*" David whispered as Carman sat down on the chair.

"So, I'm gonna sell the house." Amanda said. David's eyes grew wide and Carman smiled.

"*Why?*" David asked. Amanda smiled and shook her head.

"I don't care where we live David as long as we're together." She said. David smiled and looked at Carman.

"*Who is this and what have you done with Amanda?*" David asked in his gruff sounding voice. Carman laughed and shook his head. Amanda giggled and rubbed David's arm. David looked back at her and smiled.

"*I have news too.*" David said. Amanda clapped and Carman laughed. "*I'm not crazy. I can go home if that old doctor dude says my throat is in good enough shape.*" David said.

"Oh that's awesome." Amanda said. Carman smiled and nodded.

"I knew you could fake your way through that." Carman said. David and Amanda both laughed and David winced at the feeling it left in his throat. Amanda smiled and gently touched it. Just then Nancy came in the room.

"Your son has fooled the skeptics, Nancy." Amanda said. Nancy smiled and shook her head.

"What do you mean?" Nancy asked.

"*I passed the psychological exam.*" David said in his husky whisper. Nancy smiled and clapped her hands together.

"That's wonderful, David." She said and kissed his forehead. "Can you go home then?" Nancy asked.

"The doctor wants to have another look at his throat before he leaves." Carman said answering for his young friend.

"Oh that should be almost cleared up." Nancy said and David laughed. He winced again and everyone laughed. Nancy looked up at the clock and yawned.

"*Where is Mike?*" David asked realizing the late hour.

"With Rita overnight." Amanda answered. David nodded and looked at his mom.

"*Mom, we have decided to move.*" David said. Nancy nodded and looked at Amanda.

"I know." Nancy said. David shook his head and sighed.

"You gotta quit sleeping through everything." Carman said and Nancy and Amanda laughed.

"*Where are we going?*" David asked. Amanda giggled and looked at Carman. David looked at Carman as well and Carman raised his eyebrows.

"Apparently, she wants to go to Portland." Carman said. David looked at Amanda with astonished surprise on his face.

"*Portland. Why?*" David asked.

"Well, I thought that Portland was far enough away and we know someone there, so . . ." Amanda explained and David shook his head. He looked at his mom and she smiled at him.

"Carman has agreed to let you stay with him until you find your own place." Nancy said. David looked at Carman and Carman smiled.

"Is that ok with you?" Carman asked.

"*Yea, that's perfect.*" David said. Amanda giggled and Nancy yawned again. David smiled at her and looked at Amanda. Amanda sighed and kissed David.

"Awe, how sweet." Carman said in a funny school girl voice. David giggled and Amanda shook her head.

"I better get your mom home, she works again tomorrow." Amanda said. Nancy smiled and kissed David's forehead. They said their good byes and the ladies left.

"Wow, I'm jealous." Carman said and David laughed.

"*Why?*" David asked and took a sip from his cup. Carman leaned forward on his chair and stared at David. David smiled and raised an eyebrow. "*What?*" He asked.

"Everyone gets to kiss you but me." Carman said. David laughed and leaned closer to Carman. Carman raised his eyebrows and leaned in. David gently kissed him and Carman closed his eyes. David finished the kiss and pulled away. Carman leaned back and sighed. David giggled and shook his head.

"Happy now?" David asked.

"You are such a dick." Carman said. David laughed and took another sip from his cup. Carman swung his legs over the chair and leaned his head against the wall.

"You can't be comfortable." David whispered. Carman smiled and looked at David.

"I'm not. Thanks for noticing." Carman said. David laughed and moved to the edge of the bed.

"Come." David said patting the bed and Carman laughed. David shook his head but stayed on the far side. He leaned his head against his pillow and shut his eyes. David could hear Carman sigh and get on the bed with him. David giggled and turned his head to look at Carman. He lay flat on his back with his eyes closed and his feet crossed. *"You look more comfortable now."* David whispered and Carman giggled. He turned to face David.

"No cheap feels, I am easily exited." Carman said and turned his head back to where it was and shut his eyes. David laughed and shut his eyes too.

"Thanks for taking us to Portland with you." David whispered and Carman smiled.

"It was Amanda's demand but I'm happy to do it." Carman whispered. David giggled and cleared his throat.

"Thanks for staying with me too."

"Are you kidding? I'm having the time of my life." Carman said sarcastically and David laughed. Carman sighed and cleared his throat. David looked at him to see Carman staring at him.

"What?" David asked.

"I would like to lay a bunch of stuff out on the table before you move in." Carman said. David raised his eyebrows and nodded. "Well, no horses in the house. That's rule number one." Carman said very officially. David giggled and nodded. "No meth labs." David giggled again and waited for the next rule. Carman sighed and swallowed hard. David frowned and waited quietly beside him. Carman seemed suddenly nervous.

"*What's wrong Carman?*" David asked. Carman sighed and rolled his body to face David. David did the same and they were lying fairly close in the little hospital bed.

"Alan is my best friend." Carman said quietly and David nodded. "He means a lot to me and I don't want to hurt him." Carman explained.

"*How would you hurt him from helping me and Amanda?*" David asked. Carman smiled and shook his head.

"That won't hurt him. I think he would expect me to."

"*Then what's the problem?*" David asked. Carman sighed and gently moved a loose strand of hair from David's face. David closed his eyes and sighed.

"That's the problem." Carman whispered referring to the reaction David had to his touch. David frowned and looked into Carman's eyes. "David, remember when I called you Alan's puppy?" Carman asked. David giggled and nodded. "Well, I like kissing you. I can't like it, ok?" Carman asked. David frowned and let out a long sigh.

"*What? I don't understand what you're trying to say.*" David said. Carman sighed and shook his head.

"I know things about Alan that no one else knows. You might not like to hear this but, you're really important to him." Carman said.

"*What does that have to do with you kissing me?*" David asked. Carman cleared his throat and sighed again.

"Well, I just don't want to get too attached to you. Sexually I mean. That would bother Alan."

"What does he care? He doesn't think about who he hurts when he gets into bed with some body." David said angrily and sat up. Carman closed his eyes and sighed.

"He didn't know how you feel." Carman offered. David shook his head and took a sip of his water.

"He's your friend and you're allowed to defend him. But I doubt it would have made a difference if he knew." David said. He leaned back on the pillow and closed his eyes.

"Well, knowing Alan, it would have made a *huge* difference." Carman said putting emphasis on the word 'huge'. David shook his head and Carman sighed. "David," Carman said. David sighed again and looked at him. "I would love to get to know you sexually, don't get me wrong but, until you get this stuff sorted out with Alan, it's better that we don't." Carman said. David smiled and nodded.

"You'll be a senior citizen before that happens." David said. Carman laughed and shook his head.

"Not if you can bring yourself to talk to him." Carman said. David rolled his eyes and sighed. "Not today, I know. But someday you will forgive him." Carman added. David raised an eyebrow and Carman giggled. They lay on their backs with their eyes closed until they were both asleep.

David woke up alone in his room. He yawned and stretched the sleep out of his body. The sun was shining outside and it was peeking through the blinds. He shifted in his bed and could feel that Carman's side was still warm. He smiled and took a sip from his cup. He looked out into the hallway and could see his Irish nurse. She smiled when she noticed him and came into the room.

"Where is your good looking friend?" She asked as she checked the I.V. machine. David giggled.

"*Which one?*" David asked in his husky whisper.

"The one that slept in here with you last night." She said and smiled with raised eyebrows. David shrugged and smiled back. "I hear we are unplugging you today. You ready to go home?"

"*Yea, I love you but I gotta get out of here.*" David said. The Irish nurse giggled and left the room. David smiled and watched the hallway. He could see a couple talking quietly with a young lady doctor at the counter. He could see a nurse going through some papers at the desk. She looked up at him and smiled. David smiled back and looked up at the ceiling. The lines seemed to be brighter. He smiled and looked back at the door. He could see Carman talking to the Irish nurse. She was laughing at whatever he said and David smiled. Carman turned around on one heal and headed to David's room.

"Guess what I just heard." Carman said and David smiled.

"*I'm getting out of here today.*" David said. Carman smiled and sat down in his chair.

"Well, something you didn't sleep through." Carman said. David giggled and took another sip of his water. "Amanda has been packing all night I hear." Carman said. David raised his eyebrows and looked at Carman.

"*Really?*" He asked. Carman nodded and smiled.

"She plans on getting you guys out of here by Saturday."

"*Ok, what day is it today?*" David asked. Carman laughed and shook his head.

"It's Thursday May 2, 2005." Carman said. David nodded and Carman giggled. The doctor came in and felt David's throat.

"How is it feeling today, Mr. Smith?" The doctor asked.

"*One hundred percent.*" David answered in his horrible sounding voice. The Doctor smiled and Carman laughed.

"Well, the scratchiness should go away in a few days. I wouldn't recommend drinking carbonated beverages but, coffee or tea would be good for it. So, I will get the paper work in order and get a nurse in here to remove your intervenes, ok?" The doctor said and David nodded. The doctor left and Carman laughed.

"To bad he isn't as good looking as that doctor I saw the other day." Carman said. David giggled and shook his head.

"Did you ever see him again?" David asked. Carman laughed and shook his head.

"Nope. I'm not that lucky I guess." Carman said. David giggled and looked at the door. His doctor was talking to the Irish nurse. She smiled and nodded and headed to David's room.

"I guess you're getting evicted." She said. David smiled and Carman giggled.

"He didn't like your crumby building anyway." Carman joked. David and the nurse laughed. She removed the I.V. and wheeled the cart away. David sat up and hung his legs over the bed.

"Do I have clothes here?" David asked. Carman got up and looked in the closet. There was nothing there.

"Well, you can't walk around town in your fancy gown. I'll get some clothes here for you." Carman said and took out his phone. He left the room and David sighed. He dropped himself off the bed and took a few steps. He was a little dizzy so he sat down in Carman's chair. He looked around the room and sighed. He was happy to be leaving but suddenly wondered if he really was as ready as he wanted to be. Just then, Carman came in and smiled. "Well, clothes are on the way." Carman said and sat down on the bed. David nodded and stretched again.

"You know, this whole time, I never sat in this chair." David said. Carman smiled and looked at the door. After a few seconds, he looked back at David.

"Watch the door. That hot doctor I told you about is gonna walk by here." Carman whispered. David giggled and watched the door. A few minutes went by before a young, tall, blonde haired doctor walked in front of it. He was well built and looked to be in his early thirties. David smiled and Carman giggled. "Hot right?" Carman asked. David nodded and the doctor looked in the room. He smiled at David and Carman and went along his way down the hall.

"*Wow, hot is right.*" David said having had a pretty good look at him. Carman nodded and smiled.

"I asked him to stand there for a second." Carman said. David laughed and shook his head.

"*You did not.*" David said and laughed.

"Yea I did. I told him you were a young guy who just got the crap beat out of him for being gay and needed something nice to look at. He practically volunteered." Carman said smiling. David laughed and shook his head.

"*You're so full of shit, Carman.*" David said through his laughing. His throat hurt but he didn't care.

"I'm serious. I guess he has a gay brother that got beat by kids at school when he was young. He was happy to help."

"*You lied to him just so I could see him?*" David asked. Carman smiled and nodded. David shook his head and laughed again. They talked about the hot doctor until there was a knock at the door. Carman and David both looked. Alan stepped in with a backpack David recognized to be Amanda's.

"Hi." Alan said and Carman stood up.

"I'll be back." He said and left the room. David sighed and nodded at Alan.

"Amanda packed it all so; I don't know what she sent." Alan said and set the bag on the floor at the foot of David's bed. "Your mom said you're talking now." Alan tried. David stared at him. His heart pounded in his chest and the palms of his hands sweat. He cleared his throat and then winced. Alan sighed and put his hands in his pockets. "Amanda is just about finished all the packing. She didn't know what you wanted done in that music room so she left it for you." Alan said in an almost sheepish voice. David sighed and nodded.

"Are you mad at Carman for doing this?" David asked in his husky whisper. Alan smiled and shook his head.

"No, I would be mad if he didn't." Alan said. David nodded and looked at the bag.

"Did she pack my deodorant and cologne?" David asked. Alan shrugged and handed the bag to David.

"I don't know what she packed. She just sent me with the bag." Alan said. David opened the bag and saw his cologne and deodorant right on top along with his brush and his tooth brush and tooth paste. David smiled and shut the bag. He looked up at Alan.

"Thanks." David said. Alan smiled and nodded.

"I'll get out of your hair so you can get dressed." Alan said and left the room. David sighed and took the bag to the bathroom. He put his clothes on and then applied his cologne and deodorant. He brushed his hair and his teeth and left the bathroom. He felt dizzy again and put his hand on the bed to steady himself. Carman came into the room and smiled at him.

"You look human now." Carman said. David smiled and tried to shake the dizziness off. Carman grabbed his arm and led him out of the room. Nancy was standing at the counter and she smiled at him.

"I'll see you when I get home tonight ok." She said. David nodded and Carman took him outside. They walked slowly to Carman's truck. Parked beside it was Alan's Wine colored 1969 Mustang Fastback.

David sighed and Carman rubbed his arm. Alan got out of his car and smiled at them.

"I just wanted to see you off." Alan said. Carman left David with Alan and went to his truck. David groaned and Alan sighed. "I asked him to do this." Alan said. David shook his head and looked into Alan's eyes. He could feel his heart pounding and his legs felt weeak.

"*Why?*" David asked. Alan sighed and stepped closer to David. David tensed up and Alan stopped where he stood.

"David, I'm sorry I hurt you. I wish I could go back in time and do it over again." Alan said and ran his hand through his hair. David clenched his teeth and shook his head.

"*Don't do this. I don't want to hear you apologize or make excuses or anything else. Thank you for cutting me down out of that tree so I can see my baby be born and grow up. You owe me nothing. We are even, ok.*" David said. Tears burned his eyes and he turned away. Alan sighed and shook his head.

"I saved you because . . ." Alan stopped talking and looked down at the floor. David looked at him and Alan stared into his eyes. "I saved you because you're David. I need you. You're so important to me." Alan said and David rolled his eyes.

"*Which is why it was so important to keep your relationship with my mom away from me?*" David asked. Alan closed his eyes and turned around. David stared at his back and shook his head. "*Look, don't hurt yourself Alan. I will be fine. Thank you for the second chance.*" David said and headed toward the truck. Alan sighed and watched him walk away.

"David." Alan said. David stopped but didn't turn around. "I promise not to hurt her. I swear to you I will never hurt her. I am so sorry I hurt you." He said. David shook his head and turned around.

"*You didn't know how I felt. Just take care of her.*" David said and walked to the truck. Carman opened the door for him and waved at Alan. Alan waved back and got into his car. Carman started the truck and looked at David.

"Are you ok?" Carman asked. David shook his head and a tear ran down his face. Carman gently wiped it away and David smiled. "He loves you, you know." Carman said. David rolled his eyes and looked out the window.

"*I bet.*" David answered with a hint of sarcasm. Carman sighed and pulled the truck out of the parking lot. He pulled onto Main Street and headed for the highway.

"I guess Amanda's almost done. All that's left is the music room. We could leave tomorrow if you got it done fast enough." Carman offered. David looked at him with surprised eyes.

"*Aren't you supposed to try to keep me here long enough to talk to him or something?*" David asked. Carman smiled and shook his head.

"You're not ready to talk to him yet. When the time comes, you'll do it on your own." Carman said. David shook his head and sighed.

"*That will be a long time from now.*" Carman smiled and pulled out on to the highway. He drove in silence while David tapped the arm rest to music only he could hear. Carman smiled at him and David noticed. "*What?*" He asked. Carman shook his head and looked out the windshield.

"You two are so alike." Carman said. David looked at him and winced.

"*How can you say that?*" He asked. Carman looked at David and smiled.

"He stays mad for a long time too. Always thinking the situation over until he has beaten it to death. He also taps to music no one else can hear." Carman said. David stopped tapping and sighed. Carman giggled and pulled out to pass a little car.

"*He makes me so mad.*" David said quietly. Carman nodded and smiled.

"Wait till you have 20 some years under your belt with him." David rolled his eyes and looked out the window. Carman laughed and turned on the radio. The news was on and he shut it off. David smiled and looked at him.

"*You don't like the news?*" David asked. Carman giggled and shook his head.

"I never understood why they call it 'The News'. It's never new." Carman said. David thought about it for a second and then laughed. It hurt his throat and he winced. "No pain killers or nothing?" Carman asked and David shook his head.

"*It's just like a really bad sore throat. I guess I just have to tough it out.*" David said. Carman smiled and nodded. He slowed the truck and turned into town. David sighed and watched out the window.

"When we get there, you should shower. I have a date planned for you." Carman said. David looked at him and frowned.

"*A date?*" David asked. Carman nodded but kept a straight face. "*If its Alan, I'll kill you.*" Carman shook his head and looked at David.

"I wouldn't do that. Just shower and be ready to go in half an hour." Carman said. David rolled his eyes and Carman smiled. He pulled the truck up to the house and they both got out. David walked up to the door and Amanda met him there.

"You're late." Amanda said. David frowned and looked at Carman. He giggled and pointed up the stairs. Amanda kissed David and pointed up the stairs as well. David shook his head and went up the stairs. He went into the bathroom and got into the shower. He washed his hair and thought about Alan.

Why didn't you just tell me? He thought. Tears ran down his face as he stood in the shower and let the water beat against his skin. He was there for quite some time until there was a knock at the bathroom door.

"*Yea.*" David answered half annoyed at the interruption. The door opened and it was Amanda.

"You're going to be late for your date if you don't hurry." Amanda said. David smiled and shook his head.

"*Can't I have a hint?*" David asked. Amanda giggled and left the room. David shook his head and turned off the shower. He got out and got dressed in a nice pair of light blue jeans and a tight black t-shirt. He put on cologne and deodorant and brushed his hair. He looked at himself in the mirror and sighed. There were light bruises on his throat where the rope had pulled taught. It looked almost like hickies that had caused his skin to dry up in those places. He left the room and went down the stairs. He looked at the clock as he entered the kitchen. It was 2:30 pm. Carman smiled and stood up from the table.

"*What's going on?*" David asked and rubbed his throat with his fingers. Carman led David to the door and opened it. Outside, David could see the car that Amanda had given him that once belonged to Gabe. The big black Hearse was clean and shining in the sun. David smiled and stepped outside. Carman followed him out and they both got in. David looked at him and smiled. "*A date with my car?*" David asked and Carman smiled.

"A date with me, but you're driving." Carman said. David laughed and winced at the pain. He noticed his throat hurt worse than before.

"*I always kiss on a first date.*" David warned trying to ignore the pain and Carman laughed.

"So do I." Carman said. David laughed and started the car. The engine roared to life and David closed his eyes.

"Hello baby." David whispered. Carman smiled and looked out the windshield. *"So, where are we going?"* David asked. Carman looked at him and smiled.

"We are going to the park." Carman said. David rolled his eyes and pulled away from the house.

"The park? That's pretty gay." David said and Carman laughed. David drove and Carman said nothing. He turned into the town park and found a place to park his big car. They both got out and Carman smiled.

"Come with me." Carman said. David followed him through the park to the pond. He looked at Carman as they walked.

"What are we doing here?" David asked in his husky whisper. Carman stopped walking and sat down on a bench. David sat down next to him and stared at his face.

"We are here to talk." Carman said. David rolled his eyes and looked out on the pond.

"About what?" David asked. Carman sighed and looked out on the pond with David.

"Amanda is worried that you may have a relapse on these hurt feelings if you can't fill the hole." Carman said. David shook his head and looked at Carman.

"A relapse? That's stupid. And what do you mean fill the hole? Replace Alan or Gabe maybe? Not possible." David said. Carman grabbed David's face and kissed him. David's eyes grew wide but he joined the kiss right away. Carman's kiss was like licking satin. His breathing sped up and Carman moaned. He finished the kiss and looked at David. David blinked and swallowed hard.

"Does that help?" Carman asked. David giggled and shook his head.

"What about Alan and how mad he'll be?" David whispered. Carman shifted in his seat and cleared his throat.

"I don't plan on fucking you David. But I like kissing you and Amanda said I was allowed to." Carman said. David laughed and shook his head.

"Ok." David said with skepticism in his voice. Carman giggled and shook his head.

"David, I'm not a replacement. Amanda just wants you to be comfortable with me. She hated seeing your discomfort with Alan. She thinks if you feel like you belong there, you'll be less likely to relapse." Carman said. David laughed and shook his head.

"I would have been comfortable in your home even you didn't do that." David said. Carman nodded and looked out at the pond.

"I know. The kiss was for me." Carman confessed. David laughed again and shook his head.

"You're so confusing." Carman smiled and stood up. David stood up with him and they walked around the pond.

"I actually brought you out here to talk about Alan." David sighed and shook his head.

"I don't want to." He said and Carman nodded.

"That's ok. I'll talk, you listen." Carman said. David rolled his eyes but agreed. "Ok, where do I start? I guess you should know that if you repeat this, I'll have to kill you." Carman said. David smiled and nodded. "Ok, you know about Alan's house arrest and the shit with me and Charlie right?" Carman asked.

"Yea, Alan kicked the shit out of some guy that raped you and then Charlie had to tutor him at home. You and Charlie had some kind of an affair and it pissed off Alan, right?" David asked recapping what Alan had told him and Carman nodded.

"Alan didn't kick the shit out of him. He raped him with a dagger."
Carman said. David raised his eyebrows and cleared his throat. That
was the part that Alan had left out. All he had said was that what
he had done wasn't anything nice. He was right. Carman sighed and
continued. "Yea, so anyway, Charlie found out what really happed and
wanted to help Alan out. Alan wasn't as interested in Charlie as Charlie
would have liked so he took the second best. This was apparently me.
I didn't believe Alan's claim that Charlie had hit on him first and that
hurt him. We had a big fight about it and he moved away. When I
started seeing a pattern with Charlie and him 'tutoring' teenage boys,
I broke it off. He freaked out that I would tell the cops or his wife so
he promised to quit taking on these kids. He did and he hasn't ever
since. Alan never believed it, but I stayed in Portland all these years
just to keep an eye on him. That's why I never rewrote the bar exam.
I would have to leave Portland and I wouldn't be able to keep an eye
on Charlie. Well, it was a stupid choice. Charlie hasn't tutored since
and apparently he and his wife have gone through a ton of counseling
and shit and he hasn't been with another guy since me." Carman said.
David sighed as they turned the corner to walk around the little pond
again. "Anyway, Alan had an issue with the whole thing. He didn't
believe that Charlie had quit so he did a little investigation himself.
When he realized I was right, it was three years later and he felt it
was too late to save our lifelong friendship. One night, when I was in
college, Alan showed up to a party that one of his other friends was
having. It happened to be in my dorm and we literally ran into each
other in the hall. We had a long talk and pretty soon the party was in
my room and we had started a game of truth and dare. Anyway, Alan
was dared to kiss me and to my surprise, he did." Carman said. David
stopped and looked at him.

"*He just kissed you?*" David asked. Carman nodded and then smiled.

"David, you are an awesome kisser but that kiss was . . ." Carman stopped talking and started walking again. David walked with him. "Anyway, after that we were close again. It was that night that we invented that game we always play. The biggest rule was that we have to do it every time we see each other. That's how you got mixed up in it. Once you play it's kind of an addiction." Carman said. David smiled and nodded. "Well, so was that kiss. That's when we placed a bet. If I win, I get a night in bed with Alan." Carman said. David smiled and nodded again. He had remembered Alan telling him about the bet the last time they had visited Carman.

"*Alan said your better at it then he is and you could probably win. Why don't you do it if it's so important to you to be with him?*" David asked. Carman smiled and shook his head.

"Alan was so fucked up after what he did to that guy that I'm afraid it would scare him. I think it would be a friendship ender." Carman said. David thought about it for a second.

"*If Alan is straight, why would he make a bet like that?*" David asked. Carman smiled and stopped walking.

"I wouldn't go as far as saying Alan is straight, David. Charlie scared him so badly that he said it would take a pretty special guy if he were to explore those feelings." Carman said. David felt faint and Carman caught him. David's breathing was heavy and Carman sat him down on the ground. "Are you ok?" Carman asked.

"*God, no.*" David said and rubbed his throat with his fingers.

"David, I am the only one who knows. He would have never told you even if you told him how you felt. He is so afraid of it. Try not to freak out, or anything." Carman said quietly. David looked into his eyes.

"I knew it. I knew it but I was too afraid to talk to him about it." David said. Carman smiled and nodded.

"Well, now you know how he felt about telling you about your mom." Carman said. David shook his head in disbelief and tried to clear his throat but it hurt terribly. Carman sighed and rubbed David's back. "What are you thinking right now?" Carman asked. David looked at him and shook his head.

"Like I've been lied to for a whole year and expected to accept it in five minutes." David said and Carman sighed.

"You don't need to accept anything. I just wanted you to understand him a little better." Carman said. David sighed and stood up. Carman stood with him and looked him in the eyes. "Do you understand him better?" Carman asked and David nodded.

"It just makes me way angrier." David said. Carman smiled and they walked back to the car and got in.

"He loves you, you know." Carman repeated the same statement he had said at the hospital. David rolled his eyes and shook his head.

"Not enough." David said and Carman laughed.

"Wow, you are a bitter young man, David Smith." Carman said as David pulled away from the park. David shook his head and looked out the window. When they arrived at David's house, Amanda and Nancy had supper ready. They all ate and talked about the move. When dinner was over, David went downstairs and looked in the music room. He ran his fingers along Gabe's electric guitars. He looked at the busted drum kit that he had smashed with his father's beloved guitar. He shook his head and grabbed the two guitars that once belonged to Gabe and took them upstairs. Amanda smiled at him and he took the guitars out to his car. He set them in the back and came back into the house. He went into the living room and grabbed the beautiful guitar Alan had got him for Christmas and put it in its case.

He put the collection of music books in the case with it and took it and his amp out to the car. He shut the back and went into the house. He sat at the table and looked at Amanda.

"*Well, I'm packed.*" He said and Nancy laughed.

"You remind me of your father. If the guitars are loaded, you're ready to go." She said. Everyone laughed and Carman looked at the clock. He sighed and looked at David.

"Can I talk to you outside?" Carman asked. David nodded and they both stood up. They walked outside to Carman's truck. Carman faced David and sighed. "Would it piss you off if I stayed out at Alan's tonight?" Carman asked. David smiled and shook his head.

"*No, you should go see him. Don't tell him you told me all that stuff.*" David said in his husky whisper and put his arms around Carman. Carman smiled and hugged him.

"I will be back tomorrow to take you and your little family home. Ok?" Carman whispered. David nodded and let Carman go. Carman quickly kissed David and got into the truck. He smiled and waved as Carman drove away. He went back into the house and sat at the table with Nancy and Amanda. Little Mike was playing on the floor with a wooden spoon and a sour cream container.

"That was cute." Nancy said and Amanda giggled.

"*What was cute?*" David asked. Nancy shook her head and smiled.

"She saw you kiss Carman." Amanda whispered.

"*Oh.*" David said and looked at Little Mike. Nancy giggled and handed David a lit cigarette. He smiled and took a long drag from it.

"So, you're leaving tomorrow?" Nancy asked.

"*Yea, I think it's better to just get it over with.*" David said. Nancy nodded and sighed.

"You can't stay one more day?" She asked. David sighed and shook his head. Nancy nodded and took a drag of her cigarette.

"I think it's good that David wants to get on with his life right away." Amanda said and smiled. Nancy smiled at her and looked at her son.

"Are you running away, or moving on?" Nancy asked.

"*I am moving forward mom.*" David said and smiled at Amanda. Amanda giggled and David rubbed her stomach. Nancy smiled and nodded.

"I believe you are." She said. She giggled and touched Amanda's stomach too. "Oh I wish it was big enough to kick." Nancy said. The girls giggled over the baby while David looked out the window.

Amanda and David slept together in David's bed. He had nightmares about Gabe that woke him up over and over. Amanda woke up and rubbed his back until he fell asleep.

"I love you." She whispered. David smiled and kissed her. She cuddled up against his chest and they fell asleep for the rest of the night.

Chapter 4

With the car and truck loaded, David helped Amanda with the few things from Gabe's room in her house that she wanted to bring. He carried the boxes up to the car and loaded them in. Nancy had Mike ready to go and handed him to Amanda. They said their good byes and Amanda put him in the car. She buckled him in and got into the front seat. David hugged his mother and walked over to the car. As he opened the door, he could see Alan's car pull up in front of Carman's truck. He walked up to him with his hands in his pockets.

"I wanted to say good bye." Alan said quietly. David sighed and looked down at the ground.

"*Why?*" David asked. Alan winced at him and shook his head.

"I didn't want you to leave without saying good bye first." Alan repeated. David sighed and looked into Alan's eyes.

"*I thought we agreed we were even?*" David whispered and rubbed his throat with his fingers. Alan itched the back of his neck and sighed.

"You agreed." Alan said. David shook his head. The story Carman told him ran through his head.

"*Well, I've recently changed my mind. But that still don't make it all better.*" David said. Alan frowned and looked into David's eyes.

"Please, David. What do I have to do to make this better?" Alan pleaded quietly. David shook his head and looked at Carman. Carman smiled at him and David sighed. He looked back at Alan and stepped toward him. Alan slowly took his hands out of his pockets and seemed almost ready to block a punch or something. David stepped closer again and hugged Alan. Alan hugged back and tears filled David's eyes.

"*Please don't hurt her, Alan.*" David whispered. Alan squeezed David harder.

"I promise, David. Please be careful out there." Alan whispered. David's heart pounded in his chest as Alan held him. He breathed in Alan's sent and felt his legs weaken.

"*You need to let go of me.*" David whispered. He could hear Alan swallow hard and then sigh. He let David go and stepped back.

"Take care of yourself, ok." Alan said. David nodded and got into the car. He started the engine and pulled away.

"Zoom, Zoom!" Mike said in the back and Amanda smiled. David stared stone faced out the windshield. Carman followed behind them.

"It's nice you said good bye, David." Amanda said quietly. David shook his head and tightened his grip on the steering wheel.

"*I'm sure it was nice to look at but it killed me to do it.*" David whispered. Amanda nodded and looked out the window. They drove in silence until the first stop. Amanda got out and went into the gas station to go to the bathroom. David staid at the car and had a cigarette while Little Mike slept in the back. Carman joined him at the car.

"You doing ok?" Carman asked. David shook his head and blew the toxic smoke out of his lungs. "That was a good hug." Carman said. David looked at him and shook his head.

"*That hug was for mom.*" David said and looked back down at the ground. Carman sighed and took another drag from his cigarette.

"I had a good talk with him last night." Carman said.

"*I don't want to hear about it.*" Carman nodded and threw his cigarette on the ground and stepped on it. David looked at him and Carman smiled.

"It was a really good talk." Carman said trying to convince David to hear it.

"*Another time, Carman.*" David said quietly. Carman smiled and nodded. Amanda came out of the gas station and smiled at the men by the car.

"I'm ready when you are." Amanda said in her sweet voice. David smiled at her as she got into the car.

"You haven't said a word to her the hold trip, have you?" Carman asked. David sighed and shook his head. "You should, *she* didn't make you feel the way you do." Carman said and patted David's back. David smiled and they headed to their vehicles.

"*I'll follow you.*" David said and Carman nodded. They got into their vehicles and David leaned over and kissed Amanda. She giggled and touched her lips.

"What was that for?" She asked. David smiled and started the car.

"*I thought you could use a kiss. I know I did.*" David said. Amanda smiled and nodded. David giggled and pulled out on to the highway behind Carman.

"So, you and Carman huh?" Amanda asked. David laughed and shook his head.

"*No, he's just Carman. That kiss was just because.*" David said. Amanda giggled and shook her head. They talked about the baby and they both decided they wanted a girl. They changed the conversation for a while and they laughed talking about Carman. When they pulled into Portland, Mike had been awake for quite a while and wanted to eat. David followed Carman's red pickup truck into Carman's yard and they both parked in front of the house. David got out of the car and stretched. Amanda took Mike out of the car and let him run around the yard. Carman laughed as Mike tried to catch a frog.

"This is the perfect place for him." Amanda said and wrapped her arm around David's waist. David smiled and kissed the top of her head. She giggled and looked around the property. "Why buy a horse farm so close to the city?" Amanda asked Carman. He looked at her and smiled.

"It wasn't always so close. The city has certainly grown over the last few years." Carman said. Mike grabbed his shirt and Carman looked at him. The little boy pointed at a big black horse at the fence. "Let's go see him then." Carman said. Mike squealed as Carman picked him up. Amanda and David giggled and followed Carman and Mike to the fence. The horse snorted as Mike pet him.

"He is beautiful." Amanda said and Carman smiled.

"His name is Diablo. He is a Friesian horse. I got him about six months ago and can't seem to get any work done with him." Carman said as everyone pet the horse.

"*He seems friendly enough.*" David said. Carman raised an eyebrow and shook his head.

"Well, that's because we are on this side of the fence. That horse is going to be the death of me I think." Carman said.

"Why do you have him if he is so dangerous?" Amanda asked. Carman smiled and looked at David.

"Because he reminds me of Alan." Carman said. David giggled and shook his head. Amanda frowned and looked at Carman.

"Why?" She asked.

"Well, he is the most beautiful creature I've ever seen, but no matter what I do, he won't let me ride him." Carman said. Amanda shook her head and smiled and David laughed.

"Great, two of you." She said and Carman laughed. Mike ran across the yard after his frog again and Carman, David, and Amanda walked up to the house.

"So, pizza or Chinese?" Carman asked. Amanda and David looked at each other. David shrugged and Amanda looked at Carman.

"Well, pizza I think."

"Sounds good." Carman said. He went inside and got the cordless phone. He came out and led David and Amanda to the patio table. "What do we like?" Carman asked dialing the phone.

"Mike and I like meat lovers." Amanda answered and Carman looked at David.

"*Anything with beacon.*" David said. Carman smiled and ordered two medium meat lovers with beacon. He hung up the phone and looked at Amanda.

"You a horse person?"

"Well, my uncle has horses. I try to get out and ride every year but I think I might miss this year." Amanda answered and rubbed her stomach. David smiled and sighed.

"Well, I have a real gentle mare out here that you could ride pretty safely. She could use some exorcize." Carman offered.

"Oh that would be nice."

"*How many do you have?*" David asked in his scratchy sounding whisper. He rubbed his throat with his fingers and winced. He wished he could have left the pain behind him like he had left Alan.

"I have nine. That big black Diablo, Then that mare I was talking about. She's a little pinto mare called Pocahontas, but I call her Pokey for short." Carman said and Amanda smiled. "Then there is a gray Thoroughbred gelding named Spike and a red roan Tennessee Walker out there called Jack. I got a buck skin mountain pony named Misery, and that's exactly what she is." Carman said in a memory induced revelation. Amanda and David laughed. "Then I have the black Quarter Horse team out there. The mare is Heather and the gelding is Murphy. Then there is this little Arabian Stallion, Cocaine Safari that Jan just had to have. I just call him Cain. He is a sweet heart but needs an experienced rider. He's a little squirrelly. And, last but not least, is Holly Dunn. She is my little jenny donkey. Mikey could ride her. She's a doll." Carman said.

"I would love to have a collection of horses like that." Amanda said. David giggled and shook his head.

"What about you David? Got any horse interest?" Carman asked. David sighed and rolled his eyes.

"*I guess their alright.*" David said. Amanda giggled and shook her head. Carman looked at her with a puzzled gaze.

"You are so funny David." Amanda said then turned to Carman, "I take him out to my uncles with me and I can't keep him away from them." She said with a giggle.

"So, you're a horse man too?" Carman asked and winked.

"*I know my way around a saddle I guess.*" David said. Amanda shook her head and smiled.

"Give him a week with that Diablo and you'll see." Amanda said. David shook his head and sighed.

"A horse whisperer, huh?" Carman asked and David shook his head.

"I just understand them, that's all." David said. Mike ran up on the deck with his frog to show Carman.

"You caught him, did you?" Carman asked.

"Yea, and he is name Frank!" Mike said and Carman smiled at his enthusiasm.

"Let's find him a dish." Carman said and took Mike and his frog into the house. Amanda giggled and David grabbed her hand. She looked at him and smiled.

"I'm glad we did this." Amanda said and smiled.

"Me too." David said and leaned over to kiss Amanda. She smiled and kissed him gently on the mouth.

"I love you." She whispered and David smiled. "You said it once or twice before. Why don't you ever say it, David?" Amanda asked and David sighed.

"I'm sorry. I love you." David said and smiled. Amanda shook her head and giggled.

"Don't say it to make me happy, David. Say it because you want to." She said and squeezed David's hand. He nodded and squeezed back. Mike and Carman came outside with Frank in a large plastic container. Amanda smiled as Mike brought the container to her.

"Frank need a brother." Mike said and ran out onto the grass. David giggled and shook his head.

"That's the biggest container with a lid I own. I hope he doesn't fill it with frogs and bring it into the house." Carman said and Amanda laughed.

"I thought the rule was no horses in the house. You never said anything about frogs." David said. Carman laughed and nodded.

"I guess I didn't."

"No horses in the house is seriously a rule?" Amanda asked. Carman nodded and David laughed. "What else should I know?"

"No meth labs." David answered and Amanda giggled. Mike squealed out in the grass as he chased another frog. Carman looked across the table into David's eyes as Amanda watched Little Mike in the grass. David smiled and Carman winked.

"I might have to buy a frog tank." Carman said as Mike came to the deck with a frog in each hand. Amanda laughed and helped Mike get his frogs into the container. Carman looked up as the pizza kid came into the yard. He walked to the car and paid him. He brought the pizza up to the table and set the boxes down.

"Where do I find plates?" Amanda asked as she stood up.

"In the cupboard above the microwave." Carman said. Amanda nodded and went into the house.

"She's gonna shit when she sees that pool table." David said and Carman smiled.

"For your information, I switched the pool table out for the dining room table from the living room." Carman said and giggled. David smiled and shook his head.

"You expected this didn't you?" David asked.

"Alan did." Carman answered quietly and watched Mike collect rocks for his frogs. David sighed and looked down at the pizza boxes. Amanda came out and handed David and Carman each a plate with a fork and knife set on them.

"Come on, Mike!" Amanda called. Mike pocketed his rocks and came up to eat. They discussed a few apartments Carman knew of while they ate. Mike put in his two cents about extra rooms for his frogs and the toys he wanted to get. Carman would laugh and tell him he had it covered. When they finished their meal, Amanda took Mike in for a bath and Carman and David took the dishes and the left over pizza into the house. Carman loaded the dish washer and David put the pizza in the fridge.

"It looks nice in here with a dining table." David said. Carman sighed and leaned on the counter.

"I miss the pool table." David laughed and shook his head. Carman smiled and poured two rum and cokes and handed one to David.

"Thanks. I just hope it doesn't hurt." David said and stared into the cup.

"Well, there's only one way to find out." David raised his eyebrows and took a sip. The alcohol burned all the way down and David winced. "That's the first time I have ever seen you react to a drink." Carman said. David shivered and looked at Carman.

"It should just get easier from here, right?" David asked. Carman laughed and shrugged. He took a sip and smiled at David.

"It's not that strong." Carman said. David shook his head and took another sip. He winced again and Carman laughed.

"Laugh it up princess; I could still drink you under the table." David said and Carman laughed.

"I don't doubt that." Carman said and led David into the living room where the pool table was. They sat down on a couple of stools Carman had set up at a little table by the window. "Is she gonna be happy here for a while?" Carman asked.

"Yea, she said she was happy we did this." David answered and Carman smiled.

"That's good." Carman said and lit a cigarette. David did the same and they could hear Amanda laughing at Little Mike. "She's going to be an awesome mom." Carman said.

"Yea, she is." David said and smiled. Carman sighed and looked into David's eyes.

"Are YOU gonna be happy here for a while?" Carman asked. David stared in Carman's eyes and smiled.

"*Are you kidding?*" David asked and smiled. Carman giggled and shook his head.

"Well, I'm glad to help you guys out. It's nice to have people here. It's a big house." Carman said and took a sip from his drink then a drag from his cigarette.

"*Thanks, Carman. This is really awesome.*" David said. Carman sighed and shook his head.

"It's strange to have you here without Alan." He said.

"*Why?*" David asked in his husky whisper.

"Well, you guys are kind of a pair." Carman said. David rolled his eyes and took another burning sip of rum.

"*Not anymore.*" David whispered and Carman sighed.

"Remember that talk I told you Alan and I had?" Carman asked and David nodded. "Do you want to hear about it now?" David sighed and shook his head.

"*Carman, give me some time. I'm really not interested in talking about him.*" David said and took a sip from his drink.

"Ok, you'll be shocked." Carman said and David giggled.

"*I bet.*" David said and Carman laughed. They talked about David's throat until Amanda came out of the bathroom with Little Mike in his pajama's.

"Which room is his?" Amanda asked. Carman sat back in his stool.

"Pick one." Carman said to Mike. He smiled and went through every room down the hallway. He picked Carman's. Carman giggled and nodded. "Sure, why not?" Carman said. Amanda smiled and Mike said his good nights to David and Carman and Amanda took him into Carman's room.

"You gave up your king sized bed to a three year old." David said and laughed.

"Well, if sleeping in Uncle Carman's bed helps him sleep for the first few nights, he's welcome to it." Carman said.

"Uncle Carman, that's funny." David said and took another sip. Carman laughed and kicked David under the table. David laughed and shook his head. *"Can I ask you something?"* Carman smiled and nodded. *"How is it that a guy like you is single?"*

"Well, Jan and I were together for five years. It was a rough break up and I am just enjoying being a bachelor again. Why do you ask?" Carman answered. David smiled and shook his head.

"It's just that, you're a really hot guy, your funny, you're great with people and really easy to talk to. I think it's funny they aren't beating down your door." David said. Carman laughed and shook his head.

"Well, thank you for the compliments but, I'm not looking for a relationship I guess. I've been on a couple dates since Jan left but, I'm not interested in more than sex right now." Carman said. David laughed and shook his head.

"At least you know what you want." Carman laughed again and shook his head.

"Hardly. I have no idea what I want. I just know that right now, I want to have my house to myself and get laid once in a while." David laughed and nodded.

"I get that." David said. They looked down the hall as Amanda entered their line of sight.

"Well, he has all the pillows piled around him to keep the monsters away and has decided that Carman's room is now his room." She said and sat down on the rocking chair in the corner. Carman laughed and shook his head.

"He is welcome to it." He said. Amanda smiled and yawned.

"*Where do we sleep?*" David asked Carman seeing Amanda's fatigue. Carman raised his eyebrows and gestured to the room Alan had slept in. David sighed and looked at Carman.

"It's the second nicest bed in the house." Carman whispered. David nodded and got up. He walked over to Amanda and took her hand. He led her to the bed room and sighed before he opened the door. Carman smiled as they stepped in. David turned on the light and looked at the room. There were heavy dark curtains on the windows and matching blankets on the bed.

"Oh, this is nice." Amanda said and touched the blankets. David smiled and nodded. He pictured Alan sleeping naked in the beautiful room. He clenched his teeth and quickly dismissed the thought. Amanda sat down on the bed and sighed. "Can you go to the car and get our overnight bags?" Amanda asked.

"*Of course, Babe.*" David said and left the room. Carman smiled at him and David shook his head.

"What?" Carman asked. David sighed and put his shoes on. Carman followed him out.

"*Guess what the first thing I thought of when I went in there.*" David asked as they walked to the back of the Hearse. Carman smiled and waited for David to open the back.

"Alan sleeping naked in those big, downy blankets?" Carman asked. David sighed and handed Carman one of the bags. He took the other one out of the car and closed the door. He looked at Carman and nodded. Carman laughed and followed David back to the house.

"*Not funny.*" David said as they went into the house.

"It kind of is because that's what I think of whenever I go in there." Carman said. David shook his head and sighed.

"*Your Carman though. You're supposed to think like that about everybody.*" Carman laughed and handed the bag to David.

"I'm not that bad. You should have a great sleep in there." Carman said and David shook his head.

"*It's Alan's bed, Carman.*" David said. Carman shook his head and put a hand on David's shoulder.

"It's you and Amanda's bed now. That's how I see it."

"*Yea, well. You're not sleeping in there.*" David said and Carman smiled.

"If it makes you feel better, I AM the last person to sleep in there." Carman offered. David looked at him and smiled.

"*That does make me feel better.*" Carman smiled and hugged David.

"Have a good sleep." Carman said. David dropped the bags and wrapped his arms around Carman.

"*Thanks for all this.*" David whispered. Carman shook his head.

"Stop thanking me. We're passed that now, ok?"

"*Ok.*" David said and giggled.

"Better go to Amanda before I decide your sleeping with me." Carman whispered. David giggled and nodded his head. They let each other go and David went into the room with the bags. Amanda was already asleep and David smiled at her. He undressed and got Amanda and himself under the blankets. He cuddled up behind her and closed his eyes. The bed was incredibly comfortable and David found himself falling asleep quite easily. That night he dreamed of Alan. He dreamed that Alan was standing in front of a giant chalk board just staring at him. His beautiful light green eyes were bright and his sandy hair hung in his face. He looked as though he was ready to pounce on him. David dreamed that he stood up from the only desk in the center of the room and walked up to Alan to stand right in front of him. Alan sighed and bit his bottom lip. David tried to say something but the sound wouldn't come out. Alan put his hands up and David realized that Alan was in a glass box. He touched the glass and Alan put his hand against David's. David rubbed the glass box with his thumb and Alan smiled. Alan's mouth moved but David couldn't make out what he said. 'I can't hear you' he said in his dream. Alan moved his mouth again but David still couldn't make it out. 'What are you trying to say?" David asked. Alan stared into David's eyes and tears of blood began to fall from his eyes. David hit the box with his fists but he couldn't break through. Alan just stood there as the box quickly filled with his blood. David screamed and hit the box harder and harder but it never even cracked. The blood was up to Alan's chin now and Alan spoke. 'Don't let me go' He said calmly and David screamed again. The blood slowly filled passed Alan's mouth and nose but Alan didn't move. David cried and beat on the box. As the blood completely covered Alan's head, David sunk to the ground crying out Alan's name. Suddenly he could hear Amanda's voice but it sounded strange. He strained to hear it in his dream and suddenly he was awake.

"David, are you ok?" She asked. David was sweating and his body was vibrating. He looked at her and tried to catch his breath. "It was a night mare, Hun. Are you ok?" She asked again. David looked around the room. He managed to catch his breath and nodded. "You were dreaming about Alan." Amanda whispered. David nodded and sighed. "Want to talk about it?" She asked. David shook his head and Amanda smiled. "Ok." She whispered and laid her head on his chest. David gently rubbed her back with the hand on the arm she laid on. He stared up at the ceiling and shivered. Amanda rubbed David's leg and he smiled.

"*I'm ok.*" He whispered.

"Your voice sounded normal when you were yelling in your sleep." Amanda said in a groggy voice.

"That would explain why it hurts so much." David whispered. Amanda nodded and David could hear her breathing slow back down as she fell back to sleep. He closed his eyes and continued rubbing her back.

God that was a fucked up dream. David thought and yawned. He was soon back to sleep.

Chapter 5

As the first week went by, David's throat slowly healed but his nightmare about Alan plagued his dreams. He would wake up the same way every night. Sweating and screaming and Amanda trying to get him to talk about it. He never would and she was becoming concerned.

It was Sunday morning and David was leaning on the fence that held the big black horse, Diablo. He held a coffee in one hand and a cigarette in the other. Carman came to stand next to him.

"Good morning." Carman said and David smiled.

"Hi."

"It's not too often that someone is up and out here before I am."

"Well, I guess you'll have to start getting up even earlier." David said. Carman smiled and leaned his back against the fence.

"Amanda told me you've been having some trouble sleeping." David sighed and shook his head.

"I can sleep. I just can't STAY sleeping." David said. He took the last drag from his cigarette and stepped on it.

"Nightmares right?" Carman asked. David nodded and Carman shook his head.

"I think nightmares would be normal after what you've been through."

"Not a dream like this." David said and stared out at Diablo. Carman turned around and looked at the horse that David stared at.

"Do you wanna talk about it?" Carman asked. David sighed and shook his head.

"Not really."

"You used to talk to me about everything. Why the locked jaw?" Carman asked. David sighed and looked at Carman.

"I just don't want to talk about it." David said.

"You don't want to talk about it because it's about Alan?" David sighed and looked back out at the horse.

"How did you know that?"

"Well, I can hear you screaming at night. I can hear you saying his name. I just put two and two together."

"Oh." David said and sighed. Diablo looked up from his grazing and stared at them. David smiled at him and patted the fence. Diablo snorted and took a few steps forward than stopped. Carman smiled and shook his head.

"He knows your upset. He can feel it. You shouldn't keep this stuff inside like this. You should talk about it."

"Well, it's just a dream, Carman. One night it won't happen and then I guess, I'll be cured." David said and patted the fence again. Diablo snorted and pawed at the dry dirt in his pen. David giggled and looked at Carman. "He *is* like Alan." Carman laughed and shook his head.

"I told you." Carman said. David patted the fence again and Diablo tossed his head. Both men laughed and turned around to head back toward the house. "Amanda found an apartment to go look at today." Carman said as they sat down at the table.

"She did? That was fast."

"Well, she said she felt like a burden and wanted to get you guys your own place before you over staid your welcome." Carman explained. David smiled and took a sip of his cool coffee.

"Have we?" David asked. Carman smiled and shook his head.

"Of course not. I was actually hoping it would take longer."

"Why?" David asked laughing. Carman smiled and leaned close to him.

"I like having you here." He said quietly and winked. David smiled and shook his head.

"I bet you do." David said in a seductive sounding voice. Carman laughed and leaned back in his chair.

"The apartment is close I guess."

"How close?" David asked. Carman smiled and pointed down the highway. David turned around and followed Carman's finger. He could see a high-rise apartment passed the two over passes. "In that thing?" David asked and Carman nodded.

"I have a friend in that building and his place is gorgeous."

"How much does it cost?" David asked still staring at the large mostly glass building.

"As far as I know, the lower the floor, the cheaper the rent."

"I hope the apartment is on the first floor." Carman laughed and shook his head.

"Fifth floor Amanda said."

"Huh, where is she?" David asked and went to stand but Carman stopped him.

"She went in to the city with my car to get some special soap for Little Mike. He has a rash or something."

"A rash?" David asked sitting back down and looking at Carman.

"Yea, something about the grass or something."

"She never said anything to me."

"I guess it's a new thing. She noticed it this morning." Carman said. David raised his eyebrows and sighed.

"Hope she doesn't get lost or something."

"There is a drug store just passed the first over pass. That's where I sent her before I went looking for you."

"So she just left then?" David asked. Carman nodded and David took another sip of his cold coffee.

"Talk to me about your dream." Carman said quietly and David sighed.

"It's just a dream." David said and stood up.

"Don't walk away, David. I'm just trying to help you." Carman said. David smiled and grabbed his cup.

"Alan drowns in his own blood and I can't save him. All he says to me is don't let me go. That's when I wake up." David said and took his cup into the house. Carman followed him into the house and watched David pour his coffee.

"How does it happen?" Carman asked quietly.

"Well, he's in a glass box. He starts crying but the tears are blood. He doesn't try to get out or swim or anything. He just stands there and lets the blood fill over his head." David explained. Carman sighed and shook his head.

"What are you doing in your dream?" Carman asked as David put cream and sugar in his coffee. David stirred the additives in his cup and took a sip.

"I'm trying to break the box." Carman nodded and raised his eyebrows.

"That's creepy, dude." He said and David smiled.

"Just a dream." David said again and sat down at the table. Just then the phone rang and Carman answered it.

"Hello? . . . . Well, speak of the devil . . . . their good. Mikey has a rash, Amanda is still pregnant and David is having nightmares." David shot Carman a dirty look and he blew him a kiss. David shook his head and looked out the kitchen window. "Well, he says the dreams are pretty scary but that's all he says about them . . . . Of course I have . . . . What do you want me to do? Beat it out of him? . ." Carman laughed and shook his head. David looked at him and Carman winked. "I bet he would love that . . . . Um, Amanda found one she wants to see this afternoon . . . . It's in Paul's building . . . . Yea that new one . . . . Well I think it's good for them but they will have to decide . . . . No he hasn't." Carman said and stared at David. David rolled his eyes and took a sip from his coffee cup. Carman sighed then and cleared his throat. "I don't know if he would . . . . Ok, but I'm just the messenger . . . ." Carman laughed again and put the phone to his chest. "David, here." Carman said and held the phone out. David sighed and shook his head. "Talk to him David. You can always hang up." Carman said quietly. David rolled his eyes and took the phone. Carman smiled at him and he frowned.

"Hello." David said and cleared his throat again.

"*Hi.*" Alan's sultry voice said and David sighed.

"What do you want?" David asked quietly. Carman looked at him and sighed at his hostility as he sat down at the table with him.

"*I just want to make sure you guys are ok.*" Alan said. David rolled his eyes and looked at Carman. He smiled and sipped his coffee.

"We're fine." David answered. Alan sighed on the other end and David could hear him light a cigarette. Just then Amanda came in and Carman held his finger up to his mouth. She nodded and set Mike down in front of the T.V. before she came to sit at the table.

"He's talking to Alan." Carman whispered.

"Oh." Amanda whispered and looked at David.

"*I'm glad to hear you guys are doing well. Carman said you're seeing an apartment today.*" Alan tried. David sighed and looked at Amanda. She just smiled at him and held his hand. He did not want to be talking to this man yet.

"Yea, Amanda found it."

"*It's a nice building. I know the place, it's certainly worth a look.*" Alan said.

"Well, that's what we're doing." David said. He sighed and looked at the two people at the table with him. Carman stood up and grabbed Amanda's hand. He led her out of the room and David sighed. "Why are we talking?" David asked. Alan sighed and cleared his throat.

"*I'm worried about you.*" David rolled his eyes and lit a cigarette. He took a long drag from it and closed his eyes.

"Don't worry about us. How is mom?" David asked. The question felt like fire on his tongue.

"*She's good. She has been really busy at work.*" Alan answered. David sighed again and squinted his eyes.

"I can't do this Alan." He said and Alan sighed.

"*David, I know your still upset, but isn't there anything I can do to make this better? Summer holidays are coming up and your mother wants to see you. It would kill her if you didn't come down just because I was here.*" Alan said.

"Then, don't be there." David said and Alan sighed.

"*I wasn't going to be.*" David sighed and found himself feeling sorry for Alan.

"Alan, I don't want to do this right now." David said and closed his eyes.

"*I'm just talking David, you don't have to do anything.*" Alan said. David sighed and took a sip of his coffee.

"How could you not tell me?" David asked. Alan sighed and was silent. "Fine, don't tell me." David said and hung up the phone. He slammed it down on the table and stared at it. Amanda came into the room and sat next to him.

"You hung up on him didn't you?" Amanda asked. David looked at her and sighed.

"Yea." He answered and Amanda nodded. She ran her hand through his hair and he shut his eyes. He felt her hand move gently across his scalp and he smiled. She giggled and made a fist in his hair. David laughed and looked at her. "You're gonna be in trouble if you keep that up." David whispered. Amanda sighed and pulled her fingers out of his hair. He giggled and leaned over to Amanda. She smiled and leaned toward him. He kissed her and she giggled. David smiled and ran his hand down her stomach and to her inner thigh. She gasped and pushed his hand away.

"David. What if Carman or Mike came in?" Amanda scolded quietly. David smiled and shook his head.

"What a surprise they would get, huh?" He asked. Amanda shook her head and kissed him again. She stood up and walked over to the counter. David smiled as she got herself a glass of water and drank it down quite quickly.

"We go at one o'clock. Is it ok that I set this up?" She asked.

"Oh, yea. Of course Amanda. I trust your judgment." David said. The phone rang but Carman answered it from the other room.

"Do you think its Alan calling back?" Amanda asked. David sighed and shook his head.

"Who knows?" David asked and stood up. He walked over to Amanda and leaned her against the counter. She laughed and kissed him again. He pushed himself against her and she moaned. "You should let me fuck you before we go." David whispered. Amanda giggled and ran her hands down his back. She looked into his eyes and sighed.

"What about Little Mike?" Amanda asked and David rolled his eyes.

"Carman can watch him for a little while." He said quietly and squeezed both cheeks of her butt in his hands. Amanda laughed and shook her head.

"Tonight." Amanda said and kissed David again. He sighed and stepped back. Amanda giggled at the pathetic look on his face. She shook her head and walked over to the table with her water glass.

"You're mean to me." David said and Amanda laughed.

"I am not." She said and took another sip of her water. David smiled and dramatically readjusted the bulge in his pants.

"Yes you are." He said and came back to the table. Amanda laughed again and shook her head. David sat down and smiled at her. "How did you find this place?" He asked. Amanda raised her eyebrows and nodded her head toward Carman's office.

"Carman let me use his computer. It was so close that I couldn't resist. Mike would love to be able to see Carman's house from home, we could bring him over here all the time to play in the yard, and . . ." Amanda said and leaned close to David. "You are close enough to come over here whenever you needed to." She whispered. David laughed and shook his head.

"We have been here for a few weeks and he has already started to be a bad influence on you." David said and she giggled.

"David, I told you I don't care if you're with guys. I like Carman. I think he's cute. Don't you?" She asked. David smiled and shook his head.

"I guess."

"You *guess?* He is cute, David. And he likes you. What's wrong with that?" Amanda asked.

"He's Alan's best friend." David said. Amanda shook her head and sighed.

"So, you won't be with him because he has something to do with Alan?" Amanda asked in an irritated voice.

"No, HE won't have anything to do with me because he's friends with Alan." David corrected her. Amanda's eyes went wide and she looked behind her at the living room wall. She looked back a David and crooked her eyebrow.

"That's INTERESTING." Amanda said. David frowned at her and tilted his head to one side.

"Why do you say that?" He asked. Amanda smiled and leaned forward.

"What's the only reason in the world someone wouldn't see someone because of their friend?" Amanda asked quietly. David still looked at her with the same crooked look. "David, for someone as smart as you, you can be pretty dumb." David blinked at her.

"Why? I don't get what you're getting at." David said. Amanda smiled and looked deep into his eyes.

"I had a friend once that had a mad crush on this guy. I liked him too but I wouldn't act on it because she liked him so much." Amanda said. David raised an eyebrow and sighed.

"So?" Amanda sat back in her chair and shook her head.

"David, switch me with Carman and my friend with Alan." David thought about it and laughed.

"Sure Amanda. That's exactly what's going on here. You hit it right on the nose." David said sarcastically and Amanda rolled her eyes.

"Ask." Amanda said and David stared at her. He leaned back in his chair and looked into the living room. He could see Carman and Mike sitting on the couch. Mike was watching a cartoon on T.V. and Carman was still talking on the phone. He tilted his head back and laughed and David smiled. He put the front of his chair back down and looked at Amanda. She was looking at him with raised eye brows. "What?" He asked and Amanda shook her head.

"I think you just don't want to know. I think you like being mad because you think it gives you control of the situation. I think you like the drama." Amanda said and sipped her water. David rolled his eyes and sipped his now cold coffee.

"Well, I have no control and I hate the drama. But you were right about one thing, I don't wanna know." David said. Amanda shook her head and then smiled.

"I want to know." She said quietly and David giggled.

"Then YOU go ask." Amanda giggled now and shook her head.

"I tried that but Carman won't tell me anything."

"Well, there you go then." David said and took his cup to the sink. He looked at the clock. It was 10:30. He rinsed the cup out and set it in the dish washer.

"Why don't you want to know how these two feel?" Amanda asked. David sighed and shook his head.

"The last time I wondered how two people felt, it turned out they were both in love with me." David answered. Amanda giggled and shook her head.

"What's wrong with that?" Amanda asked thinking of herself and Gabe. David turned to face her and she smiled at him.

"Lots is wrong with that." David said and walked down the hall to the bathroom. He locked the door behind him and stared in the mirror. "I don't care, do I? I mean, what good could really come out of knowing how Alan feels?" David asked himself quietly in the mirror. He rolled his eyes and washed his face and hands. He went out of the bathroom and could see Carman and Amanda sitting at the table.

"Alan said he's sorry he didn't answer your question." Carman said as David joined them at the table.

"Oh well." David said. Carman looked at Amanda and they both shook their heads. "What?" David asked looking from one of them to the other.

"Why do you have to be so mad all the time?" Amanda asked. David sighed and shook his head.

"Why can't I be?" Carman shifted in his chair and looked at him.

"You need to get passed this if you're going to get on with the rest of your life." Carman said. Amanda nodded and looked at David. He sat silently and stared at Amanda.

"What would you have me do? Call and make up?" David asked her and she sighed.

"David, it wouldn't kill you to talk this through with him." She said gently. David shook his head and looked at Carman.

"I agree with Amanda." He said. David sighed and stood up. He walked over to the counter and looked out the window.

"I'm too mad to talk about it." David said quietly.

"Try." Amanda said. David turned around and looked at her. Her face was so sweet and young looking to him. He felt like he would melt if she kept looking at him like that. David rolled his eyes and went out to the living room. He grabbed the cordless phone and took it out into the kitchen. Amanda smiled and David shook his head. Carman got up and led David into his office.

"I'll bet this is a talk that doesn't have to be heard by anyone else." He said and David sat down in the fancy leather desk chair.

"What do I say?" David asked staring at the phone. Carman smiled and stepped out of the room. He held the door handle and looked at David.

"Tell him Amanda made you do it. Start there, the rest will come." Carman said. David rolled his eyes and dialed the phone. It rang three times.

"*Hello.*" Alan's sexy voice said on the other end. David sighed and closed his eyes.

"Hi." David said quietly. He could hear Alan clear his throat.

"*Give me a second, ok?*" Alan said. David agreed and listened to what sounded like Alan turning off the T.V. and walking out into his kitchen. He could hear him go in and out of the fridge then sit down at the table. "*Ok, hi.*" Alan said. David sighed again and cleared his throat.

"Amanda made me call you." David said taking Carman's advice.

"*Ok.*" Alan said and David closed his eyes again.

"I don't know what I'm supposed to say." David said. Alan sighed and took a sip of whatever he took out of the fridge.

"*Well, why don't you start with how mad you are?*" Alan suggested. David leaned back in the black office chair.

"Well, I'm pretty mad Alan. I can't *believe* you're with my mom." David said.

"*I know.*"

"Why?" David asked.

"*Well, I like her.*" Alan said. David rolled his eyes and shook his head.

"I meant, why didn't you tell me? I know the whole thing about easing me into it, but, you never keep a secret for this long. What stopped you, really?"

"*Well, that's a loaded question.*" Alan said. David sighed and shook his head again.

"So, you don't want to answer or what?" David asked annoyed. Alan sighed on the other end and cleared his throat.

"*It's not that I don't want to answer, I just don't know how to answer.*"

"Why don't you start with Charlie? That IS where it starts, isn't it?" David asked. Alan was quiet on the other end for a while. David waited for an answer.

"*Ok, Charlie.*" Alan said. David could imagine what Alan looked like trying to explain the hidden half of the story. He remembered what he looked like when he was uncomfortable with a question. He sighed and waited for Alan to continue. "*Charlie was my teacher and my friend. I trusted him with almost everything.*" Alan said. He paused and David shifted in his chair.

"So, what happened?" David asked. Alan sighed and David could hear him light a cigarette.

"*I didn't like him as much as he liked me.*" Alan said. David swallowed and thought back to his fear about telling Alan how he felt about him.

"Ok." Alan sighed and David could hear him grind his teeth.

"*I don't know how much you already know about this but, he hit on me and it was scary.*" Alan said.

"Why was it scary?" David asked.

"It was the way he did it. He was fairly straightforward with it." Alan explained. David rolled his eyes and shook his head.

"Why are you always so vague?" David asked. Alan was silent for a second and took a drag from his cigarette.

"David, it's not an easy thing to talk about."

"Well, you have to talk about it. You said you would do anything to make it right. Start talking." David said and leaned his head against the back of the chair. Alan sighed and took a sip of his mystery drink.

"I fell asleep on the couch reading War and Peace. I woke up with him on top of me. I freaked out and threw him off. He told me he thought I wanted him. I told him I didn't and he got mad." Alan said. David's eyes grew wide and he shifted in his chair. *"Anyway, he wasn't happy taking no for an answer, but he did. We sort of worked through it I guess and then later on I found out about him and Carman."* Alan said and sighed.

"If you weren't interested, why were you mad?" David asked. Alan was silent again and David shook his head. "Alan, if you want to talk, then talk." David said.

"I was mad because Carman was my best friend and I wanted him to be there for me." Alan said. David crinkled up his forehead.

"For what?" David asked. Alan sighed and shook his head.

"David, please think about it for a second." Alan said. David sighed and shook his head. He thought of Gabe and how he had been there for him when this whole being gay or not thing had started. He raised an eyebrow at the thought.

"You wanted Carman?" David asked. Alan took another sip from his drink.

"Yes." Alan said quietly. *"But I was so afraid after what Charlie had done that I never told him."* Alan said. David laughed and Alan fell silent.

"You have to be joking."

"No I'm not." Alan said and David shook his head.

"You expect me to believe that one bad incident with Charlie made you too scared to tell your best friend how you felt about him?" David asked then suddenly thought of how afraid he was to tell Alan how he felt.

"I guess. That's how it happened." Alan said. David was silent now. *"David, it wasn't just Charlie. I scared myself too because of the hate I had for the guy that hurt Carman."* Alan added to his explanation. David sighed and thought about the story Carman had told him in the park.

"Yea, I guess I understand that." David said and Alan sighed.

"Can I ask you about your journal?" Alan asked. David sighed and shook his head.

"Why? Everything you need to know was in them. You know it all. What's there to talk about?" David asked.

"Well, I want to tell you what I think of it." Alan said. David's breath caught in his throat and Alan noticed it. *"Can I tell you?"* David sighed and swallowed hard.

"Do I want to know?" David asked and to his surprise, Alan giggled.

"I don't know, do you?" David sighed and shook his head.

"I don't know."

"Why don't I start and you can stop me if you don't like what you hear?" Alan proposed. He agreed and Alan started. *"Well, to run the risk of sounding like a total dick, I wish you would have told me how you felt sooner."* Alan said. David rolled his eyes.

"Well, now you know how I feel about the little info you were keeping from me." David said referring to his mother and Alan sighed.

"Ok, that's fair."

"Well, go on." David said. Alan sighed again and David waited.

"David, if I had known what you were going through, that would have changed our relationship . . . Substantially." Alan said. David raised an eyebrow and shifted in the chair again.

"How?" He asked.

"I wouldn't be with your mother, I can tell you that." Alan said.

"Ok, what are you saying?"

"David, after my falling out with Carman, I never once thought about men or how fucked the whole thing with Charlie was. Then I met you." Alan said.

"So, what does that mean?" David asked. His heart pounded in his chest and his hands were sweating.

"I told Carman it would take someone pretty special to make me think about that stuff again. You punched me right in the guts with it." David swallowed hard and cleared his throat.

"That's the worst thing I've heard all year." David said quietly and Alan sighed.

"Why?" He asked quietly. David shook his head. He was feeling the same anger he felt when he saw Alan and his mom kissing.

"Alan, I am having a baby with Amanda. You are with my mom, and you lay this on me now?" David asked through clenched teeth. Alan was quiet. "Why tell me this now?" He asked.

"I didn't want to keep it from you anymore."

"Well, you should have." David said and shook his head.

"Please don't be mad, David. I just wanted you to know." Alan said quietly.

"You thought that telling me about this would be good? Why?" David asked. Alan was quiet. "Alan, you can't expect me to be cool with this." David said.

"I know." Alan said. David sighed and shook his head again.

"I don't know how to feel about this."

"*Ok.*" Alan said quietly. David tapped the desk with his fingers and shook his head.

"I need to let you go." David said. Alan sighed on the other end.

"*Ok.*"

"You can't possibly understand how bad I wanted you Alan." David said choking up. He could feel tears fill his eyes and he shut them.

"*I think I can.*" Alan said quietly. David shook his head again and cleared his throat.

"Well, I need to go." David said again trying to hide the pain that wanted to explode out of his chest.

"*Ok.*" Alan said and David hung up the phone.

"ASSHOLE!" David yelled and tossed the phone onto the desk. He let the tears fall and he put his head down on his arms on the desk. His body shook as he cried. His heart pounded in his chest and it ached. He felt like a huge hole was just dug into his stomach. There was a light knock on the door. He lifted his head and reached over to open the door. Amanda stepped in and shut the door behind her.

"David, are you ok?" She asked. David grabbed her and pulled her on top of him. Amanda gasped as he held her close to his shaking body. "Are you ok?" She asked again. David shook his head and listened to Amanda's heart in her chest.

"He is such a dick." David said quietly into Amanda's shirt. She hugged him and then backed up enough to look at him.

"What happened?" David looked up at her. She could see his tear soaked face and she sighed.

"He liked me too." David said and shook his head. Amanda's eyes grew wide and she stared at him.

"You mean how you liked him?" Amanda asked quietly. David nodded and she hugged him again. "Oh my God, David. He told you this?" She asked. David nodded again and Amanda shook her head.

"Little late huh?" She whispered. David looked up at Amanda's face and giggled.

"That's what I thought." Amanda smiled and shook her head.

"What a strange life you have David." She said and stood up. David stood with her and she hugged him again. "Are you ok?" David took a deep breath and cleared his throat.

"I'm going to be." David said and let Amanda go. She smiled at him and opened the door. Amanda went out first and David followed. He looked at Carman at the table and shook his head. "I'm done talking to him for a while, ok?" David said. Carman nodded and looked at Amanda. She shook her head and sat down at the table. David did the same.

"What happened?" Carman asked. David sighed and looked into Carman's eyes. Carman lifted an eyebrow and looked at Amanda.

"I bet you already know." Amanda said quietly. Carman looked at David and closed his eyes.

"He told you." David nodded and leaned back on the chair.

"Nice of him, huh?" David asked. Carman looked at David and smiled.

"Probably not, but now you know." He said. Amanda and Carman both looked at David. He looked back and forth from both of them and shook his head.

"No more talking about Alan, ok?" David asked but it was more of a 'new rule' tone. Carman and Amanda both nodded and David looked at the clock. He smiled and looked at Amanda. "Let's go see your new home." He said seeing it was time to see the apartment she had found for them. Amanda smiled and nodded.

"Our new home." She said to him and rubbed her stomach. David smiled at her. Carman sighed and shook his head.

"You guys go, I'll watch Mike."

"Are you sure?" Amanda asked and Carman smiled.

"He's a good kid; we should survive an hour or two." Amanda giggled and looked back at David.

"Ready to go?" She asked.

"Yep." David said and stood up. Amanda followed him out to the car and they both got in. David looked at her and shook his head.

"What?" Amanda asked. David smiled and leaned across the gearshift to kiss her. Amanda smiled and sighed.

"I love you." David whispered and Amanda blinked. He giggled and started the car.

"I love you too." She said. David smiled and backed the car out of the drive way. Amanda stared at him in disbelief.

"What?" David asked as he pulled out on to the highway toward the apartment building.

"You said it first." Amanda said. David giggled and shook his head.

"So?"

"You never say it first."

"Well, I guess you're having a good day then, aren't you?" David asked and smiled. Amanda giggled and nodded. They watched for the turn off and David took it as soon as he seen it. They pulled up to the building and David parked the car in visitor parking. When they got out, Amanda looked around them at the building and surrounding gardens.

"Wow, this looks nice." She said quietly.

"It looks expensive." David said and Amanda laughed. They walked up to the doors and went into the building. There was a door to the right that said *office*. David held Amanda's hand and knocked at the door. She giggled excitedly and David smiled at her. The door opened and David gasped.

Chapter 6

D avid stood staring at the man in the office door. Amanda
squeezed his hand and David blinked. She shook the young
man's hand and then David did.

"Hi, your Amanda and David right?" The man asked.

"That's us." Amanda said and squeezed David's hand again. He
blinked and nodded. Amanda shook her head and smiled at the man.

"Well, my name is Seth. I'm looking after the place while my
parents are away. Wanna see it?" Seth asked. Amanda nodded and he
stepped back into the office.

"What is wrong with you?" Amanda asked through clenched teeth
to David when the door shut. David swallowed and looked at her.

"Did you not SEE that guy?" David asked and Amanda giggled.

"Yes, I saw him." She whispered.

"He looks like Gabe only like, 10 times hotter." David whispered. Amanda giggled as Seth came back out of the office. David stared at him as he led them to the elevator.

"An elevator." Amanda said excitedly. David smiled at her and then looked back at Seth. He was David's height and almost exact build. He had long black hair that was just as beautiful as Gabe's had been. He had bright blue eyes that were almost scary. He had a perfectly cut jaw and his pale completion was amazing.

"So, the lease says no pets and no parties." Seth said and Amanda nodded as he spoke.

"We don't have pets." She said. She looked at David and shook her head. Seth looked at David and raised an eyebrow.

"He doesn't talk or what?" He asked. Amanda giggled and David blinked.

"Sorry, you just remind me of someone." David said and his voice squeaked. Amanda laughed as the doors to the elevator opened on the fifth floor.

"So, the unit is 509." Seth said and led the way. David squeezed Amanda's hand and she giggled. "Here we go." Seth said and opened the door. Amanda and David walked in and Amanda's mouth dropped open. David looked around and raised his eyebrows. They walked into the apartment on the side of the kitchen. There was a place for shoes and coats to the right and the kitchen and living room were directly in front and to the left.

"This is beautiful." Amanda said and stepped in. David followed her and Seth turned some lights on. The kitchen was an open concept with black counter tops and dark oak cupboards. The appliances where stainless steel and looked beautiful against the dark kitchen. The floor was a reddish colored stone tile. Amanda walked up to the counter and ran her hand along it.

"So, this suite was just renovated so everything is right out of the box." Seth explained. Amanda smiled at David and he smiled back. "The floors and everything are all new." Seth added. David looked at him and rolled his eyes.

"I think it rents itself. Look at her." David said quietly. Seth looked at Amanda and smiled. "How many rooms?" David asked.

"This one is a three bedroom with an office." Seth said reading his sheet. David raised his eyebrows and Amanda giggled. She was in the living room now trying out the electric window blinds.

"Check this out." Amanda said as she fiddled with the controls. David smiled and shook his head.

"Those come standard in every suite." Seth said. David looked at him.

"What else should we know?" He asked. Seth looked at his paper and back up to David.

"Are you a smoker?" Seth asked. David nodded yes. "Well, because this suite has no balcony, smoking is allowed inside." Seth said.

"Hear that David? You can even smoke in here." Amanda said. David smiled and they made their way to the first door in the little hall way.

"This is the bath room." Seth said and leaned in front of David to turn on the light. David smiled at Seth's closeness and Amanda giggled. They looked in the bathroom. It was a nice size. It had white tile in the bathtub shower combo and a white tile floor. The sink had a nice sized vanity and the toilet still had the fingerprint foil on the lid. "This is all new too." Seth said as Amanda looked in the cupboards in the vanity. She looked at David and smiled again. They left the bathroom and went to the room across the hall. "This one is the office." Seth said and turned the light on for them. It was a fair sized room with a nice sized window. The walls were freshly painted white and the floor was a short tan colored carpet.

"This is nice." Amanda said.

"Guitar room." David said and Seth laughed.

"You play?" He asked. David looked at him and nodded. Amanda rolled her eyes and went to the next room.

"Yea, I have a little collection of guitars that will need a home I guess." David said.

"What do you have?" Seth asked.

"Stratocasters." David answered.

"That's sweet."

"Do you play?" David asked as they joined Amanda in what Seth called room 3.

"No, but I always wanted to learn." Amanda looked at David and then giggled.

"David's an excellent teacher." She said. David shot a glare at her and she giggled again.

"Really?" Seth asked. David sighed and looked at Seth.

"I guess." David said. Amanda giggled again and tucked her hair behind her ears.

"We'll have to talk about that sometime." Seth said. David politely smiled at him and continued with the tour. Bedroom 3 was a lot like the office but had a closet. Bedroom 2 was identical to it on the other side of the hall way.

"This one could be Mike's room." Amanda said quietly.

"Look." David said and pointed out the window. She walked over to the window and peered outside. She could see the two overpasses and passed them was Carman's house.

"Yep, this would be Mike's room." Amanda said and giggled. Seth looked out the window and then back at them. "We know the guy that lives over there." Amanda said to him. Seth laughed and shook his head.

"You guys know Carman?" Seth asked. David and Amanda both stared at him.

"Yea." David said. Seth shook his head and giggled.

"He's friends with my brother." Amanda giggled and elbowed David in the ribs. David shook his head and smiled at Amanda.

"Really?" Amanda asked. "What a small world." She added and Seth smiled.

"They've known each other since school." Seth said. David remembered all the men Carman had over for Alan's birthday on the spring break trip they had taken out.

"What's his name?" David asked and Seth looked at him.

"My brother? Lance." Seth answered. David closed his eyes and pictured Lance's face perfectly. He giggled and shook his head.

"I know him." David said. Amanda looked at him and shook her head.

"Really?" Seth asked.

"Yea, does he have a red cross tattoo on his arm?" David asked. Seth nodded and laughed.

"How do you know him?" Amanda asked.

"Spring break." David said. Amanda nodded and left the room.

"You met him out at Carman's for Alan's birthday?" Seth asked. David blinked at the name and looked at Seth.

"You know Alan?" David asked. Seth nodded as they followed Amanda to the master bedroom.

"Yea, since I was in diapers." Seth said. Amanda looked around the room and giggled. David saw the two walk in closets and the on suite bathroom.

"Diapers huh?" David asked as Amanda walked into both closets and then inspected the bathroom. It looked a lot like the main bathroom but had just a shower with no tub.

"Yea, they hung out at our place all the time." Seth said as Amanda came from the bathroom and looked out the window.

"Weird." David said quietly and Amanda giggled.

"What do you think?" Amanda asked. David looked at her excited face and rolled his eyes.

"How much?" David asked and Amanda clapped her hands. Seth smiled and went through the paper.

"This one is $900 a month and the power, water and gas is included. Amanda squealed and looked at David.

"I'll give you guys a second." Seth said and left the room. Amanda smiled at David.

"Do you like it?" She asked quietly.

"Why are you asking me? I'm not the one with all the money for this right now?" David asked. Amanda giggled and shook her head.

"You need to like it too David. You have to live here." Amanda said. David smiled at her and nodded.

"I like it." David said and Amanda squealed. She hugged David and he giggled. They walked out of the room to see Seth standing at the counter.

"Can I guess that the ear-splitting squeal means you'll take it?" Seth asked. Amanda laughed and blushed.

"Looks that way." He said. Seth smiled and shook David's hand.

"Well, congratulations." Seth said and shook Amanda's hand next. She took one last look around the kitchen before they headed back to the elevator. "I will need you guys to fill out the lease in the office before you go." Seth said.

"Ok." Amanda said and squeezed David's hand. David smiled at her and shook his head.

"Excited?" He asked. Amanda looked up at him and nodded.

"So, how do you know Alan?" Seth asked as the elevator stopped and the doors opened. David sighed and Amanda squeezed his hand.

"He used to be my History teacher." David said. Seth raised an eye brow and looked at David.

"You hang out with your History teacher?" Seth asked as they walked to the office. David looked at Amanda for help and Amanda cleared her throat.

"It's a long story. How about that lease?" She asked saving David from having to explain. Seth looked at her and smiled. He took them into the office and they sat down on the two chairs in front of the desk. Seth dug through the filing cabinet and brought the lease papers to the desk. He sat down in front of them and found two pens in the drawer.

"Ok, so this just tells you the rules. You can read them over at home or we can go through them now." Seth said. David looked at Seth and found himself staring at him again. Amanda nudged his foot and he blinked. Seth smiled and looked down at the paper. He went through the agreement with them and they signed the bottom. Seth went through the other papers that Amanda and David had to sign. When all the paper work was finished, Seth stood up and shook both their hands again. "So, you can move in next weekend, we'll collect the rent and damage deposit from you then." Seth said and opened the door for them.

"Thank you so much." Amanda said and Seth smiled at her.

"Yea, thanks for the show. We'll see you next weekend." David said. Seth smiled at him and cleared his throat.

"Looking forward to it." He said. Amanda giggled as David seemed to become extremely uncomfortable with the statement. They walked out to the car and got in. Amanda giggled as David took a deep breath and started the car.

"What?" David asked. Amanda laughed and shook her head.

"He's cute huh?" David giggled and looked at Amanda.

"Yea, I noticed." He said. Amanda laughed again and shook her head.

"NOTICED? I thought you were going to trip over your tongue in there."

"Really? I wasn't that bad was I?" David asked as he pulled out on the highway toward Carman's house. Amanda nodded and he laughed. "Are you happy with the apartment?"

"I love the apartment." Amanda answered excitedly. David smiled and stopped at the only set of lights between their new home and Carman's house. David looked at Amanda and smiled.

"I think it's gonna be cool living there."

"Especially if Seth spends a lot of time at work." Amanda bugged and David giggled. He shook his head and started driving again when the light turned green.

"One thing at a time here girl. I think I've had enough heart-ache from men lately." Amanda smiled and nodded. David slowed the car and turned into Carman's yard. He was walking his little donkey, Holly Dunn around with Mike on her back. Amanda giggled at Little Mikes excited face as they got out of the car.

"So, how did it go?" Carman asked as Little Mike giggled and pet the donkey's neck.

"We took it." Amanda said excitedly.

"Oh really? You don't want to see anything else?" Carman asked.

"Nope." Amanda said and went to Mike's side.

"Go, Go!" He said and Amanda laughed. She took the rope from Carman and walked the little donkey away. Carman smiled at David.

"So, when do you move in?" Carman asked as they walked from the car to the little patio table on the deck.

"Next weekend." David answered. Carman nodded as they sat down at the table.

"Who showed the place to you?" Carman asked. David rolled his eyes and watched Amanda walk the donkey in a wide circle.

"Yea, you could have warned me." David said. Carman giggled and shook his head.

"Who did it? Lance?" Carman asked. David shook his head and sighed.

"His little brother, Seth." David said and gave Carman a dirty look. Carman laughed and nodded.

"Lucky you." He said. David laughed and shook his head. "Tell me about the place." Carman added and David sighed.

"Well, it's all renovated and looks pretty nice. Its $900 a month and gas, power and water is included." David said. Carman raised his eyebrows.

"That's not bad." He said.

"And, we can see your place from every room in the house." David said.

"No buying a telescope." Carman said. David laughed and shook his head.

"Don't need one, I have a pair of binoculars." Carman laughed and shook his head.

"What do you think of Seth?" He asked. David sighed and looked at Amanda and Mike again. The donkey was eating grass and Mike was hugging her neck. Amanda was petting her and talking to Mike about the different parts of the animal.

"He is something." David answered referring to Seth and Carman giggled.

"Tell me what you really think." David looked at him and raised his eye brows.

"Why?" David asked. Carman giggled again and shook his head.

"I'm curious."

"Well, he's hot." David said. Carman laughed and nodded.

"He is that."

"He kind of reminds me of Gabe." David said. Carman smiled and nodded.

"I thought you might say that. Does that bother you?"

"No, what bothers me is that he knows all you guys." David said. Carman giggled and shook his head.

"Well, that's what happens when you live in the same place your whole life."

"Yea, well I certainly didn't expect to meet someone else who knew Alan." David said and lit a cigarette. Carman sighed and watched Amanda take Mike for another wide circle. He looked back at David and sighed.

"How are you doing with that little bit of info?" Carman asked. David sighed and shook his head at the memory of his earlier phone conversation with Alan.

"I wasn't expecting it, that's for sure."

"I told you he loved you." Carman said. David looked at him and blinked.

"You knew all that stuff?" David asked.

"I asked if you wanted to know what we talked about, you said you didn't." Carman said and sighed. David rolled his eyes and sighed as well.

"Yea, I did, didn't I?" Carman nodded and David took a puff from his cigarette. They could hear Mike laughing and they both looked. Amanda was feeding Holly Dunn a candy from her pocket. Holly Dunn was making a funny face which was making Mike laugh. Carman smiled and shook his head. David looked at him and sighed. Carman smiled at David and shook his head.

"It may seem like a lot to process right now, but it will get easier." David rolled his eyes.

"Why didn't he just do it with you?" David asked. Carman laughed and shook his head.

"Not all friendships can go to sex and turn out as well as you and Amanda did." Carman said. David smiled and looked at Amanda.

"Well, I think Alan has a lot of crap on his plate now." David said. Carman nodded and sighed.

"Yes he does." David looked at him.

"So, do you think I'm wrong for being mad at him about it?"

"Well, you can't help how you feel. Tell me why you're mad." Carman said. David sighed and looked into Carman's eyes.

"He's with my mom and I'm a state away. What's not to be mad about?" David asked. Carman sighed and nodded.

"Ok, so bad timing. What else?" Carman asked.

"Well, I wish I had made a move or something before all this happened." David said quietly. Carman smiled and shook his head.

"David, don't be mad at yourself. You guys will figure it all out someday." He said. David rolled his eyes and looked back out at Amanda. She was trying to convince Mike to get off the donkey. David giggled at Mike's persistence to stay on. Carman smiled and shook his head.

"You can leave him up there. She won't go anywhere." Carman said and Amanda sighed. "You can trust her, Amanda." He added. Amanda stood out in the yard and let the rope fall. Holly Dunn walked over to the short bushes at the side of the fence and nibbled on them. Mike clapped his hands and Holly Dunn swished her tail. David smiled and Carman laughed. Amanda slowly walked toward the house never taking her eyes off her little brother.

"Are you sure?" Amanda asked as she got to the stairs.

"Oh, yea. I wouldn't even put her in the pen with the other ones if I was sure she wouldn't follow her gut to the highway." Carman said. Amanda smiled and watched her little brother.

"Will she buck him off?" Amanda asked. Carman laughed and slapped the table.

"I bet she couldn't buck if she had nothing on her back let alone that little guy. He's pretty safe up there." Carman reassured her and she smiled. She sat down next to Carman so she could keep her eyes on Mike. "So, are you excited about your new place?" Carman asked trying to get her mind off the non-pending doom that her little brother was in. She smiled and looked at him.

"Oh, Carman. It's so pretty. I'm going to do furniture shopping starting tomorrow. I think light colors would look best." She said excitedly. David smiled and shook his head.

"Light colors? Won't you hate yourself for that when we have two kids running around there?" David asked. Amanda giggled and shook her head.

"I was thinking leather or something." She said.

"Leather? That's sounds nice." Carman said. Amanda giggled and looked at David. He smiled at her.

"Whatever you want." David said. Carman giggled and shook his head.

"You guys are so cute." He said. Amanda laughed and looked at her watch.

"Oh, I gotta get the supper in the oven." Amanda said and stood up. She looked at David and smiled. "Please keep an eye on him." She said referring to Mike. David looked at him. He was hugging the donkey's neck again while she grazed.

"I think I got it covered." David said and giggled. Amanda ran her hand through his hair and went into the house. David smiled and watched her go in.

"Boy David, if I was straight." Carman said. David looked at him and giggled.

"Yea, yea. But you're not so, don't even think about it." David said. Carman laughed and shook his head. They talked about the new apartment and Seth. Carman found it funny that David thought he was hot.

"Why is that so funny? He's a babe." David said. Carman smiled and shook his head.

"Yea, well. Good luck with that." Carman said. David laughed and shook his head.

"Why do you say that?" David asked. Carman smiled and looked at Mike. It looked as though he had fallen asleep on the back of the donkey. Carman giggled and got up. David followed him. They walked over to Holly Dunn. Carman grabbed the rope and David gently took Mike off of her back. "So, gonna tell me?" David asked. Carman sighed and shook his head.

"Get to know him first. You'll figure it out." Carman said. David shook his head and carried Mike in his arms while Carman put the donkey back into the pen. He took the rope off and closed the gate. They walked back to the house together and David took Mike into Carman's room. He laid the boy on the bed and covered him up. He cuddled up with the large pillows and David smiled at him. He walked out of the room to where Carman and Amanda sat at the table.

"Well, he should sleep for a while." David said. Amanda smiled and looked at Carman.

"Can we bring him here to play often after we move?" She asked. Carman looked at her as though she was stoned.

"Are you kidding? You guys can call this your new home away from home. You're always welcome here." Carman said. David and Amanda smiled. They discussed the move and how it would work. Carman said he would make sure to have the whole weekend off so he could help. When dinner was ready, Amanda dished it out and David got Mike up for it. He was whiney but was happy to see Amanda's lasagna. They chatted about the horses over diner. When they were finished, Amanda took Mike to the bathroom for a bath and David and Carman did the dishes.

"So, remember that time we kissed when Alan and I came out here?" David asked. Carman raised his eyebrows and smiled.

"Yes I do." Carman answered in a seductive sounding voice. David giggled and set a plate in the dishwasher.

"Do you remember what you said about Alan's dick before we kissed?" David asked. Carman giggled and nodded.

"I'm afraid of it?" Carman asked. David nodded and leaned against the counter.

"Why?" David asked. Carman sighed and grabbed a wash cloth. He wet it with hot water and took it to the table. He started to wipe the table and looked at David.

"That guy that raped me had a really big dick. Like huge. I've been scared of guys that size ever since. I've even broke off relationships with some really nice guys because of their size." Carman explained. David raised his eyebrows and shook his head.

"So Alan is . . ."

"Well endowed?" Carman asked cutting him off and David nodded. "Yea, he is." Carman said. He finished wiping the table and took the cloth back to the sink. "I have a strict seven inch and smaller policy now." Carman said. David giggled and shook his head.

"That's sad, Carman." Carman laughed and shook his head.

"Well, I like to walk after. And not bleeding is a good thing." Carman said. David sighed and thought about Gabe's comment about not being able to walk right after being with David.

"So, how do you go about getting a measurement?" David asked. Carman laughed and shook his head.

"Making out. They get hard and you can sometimes guess." Carman answered. David giggled and shook his head.

"Ok." David said. Carman looked at him and smiled.

"Or you can just ask. If you know the guy well enough of course." He added.

"Did you ask Alan?" Carman laughed and shook his head.

"We didn't shower in stalls after gym class like you guys do now."

"Oh." David said. Carman shook his head and handed David the last dish for the washer.

"Why did you ask?" Carman asked. David shook his head and smiled.

"I was just thinking about it." David said. They went to the table and sat down.

"You were thinking about Alan's dick?" Carman asked. David smiled and lit a cigarette. Carman giggled and lit one of his own. "You can't be that mad if you're thinking about that." David laughed and shook his head.

"It was just a passing thought." He said and took a drag from his cigarette. Carman giggled and shook his head.

"You know. I bet Alan would like to show you." David coughed and then laughed.

"Shut up, Carman." He said. Carman laughed and shook his head. They talked about the guys that Carman had turned down due to the size of their penises. One of them was Seth's brother Lance. David laughed at Carman's ridiculous stories. Amanda came out of the bathroom with Mike and took him straight to bed. David smiled and shook his head.

"No good night hugs tonight I guess." Carman whispered. David giggled and shook his head. Amanda walked out of the room and quietly shut the door. She tiptoed to the table and Carman giggled.

"He just about fell asleep in the bathtub. I barely got his P.J.'s on." She said as she sat down next to David.

"Awe, poor guy." Carman said. David smiled and set his hand on Amanda's leg. She smiled at him and Carman giggled. "You've already knocked her up, what else do you want?" He asked. David laughed and shook his head. Amanda blushed and squirmed in her chair.

"Speaking of that, I need a doctor." Amanda said.

"Mine is awesome. I'll give you the number tomorrow." Carman said.

"Oh, thank you Carman." Amanda said. David smiled at him and then looked back at her.

"How are you feeling?" David asked. Amanda smiled at him and sighed.

"Tired." David smiled and looked at the clock. It was 7:30.

"Little early for bed." David said. Amanda smiled and shook her head.

"What were you guys talking about before I came out?" Amanda asked. David giggled and looked at Carman. He leaned back in his chair and smiled.

"Alan's dick." Carman answered. David laughed and Amanda seemed shocked.

"Were you really?" Carman laughed and rolled his cigarette in the ashtray. David sighed and nodded. "Oh my God." Amanda said and shook her head. David and Carman laughed and then Amanda joined them. They didn't explain the conversation to her. They changed it to the furniture shopping Amanda had planned.

"When are we going?" David asked. Amanda looked at him in horror. "What?" David asked.

"The last time you went shopping on a whim, you bought a guitar." Amanda said. David laughed and shook his head.

"You need a job." Carman said. David sighed and nodded. "Come work with me while Amanda shops tomorrow. You can see what you think. If you do a good job, I might even pay you." Carman said. David raised his eyebrows.

"I should probably go with Amanda."

"Don't be silly. I will only pick out what I like. I will arrange to have it delivered on the weekend." She said. David looked at her and smiled. He looked back at Carman and sighed.

"When do we go?" David asked.

"8:00 am."

"Ok, sounds good." David said. Amanda smiled and yawned. David looked at the clock. She had lasted another hour and David smiled. "Go to bed baby. I'll be there in a second." He said and held up his cigarette as a time limit. Amanda smiled at him and looked at Carman.

"Good night." She said. Carman and David said their good nights and Amanda went to bed. David sighed and shook his head.

"I hate computers." David said looking at Carman. Carman laughed and took a drag from his cigarette.

"So do I." Carman said. David laughed and shook his head.

"Then why do you do it?" David asked.

"Well, it's easier than being a teacher." Carman said and David laughed.

"Nice." David said.

"What? It's true. I couldn't stand in front of a bunch of hot young guys all day long. I would get fired on the first day." Carman said. David laughed again and shook his head. He took the last drag from his cigarette and put it out.

"Well, it's early but Amanda needs me." He said. Carman smiled and nodded.

"That's ok. I have a little work to do before bed anyway. There's an alarm clock in there in the bed side table." Carman said. David nodded and stood up. He headed toward the bed room. "Hey David." Carman said and David looked at him.

"Yea?" David asked.

"Do we know each other really well?" Carman asked. David giggled and nodded. "Can I ask then?" Carman asked. David looked at him with a puzzled gaze. Carman giggled and shook his head. "How big?" He asked. David giggled and shook his head.

"Maybe I'll show you someday." David said and Carman laughed. David walked into his room and got undressed. He crawled in behind Amanda and slowly ran his hand up her side to her breast. Amanda giggled and pushed herself against David's body. David kissed her neck and squeezed the breast he held in his hand. Amanda moaned and brought her hand up to play with David's hair. David pushed his growing erection against Amanda's ass. She moaned again and rolled over to face him. She kissed him and David pulled her hips against his. Amanda clawed at his back and he moaned. He rolled Amanda onto her back and slowly laid himself on top of her. She closed her eyes as David kissed his way down her naked body. He stopped at her stomach and kissed it gently. Amanda giggled and pushed him farther down. He laughed and kissed the inside of her leg. She moaned and David smiled. He kissed her leg again and Amanda giggled. He licked the inside of her thigh up to her vagina. Amanda moaned as David kissed and licked her clit. She pulled his hair and moaned. David licked harder and Amanda bucked against him. He worked on her until she climaxed. David looked up at her and smiled. Amanda pulled him on top of her by the shoulders and he kissed her. She pulled his hair and pushed her hips against his. David positioned himself and pushed his penis deep inside her. She moaned and clawed at David's back. He moaned and pushed himself inside of her as far as he could. Amanda dug her nails in to David in pain and he backed off. "Sorry." David whispered through his heavy breathing. Amanda smiled at him and kissed him with a passion that David couldn't help but moan to. He picked up his pace and Amanda climaxed. He smiled and arched his back. He moved faster and Amanda moaned louder. He could feel his orgasm build as he moved. Amanda closed her eyes and ran her fingernails gently down his arms. David's body shook as he climaxed. Amanda kissed his arm and he careful lay down on top of her. Amanda rubbed his back and kissed his shoulder.

"I love you." She whispered. David looked at her and smiled.

"I love you too." He said and kissed her. She sighed and hugged him. David smiled. She held him like that for quite some time. When David felt as though he might fall asleep where he lay, He lifted himself off of her and rolled over onto his back. Amanda cuddled up to him and kissed his shoulder again.

"You look so hot after sex." She said. David giggled and looked at her.

"I do?" He asked. Amanda smiled and nodded. She rested her head on David's chest and he rubbed her back until they both fell asleep.

Chapter 7

For the next few days, Amanda organized sitting for Mike and found herself a good doctor. David worked with Carman and was picking it up quite quickly. Amanda had found the furniture she wanted and had it arranged to be delivered on the following Saturday. It was Thursday morning and David and Carman seemed to have the day off. David was ready for the day and joined Carman at the table.

"Good morning." Carman said. He seemed a little out of sorts. David got himself a coffee and sat down with him at the table.

"You sound grouchy." David said as he lit himself his morning cigarette. Carman looked up at him from his newspaper and half smiled.

"I am grouchy today."

"What's the matter?" David asked. Carman sighed and shook his head.

"It's Alan." Carman said. David raised his eyebrows and took a sip from his coffee. "He's not talking to me. I mean, he'll talk on the phone or whatever, but he's not TALKING to me." Carman explained.

"Why do you think that is?" David asked. He rolled his cigarette in the ashtray thinking of the discussion he and Alan had the previous Sunday.

"I don't know. He usually talks to me but he's being distant or something." Carman answered. He lit a cigarette and blew the toxic smoke out in a long, exaggerated line. David looked across the table at the phone then back to Carman.

"Is it because of the talk we had?" David asked quietly. Carman shook his head and shrugged. He turned a page of his newspaper then looked up at David.

"Don't worry about it. I'll figure it out." Carman said and looked back down at his paper. David looked up at the time and sighed. It was 7:00 am. He got up and picked up the phone. Carman rolled his eyes and shook his head. "Don't bother David." He said. David frowned at him and sat down at the table with the phone.

"You think I want to live with you for another two days while you're whiney like this?" David asked. Carman giggled and shook his head. David smiled and dialed the phone. He waited as it rang on the other end. With every ring, his stomach flipped. Finally on the fourth ring, Alan answered.

"*Hello.*" Alan said with his sexy drawl. David closed his eyes for a second then answered,

"Hi."

"*Oh, David hi.*" Alan said more excitedly than David would have liked. He sighed and looked at Carman. Carman just raised his eyebrows. "*Is everything ok?*" Alan asked.

"No, actually. Carman feels like your keeping something from him and I want to know what it is." David said. Alan giggled on the other end and it made David smile. Carman smiled at David's reaction to Alan's giggle and David quickly fixed his face.

"*He can't say this to me himself?*" Alan asked and David sighed.

"He doesn't know I'm calling you. I have to live with him and you're making it tuff. What's going on?"

"*Nothing. I'm not sure what he wants to know so it's hard to tell him.*" Alan said. David looked at Carman and scowled. Carman smiled and left the table. David shook his head and realized that it was all a ploy to get him to talk to Alan again.

"Well, I think I just figured it out." David said and Alan giggled.

"*What's that?*" Alan asked. David sighed and shook his head. He took another drag from his cigarette and closed his eyes.

"He told me that shit just so I would call you." Alan laughed.

"*Yea, that sounds like Carman.*" Alan said. "*How did you come up with that?*"

"Well, the look on his face when I was telling you that."

"*I thought you said he didn't know you were calling.*" Alan said. David giggled and shook his head.

"I thought I was helping him out." David said and Alan laughed again.

"*Well, since you have me on the phone, is there anything you want to talk to me about?*" Alan asked. David's mind swam with all the things he wanted to say but Alan's relationship with his mother seemed to stay his tongue.

"Nothing now." David said. Alan sighed and David could hear him light a cigarette.

"*Can I tell you a story?*" Alan asked quietly. David swallowed hard and shifted in his chair.

"Ok."

"Ok, I once had this friend. He was about your age, maybe older, anyway. He was a lawyer's son and was expected to go far in his life. He wasn't turning out how his parents wanted and they were becoming harder and harder on him. He got himself in a little trouble and they decided it was best he didn't live with them anymore." Alan said. David could hear him take a drag of his cigarette. David did the same then put it out. Alan continued, *"Anyway, after a while, he met this guy who was so intriguing and so beautiful that the other crap in his life didn't seem to matter anymore. As he got to know him, he realized his feelings for this guy had grown passed friendship and it scared him."* Alan said. David rolled his eyes and cleared his throat.

"So what happened?" David asked and Alan sighed.

"Well, my friend screwed it up." Alan said. David was silent for a while. Alan was silent as well. *"The point is David; I would have loved to see my friend make up with this guy."* Alan said quietly. David sighed and shook his head.

"Do you think it's possible? I mean, how bad did your friend screw up?" David asked. He took a sip of his coffee while he listened to Alan take another drag from his cigarette.

"Well, my friend screwed it up pretty bad but, I think with a little compromise, they could make up. They were pretty close to just throwing it away." Alan said. David sighed again and shook his head.

"How sorry is this friend of yours?" David asked and Alan sighed this time.

"Pretty sorry. He would get down on his knees and beg for forgiveness if he thought it would help." Alan said. David laughed and Alan joined him.

"Well, maybe the guy needs more time to get over whatever your friend did."

"That could be. All I know is, my friend is lost without him." Alan said. David felt his stomach flip and his hands start to sweat.

"Sounds to me like your friend had some pretty strong feelings for this guy." David said quietly. His heart pounded in his chest.

"I'm pretty sure he does." Alan said. David sighed and closed his eyes.

"Well, my advice for your friend is to give the guy a little more time. These kinds of things are difficult to fix in a day."

"I'll tell him. I'm sure he would understand that." Alan said. David giggled and shook his head.

"Anything else?" David asked and Alan giggled.

"There is one thing." Alan said and paused. David's stomach flipped again at the sound of Alan's voice.

"What's that?" David asked in a half whisper. Alan sighed and cleared his throat.

"I think my friend is a little scared of what would happen if he can't get over the feelings he has for this guy. The situation as it is, to get as close as they were before would be painful for both of them." Alan said. David felt like he could scream. The flipping in his stomach was so intense that he felt almost dizzy.

"Well, I guess they would have to work through that to." David said. He was surprised at how even his voice sounded.

"Yea, they would." Alan said. David sighed and shook his head.

"If I was that guy, I wouldn't leave it for too long. It sounds like your friend was pretty important to him even if your friend is the asshole of the century." Alan laughed.

"Well, my friend can be that way. He certainly deserves to have to wait for his forgiveness. But, in his defense, he didn't really know the whole story." Alan said. David sighed and nodded.

"Maybe the guy was afraid your friend would hate him for it?" David asked.

"*From what I know of this friend of mine, he would have probably been pretty happy to get the whole story right away. It would have changed a lot of things between those two I think.*" Alan answered. David sighed and gently hit the phone against his forehead.

"Alan, you're a teacher, you're with my mom, your way older than me. How could knowing have made a difference?" David asked quietly. Alan sighed. He was silent on the other end for a while. David closed his eyes and tried to steady the flipping in his stomach.

"*I don't know.*" Alan said. David sighed and shook his head.

"You can't understand what this has done to me." David said quietly. He could feel a lump grow in his throat.

"*Your right. But I do know what it's done to me and it isn't pleasant.*" Alan said. David cleared his throat and looked at the time. It was 7:30.

"How's mom?" David asked and Alan sighed.

"*Happy I think.*" Alan answered.

"That's good Alan. Keep it that way."

"*I'm trying.*" Alan said. David sighed and fought the tears forming in his eyes.

"I have to go." David said. His voice broke in mid-sentence.

"*Ok, please try to have a good day.*" David sighed.

"You too."

"*Bye.*" David hung up the phone and rested his head on the table.

"I hate you Carman." David said fairly loud. Carman laughed from the office and came out into the kitchen.

"Why? It sounded like a good talk." Carman said. David looked up at him and shook his head.

"I'm not ready to deal with this yet." David said. Carman sighed and sat down next to David.

"David, just get the ball rolling. The rest will happen on its own."

"It will never be the same." David said. Carman smiled and rubbed David's arm.

"You're right. But something is better than nothing. You can't tell me you don't miss him." Carman said. David sighed and shook his head.

"I am too mad to miss him." David said and took a sip of his coffee. Carman giggled and shook his head.

"You love him that's why." Carman said. David rolled his eyes and stood up.

"Carman, cut it out." David said. Carman giggled and slapped David's backside as he walked passed him to the counter. David laughed and shook his head.

"I'll tell you one thing, he don't know what he's missing." Carman said checking David out from behind. David laughed again and poured another coffee.

"Neither do you." He said. Carman laughed and went back to the office. David smiled and took his coffee to the bedroom he and Amanda were staying in. Mike was in bed with her and they were both sleeping. David smiled and shut the door. He walked back down the hall and stopped at the office door. Carman was typing up some invoices for the next day. "10 ½ and pretty thick." David said. Carman stopped typing and turned to look at David.

"What are you talking about?" Carman asked. David giggled and walked away. He pulled his shoes on and went outside. It was a beautiful spring day. The sun was shining and the sky had hardly a cloud. He walked down the steps and went to the fence that held Diablo. He stared out at the big black horse and smiled.

Fucking Alan. As nice as it is to hear that stuff but it's like a carrot on a string. Why tell me all this now? I wonder what he would have done. He's a teacher, there has to be some kind of rules or something against that. God I wish I wasn't such a pussy. I would ask him right out. 'Would you be with me Alan? Would you hold me and kiss me?' Fuck I'm dreaming. What about my mom? Something like that would devastate her. Why does he have to be with her? God that sucks. David thought to himself as he stared out at Diablo. He sipped his coffee and turned around. He could see Amanda walking toward him in her house coat.

"Hi." She said.

"Hi." David said and hugged and kissed her. "How did you sleep?" David asked.

"Um, good until Mike came in. He kicks." Amanda said. David smiled and nodded.

"That's why I got up."

"It's nice out today." She said and took a deep breath into her lungs. David smiled at her and shook his head.

"You're beautiful." David whispered. Amanda rolled her eyes and looked at him.

"I'm not interested this morning." She said. David laughed and they walked up to the house together. "Are you hungry?" She asked.

"Yuck, no way. I hate breakfast." David said. Amanda giggled and walked up the steps.

"Well, I'm hungry." She said and rubbed her stomach. David giggled and shook his head.

"You or the baby?" Amanda smiled and David opened the door for her. Carman was up at the counter making a fresh pot of coffee and Mike was playing with a little truck on the floor. "I think we need to feed the kids." David said as they walked in. Carman turned around and smiled.

"Hungry?" He asked Amanda. She nodded and sat down at the table. Carman started to make breakfast with David's help. "I figured it out." Carman whispered as David buttered some toast and Carman scrambled the eggs. David giggled and shook his head.

"Did you?" He asked. Carman giggled and went back to the eggs.

"That's huge, David." Carman said quietly. He seemed nervous just talking about it. David looked behind him and seen Amanda getting Mike into his highchair. He leaned close to Carman and whispered.

"I'm good with it though." Carman blushed and seemed to shiver. David giggled and finished buttering the toast. When the eggs were ready, he brought plates to the table and set one in front of Amanda and one in front of Mike. He set one down for Carman and then helped Carman take the food to the table. David drank coffee while the other three ate.

"I think I'm going to take Mike to the mom's and tot's thing today." Amanda said.

"That's a great idea." Carman said.

"What's a mom's and tot's thing?" David asked. Amanda giggled and looked at him.

"It's a big play date kind of thing. The mom's get to meet each other and the kids get to play together. I think it would be good for Mike and I would like to meet some of the ladies around here." Amanda said.

"That sounds boring." David said and Carman laughed.

"Well, I wasn't going to bring you." Amanda said. David laughed and shook his head.

"I was kidding. It does sound like a good idea. When does it start?" David asked.

"Ten am. Until 1:00. They provide lunch and stuff." Amanda said.

"Want me to take you?" David asked.

"Actually, I thought I would just take the car in case Mike got cranky or something and didn't want to stay." Amanda said. David nodded and looked at Mike.

"You'll tell me if there's any hot mama's there right?" David asked. Mike giggled and nodded. Carman laughed and Amanda shook her head.

"You're corrupting him."

"Well, someone has to." David said. Carman and Amanda laughed. They finished their meal and David took the plates up to the counter. He started rinsing off the dishes as Amanda took Mike down the hall to get him dressed. Carman came up to the counter and started loading the rinsed dishes into the dishwasher. "Carman, why the red face?" David asked. Carman would hardly look at him.

"What red face?" Carman asked putting a dish in the machine. David sighed and shook his head.

"That red face." David said as he continued rinsing. Carman sighed and looked at David.

"10 ½ inches?" Carman asked. David giggled and nodded.

"About that." David said. Carman shivered and shook his head. "Carman, I'm still David. I just come with attachments." David said and giggled. Carman shook his head and sighed.

"Yea, huge ones." Carman said quietly. David realized that Carman's fear was genuine.

"Carman, I wouldn't ever hurt you." Carman sighed and nodded.

"I know that, it's the very thought that freaks me out."

"Why are you thinking about it? I thought there was an Alan rule or something." David said and rinsed the last dish. He shut the water off and leaned against the counter. Carman rolled his eyes and sighed.

"There is but I still think about it." Carman whispered. David raised his eyebrows and smiled.

"Cool." David said and walked over to the table with a wash cloth. Carman shook his head and looked at David.

"Cool?" Carman asked. David smiled and looked at him.

"I think it's cool you think about it. It's nice to be a fantasy." David said then continued wiping the table. Carman laughed and shook his head.

"I bet." Carman said. Amanda came out with Mike and checked the time. It was closing in on 9:00am.

"I gotta shower, would you watch him?" Amanda asked. David smiled and nodded. She smiled back and headed to the bathroom.

"10 ½ inches." Carman said under his breath. David laughed and brought the cloth back to the counter. He leaned close to Carman and whispered.

"And thick too." Carman shot him a dirty look and David giggled. "Come on Carman. Relax." David said and took Mike some spoons to play with.

"Relax? The thing is David, I think your lying to bug me." Carman said. David laughed and shook his head.

"Too bad there's that Alan rule standing between you and the truth, huh?" David asked and Carman rolled his eyes.

"Alan rule." Carman said under his breath. David giggled and sat down at the table. Carman sighed and went to the office. David laughed again and grabbed the paper. He read over the auto finder section until Amanda was out of the shower. She came to the table dressed in a long blue skirt and a white t-shirt.

"You look nice." David said.

"Thank you." She said and sat down. "You guys don't work today?" She asked.

"Maybe this afternoon." David said closing the paper and putting it aside. Amanda smiled and grabbed his hand.

"I have an ultrasound on the 27th." She said. David raised his eyebrows.

"What do you think it looks like?" David asked.

"Well, it's the 17th of May today and I conceived on the 14th of February so I would guess it looks like it's been in there for three months." Amanda said and they both giggled.

"What does that look like?" David asked. Amanda sighed and squeezed his hand.

"It's only the end of the first trimester. I have no idea. Maybe like a big piece of rice or something like that. I'm getting an ultrasound because there is a pain in there that feels funny." Amanda said. David frowned and looked into her eyes.

"Is something wrong?" He asked.

"I don't know. That's why I'm going." David nodded.

"Are you scared?"

"No." Amanda said and smiled. She rubbed her stomach and David sighed.

"Can I come?" David asked. Amanda smiled and nodded. He smiled back at her and touched her stomach. She looked up at the clock. It was 9:30.

"I better go." Amanda said and kissed David.

"Be careful." David said and smiled at her. She nodded and got Mike ready to go. David watched her pull away and sighed. He went back into the house and got a new coffee. He could hear Carman swearing at his computer and giggled. He walked down the hall to the office. He looked in and saw Carman fighting with a paper jam in the printer.

"Fucking thing." Carman cursed and David laughed. Carman looked behind him at David and shook his head. "I hate these things." Carman said and went back to work.

"Is it the printer or the guy using it?" David asked. Carman shook his head.

"It is certainly the printer." He insisted. David giggled and stepped into the room. He set his coffee on the desk and looked at the printer with Carman.

"How many pages are jammed?" David asked. Carman cringed at David's closeness and David blinked. "Carman?" David said the name in a questioning tone.

"Sorry, it's not you." Carman said and sat down in the chair. David sighed and pulled the paper out of the printer. He handed it to Carman and he tossed it on the desk. The printer started back up again and printed the last three pages Carman needed.

"Are you ok?" David asked and picked his coffee cup off the desk and took a sip.

"Yea, I'm just thinking." Carman said. David rolled his eyes and leaned against the metal filing cabinet.

"What are you thinking about?" David asked quietly. Carman sighed and looked at him.

"I know that us fucking around the way we do is all in fun. But just the thought of that kind of size is terrifying to me. I can't get passed it. My whole life I've been so scared since that guy and I can't shake it. Pretty lame huh?" Carman asked. David smiled and shook his head.

"Carman, I'm the same guy." David said. Carman smiled and nodded.

"I know, just knowing is scary. It just takes a little time. I got used to the thought of the size of Alan, I'll get used to you too."

"You saw Alan's, I could be lying." David offered with raised eyebrows. Carman giggled.

"Are you?"

"No, but that's not the point. The point is, it's not like you have anything to get over. You haven't SEEN it." David said.

"I know. It's the thought alone that does it, David." Carman said and got up. He took the pages from the printer and put them in the pile with the others. He looked at David and smiled. "I guess you would have to be with a big guy to understand." Carman said. He put the papers in his briefcase and clicked it shut.

"Gabe was bigger than me." David said. Carman's eyes grew wide and he shivered.

"That's not helpful." Carman said. David shook his head and smiled.

"You know what's even less helpful?" David asked. Carman sighed and looked at David. He still had his hands on the briefcase.

"What?" Carman asked. David itched the side of his neck and sighed.

"I've never been fucked by a guy." David said. Carman rolled his eyes and shook his head.

"I thought you were with Gabe."

"I was, but I did the fucking, he was too scared he would hurt me." David explained.

"David, *you* could hurt someone if you're as big as you say you are." Carman said. David sighed and nodded.

"Well, Gabe liked it." David said and went to the door. Carman sighed and rolled his eyes.

"I bet." He said and followed David out of the room. They went to the kitchen table and Carman slumped himself down in the chair. "I don't think I'll ever get over this." He said. David sat with Carman at the table and lit a cigarette. He handed it to Carman and then lit one for himself.

"Well, what about doing it on your own terms?" David asked. Carman looked at David with a shocked expression. "Not me, there's that Alan rule and everything. I was talking about the next one that comes around." David said and giggled. Carman sighed a breath of relief and shook his head.

"I don't know if I could ever trust anyone enough." Carman said. David thought it was strange to see Carman acting this way.

"Well, can I give you something to think about for a while?" David asked. Carman looked at him and nodded. "Ditch the Alan rule for long enough to see how scary it really is. We don't have to do anything, just enough to see how you feel about it with me. You trust *me* don't you?" David asked. Carman stared at him and took a drag from his cigarette.

"I gotta think about it. I trust you David but, Alan really likes you and . . ." Carman said and David cut him off.

"Carman, I think he's off the market, don't you?" David asked with raised eyebrows. Carman sighed and nodded.

"Let me think about it." David smiled and stood up.

"You're so funny." David said and went up to the sink. He dumped his coffee and stretched his arms up in the air. Carman looked at him and shook his head.

"Are you even attracted to me or are you just trying to be nice?" Carman asked. David finished his stretched and turned around. He was a little shocked at Carman's question.

"That was blunt." David said. Carman sighed but still stared at David. He sighed and leaned against the counter. He smiled at Carman and shook his head.

"Do you think I kissed you because I know you? I kissed you because I think you are very attractive and I think you're a nice guy." David said. Carman raised his eyebrows and tapped the table. David giggled. "What?" He asked. Carman shook his head and leaned back in his chair.

"I meant sexually, you kiss your mother. Kissing is nothing." Carman said.

"Yes Carman, You're hot and I want you." David said and Carman laughed. "Happy now?" Carman nodded and David laughed. They decided to go out and take the garbage to the dump before Amanda got home. They were on their way home when Carman looked at David and smiled. "What?" David asked as he watched out the windshield.

"I was wondering, if you and Alan ever got together, would you risk the pain and let him fuck you?" Carman asked. David giggled and looked at Carman.

"Probably." David answered. Carman nodded and drove the rest of the way in silence. When they pulled into the yard, they took the large barrels back to the side of the house and went inside. Carman looked at the clock and sighed.

"Well, Amanda should be home soon. What would you like to do this afternoon when she gets back?" Carman asked. David shrugged and sat down on the couch.

"I'm kind of tired today." David said. Carman nodded and sat in the chair kitty corner from the couch.

"I bought a board game last week if you're interested." Carman said.

"Sure." David said and they watched T.V. until Amanda came home. They set the game up on the table and put a show on for Mike. They played the game twice and Amanda won both times. Carman would look at David every once in a while and Amanda would giggle. When it was time to make dinner, Amanda went up to the counter and David and Carman cleaned up the game. Carman stared at David as they worked. "What?" David whispered in an almost inaudible voice.

"I think you're hot." Carman whispered and David giggled.

"Well, you're right. I am." David whispered back and Carman laughed. Amanda looked back at them and shook her head. David and Carman both giggled and Carman took the game back into the office. David walked up to Amanda and hugged her around the waist.

"I'm cooking." Amanda said and David kissed her cheek. She was peeling potatoes and putting them into a pot.

"I know, I just wanted to touch you." David whispered and Amanda giggled.

"From the looks of things, you want to touch Carman too." Amanda whispered. David sighed and shook his head.

"He thinks I'm scary." David said and rubbed his groin against Amanda's back. She laughed and shook her head.

"You are." Amanda said and David giggled.

"I am not." Amanda sighed and turned around in David's arms. She looked up at him and smiled.

"David, you're not a little boy. You're fairly intimidating you know." Amanda said. David rolled his eyes and stepped back.

"You're not scared of me."

"I would be if you wanted to put that thing in my ass." Amanda said. David laughed and shook his head. He took the pot of potatoes and put water in it for Amanda and set it on the stove. "Thank you." Amanda said and kissed David. He smiled and went back to the table. Carman hadn't left the office yet and Mike was sleeping on the couch.

"You know what I think." David said. Amanda raised her eyebrows and faced him.

"What?" She asked as she headed to the fridge and took some chicken out.

"I think he just needs to do it and get over it." David said. Amanda shook her head and giggled.

"Yes, well. Not everyone can be as brave as me. I mean, look what happens." Amanda said and rubbed her stomach. David laughed and went to the office. Carman was crouched down going through some papers in the filing cabinet.

"What are you doing?" David asked. Carman looked up and smiled.

"I'm looking for the paperwork on this printer." Carman answered. David looked at the printer and seen that Carman had the top taken off of it.

"Aren't you supposed to know how this stuff works?"

"I do, but this is an old printer and I don't know if I can still get the part I want." Carman said. David sighed and walked up to kneel behind Carman. He slowly ran his hands from Carman's shoulders down to his chest. Carman shut his eyes and leaned the back of his head against David's chest. David smiled and scratched his fingernails back up to Carman's shoulders. Carman smiled and shook his head. He opened his eyes and looked up at David. "You are really something David." Carman whispered. David smiled and walked toward the door.

"That wasn't so bad, was it?" David asked. Carman shook his head and David left the room. Amanda was in the living room with Mike. She saw him and smiled. David walked over to where she was sitting on the couch and sat next to her.

"So, what was that about? It was pretty quiet in there." Amanda asked. David smiled and put his hand on her leg.

"Just helping him out with a little fear he has." David said. Amanda looked at him and found.

"How?"

"Well, he is really scared of big men." David said putting emphases on 'big men'. Amanda nodded and David continued. "I don't want him to be scared of me." David whispered. Amanda smiled and blushed.

"Are you thinking about sleeping with him?" She asked. David giggled and shook his head.

"I'm always thinking about sleeping with him. Remember the Alan thing?" David asked and Amanda nodded. "That's why we don't. I'm not looking to sleep with him, I just want to help him with his size issue. Apparently he's had a hard time with relationships because of it." David explained.

"That's really sad." Amanda said. David sighed and nodded. "I think it's nice of you David. No matter how weird it is."

"Weird?" David asked. Amanda giggled and nodded.

"It's a weird thing to try to help a friend with." Amanda whispered. David smiled and kissed her cheek.

"I guess it kind of is." David said. They watched their T.V. show until supper was ready. It went as usual. They discussed the apartment and the furniture Amanda bought as they ate and afterward, Carman and David did the dishes while Amanda bathed Mike.

"You know. That was a really sexy thing you did in the office." Carman said as he wiped the table and David washed the potato pot. David giggled and shook his head.

"Not scary?" David asked.

"Not really. I liked it." Carman answered. David smiled and put the pot in the adjacent sink to be dried. He started to work on the chicken pan.

"Do we work tomorrow?" David asked. Carman came back to the counter and grabbed the potato pot out of the sink.

"Yea, it's an easy day though. One office program malfunction, and then, we're installing a new computer program in my friend's office." Carman said as he dried the pot. David nodded and flipped the pan he was working on over.

"Who's the friend?" David asked. Carman smiled and put the pot away.

"Lance." Carman said. David smiled and rinsed the soap off of the chicken pan and set it in the sink for Carman to dry.

"Oh." David said and Carman laughed.

"Seth will be there." Carman said. David sighed and looked at Carman.

"That's cool." David said trying to hide his embarrassing excitement. Carman rolled his eyes and put the chicken pan away. David pulled the plug out of the sink and rinsed it out.

"You know, I really don't need you tomorrow if you wanted to spend the day grocery shopping with Amanda." Carman said in a nonchalant voice. David sighed and shook his head.

"No, I could use the practice. How often do I get to see an install?" David asked. Carman laughed and threw the towel he was using toward the laundry room door.

"That's what we usually do." Carman said.

"I know, but what's the harm in seeing one more?" David asked. Carman smiled and shook his head.

"Ok, if you insist." Carman said. David nodded and Carman giggled again. They made themselves a Rum and went to the pool table. Carman set up a game and let David break. He sank one solid ball. Carman raised his eyebrows and David giggled. He aimed his next shot and missed. It was Carman's turn. He lined up his shot and sunk two striped balls in one shot. They both laughed and Carman stared into David's eyes. David smiled at him and took a sip of his drink.

"What are you thinking about?" David asked quietly. Carman cleared his throat and took another shot. He missed and David giggled.

"I was thinking about you." Carman said and stepped aside to let David take his shot. He sunk another ball and smiled. He looked at Carman and bit his bottom lip.

"Do I want to know what you were thinking about me for?" David asked. He lined up but missed by a long shot. Carman giggled and lined up his cue for his shot.

"Well, maybe it's none of your business." Carman said as he shot and missed. David laughed and took a sip of his drink.

"If I'm in your thought, I think it counts as my business." David said and took his turn. He sunk a ball and set up for the next shot.

"I don't think it works that way." Carman said and David giggled. He took his shot and sunk another ball. He did this another time before it was Carman's turn. As they passed each other, David smelled Carman's hair and Carman giggled. "You're really laying it on pretty thick today." Carman said as he took his shot. He missed and David laughed at him.

"Well, it helps me win when your mind is elsewhere." David said as he set up for his shot.

"So you're cheating?" Carman asked. David nodded and took the shot. He sunk another ball and Carman shook his head. David lined up for his next shot, just before he took it, Carman said. "I have no gag reflex." David moved the cue funny and the cue ball bounced off the table. Carman laughed and David shook his head.

"Nice, Carman." David said. Carman winked at him and put the cue ball on the table where he wanted it. He sunk two balls before it was David's turn again. "Really?" David asked thinking of Carman's comment. Carman laughed and nodded. David raised his eyebrows and took his next shot. He missed and Carman laughed.

"Now who can't concentrate?" Carman asked. They bantered back and forth until the game was over. Amanda clapped from behind them when Carman won the game. David turned to face her and laughed.

"Traitor." He said and Amanda giggled. David handed her the cue and she played a game with Carman. He won quite easily. When they were finished, David and Amanda went to bed. Carman said he wasn't far behind. When Amanda and David where cuddled up in bed, Amanda sighed and looked at David.

"I can't wait to get into our new place." She whispered. David smiled and nodded.

"Me too. It will be nice." He said. Amanda rested her head on his chest and David rubbed her back until she fell asleep. David thought about Carman and his gag reflex and smiled.

No gag reflex and you're scared of big men. I have GOT to fix that. David thought to himself. He smiled at the thought and shut his eyes. It wasn't long before he was asleep as well.

Chapter 8

Friday morning went as slow as molasses as far as David was concerned. It seemed to take Carman forever to get ready for work. When he finally decided he was ready to go. David practically ran out to the truck. Carman giggled as he got in.

"Why are you in such a hurry?" Carman asked. David sighed and shook his head.

"No reason."

"Yea right. I bet you used to run to school too, didn't you?" Carman asked. David rolled his eyes and looked at Carman.

"History was in the afternoon. I had to get through slow ass mornings then too. Don't judge me, Carman. Seth is fucking hot." David said defending himself. Carman laughed and turned onto the highway.

"I'm not judging you. I think it's cute."

"Cute? I never do anything cute."

"No? Ok. How about running out to the truck to try to get the morning to go faster just so you can see Seth?" Carman asked. David shook his head and sighed.

"That's not cute, that's eager." Carman laughed again and shook his head.

"You know, you're not gonna be happy about this but, Seth is straight." Carman said. David looked at him and smiled.

"Who cares? He's still nice to look at." Carman nodded.

"Yes he is." He said as he turned onto a busy street with a lot of high-rise office buildings. "Look for 1205." Carman said. David looked out the window and counted the numbers off to Carman. When they reached the right building, Carman pulled in front and they got out. "Floor 16." Carman said as he read off a piece of paper.

"So, how about your little fear. Think any more about that?" David asked as they entered the building. Carman looked at him and smiled.

"I think about it all the time." Carman said as he pushed the button for the elevator.

"I meant getting over it." Carman sighed and watched people come in and out of the building.

"I'm still thinking about it." He answered. Just then the elevator doors opened and two people got out. Carman and David got in.

"What have you thought of so far?" David asked as Carman watched the numbers light up at each floor. Carman sighed and looked at David.

"If it wasn't for Alan, I would have taken you up on that offer in the office when you raked me with your fingernails." Carman said quietly. David smiled and could feel his stomach flip. They had reached the 10th floor when a woman came into the elevator. Carman giggled and nudged David. David looked at him and Carman winked. "So, I was thinking. If you and your mom say it's alright, I thought we would start filming tonight." Carman said and winked at David again. David smiled and cleared his throat.

"Do you think the goat will be ready by tonight?" David asked. Carman smiled as the woman took a small step farther away from them.

"Oh, he'll be ready. I just hope your mom shaved this time." Carman said.

"Oh yea, she looks great. I did it myself." David said. The woman stepped out at the 14th floor and as soon as the doors closed, Carman and David burst out laughing.

"That was awesome." Carman said.

"Your way cooler when you're not freaking out about Alan and my dick." David said. Carman giggled and shook his head.

"I wasn't expecting you to be as crude as you were. And I'm not freaking out about Alan." Carman said. The elevator doors opened for their floor and they stepped out.

"You do so." David said as they made their way to the office that had the program malfunction.

"I do not. I'm just worried about him. He tells me things he doesn't tell you about all this you know." Carman said quietly as they entered the room. A woman at the counter led them to the computer that was having the problem. Carman sat down at it and the woman left the room. David pulled a chair beside Carman and looked at him. Carman looked at David and smiled. "What?" Carman asked.

"What does he say?" David asked. Carman sighed and brought up the program that was having the problem.

"I thought you didn't want to talk about Alan." Carman said. David scratched the back of his neck and watched Carman type a mile a minute on the programming page.

"Well, I do today." David said quietly. Carman sighed and looked into David's eyes.

"You made him promise not to hurt your mom, right?" Carman asked. David nodded and Carman went back to the computer. "That's what he's doing. Not hurting your mom. Telling you how he feels in a nut shell is one thing. Elaborating on it and doing what he would like to do would hurt your mom." Carman said as he typed. He pressed enter and then sat back in his chair.

"What does that mean?" David asked.

"That means we wait to see if what I did fixed the problem." Carman answered. David rolled his eyes.

"Not the computer. What does Alan want to do?" David asked. Carman sighed and looked into David's eyes.

"Things you would like." Carman said and giggled. David's face went red and he could feel his stomach flip. "Does talking about it to me land in the 'don't hurt your mom' rules?" Carman asked. David raised his eyebrows and then smiled.

"Does testing out your gag reflex on something a lot bigger than your used to land in the 'Alan rules'?" David asked. Carman sighed and looked back at the screen. The little bar on the bottom was half full and Carman shut his eyes.

"It falls in the 'Scare me half to death' rules." Carman said quietly. David sighed and shook his head.

"Sorry." Carman smiled and looked at David. He moved his eyes slowly down David's body then back up to his face. David just stared at him. Carman shivered and looked back at the computer. "What?" David whispered. Carman swallowed hard and looked back into David's eyes again.

"I wish I was younger and less attached to Alan." Carman said.

"What does that mean?"

"This fear I have has gotten worse with age. And well, your Alan's puppy." Carman said and David shook his head.

"Well, call the pound for animal cruelty." David said. Carman smiled and tapped the desk. The bar at the bottom of the computer screen was almost full.

"Alan is very turned on by you." Carman whispered. David coughed and Carman giggled.

"Like shit he is." David said. Carman laughed and nodded.

"He said it's mostly your eyes and when you sing."

"Yea right." David said and rolled his eyes. The computer beeped and the program began running. Carman smiled and looked at David.

"Well, it's true." He said. He got up and patted the computer. "I'm a genius." He said. David looked at the computer and shook his head.

"What did you do?"

"I told it to work or I would kick its hard drive." Carman said. David laughed and shook his head. They left the room and Carman handed the bill to the receptionist. They left the main room and got back into the elevator.

"He told you that crap?" David asked. Carman was irritated now and pushed the button that stops the elevator.

"David, he tells me everything. He's afraid to tell you because he thinks that constitutes as hurting your mom. He tells me because he wants to get it off his chest and out of his head. BOTH of them." Carman said. David blinked at his friend's tone and then looked down at the floor. "I think you should try to be a little more understanding with him. He was your teacher so there was a boundary there. Not only the legalities of the teacher student thing, but also the trust that was shaken when he was young with Charlie. He couldn't tell you this shit. When he met your mother, he wasn't thinking you had any interest. Their relationship just started out as meetings about you over coffee. It escalated from there after the shit with Gabe. She needed somebody and Alan was there. Another thing is, you hid your feelings from him really well. He can usually see it but with you he didn't. He knew you were interested in men, just not how interested you were in him. Cut him some slack already. If it where up to him and that wasn't your mother he was with, He would be down here showing off HIS gag reflex!" Carman scolded and pushed the button to resume the elevator ride. David stood there stunned and Carman watched the numbers count down. When they got to the bottom floor they stepped out and he led the way to the truck. David got in and sat quietly in the passenger seat. Carman sighed and looked at him. "Look, I didn't mean to get mad. I guess this is just another case of someone not knowing the whole story." Carman said. David looked at him and his face was pale. Carman looked at his white face with wide eyes. "Are you ok?" He asked. David swallowed hard and took a deep breath.

"I don't think I know what to say." David choked out. Carman smiled and started the truck.

"You don't need to say anything. I shouldn't have said anything for that matter." Carman said as he pulled out onto the busy street.

'I'm glad you did." David said quietly. Carman frowned and looked at him.

"Why? I would think news like that would suck."

"Well, actually. It's exactly what I was too afraid to ask. It's the shit that was always avoided." David said. Carman raised his eyebrows and looked out the windshield as he made his way through the busy city to Lance's office.

"How do you feel about it?" Carman asked as he turned onto a less busy street. David sighed and shook his head.

"I don't know. How would you feel?"

"How would I feel if Alan Black wanted to fuck me so bad it hurt? Well let me see . . ." Carman said sarcastically and rolled his eyes. David giggled and shook his head.

"Yea, I get it. But I thought you were scared of big guys."

"I guess I would be getting over that in a big damn hurry." David laughed and looked out the window. They had entered a fancy section of town and David recognized some of the houses.

"Hey, Charlie lives down here." David said

"Yea but we're not going down that far." Carman said as he pulled over in front of a huge Victorian styled house.

"So bad it hurts?" David asked repeating the words as Carman shut off the truck. He laughed and nodded.

"That's what he said." Carman said and got out of the truck. David shook his head and followed him to the house. The house was white with black trim. The door way was covered with a stone arch. Carman smiled at David and leaned close to him. "The rules apply here too." Carman whispered. David smiled and they both took a deep breath.

"DEAD MAN WALKEN!" They yelled in unison. David giggled as they waited for the door to be answered.

"Listen, Think about it this way. Whenever you pull your head out of your ass enough to hang out with Alan again, imagine how easy it will be for YOU to win now." Carman whispered. David laughed and shook his head.

"You are evil." David whispered back and Carman laughed. Just then the door opened and Seth stood in front of them. David buckled slightly and Carman giggled.

"Hi little bro. He ready for us?" Carman asked.

"Is he ever ready for you Carman?" Seth asked. Carman laughed and stepped into the house. "Hi." Seth said to David.

"Hi" David said and Seth stepped out of the way to let him in. He walked into the house and looked around. It was decorated like a show home and smelled really clean.

"Lance is downstairs." Seth said. Carman looked at David and winked.

"Is he ready?" Carman asked Seth again. Seth shook his head and smiled. David watched as his hair tossed around his broad shoulders and sexy shaped jaw.

"Go look old man." Seth said and Carman laughed. Seth smiled at David and David cleared his throat. Carman laughed again and headed for the stairs. David followed and Seth followed behind David. They got down to the basement and David was amazed at the beautiful pool table and red oak bar. There was a big screen T.V. over the fake fireplace and it was lit like a bar. Carman went behind the bar and dug out a towel. He threw it over his shoulder and Seth laughed. "You know the drill, right?" Seth asked David quietly. David smiled at him and nodded. "The bar tender is in!" Seth called and went to the bar and sat down. David sat down on a stool that was two down from Seth and Carman giggled. Seth moved to sit next to David and he sighed. Carman giggled and suddenly David could feel hands run around his hips. He looked to the right quickly to see Lance standing behind him. David giggled and shook his head.

"Hello good looking. How did we get so lucky?" Lance asked and kissed David on the cheek. David laughed and shook his head again.

"I stole it from Alan." Carman said and Lance laughed.

"That didn't take long." Lance said and sat next to his little brother.

"What are you having?" Carman asked and David smiled. Carman giggled and pulled out a bottle of 18 year old scotch and poured David's drink.

"Ooo, well. If we're being serious, we better have a couple of those." Lance said and Carman smiled. He poured one for Lance and then looked at Seth. Seth smiled and ran his hand through his hair. David shifted in his chair and Carman giggled.

"The same I guess." Seth said and Lance raised his eyebrows.

"Showing off for the new guy or what?" He asked. Seth looked at David and then back at Lance.

"It won't be easy." Seth said and Carman laughed. He handed out the drinks and poured one for himself but staid standing where he was.

"Since this is David and Seth's first time to play together, they have to go first." Carman said and smiled at David. David sighed and glared back. Lance giggled and took a sip of his drink. Seth looked at David and David held up one finger at him to inform him to wait. He pounded the drink back and handed the glass to Carman. Lance giggled as David kept his finger up in front of Seth's face while Carman poured. He handed the glass back to David. He took a big sip of the very full glass Carman gave him then dropped the finger.

"Ok." David said and looked at Seth. Lance giggled again and leaned on the bar so he could see better. Seth tossed his hair to one side and stared into David's eyes. David held his gaze and waited.

"So, do you swallow everything that easy or does the age have something to do with it?" Seth asked referring to the Scotch in sexy bedroom drawl. David stared at him and sighed. Carman and Lance both waited in silence. David stared deep into Seth's eyes until Seth's eyelids drooped.

"Age is everything." David whispered and Seth slowly licked his lips. He stared at David then picked up his glass.

"Show me." Seth said. David took Seth's cup from him and slowly touched it to his lips. He lightly ran his tongue along the lip of the glass then in one quick movement he slammed the whole drink. He set the glass down and swallowed the strong liquid as slow as he could. Carman giggled as Seth shifted uncomfortably in his chair. David held his gaze while he thought of something else to say. He leaned closer to David and bit his bottom lip. "Watching you do that makes me hard as a rock." Seth whispered. Lance and Carman both giggled and waited for David's reply. David leaned closer to Seth and deepened his stare.

"Show me." David whispered and Seth broke. He laughed and sat back in his chair. Lance and Carman clapped and David took a deep breath. Seth shook his head and looked at him.

"Fuck man, you're like, as good as Alan. Have you ever done it against him?" David smiled and nodded.

"It's incredible to watch." Carman said and refilled Seth's cup. Lance shook his head and looked at Carman.

"A few more games with that kid and Seth might be worth playing against." Lance said. David laughed and shook his head.

"Do Carman." Seth said and David smiled at the innuendo. Carman sighed and got close to him. David giggled and took a sip from his glass.

"Do Carman?" David asked in a sexy drawl. Carman sighed but kept a straight face. "Would you let me do you Carman?" David asked quietly leaning on the bar so he was really close to Carman's face. He swallowed hard and looked into David's eyes.

"If you can last through a blow job, I'll let you do me." Carman said. David raised an eyebrow and ran his thumb along his bottom lip.

"Try me." David whispered. Carman smirked and it struck David as quite sexy. He stared into Carman's eyes and waited. He moved closer until they were almost kissing and David closed his eyes.

"I would love to." Carman whispered. David swallowed and opened his eyes. He stared at Carman and sighed. Carman raised an eyebrow and David moved a little closer. They could almost feel the little hairs on each other's lips.

"Then do it." David whispered with his eyes closed. Lance shifted in his seat and Seth giggled. Carman sighed and swallowed hard. He smiled and kissed David. David was so shocked he pulled away and started laughing. Lance and Seth both laughed and clapped their hands. Carman smiled at David and winked. David shook his head and drank the last of the hard scotch in his glass.

"That was awesome." Seth said.

"It's the only way I can beat him." Carman said. David laughed and shook his head.

"Can Alan beat him?" Lance asked. Carman and David smiled and Carman looked at Lance.

"Alan and David are tied right now."

"Did he have to kiss you?" Seth asked. David and Carman laughed.

"No, he's the master." David said and Lance giggled. Carman came around the bar and he and Lance left to install the computer. Seth and David still sat at the bar. David suddenly felt very uncomfortable and Seth could tell.

"So, I hate to ask this but, Am I still the lone straight guy in this gay parade or are you and Carman just really close?" Seth asked. David laughed and looked at Seth.

"You're alone." David said. Seth nodded and rolled his eyes.

"Never a hot chick around here." Seth complained and David shook his head.

"So, you're surrounded by gay guys and you managed to stay straight?" David asked. Seth smiled and nodded.

"Never even an experiment." Seth said and tossed his hair again. David cleared his throat and tried to hide the interest he had in Seth. His hair was killing him.

"It must be strange to be the weird one." David said and they both laughed.

"Yea, I guess it's better than being the only gay guy."

"That's true." David said remembering what it was like thinking all he had to learn from was a dirt bag like Todd.

"So, are you all the way or Bi like Lance?" Seth asked. The question rolled out of his mouth as if he were asking about the weather.

"Um, Bi I guess. I have a baby on the way with my girlfriend."

"She's cool with you and guys?"

"So far." David said. Seth nodded and got up.

"Come with me." Seth said and David looked toward the office. "Trust me, they won't get to that computer until after an epic tongue battle that will end with Carman stopping Lance before it goes too far. I swear that guy is faking the whole gay thing." Seth said. David shook his head and giggled. He got up and followed Seth up to his room. He closed the door behind him and they both sat on Seth's bed. Seth reached over and pressed play on his C.D. player. He had Manson in his stereo and David smiled. "So, I take it your new meat." Seth said as he lit a cigarette. David raised his eyebrows and crossed his legs under himself.

"You know your stuff. How can you tell?" David asked. Seth smiled and tossed his hair over his shoulder. David cleared his throat again and looked away. Seth giggled and shook his head.

"That's how I can tell. You're way too obvious." Seth said and David giggled.

"Really?" Seth laughed and faced David. He crossed his legs like David and let his hair fall in front of his shoulders. David swallowed hard and Seth giggled.

"Ok, hair is obviously your thing, right?" Seth asked. David sighed and nodded. "What is it you like so much about it?" Seth asked. David raised his eyebrows and cleared his throat again.

"Well, it's just hair like yours. I don't know what it is I just find it really sexy." David answered. He found it incredibly easy to talk to Seth.

"Ok, so what happens if I do this?" Seth asked and ran his hand slowly through his hair. His hand combed through the black silk looking hair and David shuttered. He thought of how it felt when Gabe's hair would shroud him when they were in bed together. He sighed and closed his eyes. "Wow, that's an interesting reaction." Seth said. David opened his eyes and looked at Seth with a puzzled gaze. Seth smiled and shook his head. "I was expecting words not the actual thing." Seth said and giggled. David laughed and shook his head.

"Why the questions?" He asked. Seth smiled and cleared his throat.

"In a world like this, half the battle is acting straight. It sucks but some people are really pissed with you gay dudes. They think your freaks of nature or something."

"Ok, so why the questions?" David asked again.

"I can help you fake it." Seth said and tossed his hair again. David sighed and shook his head.

"How is throwing your hair around like that going to help?"

"Well, I'm desensitizing you. The more you see it, the less of an effect it has. You don't want to be caught in a place full of long haired homo-phobics and be so damn obvious." Seth explained and let his hair fall like fine strings of black silk across his shoulders again. David raised his eyebrows and thought of being in a room full of Gabe look a likes. He shuttered.

"Ok, I can see what you mean. What else?" David asked and Seth shrugged.

"What else do you like?" David mock laughed and shook his head. "Besides me." Seth added and smiled. David giggled and shook his head.

"Um, it's hard to explain." David said and Seth rolled his eyes.

"Who's hotter, Carman or Lance?" Seth asked.

"Carman." David answered without hesitation and Seth nodded.

"Ok, Me or Carman?" Seth asked. David giggled and shook his head.

"You." David answered and Seth raised an eyebrow.

"ok, Me or Alan?" The question drug David's heart into his throat. He was instantly nervous and Seth could see it. "Uh huh." He said and shook his head. David raised an eyebrow and stared at Seth. He sighed and got up. He went to his little book shelf and took out a brown book. He brought it back to the bed and set it in front of David. It was an old year book. Seth sat cross-legged again in front of David and tossed his hair behind his back. David smiled and Seth giggled. "Ok, look through it." Seth said. David swallowed and opened the book. He flipped through a few pages with Seth staring at his face. He got to the junior prom page and stopped. Seth smiled and ran his hand over the page. "See that beautiful guy with all the hair?" Seth asked.

"Yea." David said.

"That's Carman." Seth said and David raised his eyebrows. Seth turned the page and David's heart caught in his throat. "I bet you can guess who that is." Seth said quietly. David stared at the young man on the page. He was dressed in a black, priest collared suit. His shirt wasn't tucked in and it hung below his black suit jacket. His long sandy hair hung around his shoulders and it made his light green eyes pierce the page. Seth smiled and shook his head.

"That's Alan." David said quietly and touched the page. He ran his hand along the side of Alan's face and down to his throat. David sighed and looked up at Seth. Seth raised his eyebrows and smiled.

"So, Alan is what you like." David nodded and looked back down at the page. Seth sighed and got back off the bed. He walked to the book case again and took a small photo album from the top shelf. He brought it back and threw it in front of David. "Give that a gander." Seth said. David picked up the book while Seth sat back down on the bed to face David and crossed his legs again. He tossed his hair over his shoulder again and David looked up at him. Seth smiled and shook his head. "Just look at the pictures." Seth said quietly and David looked back down at the book. On the first page was a picture of Carman and Alan. They were sitting on an old couch with a beer in each of their hands. Carman was giving the finger and Alan was laughing at something off to the right. David smiled and turned the page. The next photo was of just Carman. He was riding a big white horse. David recognized the horse to be the Arabian stallion, Cocaine safari. David turned the page and stopped. The next picture was of Alan. It was a side profile in the winter. The picture was taken in black and white but it looked to be relatively new. He was wearing his leather jacket and looking off into the distance somewhere. His eyes were squinted slightly and the stray hairs that David loved were hanging in his face just as David liked. He could feel his heart pound in his chest and his hands start to sweat. His breathing picked up a little and he swallowed hard. Just before his chest could expel the pain it held, Seth took the book. David looked up at him and watched him take the picture out of the album. "Here" Seth said and handed the picture to David. David looked from the picture to Seth and Seth smiled. "Keep it. I don't know what it is but, I've never seen anyone look at a picture and react like that. I thought Carman had it bad for him." Seth said. David shook his head and closed his eyes.

"Thanks." David said quietly and stared at the man he missed so much. "You know, I've only been gone for three weeks." David said and looked up at Seth. Seth sighed and put the books away.

"Three weeks is a long time when you feel like that about somebody." Seth said and came back to the bed. David put the picture in his inside jacket pocket and sighed. "Tell me about it." Seth said. David sighed and shook his head.

"Well, I've known him since September. He was the first guy I ever liked."

"Wow, so you're *really* fresh." Seth said and David laughed.

"Yea, I guess so."

"Ok, so what happened?" Seth asked.

"Well, my mom thought I needed a mentor or something since my dad died and set this big brother deal up with Alan. When I got to know him better I liked him even more, I even fell in . . ." David stopped talking and looked down at the bed.

"You fell in love with him?" Seth asked. David sighed and nodded. "Whoa, ok. So then what?" Seth asked. David sighed and shook his head.

"Well, nothing I guess. I learned a lot from a guy named Gabe and just after he told me *he* was in love with me, he died." David said and closed his eyes.

"So this Gabe was your first everything or what?" Seth asked. David looked at him and nodded.

"You look like him." David said and smiled. Seth raised his eyebrows.

"Well, at least you have good taste." He said and they both laughed. "Ok, so Gabe is gone. What happened next?" Seth asked.

David took a deep breath in from his nose and sighed it out in an exaggerated breath.

"I knocked up his sister." David said. Seth laughed and shook his head. David laughed with him and ran his hand through his hair.

"Well, that's one way to heal over a death I guess."

"It's not like that. Amanda and I have been friends since we were little and Gabe was her older brother." David said. Seth nodded and stared into David's eyes.

"So, through all this, you had a thing for Alan?" Seth asked.

"Yea, and it was getting worse. Soon we were inseparable. I was just about ready to face the gauntlet and tell him how I felt when . . ." David stopped talking again and clenched his teeth.

"Ok, what happened? Teeth clenching is anger." Seth said and raised his eyebrows. David sighed and shook his head.

"He's fucking my mom." David said. Seth burst out laughing and David shook his head.

"Oh, dude! That's so harsh!" Seth said through his laughing. David rolled his eyes and Seth composed himself.

"So that's why you're staying with Carman?" Seth asked after the laughing subsided. David nodded thinking that leaving out the suicide attempt was a good idea for now. "Wow, that would really suck." Seth said.

"Well, it gets worse." David said. Seth raised his eyebrows and David shook his head. "Apparently, he was into me the whole time and if I would have spoken up sooner, well, you get the picture." David explained. Seth shook his head and giggled.

"Wow, its way easier being straight man." Seth said and David laughed. He thought of how easy it was to be with Amanda.

"That's true." David said. Seth shook his head again and looked into David's eyes.

"I bet you hate his guts now." David stared into Seth's striking blue eyes and shivered. Seth giggled and tossed his hair again. David laughed and rolled his eyes.

"I don't hate him. I'm just really mad." David said. Seth sighed and stood up.

"Come on." Seth said and pulled David up to his feet. He followed him back down to the basement and sat down at the bar.

"Hi there, convert him yet?" Lance asked. David giggled and looked at Seth.

"Yea, I have finally found what I've been missing all these years." Seth said sarcastically. David, Lance and Carman all laughed. Carman looked at David and David smiled. Seth and David sat down at the bar with Lance. "David needs a drink." Seth said and patted David's back. David smiled at Seth and Carman giggled. He poured David a drink and handed it to him. David sipped it and looked at Lance.

"Get your hard drive all unloaded?" David asked in a sexy drawl. Lance and Carman giggled and Lance looked at David.

"My hard drive was too large. The computer wouldn't accept it." Lance said and Carman rolled his eyes.

"That's too bad. I bet your hard drive has a lot to offer a little computer like that one." David said. Seth was confused but Carman giggled.

"Oh I think that computer would be so full it wouldn't know what to do with its self." Lance said and stared into David's eyes. David leaned closer to Lance and sighed.

"From what I hear about that little computer, it can really eat up your ram." David whispered. Lance laughed and shook his head. David snorted and looked at Carman. Carman shook his head and looked up at the time.

"Well, we're off the clock. It's over time now." Carman said. David looked at the clock and laughed. It was only 2:30.

"I'm not paying over time." Lance said and David laughed. Carman shook his head and smiled. Seth tapped David on the shoulder and David looked at him. He sighed and tossed his hair so it rested on David's shoulder. David sat arrow straight and stared at him. Carman and Lance waited to see what happened. Seth smiled and bit his bottom lip.

"Touch it." Seth whispered and David giggled. Seth laughed and Carman shook his head.

"David, I'm disappointed." Lance said. David laughed and elbowed Seth in the side. He laughed and elbowed David back. The four of them talked about Amanda and the coming baby and their pending move. Seth agreed to help and after they finished their last drinks, Carman and David got ready to go. Seth and David went up first and Seth stopped David at the door. David looked at him and sighed.

"What are you gonna do, kiss me?" He asked. Seth smiled and shook his head.

"You would like that wouldn't you?" He asked in a quiet whisper. David swallowed hard and Seth giggled. "God you're easy."

"I know." David said. Seth laughed and stared into David's eyes.

"I stopped you to ask a question." Seth said.

"Ok, shoot."

"What was the hard drive stuff?" Seth asked. David looked toward the stairs and didn't see Carman yet.

"Well, Carman isn't with Lance because he's hung to well." David whispered. Seth raised his eyebrows and looked at the stairs.

"Really?" Seth asked looking back at David. David nodded and smiled. "That makes a lot more sense now." Seth said and giggled. David laughed and Seth ran his hand through his hair.

"Stop doing that." David whispered and Seth laughed. Just then Carman and Lance came up the stairs.

"Ready to go?" Carman asked. David nodded and shook Lance's hand.

"Don't be a stranger good looking." Lance said and David laughed.

"Well, I'll try not to be." David said and looked at Seth. Carman laughed at the look David gave Seth and Lance rolled his eyes.

"He turns them on and I get them off." Lance said and Carman laughed. Seth rolled his eyes and looked at David.

"Not this one." Seth said and Carman raised his eyebrows. David felt his breath catch in his throat and Seth smiled.

"Well, that's interesting." Lance said and Carman opened the door.

"See ya." Seth said quietly and smiled at David.

"Ok." David said and went out of the house. Carman followed him to the truck and got in.

"What the fuck was that?" Carman said giggling. David looked at Carman and shrugged. His face was still in shock and he couldn't help but giggle. Carman honked the horn and drove away.

"That WAS weird wasn't it?" David asked. Carman laughed and nodded.

"No shit. What happened while me and Lance were . . . working." Carman asked. David laughed and dug into his pocket. He pulled out the picture and handed it to Carman. Carman stopped at a red light and looked at the picture. "Wow, nice picture. He gave you this?"

"Yea, we were looking at some old pictures and he said I could have that one." David said. Carman raised his eyebrows and handed the picture back.

"That's a really sexy picture of Alan." Carman said and shook his head. David looked at the picture again and then put it back in his pocket. Carman started driving and sighed. "So, you talked about Alan I take it then." Carman said.

"Yea, it just sort of came up." David said and looked out the window.

"So what's with the moment at the door then if all you guys did was talk?"

"I don't know." David said and looked at Carman. "What was with the hour long program if all you did was work?" David asked and Carman laughed.

"It's a thing. Lance likes to kiss me so I let him."

"Uh, huh. Isn't he one of the guys you broke up with because of the size thing?" David asked. Carman sighed and nodded. David giggled and shook his head.

"He doesn't care though at least." Carman said. David sighed and scratched the back of his head.

"Why don't you let him help you get over it if you're too scared of corrupting Alan's puppy?"

"Well, if you must know, I trust Alan's puppy more than I trust Lance." Carman said and smiled. David giggled and shook his head. Carman turned onto the freeway and headed toward his house.

"Seth is really hot." David said under his breath and Carman laughed. David looked at him and giggled.

"Well, straight guys are even hotter because you can't have them." Carman said and David shook his head.

"No. Seth is just hot."

"Well, he is. I agree with you there." Carman said and they both laughed. He slowed the truck then and looked at David. David raised his eyebrows and stared at him. "If I did want to do this with you, would you stop no matter what and never tell a soul?" Carman asked. David pursed his lips and cleared his throat.

"Yes." David said quietly and Carman sighed. He sped the truck back up and got on to the road that leads to his house.

"I'm not saying I am, I just wanted to know." Carman said quietly.

"Ok, that's cool." David said and smiled. Carman looked so nervous and David found it oddly attractive. "What's holding you up still?" David asked quietly. Carman sighed and shook his head.

"Alan." He answered. David nodded and looked out the windshield. They could see Carman's house now and Carman slowed the truck to get ready for the turn. "You're his puppy and I can't get passed that." Carman said.

"Well, you know where I am if you ever do." David said and ran his hand up Carman's leg. Carman cleared his throat and shook his head. David laughed and pulled his hand away.

"You're cruel." Carman said and parked the truck. They could see that Amanda was still gone.

"We're alone." David said trying to sound persuasive. Carman laughed and shook his head. He looked at David and sighed.

"David, I can't." Carman said nervously and looked away.

"I know. I was just bugging you." Carman smiled and traced David's jaw with his finger. David parted his lips and closed his eyes. Even though he had Amanda, the touch of a man was so nice to him. Carman sighed and ran his thumb along David's bottom lip.

"I want to, but I can't." Carman whispered.

Chapter 9

Seth was at Carman's place at 8:30 to help with the move. The day before, Carman and David had loaded everything back into the truck and car from the garage and had it ready to go. Amanda was busy packing up their clothes and things they had in the house while Carman, Seth and David had coffee at the kitchen table.

"When does the furniture arrive?" Carman asked as he took a sip of his coffee.

"One o'clock or something like that. Those guys are never on time so who knows." David answered. Seth giggled and shook his head.

"What about the phone and stuff?" Seth asked.

"All done." David answered and lit a cigarette. Amanda walked into the kitchen to get a drink of water. She was wearing a pair of tight blue jeans and a yellow tank top. Her long blonde hair was tied back in a ponytail and she was wearing a bandana on her head. Seth raised his eyebrows and Carman laughed. David looked at Seth and squinted his eyes. Amanda turned and seen the production at the table. She giggled and shook her head.

"What's the matter David, jealous?" Amanda asked. Seth and Carman laughed at the comment but all David did was look at her and smile.

"Why would I be jealous?" He asked and Carman giggled.

"Cause he likes her and not you." He said. David, Seth and Amanda all laughed. She shook her head and went back down the hall to finish packing. David shook his head and took a drag from his cigarette. Seth tossed his hair and David sighed.

"This desensitizing thing isn't working out so well." Carman said. Seth giggled and shook his head.

"It will eventually."

"Don't count on it." David said and Carman laughed. They finished their coffees and got up to carry out the suit cases for Amanda. When everything was loaded, they headed into town. Seth rode with Carman in the truck and David, Amanda and Little Mike road in the car.

"I hope you don't think I'm interested in Seth." Amanda said quietly as they turned onto the highway. David giggled and shook his head.

"I didn't think about it. Are you?" He asked. Amanda laughed and looked at David.

"Are you kidding? I don't like long hair on a guy."

"Oh, I was going to grow mine out." David said.

"Well, you can. I might like it on you but normally I don't."

"What would happen if Seth cut his hair?"

"Well, that's a different story." Amanda said. David laughed and shook his head. She reached out and held his hand as they drove. He slowed the car and turned off the highway to get into the apartment building. Carman and David both parked as close as they could to the doors. They got out of their vehicles and Seth went in to get the keys.

"Fuck he's hot." David whispered to Carman as they waited. Carman giggled and shook his head.

"You're hopeless." Carman said. Amanda laughed over hearing the conversation.

"You should have seen him when this all started happening. You think he's hopeless now." She said and took Mike out of the car. Carman laughed and looked at David.

"Well, what were you like?" He asked. David rolled his eyes and sighed.

"Carman, I don't know what she's talking about." Carman and Amanda laughed. Seth waved them in and Carman and David both grabbed a box out of the back of the truck. They all went in and set the boxes down in the hall.

"Go ahead, I'll pay all the stuff." Amanda said. David nodded and Seth handed him the keys. Their fingers touched and David stomach involuntarily jumped causing him to swallow hard. Seth smiled and took Amanda into the office. David sighed and picked up his box. When he stood, he noticed Carman was giggling at him.

"What?" David asked as they headed to the elevator with their loads. Carman shook his head and leaned against the wall.

"You're so obvious." David sighed and shook his head.

"I really don't mean to be." He said. The door opened and they stepped in.

"I don't remember you being this bad before." Carman said as they waited for the doors to close. David sighed and leaned his back against the blue wall in the back of the elevator.

"I don't know what it is." Carman sighed and leaned right next to David.

"When was the last time you were with a guy?"

"Gabe." David answered. The elevator started its climb.

"That's what's wrong then. Don't you find yourself acting like that when you and Amanda haven't done it for a while?"

"Well, yea, but it's not as bad."

"Well, you and Amanda do it more often. If you had to wait longer between times you were together, it might be as bad." Carman said. The elevator stopped and the two men stepped out. They walked to room 509 and David unlocked the door. He walked in first and stepped into the kitchen. He saw a basket of fruit on the counter with a card on it. Carman raised his eyebrows as he stepped in next to David. "Let Amanda open it." He said. David smiled and nodded. They set their boxes down and headed back down for the next ones.

"Maybe your right." David said as they entered the elevator. Carman smiled and looked into David's eyes.

"About being too long since you were with a guy?" Carman asked. David nodded. "You know, being as young as you are, I think you're more easily excited. As you get older it will get easier." Carman said. David rolled his eyes and shook his head.

"Coming from the guy that can't go to his buddies place without making out for half an hour." Carman laughed.

"You're just jealous that I have an outlet and you don't."

"I could but he's scared of me." David said back referring to Carman. The elevator doors opened and Amanda was standing in the hall holding the light overnight bags. Mike was carrying his pillow.

"I helping." Mike said. David smiled and he and Carman stepped out of the way for Amanda and Mike.

"You could start unpacking or going through things if you want. We can carry the rest up." David said to Amanda.

"I wasn't planning on carrying anything else." Amanda said and Carman laughed.

"Open the thing on the counter." He said as the doors closed. David giggled and they walked out to the truck. Seth was in the back stacking the boxes on the tail gate.

"Well, you're paid up for three months big boy." Seth said as they got to the truck and loaded their arms with two boxes each.

"That's good. My boss fucks me all the time so it could take that long to come up with another month's rent." David said. Carman laughed and shook his head.

"You wish." Carman said and they all laughed. David and Carman headed back in. They got into the elevator and Carman looked at David.

"Your outlet wouldn't be so scared of you if he was sure you would be careful." David smiled and shook his head.

"Carman, as long as there is that Alan rule, you'll never know." David answered. Carman sighed and watched the numbers count up to 5. The doors opened and they walked to the apartment. Amanda was setting the fruit in the fridge.

"It's from the land lords. They said thanks for moving in and enjoy your new home." She said as the men set their boxes down.

"Well, that's nice." David said. Amanda smiled and set the basket on the counter. She looked at the boxes.

"There is a blue box that says kitchen on it. Can that come up next?" She asked. Carman and David agreed and they headed back out to the elevator. When they got in, Carman stopped it. He pushed David against the wall and locked him into a hungry kiss. David closed his eyes and raked his fingernails down Carman's sides. Carman moaned. He held David against the wall and pressed his body against his.

"The Alan rule is important." Carman whispered still pressed against David.

"Well, I hate the Alan rule right now." David whispered back. Carman smiled and backed away. David groaned and Carman laughed.

"If we could make out without you getting hard and me wanting to fuck, I would do it all the time." Carman said and David smiled.

"What's wrong with wanting to fuck?" David asked. Carman rolled his eyes and started the elevator. "Why isn't kissing against the rules?"

"It is but I can't help it sometimes." Carman whispered and David laughed.

"And I'm hopeless." David said under his breath. Carman giggled and the doors opened. Seth was busy bringing the boxes into the hall way.

"Is there one that says kitchen on it?" Carman asked. Seth looked out the door.

"I'll go look." He said and left the building.

"Why is it ok to break the rules a little bit and not all the way?" David asked as he picked up two of the boxes in the hall. Carman laughed and shook his head.

"Alan." Carman said. David rolled his eyes. Seth came back in with two boxes. One was the blue kitchen box. Carman took the two out of his hands and turned toward the elevator.

"The truck is almost empty." Seth said.

"My keys are in my pocket. There is stuff in the car." David said trying to steady the boxes in his arms. Seth walked up to David and looked at him.

"Which pocket?" He asked. David closed his eyes and sighed.

"Front right pants pocket." David answered. Seth giggled and pushed his hand into David's pocket. David stood very still as Seth slowly pulled the keys out.

"Thanks." Seth said and walked outside. David opened his eyes and Carman laughed.

"Good thing we didn't kiss for too long before THAT, huh?" Carman asked as the elevator doors opened. David shook his head and stepped in with Carman.

"You're a dick." Carman laughed and shook his head.

"I'm not the one who told him where the keys were."

"I didn't think he would dig in my pockets."

"Never underestimate Seth." Carman said. David smiled and looked into Carman's eyes.

"I'm still trying to learn not to underestimate you. Don't put Seth in the mix."

"Why? What did I do?" Carman asked.

"The only time you kiss me is when I least expect it." David answered. The doors opened and they stepped out.

"That's what makes them so good."

"No, YOU are what make them so good." David said quietly as they walked into the apartment.

"Yes, perfect. That's the one." Amanda said as she seen the box in Carman's arm. They set the boxes down and Mike giggled.

"David and Carman strong." He said and they both laughed.

"Thank god there's no stairs to climb." Carman said. David giggled and they left to the elevator again. They stepped in and David stood in front of the controls. Carman laughed and shook his head. "What are you doing?" He asked.

"I was thinking. You might be right about this whole 'it's been awhile thing.' I don't think it's fair for you to stop the elevator and make it worse." David said. Carman laughed again and shook his head.

"Sorry. I promise to behave myself."

"Yea right." David said but stepped away. Carman pushed the ground floor button and the doors closed. He leaned toward David and ran his hand through David's hair. "Ass hole." David whispered and Carman smiled.

"I am not." Carman whispered and gently kissed David. He pulled away just as the doors opened. They stepped out to see Seth out at David's car. He had half of the car emptied already. "Well, he has the easier job I think." Carman said.

"Yea, he should have to ride in that elevator with you." David said quietly and picked up Gabe's guitars. Carman laughed and picked up a stack of three small boxes. They got back in the elevator and David put the guitars down. He pushed the stop button and Carman laughed.

"That's not fair, my arms are full and I can't defend myself." Carman said quietly. David smiled and took the boxes from Carman. He set them down and stared into Carman's eyes.

"I am not as cruel as you. I just have something to say." David said. Carman sighed and shook his head. "I think you want to try but you're scared of Alan. I think you break the easy rules to try to talk yourself into the big no-no rule. I bet if I was persistent enough and as cruel as you, it wouldn't take much to convince you to do it." David said. Carman rolled his eyes and sighed.

"David, I like you ok. I like how you kiss and I would love to do more. I am honestly afraid though. The Alan rule is there but it's not the only thing that stops me."

"Well, I don't think I could make out with you for a long period of time and not get hard, so what do you want to do about it?" David asked. Carman sighed and shook his head.

"I don't know." He answered.

"Think about it and let me know then." David said and started the elevator again. Carman sighed and picked up his boxes. David picked up the guitars and watched the numbers. The doors opened and they stepped out. They took their things to the apartment and David went right to the music room with the guitars. He leaned them against the wall and sighed. He met Carman at the door and they went back to the elevator. It had gone down so they had to wait.

"Are you mad at me?" Carman asked. David giggled and shook his head.

"No. Why would you ask that?"

"Well, the random kissing. It seems to me like it pisses you off." Carman explained. David smiled and looked into Carman's eyes.

"The only thing that pisses me off is that I have to stop because you're scared of the result." David said. Carman sighed and nodded. They watched the elevator numbers count back up to 5 and the doors opened. Seth stepped out with three boxes in his arms.

"Where do I take them?" Seth asked.

"Amanda will tell you." Carman said and they stepped into the lift. They watched Seth walk to the apartment as the doors closed.

"You know, there are four layers of clothing between you and my dick." David said. Carman laughed and shook his head.

"Clothes come off eventually though."

"They don't have to." David argued. Carman sighed and cleared his throat.

"David, I would be able to feel it and that's scary enough."

"Ok, suit yourself." David said. Carman shook his head and waited for the doors to open. When they did they stepped out and Carman grabbed David's arm. David smiled and faced Carman. He stared into David's eyes and sighed.

"I wish you weren't Alan's puppy. Those four layers of clothing thing is a really good line." Carman said. David giggled and quickly kissed Carman. Carman smiled and they both grabbed two large boxes. They got back into the elevator and rode it up. Seth met them at the top and decided to wait. They put their boxes in the living room and met Seth at the elevator. They all got in.

"Why is it that your elevator ride is so much slower than mine?" Seth asked. David and Carman laughed. "You know, you're old enough to be his father." Seth said to Carman and David laughed.

"You're just jealous." Carman said. The doors opened and Seth was laughing.

"You wish old man." Seth said. Carman and Seth each grabbed two boxes and David grabbed his amp and the suit case he had his music books in. They all stepped into the elevator and Seth pressed the floor 5 button.

"It will be nice when you're all moved in and ready to have everybody over for a drink." Carman said as he shifted the boxes in his arms. David giggled and shook his head.

"I won't have a nice bar to sit at though." David said. Seth smiled and shook his head.

"I bet you would build something just to play that game." Seth joked. They all laughed and waited for the doors to open. They stepped out and took the things they carried into the apartment. Amanda had two boxes emptied and crushed on the floor.

"Can you take those down with you?" She asked as David came out of the music room.

"Of course." David said and she smiled.

"Wow, crack that whip baby." Seth said. The boys all laughed and headed back out the door. David set the boxes against the back wall of the elevator when they stepped in. "Do you ever say no to her?" Seth asked. David giggled and shook his head.

"When you start saying no to the woman your with, you stop getting laid." David said and Carman laughed.

"I can't believe I'm getting chick advice from you." Seth said. David and Carman laughed and David shook his head.

"Well, you teach, I teach." David said.

"Speaking of teaching, how about those guitar lessons?" Seth asked as the doors to the elevator opened. David smiled and stepped out.

"Well, let me get all moved in first and then we'll talk about it." David said.

"You teach, I'll teach." Seth said in a sexy drawl and Carman giggled at the red face it gave David. They gathered up the last of the boxes and piled them in the elevator. They all got in when it was full.

"You know, David is actually very good with a guitar." Carman said. Seth raised his eyebrows and smiled.

"As good as Alan?" Seth asked.

"No one is as good as Alan." David and Carman said in unison in the same distant sounding voice. Everyone laughed. When they reached the fifth floor, Carman held the elevator door open while Seth and David unloaded all the boxes.

"You know, it would have been a lot less trips if we had thought of this before." Carman said and David and Seth laughed. They carried the rest of the boxes into the apartment and Amanda smiled.

"All done?" She asked and kissed David.

"Well, it's not like we have a lot of stuff." David said and she smiled.

"Well, let's go for lunch before the furniture comes." Carman said. Amanda got Little Mike ready and they all headed to the elevator.

"I want pizza." Mike said and smiled at Carman. Carman crinkled up his nose and gave the little boy a funny look.

"That's all you ever want." He said and Mike laughed.

"I like pizza." Mike said back. Everyone laughed as they got into the elevator. Seth stood close to David and David could feel himself vibrate next to the young, more attractive version on Gabe.

"Pizza is fine bud." Carman said and Amanda and Mike giggled. Seth gently rubbed his arm against David's and David cleared his throat and looked at him. Seth kept looking ahead at the elevator doors. David sighed and shook his head. Seth giggled as the doors opened.

"You're a dick." David whispered and Seth laughed. They all went outside and Seth and Carman got into Carman's truck. Amanda loaded Mike into the car before she and David got into the front.

"You're acting strange." Amanda said as David pulled the car out to follow Carman.

"I'm having a strange day." David answered and stared out the windshield.

"Why?"

"Well, first, Carman and his random kissing in the elevator. Then there's Seth. I don't know what the story is on that guy but, he's not very nice." David explained. Amanda giggled and shook her head.

"Well, Carman I understand but, Seth, what makes him not very nice?" Amanda asked.

"He's straight one minute and then I feel like he's secretly hitting on me the next."

"Why don't you ask him about it?" Amanda offered. David smiled and shook his head.

"I think I'm going to be cleverer than that." David said with a devious smile and Amanda laughed. David turned right to follow Carman into the pizza parlor.

"What do you plan to do?" Amanda asked as David parked the car. David giggled and shook his head.

"I plan to wait it out and see how brave he gets first." David answered and shut off the car.

"Then what?"

"I'm not sure yet." David said and opened the door. Amanda giggled and got herself and Little Mike out of the car. They all went into the diner together and the waitress found them a suitable table. Amanda purposely sat next to Carman and put Mike on the other side of her so David would have to sit next to Seth. David shook his head and she giggled. The waitress took their drink orders and left a large menu on the table. They picked what they wanted and waited for the waitress to return.

"It's going to be nice to have the furniture in there." Amanda said.

"Yea, I haven't even seen it." David said. Carman giggled and took a sip of his drink. Mike played with the crayons and paper the waitress had given him. Seth let his left leg fall to the side and it rested against David's. David sighed and pushed his leg against it. Seth giggled but never pulled his away. Carman smiled at David and shook his head.

"Well, the couch and chair are a light olive color and they are leather." Amanda said. David nodded and pushed his leg harder against Seth's. "The bedroom set I picked out for Mike is white with blue clouds on it. I know it sounds dumb but you should see it. It's actually really nice." Amanda continued. David smiled as Seth pushed his leg against David's as well. "Oh, and going back to the living room. I got two end tables and a coffee table that is all metal has glass tops and I also found these two brass lamps. They are probably the coolest thing I found in the whole place." Amanda said excitedly. David lifted his leg slightly so it rubbed against Seth's. To David's surprise, Seth reciprocated. David cleared his throat and took a sip of his drink and

Seth giggled. Amanda continued, "For our bedroom, I got a metal bed frame that has these twirled leaf things on the head and foot boards. It's really cool actually. I got the cheap mattress and box spring but that was only because of the dressers that came with them. They are so dark their almost black. Oh, David they are so cool." She said. David smiled at her and Seth rubbed their legs together again. David sighed and pushed against Seth. He took a sip of his drink and tossed his hair. Carman shook his head and looked over his shoulder for the waitress.

"I'm getting hungry." Carman said to little Mike. Mike giggled and nodded his head.

"I want pizza." Mike said and Carman laughed. Seth bit his bottom lip and reached across David to the drink menu. When he recoiled, he ran his arm along David's chest.

"Oh, sorry." Seth said so convincingly that both David and Carman laughed. Amanda looked at them with a confused gaze and shook her head.

"What's so funny?" She asked. David giggled and Carman looked behind him again for the waitress. Seth smiled and looked at Amanda.

"Nothing. They just laugh randomly because their heads aren't attached properly." He said. Carman and David both laughed but Amanda just shook her head. The waitress finally arrived with their meal and set out a plate in front of everyone. Carman put a piece on Mike's plate first and then one on his own. He passed the spatula to Amanda and she did the same. She set the spatula just out of David's reach so he would have to reach across Seth for it. He took the hint and went for the spatula. Seth smiled and leaned back to give David room. He slowly trusted his hips up just enough for David to see him do it. He closed his eyes for a second and Seth giggled. He got his piece of pizza and handed the spatula to Seth. "Thank you." Seth said and

David shook his head. They ate their meal while Amanda talked about the new furniture. She was very excited about the round, wooden, 6 chaired table she had found. When they were finished eating, Carman had the waitress put the last of it in a to go container. Seth got a tooth pick and popped it into his mouth.

"Well, I bet the stuff you found is awesome babe." David said to Amanda and she smiled.

"Thank you. You'll love it." She said and took Mike to the bathroom to wash the pizza sauce off his face and hands. Carman looked across the table at Seth and David and shook his head.

"What is up with you guys?" He asked. David and Seth both looked at each other and then back at Carman.

"Nothing." They said in unison. Carman rolled his eyes and shook his head.

"Uh, huh." He said and took the check up to the counter. David shot a look at Seth and scowled. Seth giggled and held David's gaze.

"What?" He asked.

"There's desensitizing and then there's turning me on. What are you trying to do?" David whispered. Seth smiled and stared into David's eyes.

"Both." He whispered. David was shocked. He opened his mouth but nothing would come out. Seth laughed and tossed his tooth pick onto the table. "David, I like to tease you because it's easy. Does it really bother you that bad? You're a total ego stroke." Seth explained. David sighed and leaned his back against his chair.

"Well, it's not very nice." David whispered and Seth giggled. He ran his leg up David's again and David looked at him.

"What's not nice about that?" Seth asked in his sexy drawl. David sighed and shook his head. Amanda and Mike came back to the table and David and Seth both stood up.

"Ready to go?" David asked her and she smiled.

"Yep, where's Carman?"

"Paying for lunch." David said. They walked up to the counter and Carman was just finished paying.

"Well, let's go move you in." Carman said. Amanda giggled and turned to leave. "Ride with me Amanda." Carman said and David shot him a look that could have killed a lesser man where he stood. Carman smiled and led Amanda and Mike to the truck.

"See you at home." Amanda said playfully knowing what Carman had done and David shook his head. He and Seth walked to the car and both got in. David stared out the windshield before starting the car.

"Forgot how it works or what?" Seth asked as he stared at David's hand on the key in the ignition. David closed his eyes and turned the key. Carman had already left.

"Why? Why do this?" David asked. Seth looked at him and blinked. David looked at him and waited for his answer but he said nothing and David shook his head. "Seth, you are probably the perfect guy to desensitize me or whatever but, what your doing is a little harsh." David said and Seth laughed.

"David, I was serious in there. But, to be less harsh, I'll tell you something. I like that you like me. I think it's cool. I'm sorry if I bug you." Seth said. David shook his head and pulled the car out of the parking lot.

"That's not very heterosexual of you." David said. Seth laughed and shook his head.

"Maybe, not, but I'm not as normal as the other ass holes that call themselves men on this planet." Seth said and David giggled. He turned the car on to the street the apartments were on.

"That is very true. So is this thing with all gay guys or what?" David asked. Seth smiled and shook his head.

"No, just you. I think it's cool what I do for you."

"Well, I don't." David said. He pulled up to a red light and stopped.

"Why not?" Seth asked. David sighed and shook his head.

"I don't like it because I can't do it back."

"Sure you can." Seth said and giggled. David shook his head then looked at Seth.

"And where do you draw the line?" Seth thought for a while as David drove. They were almost at the building when Seth finally answered.

"I think I have to figure it out as we go along." He said. David laughed and shook his head. He pulled up and parked in the 509 parking stall and shut off the car.

"That's a terrible idea." David said and Seth laughed.

"Why?"

"Well, what happens if you find your line when it's too late?" David asked as he shut off the car and looked at Seth. Seth tossed his hair and smiled at David.

"Ok, I would go farther than the leg thing at the diner but probably not as far as kissing or something like that." David giggled and shook his head.

"Ok. Is that final or should we leave it open for discussion?"

"Um, let's leave it open." Seth said. David laughed and they got out of the car. They went into the building together and waited for the elevator to come down to get them. Seth tossed his hair again and David shook his head.

"The hair thing is mean." He said quietly and Seth giggled.

"I know."

"Then why do you do it?" David asked. Seth sighed and itched the back of his head.

"Well, in the spirit of our new little game here, I guess I'm waiting to see what you do."

"So, it's my turn and you can't do anything else till I go?" David asked. The doors opened and they got in.

"Ok, sounds good. But in my defense, I toss my hair out of habit so it shouldn't count." Seth said. David sighed and agreed to the hair terms. The doors opened and they stepped out. Seth stepped out first and turned to face David. David stopped and looked at him.

"What?" David asked realizing Seth wasn't getting out of the way. Seth smiled and grabbed David's hand. He gave it up easily and Seth brought it up to his long, silky, black hair. He closed his eyes and ran David's hand through it. David swallowed hard and stared at Seth's young, beautiful face. When his hand reached the end of its arousing trip through Seth's hair, Seth opened his eyes and smiled at David.

"Your move" He whispered and walked to the apartment. David took a deep breath and joined Seth, Amanda and Carman in his new kitchen.

"We should have picked up beer." Carman said looking at the little collection of fruit in the big two door fridge. Amanda giggled and handed David her wallet.

"You and Seth go get beer." She said. David sighed and shook his head.

"I have money." He said and looked at Carman as if to say 'help me'. Carman giggled and shook his head.

"Hurry up, I'm thirsty." He said and Seth giggled.

"I know the best place." Seth said.

"Yea, go to Chester's." Carman said. Seth nodded and David kissed Amanda before they left the room. They got into the elevator and David could hear Amanda and Carman laughing as the door closed.

"And you say I'm mean." Seth said. David sighed and looked at Seth.

"You are. Their being funny. If Carman was me I would have done the same thing to him." David said and Seth smiled.

"So, it's your move." Seth said. David stretched and looked at the numbers. They counted down to 1 and the doors opened. Seth stepped out of the elevator and David checked him out as he walked.

"Nice." David said quietly and Seth giggled.

"Is that all you got?" Seth asked as they walked out to the car. David laughed and shook his head. He unlocked the doors and they both got into the car.

"See, you have the advantage because what you do turns me on. How can I be expected to have the same effect on you?" David asked as he started the car. Seth laughed and directed David to turn right and get on the first exit off the main road.

"Look, the first time I saw you, I thought your reaction was really cool. I thought about it for like a week. Then when you showed up at the house, and played that game the way you do, it was like an eye opener to me. I'm not saying I'm gay or even that interested sexually, it's just that you have this thing about you that I find kind of exciting. If you know what I mean." Seth said. David giggled and shook his head.

"Ok, so you're not gay but I turn you on?" David asked. Seth pointed to the coming road and David slowed to turn left.

"Well, sort of I guess." Seth said.

"I don't get it."

"Ok, ever had a thing for somebody you never would?" Seth asked. David laughed and nodded. He thought of Alan and how much he beat himself up over the way he felt about him. "Ok, same thing. I'm not jacking off over you or anything but I like what you do for me." Seth explained.

"This ego stroke or whatever you mentioned before?" David asked and Seth nodded. "So, how does it work? I mean like, how does it make you feel?" David asked. Seth was becoming more and more interesting to him the more he spoke.

"Well, you kind of turn me on but not." Seth said. David laughed and shook his head.

"What does that mean?" Seth laughed and tossed his hair. David could smell his shampoo and smiled.

"I don't know how to explain it. It's like watching a really dirty porn that isn't getting you off but you can't look away either." This time David laughed. He stopped the car for a red light.

"I'm a dirty porn?" David asked.

"Yea, like the kind that looks painful or wrong but you can't stop watching." Seth explained. David raised his eyebrows and shook his head.

"Painful and wrong. Wow." David said and Seth laughed.

"That's the best way I can explain it." David smiled and looked at Seth.

"Where am I going?" He asked stopping at the next red light. Seth looked out the windshield.

"Next set of lights turn right." Seth said and ran his hand through his hair. David sighed and shook his head. "Hair stuff doesn't count." Seth reminded him.

"I know. Isn't it still my turn anyway?"

"No, you had the 'nice' comment about my ass remember?" Seth asked. David giggled and nodded.

"Your move then." David said and made his right hand turn at the set of lights Seth told him to. Seth smiled and looked at David. He moved in his seat so he was closer. David took a deep breath and waited to see what Seth would do. He saw a sign for Chester's Liquor and focused on it. Seth blew on the side of David's neck and David shivered. Seth giggled and moved away. "That's it?" David asked. His voice squeaked and Seth giggled. David pulled up at the liquor store and went inside. He found a 24 pack of Carman's favorite beer and took it to the counter. He paid for it and took it out to the car. He set it in the back seat and got back in. He looked at Seth and leaned close to him. Seth smiled and waited patiently for David to make his move. David smelled Seth's hair and kissed him gently on the neck. Seth shook and giggled. David sat back and pulled the car away from the store.

"That's pretty close to the line." Seth said and David giggled.

"Well, how close? Like crossed a little or could have been worse?" David asked. Seth laughed and shook his head.

"Like right against it." Seth said putting his hands together in front of his face. David laughed and turned the car on to the main road. Seth told David he could take the same way home. "So I guess it's my move, huh?" Seth asked. David nodded and stared out the windshield while Seth thought of what to do next. He had passed the first two lights and was coming up to the last set before he had to turn onto the main road when Seth leaned over and kissed David's neck. He kept himself there for about three seconds before he pulled away. David looked at him and shook his head.

"I thought kissing was a no go. You said what I did was right against the line. What the hell was that?" David asked laughing. Seth shrugged and tossed his hair.

"Your move." He said and David shook his head.

"What I want to do is too hard to do when I'm driving." David said in a sexy sounding voice. Seth laughed and shook his head.

"Did I kick you across the line?"

"It's your line." David said and turned onto the main road. Seth laughed and readjusted himself so he could face David.

"Ok, sorry, I had a brave moment." Seth said in an almost pleading voice. David smiled and shook his head.

"The line is for me. You kiss me all you want. I get the rules." He said. Seth sighed and shook his head.

"That's hardly fair though."

"Then change the rules." David said. Seth took a deep breath and looked out the windshield.

"I can't. Your right, the line is there for you." He said and smiled. David laughed and shook his head. They sat in silence until they could see the building.

"I want to feel you up." David said and Seth choked on a cough. David laughed and looked at Seth.

"What?" Seth asked genuinely surprised.

"Your move." David said and Seth took a breath of relief.

"Fuck, I thought you were serious."

"I am, but in the spirit of the game, this is a lot more intense for me than it is for you so, you'll have to deal with these honest outbursts." David said in a very even voice. Seth smiled and nodded. David turned the car into the apartment building parking lot and parked in his stall. Seth sighed and looked at David.

"What would you touch first?" Seth asked in a bedroom sounding voice. David shut off the car and looked at Seth.

"Well, I would start with your hair and work my way down." David said. Seth giggled and they both got out of the car. David grabbed the beer out of the back and locked up the car. They walked into the building and waited for the elevator. "Does that count as my turn?" David asked.

"Um, yes I think so. It was pretty hot so it was a turn." Seth said. David laughed and shook his head. The doors opened and they stepped in.

"What if touching everything from the waist up was still on the right side of the line?" Seth asked. David raised his eyebrows and stopped the elevator. Seth laughed and stared at him. David stood looking over Seth's well-built body for quite a while. He sighed and shook his head. It seemed that doing more than that may be crossing the line so he started the elevator. Seth took a deep breath and blinked at David. "That's the coolest move yet I think." Seth said.

"Why?" David asked.

"I was expecting to have every inch of my torso hand examined. It's sexier that you thought about it instead of actually doing it." David smiled and raised his eyebrows.

"Well, I thought I would save it for later." He said and Seth laughed. The doors opened and they went into the apartment.

"You know, it's almost 3:00 and the furniture isn't here yet." Amanda said as she took the case of beer from David and put it in the fridge. She took one out for each of the men and got herself a glass of water.

"Want me to call?" Amanda nodded and David went to the phone sitting on the floor in the living room. He found out that the driver was on his way and would arrive within the next few minutes. The four of them talked about the best way to move the furniture in until the door buzzer rang.

When all the furniture was up in the apartment, the first thing David and Carman did was build the table. Carman put the chairs together while David built the table. Seth helped Amanda set up the living room the way she liked and put the end tables together. When they were finished, they all sat at the table for a break.

"I like that couch." David said staring at the piece of furniture that seemed to be the perfect color against the blinds and floor.

"I thought you would. I was hoping it would look a little darker but I think the colors work." Amanda said. David nodded and ran his foot up Seth's leg under the table. Seth smiled and licked the mouth of his beer bottle. No one noticed but David.

"I'm interested to see these dressers." Carman said inspecting the picture on the box.

"They are so awesome Carman." Amanda said and giggled. David bit his bottom lip and squinted his eyes at Seth. Seth smiled and ran his foot up David's leg this time. Carman got up and drug the box to the master bed room. David got up and went with him. They opened the box and took the dark four drawer dresser out of it.

"At least this comes in one piece." David said and Carman laughed.

"How are you doing? That was pretty mean to send you alone with Seth again." Carman said quietly. David smiled and shook his head. They moved the dresser under the smaller window and got the handles out of the bag they were taped into.

"Well, that Alan rule is sucking worse and worse." David whispered and Carman giggled. He leaned over and kissed David. David closed his eyes and massaged Carman's soft tongue with his. Carman whimpered and kissed more deeply. They kissed like this for a few minutes before David pulled away and took a deep breath. "I gotta stop." David whispered. Carman smiled and went back to the drawer handles.

"You know, you can kiss a lot longer than I can without getting hard." Carman whispered. David giggled and shook his head.

"No I can't, I just didn't want you to notice." David whispered back. Carman raised his eyebrows and sighed.

"Well, that's nice of you I guess." He said. They finished the handles and went to get the matching dresser. Amanda and Seth were putting Mike's bed together in his new room. He was laughing and jumping on the little mattress on the floor. David and Carman drug the second dresser to the master bedroom.

"I really think I could turn Seth if I tried hard enough." David whispered as they pulled the dresser out of the box.

"What? Why do you say that?" Carman asked.

"Well, I turn him on like a dirty porn he can't look away from." Carman laughed so hard there were tears in his eyes.

"That's new." Carman said. David rolled his eyes and they pushed the dresser under the matching window. Carman got the bag of hardware and they got to work putting the handles on the drawers. "What does that even mean?" Carman asked and David laughed.

"I don't get it but I think it means that he likes to tease and flirt but wouldn't do anything too sexual." David explained. Carman sighed and shook his head.

"So between Seth, Amanda and me you should be horny all the time then." David laughed and nodded.

"It's looking that way. Amanda gets all the benefits though." David said. They both laughed and left the room. They didn't take long getting the rest of the bedroom furniture put together. Amanda put the new sheets and blankets on each bed and was satisfied with their set up for now. David and Carman decided to order Chinese food for supper while Amanda started to put their clothes in her new dressers. Seth played with Mike on the floor and Mike decided that anyone who looked just like Gabe was allowed to play in his new room.

Chapter 10

For the next couple of days, David and Amanda collected things for their new home when David was off work. They had found themselves an entertainment stand and a T.V. and DVD player. Amanda bought them a coffee maker and a toaster and she found Little Mike a treasure chest toy box. Carman had brought over a filing cabinet for the paper work that Amanda had of Gabe's and any future paper work they would have. Amanda picked a corner in the living room that she wanted a desk and computer in so the filing cabinet was set there. On Thursday morning, Carman game over early for coffee.

"So, I was thinking." Carman said as David sat down at the pretty round table with a coffee for each of them.

"What's that?" David asked as he sat down.

"Maybe we should invite Alan and your mom down and have a little house warming thing for you guys." Carman suggested. David sighed and looked around. Amanda had the place looking very nice and homey. It was clean and bright and almost exactly how they wanted it.

"Ok, well that's an idea I guess." David said thinking of the uncomfortable situation it was going to be. Carman sighed and shook his head.

"How long will you live in here before you have your mother down? They come as a pair now you know."

"I know that I just don't like it." David said and sipped his coffee.

"Ok, you don't have to but can't you play nice for a few hours?"

"Carman, of course I can it's just that, what if he stares at me or something like he used to? Then what?" David asked. Carman sighed and nodded.

"If I talked to him about it first and he promises to be good, would you be willing to have them down?" David raised an eyebrow and looked across the table at Carman. He was wearing his jean jacket that seemed to match his eyes. David smiled at the attractiveness of him. It seemed the longer he knew him, the more attractive he was becoming.

"Ok, but he's staying out at your place." David finally said and Carman smiled.

"Of course." Carman said and giggled. He seemed so proud of himself. David rolled his eyes and sipped his coffee again.

"You know, if you start jumping up and down, I'll have to kick your ass."

"Of all the things you could do to my ass, you choose to kick it?" Carman asked. David laughed and shook his head.

"No, but it seems you aren't afraid of feet so I guess I gotta take what I can get." David shot back. Carman laughed and they discussed their coming day while they finished their coffees. David went in to the bedroom and kissed Amanda before they left. They got into the truck together and Carman pulled away.

"Would it be wrong to ask a favor of you that is of a sexual nature?" Carman blurted out as they traveled down the busy street. David laughed and shook his head.

"That would depend on the favor I guess." He answered and looked at Carman. Carman smiled and shook his head.

"Well, it's about Seth." David giggled and felt his stomach flip. "He told me you said something to him on the phone the other day and it got him thinking."

"What was it?" David asked racking his brain over the last few phone conversations he had with Seth.

"Well, he told me that you said you had a thing for muscular stomachs and broad shoulders." Carman said. David laughed and nodded. He could recall the conversation now and thought that of all the things that were said, the shoulder and stomach thing stood out.

"Ok, so?" David asked. Carman shifted in his seat and turned the corner to the street their first job was on.

"So, I thought about it and was wondering how hard it would be to get you out of your shirt." Carman said in a nervous sounding voice. David laughed and ripped his shirt off over his head. Carman giggled but looked David over. He raised his eyebrows and looked back to the road.

"Is that all?" David asked. Carman giggled and nodded. David put his shirt back on and shook his head. "That was stupid Carman." David said and looked at Carman's nervous expression.

"Well, I'm not the one who wanted to see." Carman said and giggled. David smiled and shook his head.

"Seth does?" He asked.

"That's the story." Carman answered and parked in front of a small dentist office. They got out of the car and walked up to the doors.

"What do I get out of this? Did he say?" David asked as they went in. Carman giggled and nodded. He said nothing as the receptionist took them to the computer that needed work. It had some kind of virus and Carman thought it would be best to just reprogram the whole thing. He took out his disks and got to work.

"He said you might ask that." Carman whispered as he started clearing the old program off the computer. David went through the briefcase and got out the flash drives for Carman to save as much as he could on them.

"And?" David asked as he handed the little instruments to Carman.

"Well, he said he would move the line a little. Whatever that means." David giggled and shook his head.

"Uh, huh." Carman looked at him and crooked his eyebrow.

"What is going on with you guys anyway?"

"We are playing our own ongoing version of that game. The only thing is, it doesn't matter if we break or not. It's more of a really bad teasing type of thing. I think it's unfair because he has the advantage of being straight." David explained.

"Ok, so what's the line?" Carman asked as he handed a loaded flash drive to David and a piece of paper with the list of things on it. David put them in a case and wrote out the list in neat writing for the receptionist and set it aside.

"Nothing physical, like kissing or whatever. He's aloud to kiss me but I can't kiss him. I think it sucks but that's the rule. Also, I can touch whatever I want from the waist up." David answered. Carman laughed and shook his head.

"Wow, he does have the advantage doesn't he?"

"No shit. So I take my shirt off and he pushes the line? That's the deal?" David asked. Carman laughed and nodded. "That's weird. I don't get what he's getting out of it." David added. Carman started loading another flash drive and sat back in his chair.

"He didn't say. I think he's setting you up for a pretty major move though. I would plan for anything if I was you." Carman said and stared into David's eyes. They finished the flash drives and Carman started the reprogramming. David took the drives to the other computer and started loading them onto it.

"How about *your* little problem?" David whispered across the desk. Carman sighed and looked at David.

"Still thinking."

"Well, hurry up. I want to make out." David whispered and Carman laughed. They worked on the computers until Carman was satisfied they would work properly. He gave the receptionist the bill and they headed back to the truck. They got in and Carman looked at David.

"So, four layers of clothing and nothing ever has to come off?" Carman asked.

"Nope, you're perfectly safe. Wear jeans so you're even safer if you want." David said. Carman sighed and pulled out onto the road. He drove to the next location which was just a computer removal thing.

"If I freak out, you'll stop right?" Carman asked. David giggled and nodded. Carman sighed and they went into the building. They collected the four old computers and got them into the back of Carman's truck. They got back in and headed toward the waste management station. "What if I don't?" Carman asked.

"What if you don't what?" David asked and Carman shook his head.

"What if I don't freak out?"

"Well, we do what you're comfortable with. Are you considering this or what?" David asked feeling a rush of sudden excitement.

"I've been considering it since you mentioned it. I'm just not sure if I can get passed the Alan thing."

"Well, how about this. I will talk to Alan about it." David said. His stomach flipped at the thought. Carman was silent and appeared almost terrified at the offer. "What? You have been doing nothing but help me and Amanda through all of this. What's wrong with helping you? Your thing is actually a fear that I can help you with. Wouldn't Alan be happy I offered?" David asked. Carman sighed and cleared his throat.

"You really think you could sit through a conversation like that with Alan? I mean especially now that you know he felt the same way you did?"

"Well, I don't know. Should I try or not?" David asked. Carman thought about it while he drove. David stared at his handsome face and felt his groin tighten at the thought of Carman's hands on him. He looked away and concentrated on calming himself down. He had gotten very good at it for Carman's sake. Carman pulled into the dump and parked the truck at the computer disposal sight. They both got out and tossed the old things into the bin. When they were finished, they got back in and Carman looked at him.

"David, I'll make my decision on what Alan says. *If* you manage to talk to him about it." David smiled and nodded. "But, please don't do it in a way that will hurt him. Try to be nice when you talk to him about it, ok?" David smiled.

"Carman, I would plan on waiting a while. I have to get the guts to talk to him about it." David said. Carman laughed and drove to the next job. It was another program install but there was really nothing for David to do. He leaned against the desk and watched Carman work. He found himself staring at Carman's face as opposed to watching what he was doing. Carman seemed to notice and smiled.

"Are you checking me out?" Carman asked in a quiet whisper. David giggled and nodded.

"I'm trying to imagine what you look like with YOUR shirt off." David whispered. Carman smiled and shook his head.

"Well, not as nice as you do."

"Let me be the judge of that." David said and leaned closer to Carman. Carman laughed and nudged him away. They giggled about it and Carman finished his work. He dropped off the bill and they went out to the truck. They got in and as soon as David shut the door, Carman took his shirt off and David giggled. Carman was very nicely built and David raised his eyebrows. It didn't take long before David looked away and shut his eyes.

"That bad?" Carman asked putting his shirt back on. David laughed and looked back at Carman.

"No, but if I sit here and stare at you with your shirt off, well . . . Let's just say you won't be so calm for the rest of the day." David said and cleared his throat. Carman laughed and pulled away from the building.

"Ok, well that's good I guess." He said. David smiled and ran his hand through his hair.

"You are very easy to look at Carman." David complimented quietly and Carman smiled. He turned into a cell phone store and they both got out.

"Well, you aren't. I thought I might have to see the rest of you if you didn't get that shirt back on." Carman said as he led David into the store. David giggled and grabbed Carman's backside as they walked in. Carman laughed and shook his head. They went up to the display counter and both looked in. "Pick one." Carman said. David frowned at him and sighed.

"Why?"

"Well, you need one for work and I thought you would like to pick out your own." Carman answered and David raised his eyebrows. He looked through the phones and picked a black one that had a key board for texting. Carman bought the phone and added it to his plan. He programmed Seth's, Alan's and his own cell phone numbers in to the phone and handed it to David. "Now you can't hide from me." Carman said and David laughed.

"It has an off button." David said and scrolled through the phone. He saw Alan's number and looked at Carman.

"Just in case." Carman said knowing what David had seen and they left the store. David followed him out and they got into the truck. He went through the phone and picked his favorite ringer and wall paper. When he finally quit playing with it, he put it in his pocket and stared at Carman.

"So you want to see the rest of me, huh?" David asked and Carman laughed.

"Well, yea if I wasn't so scared of your gun there cowboy." Carman answered as he drove to the little diner for lunch. They had chosen it because of the guy that worked behind the counter. All they ever had there was French fries and a coffee but it was the view they liked.

"Well, what if you knew it wasn't loaded?" David asked. Carman burst out laughing shook his head.

"It's always loaded you dip shit." Carman said. They both laughed and David shook his head.

"Just trying to make it a little easier for you."

"Yea well, whether or not you have led in your pencil doesn't help the situation." Carman said and they both laughed again. He parked the truck in front of the diner and they went in. They both smiled when they seen the view they had waited all morning to see. He smiled at them and they sat down at their usual table. He brought them over their coffees and they ordered French fries like they always did.

"Fuck he's hot." David whispered and Carman nodded. The man looked to be in his late twenties or early thirties. He had blonde hair that was buzz cut. He wore an earring that looked like a scull with a diamond on it. He was short but built like a model. He wore baggy jeans that often showed off his muscular stomach. He had brown eyes that seemed perfectly placed on his beautiful face.

"I bet he's straight." Carman whispered. David giggled and shook his head.

"Don't ruin the fantasy old man."

"Who's hotter? Café guy or Seth?" Carman asked. David sighed and stared at the Café guy. He looked at Carman and rolled his eyes.

"Seth." David whispered. Carman laughed and shook his head.

"Yea, it's a bad comparison isn't it?"

"Yea, its two different kinds of hot." David said. Carman giggled and nodded. They watched him as he wiped the counter. He would look up at them every so often and smile. They would smile back and he would go back to his work. "I think he's into you." David whispered and Carman laughed.

"What? Why would you say that?"

"Well, watch when he brings the fries. He totally checks you out."

"Oh, he does not." Carman said and laughed again. David giggled and watched as the Café guy got their meal ready. David giggled as the man approached and Carman kicked him under the table. David smiled and watched as the man gave Carman the once over as he handed them their meals. He walked away and David giggled again.

"Did you see it this time?" David asked quietly and Carman laughed.

"I don't know. Maybe he just likes my shirt." Carman said. David laughed and popped a French fry into his mouth. He got up and walked over to the counter. Carman shot him a dirty look but David continued. The man came up to him and smiled. His teeth were perfectly straight and white.

"Hi, we come in here a lot and we just realized that we don't know your name." David said. The man smiled and looked at Carman. He looked back at David.

"My name is Jake." He said. David smiled and nodded.

"Well, I'm David and that's Carman." He said nodding his head in the direction of his table.

"Well, it's nice to finally know your names too." Jake said and David smiled at Carman. He looked back at Jake and sighed.

"This might be a little odd but, I couldn't help but notice the way you look at my friend." David said quietly and Jake blushed.

"Oh, um I'm sorry. I don't mean to make him uncomfortable." Jake said and shifted where he stood. David laughed and shook his head.

"Are you gay?" David whispered. Jake blushed again but looked unsure if he should answer. David smiled and shook his head. "Look, if you ever get the guts, ask him for his number. He'll give it to you." David said and walked back to the table. Carman shook his head as David sat back down in his chair. "His name is Jake and I'm pretty sure he's gay." David said and ate another French fry.

"You are the bravest guy I've ever had lunch with." Carman said and sipped his coffee. David laughed and shook his head.

"Well, someone has to look after your interests."

"Yea, yea. I bet you're always thinking of my *interests*." Carman said putting emphasis on the word interests. David laughed.

"You're welcome." He said. They finished their meal and Carman went up to the counter to pay. Jake smiled at him and rang the bill through. David watched as Jake quickly wrote something on the back of the receipt and handed it to Carman. Carman smiled and he and David went out to the truck. They got in and Carman looked at the back of his receipt.

"It's his fucking number." Carman said and David giggled.

"Well, there you go. Are you gonna call him?" David asked. Carman sighed and started the truck.

"We'll see." He said and pulled away from the diner. David shook his head and looked out the window. There was a lot of traffic and it was slow going. The next job they had was on the other side of town and it looked as though it would take a while. "So, about Seth." Carman said breaking the silence and David giggled. He looked at Carman and sighed.

"What about Seth?"

"Well, are you prepared to scare the hell out of a straight guy?" Carman asked. David smiled and shook his head.

"No. I don't plan on it either. I will be nice."

"I bet you will. But Seth is straight and might not appreciate how nice you can be." David laughed.

"Carman, that's not what I meant. And besides, how do you know how nice I can be?"

"I was guessing." Carman said and changed lanes.

"Well, get your head out of your ass and let me show you." David said and Carman laughed.

"You can be so crude."

"Yea, I know." David said and they both laughed. They talked about Jake as they drove through the congested traffic. They finally made it through and got to their next job. It was an office building and the job was a computer upgrade. Carman took the new computer out of the back seat and they went inside. They were led by a fat little receptionist to the computer that needed to be changed and they got to work. Carman started copying all the data onto disks while David unpacked the new computer.

"What if I said I wanted to have that make out session right now? What would you say?" Carman asked quietly while they worked. David sighed as he pulled the cords out of the box.

"Well, I would probably say let's go." David answered and Carman giggled.

"I'm being serious." Carman said and David sighed.

"Well, I would Carman. I think when you're ready for that, it'll be a now or never thing." David said. He sorted out the cords and plugged in what he needed to into the monitor and the tower. Carman sighed and took the first disk out of the machine. He put in the next one and looked around. They seemed to be alone. He looked at David and cleared his throat. David looked at him and smiled. "What?" David asked and Carman leaned back in his chair so he was closer to where David worked.

"What if that time was right now?" Carman asked and David raised his eyebrows. He sighed and looked at the computer he was working on. He looked back at Carman and smiled.

"Well, hurry up with those disks then." David said and Carman laughed.

"Ok, so you're willing as soon as I am. I get it." Carman said and got back to work. He disassembled the old computer and David put the new one in its place. David hauled the old one out to the truck and came back into the building. Carman was just setting up the computer program as David walked in. He walked over to Carman and ran his hand across Carman's chest. He picked up the computer box and smiled at Carman as he went to the door. "You're terrible." Carman said looking to be sure no one noticed David's advance and David laughed. He took the box out to the truck and got into the passenger side. He waited for Carman to finish. After a few minutes, Carman walked out and got into the truck. He looked over his paper and smiled. "We're done. All we gotta do is get this pile to the dump." Carman said and started the truck.

"Carman, are you ready now?" David asked. Carman smiled and shook his head.

"If I was, you'd know about it. The only thing stopping me now is Alan." Carman said and turned toward the transfer station. David sighed and looked out the window.

"I'm not looking forward to that conversation." David said quietly and Carman smiled.

"Can I give you a piece of advice?"

"Sure." David said and stared at Carman's face.

"Alan is the kind of guy that would do anything for a friend. If you want to do this, he's going give the ok. Not that I need permission but, I need to know if it would hurt him. I don't care about what he thinks is right or not as far as helping me with this go's. If it's going to hurt him, I don't know if he'll tell you." Carman said. David sighed and nodded.

"When are you asking him to come?" David asked. Carman cleared his throat and looked at David.

"They will be here tomorrow." Carman confessed and David's eyes grew wide.

"Tomorrow! You already talked to them?"

"Well, I knew you would say yes so I thought, what's the harm in inviting them?" Carman asked. David shook his head and fought the fluttering in his stomach. Carman sighed and looked over at him. "I'm sorry." He said quietly and David smiled.

"It's ok. Just quit doing shit like that." David scolded and Carman nodded.

"That's the last time this week." He said. David laughed and shook his head.

"You owe me now."

"You're going to bribe me?" Carman asked with a hint of mock terror in his voice. David laughed and nodded.

"Well, yea." David said and Carman sighed.

"Ok, what do I owe you?" Carman asked. He seemed to brace himself for impact. David smiled and ran his hand through his hair.

"10 minutes of making out no matter what happens." David said. Carman raised his eyebrows and smiled.

"Done." Carman said. "You do realize that by the time I have a moment to pay up, you would have talked to Alan already." Carman added. David smiled and looked at Carman.

"What if I said you had to pay up now?"

"Then I guess you'll have to add that in with the talk with Alan." Carman said. David thought about it for a second and felt suddenly strange.

"What if that bugs him or something?" David asked. Carman raised his eyebrows and looked at David.

"Since when do you care?"

"I don't know." David said and looked out the windshield. Carman smiled but didn't bring it up again. They got to the dump and David unloaded the old computer. He got back in and Carman leaned over and kissed him. David closed his eyes and ran his hand up Carman's arm to his shoulder. He rested it there for a second then moved it to Carman's jaw. Carman shifted in his seat and ran his hand through David's hair. David whimpered and kissed more deeply. Carman moaned and ran his hand down David's back to his hip. David's breathing picked up and he was suddenly aware of his building erection. He tried to pull away but Carman pulled him back into the kiss. "Carman, I need to stop." David whispered and Carman smiled.

"No you don't." Carman breathed and pulled David's hair. David moaned and playfully bit Carman's bottom lip. "Am I paid up yet?" Carman breathed as David gripped Carman's shoulder and tried to steady his pounding heart. David nodded and Carman slowed the kiss.

"You are so cruel." David whispered and Carman smiled.

"I don't mean to be." Carman whispered back and ran his hand across David's chest. David closed his eyes and took a deep breath.

"Well, you are." David said with eyes still closed. Carman smiled and kissed him again. David made a fist and relaxed it. "Carman, let me touch you." David said. Carman swallowed hard and David giggled. "Your chest." David said and Carman seemed to instantly relax. He grabbed David's hand and guided it to the bottom of his shirt. David kissed Carman and slowly ran his hand up over the muscular lines in his stomach and rested it on Carman's chest. He could feel Carman breathing heavy and his heart pounding as he kissed a little deeper. Carman put his hand over David's and held it in his shirt.

"Your hand is cold." Carman whispered and David giggled.

"Well, your body is hot and I'm not talking about temperature." David whispered back and Carman smiled. They finished the kiss and David slowly removed his hand. "You're paid up." David said and shifted in his seat. His erection felt crushed in his tight jeans but he thought readjusting would scare Carman. Carman smiled and started the truck.

"I won't look, fix it." Carman said knowing the problem instantly and David laughed. Carman closed his eyes so he could readjust himself.

"Ok, I'm good." He said and Carman opened his eyes. He pulled away from the dump and headed toward David's apartment building.

"That was awesome David." Carman said and David giggled.

"Yea it was. I love kissing you." David said and Carman shook his head.

"You know, Alan is a better kisser than me."

"I don't know that and will probably never know." David said and looked out the window.

"I think you will someday. Just remember that your special and he loves you."

"Oh fuck Carman. Give it up. I'm not stealing my mom's boyfriend from her." David said and Carman laughed. He looked David up and down and shook his head. David giggled and looked back out the window.

"I hope you have that talk with him." Carman said and swallowed hard. David sighed and turned to face Carman. He ran his hand up Carman's leg and the farther he moved up, the straighter Carman's back would get. David stopped at mid-thigh and looked at Carman.

"Your leg is twitching." David whispered and Carman giggled.

"Well, yours would too" Carman said and David smiled. He took his hand away and sat back in his chair. They both laughed and Carman drove to David's. They pulled up and Carman shut off the truck. They got out and went inside. The elevator was waiting for them and they went upstairs.

"Carman, if it wasn't for Alan, how hard would it be to get you in my bed?" David asked quite seriously. Carman laughed and shook his head.

"Well, let's just say that after a day like today, I wouldn't be stopping at the kitchen when we got to your apartment." Carman answered and David giggled. The doors opened and they went into 509. Amanda looked up from the table and smiled.

"Oh my God, get over here!" She said and Carman and David looked at each other.

"What is it?" David asked as they both took a seat at the table.

"Gabe had a kid!" Amanda said. David was silent and Carman raised his eyebrows.

"What?" Carman asked. David was still silent. Amanda handed him some papers and he read them over. "Holy shit." He whispered and handed the papers to David. David slowly took them and read the first sheet.

> Dear Gabe,
>
> I didn't want to tell you because I didn't want you to be mad. I had a baby last month and she belongs to you. I attached a copy of her birth certificate for you to see. I named her Beth. Please don't be mad that I didn't tell you. I don't want anything from you I just thought you should know.
>
> I miss you terribly and if you wanted to see her, you could. I love you and wish you all the best.
>
> Lyn.

David raised an eyebrow and looked at the birth certificate.

"So, a letter from some girl? That's not proof." David said and handed the paper back to Amanda. She handed him another paper and David looked it over. It was a paternity test that Gabe had asked for. Beth was definitely his. "Holy shit." David said and Amanda nodded.

"I know. I called the number on the birth certificate but it was out of service. The little girl would be 11 now." Amanda said and looked into David's eyes.

"You didn't know about this?" Carman asked Amanda.

"I didn't know Gabe was gay let alone had a kid. This is all news to me. His life was a closed book all the time I knew him." Amanda answered and looked over the paternity test again. David sighed and shook his head.

"So, what do you want to do?" He asked still not sure how he felt about the news. Amanda blinked at him and shook her head.

"I want to find her David. I mean, she's Gabe's daughter. We have to find her." Amanda said and David smiled.

"Ok. How do we do that?" Carman smiled and leaned forward.

"I think it's time we bought you guys a computer." Carman said. David nodded and looked at Amanda.

"Oh my God David. Gabe was a father! Do you think he ever had anything to do with her?"

"I don't know. He never said anything to me about it." David said and itched the back of his neck.

"Well, from what I've heard of Gabe, his life was certainly his own. It's hard to guess. I say we ask her." Carman said and Amanda giggled.

"Oh David, I'm an auntie!"

Chapter 11

David and Carman set Amanda up with a computer to start her search for her estranged niece the next day after work. She got right down to searching as soon as Carman set up the program for her. They sat down at the table and David stared at the clock waiting for Alan and his mom.

"They should be here in the next hour or so." Carman said quietly as he took a sip of the beer Amanda had set him up with when he walked in the door. David nodded but never took his eyes off the clock. "You know, you're making me nervous. You could at least blink." Carman said and David looked at him.

"Carman, I don't know what to do with myself. I feel so edgy." David said quietly and Carman smiled.

"I know. It will be ok David." He reassured and David rolled his eyes. He looked back at the clock and Carman kicked him lightly under the table. David looked back at Carman's smiling face and sighed. "Cut it out." Carman whispered and blew a kiss at him. David smiled and shook his head.

"That doesn't help." David said. Amanda giggled and David looked over at her. She shook her head and looked back at her computer.

"You guys should seriously just do it and get it over with." She said as she stared at the screen. David and Carman both laughed and took a sip of their drinks.

"She's right you know." David said and Carman rolled his eyes. David giggled and looked back at the clock. The time seemed to be flying by and David could feel his stomach flip. He took a deep breath and closed his eyes.

"Don't think about it." Carman whispered and ran his foot up David's leg. David smiled and looked at him.

"You know, that isn't helpful either." He said and kicked at Carman's foot. Carman laughed and looked over at Amanda.

"How do I calm him down?" He asked and Amanda laughed.

"Well, I find that a blow job often works." She said and David laughed. Carman shook his head and looked back at David.

"She's as bad as you are." Amanda laughed and cleared her throat.

"I resent that." She said and both David and Carman laughed. Carman looked back into David's eyes and David met his gaze. They stared at each other until the door buzzer rang. David jolted out of the staring match and closed his eyes and Amanda jumped up. "So you're just going to sit there?" She asked and giggled. She pushed the button. "Hello." She said.

"DEAD MAN WALKEN!" Alan's voice said. Carman smiled and David stood up.

"I got to get out of here for a second." He said and went into the bathroom. He locked the door behind him and closed his eyes.

Oh GOD! What do I say? What do I do? Mom will be here too. Is that enough to make him being here ok? God I feel sick. Why did he have to tell me all that stuff? Fuck I'm not going to make it through this visit. I gotta get out of this but how? Amanda will never let me leave. Carman would kick my ass if I left. What would mom think? David rested the back of his head against the bathroom door and took a few deep breaths.

Ok David. Get your shit together and get out there. It's your mom. Focus on your mom. Don't even look at him if you don't have to. He said to himself and opened his eyes.

"I can do this." He said out loud to himself and stepped out of the bathroom. He could hear Alan and Carman laughing. He could hear Amanda and his mom talking about what was on the screen of the computer. He took another deep breath and walked out of the hall way. His eyes met Alan's instantly. His stomach flipped and he felt dizzy. Alan looked amazing. He was wearing his leather jacket and a tight white t-shirt underneath of it. He was wearing David's favorite pair of tight light colored blue jeans that clung to him like a pair of rubber gloves.

"Hi." Alan said and David nodded. All he could do was stare at him. Alan smiled and raised his eyebrows. "Lost your voice?" He asked and Carman sighed. David looked over at his mother who was smiling at him. She looked well rested and happy to see him. He stood motionless for a second before Carman suddenly pulled him into the master bedroom. He shut the door and stared into David's eyes.

"Get it together. You look like you just stepped into hell." Carman said and rubbed both of David's arms.

"Did you see him?" David whispered and his voice cracked.

"Yes I did. He looks amazing as always. You need to try to ignore it." Carman whispered and hugged David. David closed his eyes and wrapped his arms around Carman.

"I can't do this." David whispered with a voice that sounded as if fear had touched it with its clammy hand.

"Yes you can and you will." Carman said and pulled away. "Pull it together then come out ok." Carman said. David nodded and Carman left the room. David took a few deep breaths and grabbed the door handle. He stood there staring at the knob but couldn't bring himself to turn it. A knock on the other side made him jump.

"*Open the door son.*" Nancy said and David sighed. He opened the door and Nancy walked in. She hugged her son and David held her tight.

"Oh mom. I missed you." David whispered as he held his mother.

"I missed you too dear." She said. They stood holding each other for quite a while then Nancy finally let go. "Will you come out and see him now?" Nancy asked and David sighed. He looked at the door handle and then back at his mom.

"You go. I'll be out in a second." Nancy looked at him with a crooked eyebrow. "I promise mom, one minute." David insisted. Nance smiled and rubbed her sons arm. She stepped out of the room and David took another shaky breath. "Ok." David said and opened the door. He stepped out and walked into the kitchen. Nancy was at the computer with Amanda. They all looked at him and he sighed. He walked up to Alan and swallowed hard.

"Hi." Alan said again and David stared into his eyes.

"Hi." David said and took a deep breath. Alan smiled and looked at Carman.

"Let's sit." Carman said and Alan smiled at David. David looked at Carman and nodded. Alan and David sat down at the same time.

"Nice place." Alan offered up as conversation. David nodded but never took his eyes off Alan's. Alan shifted in his chair and looked at Nancy. Nancy smiled at him and he looked back at David. "Let's go." Alan said and David's eyes grew wide. He looked at Carman and Carman smiled.

"Go." Carman said and Nancy got up and came to the table. She handed David his jacket and smiled.

"You guys should talk alone." She said and David sighed. He looked at Alan and took a deep breath. He stood up and Alan followed. They walked to the door and Amanda kissed David before he left the house with Mr. Alan Black. They got into the elevator and rode down it silence.

"My car or yours?" Alan asked. David thought of the night he had made love to Gabe in that car and shivered.

"Yours." David answered and Alan nodded. They walked outside and got into the wine colored 1969 Mustang Fastback. Alan started the car and pulled out of the parking lot. David sat silently staring at his hands on his lap.

"Ok, I know this is hard for you but, let's talk." Alan said. David took another deep breath and looked at Alan.

"You look great." David blurted out and Alan smiled. He looked at David and sighed.

"That's what I was thinking." Alan said and David shook his head.

"This is weird." David said quietly and Alan laughed. The sound was like a dagger of lust into David's gut.

"It doesn't have to be."

"Well, it is." David said. Alan sighed and turned onto the freeway.

"Ok, want me to go first?" Alan asked. David looked at him and nodded. Alan took a deep breath and stared out the windshield. "This isn't going to be easy to hear but I plan on going against our deal and keeping something from your mom. It might hurt her if she ever found out but the only way she would is if you told her. Are you with me so far?" Alan asked. David took a deep breath and nodded. "Ok, David, I can't live in a world that you're not a part of. We need to get over this little fight or whatever it is and get on with our lives." Alan said. David looked at him with a confused gaze.

"How does that hurt mom?" David asked. Alan smiled and shook his head.

"That wouldn't, that would make her day." Alan said.

"Ok, so what are we talking about here then?" David asked. He felt both angry and surprisingly aroused.

"I don't know how else to say this but, I need you." Alan said. David shook his head and sighed.

"You're always so fucking vague Alan! What are you trying to say?" David yelled. Alan gripped the steering wheel and took a deep breath. David rolled his eyes and shifted in his seat so he was facing Alan. "Can I tell you a story?" David asked in a cocky tone. Alan looked at him and nodded. "I have this friend who has this problem. I can help him with it but he is afraid how his other friend would feel about it because his other friend has some kind of mystery feelings for me. With me so far?" David asked. Alan swallowed hard and nodded. David took a deep breath and continued. "So, This other friend happens to be with someone very important to me so I'm thinking, what the fuck does he care? But, this friend of mine thinks his feelings are important so now I'm at an impasse. What would you do if you were me?" David asked. Alan sighed and shook his head.

"Well, I would want to know what the other friends deal is." Alan said and David rolled his eyes.

"So, start talking and cut it out with the riddles and vague descriptions." David scolded. Alan looked at David and took a deep breath. He looked back out the windshield and shook his head.

"What do you want to know?" Alan asked. David shook his head and looked away. He could feel his chest tightening with his anger and frustration. He could feel his face heat as he thought of what else he could say. He turned to Alan and blurted out,

"Alan, I'm in love with you. I've wanted you so bad since the moment I met you and you don't know what I want to hear? You can't come up with a single thing to say?" David yelled. Alan closed his eyes for a second and then pulled off the freeway. He pulled over in front of an old house and parked the car. He looked at David and sighed.

"David, I made you a promise and I'm doing everything I can to keep it." He whispered.

"That's good. I thought you weren't above keeping secrets." David snapped back. Alan shook his head and glared at David. David blinked and stared into Alan's light green eyes.

"I don't know what to say." Alan said through clenched teeth. David shook his head and turned away from Alan.

"Then why did you drag me out here?" David asked. Alan sighed and tapped the steering wheel.

"I wanted to tell you that I feel something for you I never felt for anyone else and it scares me." Alan said quietly and David shook his head. He turned to Alan and sighed.

"You and Carman both I guess." David said and got out of the car. He walked about a block away before Alan caught up with him on foot.

"David, please don't walk away." He said. David stopped and faced Alan. It was starting to get dark and Alan was even sexier in the sunset.

"What do you want from me? I said we were even and I'm happy if mom's happy. What else do you want?" David asked. Alan shook his head and clenched his teeth.

"I want you to stop hating me." Alan said. David shook his head and hugged Alan. Alan was shocked but hugged back.

"I don't hate you. I love you. The problem is I hate loving you." David whispered. Alan swallowed hard and nodded. "Why can't you just, not be you? That would be easier." David whispered and Alan giggled.

"Could you quit being you too then?" Alan asked and David laughed. Alan giggled and held David tighter. David did the same and closed his eyes.

"God I missed you. But don't tell anyone I told you that." David whispered into Alan's hair. Alan giggled again and nodded.

"Me too." Alan whispered and rubbed David's back. David whimpered and Alan giggled again. "Are you ok?" Alan asked. David shook his head and pulled away.

"I would kiss you but that would certainly be on the hurting mom list." David whispered and Alan smiled. He ran his hand through David's hair and sighed.

"You're beautiful David." Alan said and pulled his hand away. David stared into Alan's eyes and seemed to hang on every word.

"We should go." David whispered and Alan nodded. They walked back to the car and got in. Alan started the engine and looked at David.

"That story you told me, who's your friend?" Alan asked. David giggled and looked at Alan.

"Carman." David answered and Alan raised his eyebrows. He pulled out onto the road and started to head back to David's house.

"What's the problem?" Alan asked and David giggled.

"Well, he's afraid of well-endowed men." David said and both Alan and David laughed.

"Yea, I know that. What can you do for him?" Alan asked. David giggled and looked at Alan. Alan looked back at him and raised his eyebrows. "Oh." Alan said figuring it out on his own and David laughed. Alan shook his head and shifted in his seat. "So, what would you do?" Alan asked.

"Well, that depends on you." David said and turned in his seat to face Alan. Alan frowned and looked at David.

"Why?"

"Ok, don't think about Carman or his fear. Don't think about all the guys he's dumped because of this fear ok." David said. Alan nodded and stopped at a red light. "You need to think about me and how you feel about me. Then consider Carman and me in bed together." David said. Alan took a deep breath and looked at David. He cleared his throat and looked back out the windshield.

"Well, I'm with your mom." Alan said and David nodded. "So, that being said, it would be unfair to tell you not to." Alan drove forward as the light turned green.

"Well, forget about that. See Carman's problem is, he thinks you'll be mad at him cause I'm your puppy." David said and Alan laughed.

"My puppy." Alan repeated under his breath and shook his head. David sighed and stared at Alan's sexy face and body. Alan saw him do it and he smiled.

"I'll tell you what. You use your own discretion." David rolled his eyes. Alan sighed and stopped at the next red light. "David, the truth is I would be really mad if you did it. It's not fair to say that because of the current situation so it shouldn't be up to me." Alan said. David shook his head and looked at Alan.

"What would you do if you were me?" David asked.

"Well, are you me?" Alan asked. David giggled and nodded. "That's not fair, my mother was a bitch so I wouldn't care how she felt if I was you and you were me." Alan answered.

"Ok, well that's not helpful." David said and sighed. Alan shook his head and laughed.

"You know, this Carman thing is a rough call."

"Yea well. I promised I would talk to you about it first." David said. Alan sighed and turned onto David's road.

"Well, all I have to say about it is, you decide." Alan said. David shook his head and watched Alan as he pulled into the parking lot at David's building.

"That's not fair." David said quietly and Alan smiled.

"I know." He said and shut off the car. He faced David and sighed. "If it was different circumstances I would give you a reason not to." Alan said quietly. David felt his stomach flip and he took a deep breath.

"What would you do?" David asked with a shaky voice and Alan giggled. He leaned closer to David and David could smell his intoxicating cologne and feel his breath on his face.

"If I had the guts, I would kiss you." Alan whispered and bit his bottom lip. David closed his eyes and sighed.

"Alan, I hate you right now." David whispered and Alan smiled.

"Sorry." Alan whispered and backed away. David sighed and got out of the car. Alan did the same and locked it up. They walked into the apartment building and got into the elevator.

"Help him if you can David." Alan said quietly. David looked at him and sighed.

"Alan, how will you feel about it?"

"Honestly?" Alan asked. David giggled and nodded. Alan sighed and stopped the elevator and looked at David. David's heart pounded in his chest and his hands where instantly sweating. "I would like to be Carman that day." Alan said seductively and sighed. David whimpered and Alan giggled.

"Well, that's interesting." David squeaked out and Alan laughed. He started the elevator again and David stared at him. "You're a dick." David whispered and Alan laughed again.

"Sorry." Alan whispered and the doors opened. They walked to David's apartment together and walked in.

"So, did you duke it out?" Carman asked as they came into the kitchen.

"Yea, he kicked my ass. I've learned my lesson." Alan said and Carman and David laughed. Amanda and Nancy looked up from the baby book they were looking at and smiled. Carman handed both David and Alan a beer and they sat down at the table. David smiled at Carman and Alan giggled.

"So, are we all friends again?" Carman asked quietly. Alan and David looked at each other and nodded. "Oh good. I was worried I would have to make you kiss and make up." He added and Alan laughed. David shook his head and held Alan's gaze. Carman smiled and sat back in his chair. "Well, I'm glad to see some things never change." Carman said watching Alan and David stare at each other. David laughed and looked at Carman.

"You know something; I bet you would love to know how fast things can change." David said. Alan laughed and looked at Carman.

"What are you talking about?" Carman asked. David rolled his eyes and moved close enough to whisper in Carman's ear.

"Limp to hard, Carman." David said and Carman coughed. Alan laughed and shook his head.

"If we were just playing Carman, you just lost." He said and Carman laughed.

"I want a do over." Carman said and they could hear Amanda and Nancy giggle. David looked at Amanda and she smiled at him. He winked at her and looked back at Carman.

"Ok, do over." David said and ironed out his face. Alan sat silently as Carman leaned into David. He put his mouth close to David's ear and whispered. "I want you." David smiled and turned his head to whisper in Carman's ear.

"Well, I got the go ahead whenever you're ready." David said and Carman's eyes went wide. Alan giggled and waited to see what Carman would do. Carman looked at Alan and leaned over to whisper in Alan's ear. Alan smiled and leaned forward.

"He says he wants your body." Carman whispered and Alan smiled. He looked at David and whispered in Carman's ear.

"Well, tell him he can have it if he wants it." Alan whispered. David heard it and laughed. Carman looked at Alan and took a deep breath. He leaned in to Alan and whispered,

"What would you do if he did?" Carman asked and Alan smiled. He turned his head and stared into Carman's eyes.

"Let him." Alan said and Carman laughed. David shook his head and took a sip of his beer.

"You guys aren't going to fight over me are you?" David asked and Amanda and Nancy burst out laughing. Carman and Alan joined them and shook their heads. They talked about Carman and David's work as the night went on. David gave Alan his new cell phone number and that started a conversation about Jake. Carman explained the whole story to Alan and how David got the info. Alan laughed but never seemed to keep his eyes off David. Amanda and Nancy tired out way before the boys did and they both went to bed in David and Amanda's room.

"You lost your bed." Carman said giggling and looked at Alan. Alan raised his eyebrows and shook his head.

"I have a couch." David said quickly and smiled. Carman giggled again and shook his head.

"Staying with me?" Carman asked Alan and he nodded.

"I guess so. Don't you have three bedrooms?" Alan asked David and David nodded.

"I do but there's nothing in the other room." David said and smiled at Alan. Alan shook his head and looked at Carman. He looked up at the clock and seen it was after midnight.

"Well, should we go then?" Alan asked. Carman yawned and looked at the clock as well.

"Yea I guess." He said and stood up. David and Alan stood with him and David walked them to the door.

"Let your mom know where I am when she gets up?" Alan asked. David smiled and nodded.

"See you tomorrow." Carman said and David nodded. He left the apartment and Alan stood in front of David.

"Well." Alan said and David giggled. He hugged Alan and pressed his body right up against him. Alan sighed and held David in a tight hug. "You feel good." Alan said. David sighed and shook his head.

"Alan, we either have to do something about this or pretend it isn't there. I can't do it this way." David whispered and Alan smiled. He backed away from David and looked into his eyes.

"Ok, what do you want to do?" Alan whispered and David rolled his eyes.

"Well, I love my mom." David said and Alan laughed.

"Ok, that's a pretty clear answer." Alan said. David sighed and held Alan's penetrating gaze.

"What do you want?" He asked and Alan cleared his throat.

"Well, I really like your mom and I think things are getting a little more serious every day." Alan answered. David sighed and nodded.

"Ok then. We pretend it isn't there." David said quietly. Alan nodded and ran his hand along David's jaw line.

"I wish things were a little different." He said and dropped his hand. David smiled and looked out in the hall way at Carman.

"Well they aren't right? So we have to keep it this way." David said and took a deep breath. Alan nodded and smiled.

"You are far to wise for your age." Alan said. David laughed and shook his head.

"Good night Alan." David said and Alan smiled.

"Good night David." He answered and stepped out into the hall he went to stand next to Carman and David waved at them. Carman smiled and shook his head. Alan looked back at David and squinted his eyes.

"No touching my puppy." David said and Alan laughed. Carman shook his head and giggled.

"Which one is your puppy?" Carman asked and David smiled.

"You are." He said and closed the door. He could hear Alan and Carman laughing as they stepped into the elevator. David walked down the hall to his room and peeked in at Amanda and his mom. They were both sleeping and he smiled. He shut the door and looked in on Little Mike. He was sprawled out on his bed and David giggled. He stepped in and covered up the little boy. He went out into the kitchen and shut the lights off. He went into the living room and lay down on the couch. He reached up and shut the lamp off. He closed his eyes and thought of Alan.

Ok, I have to pretend I don't want Alan. That should be the hardest thing I've ever done. It's cool that he wants me though. I wish I had a bitch for a mom that I would do anything to piss off. That would be me leaving with Alan and not Carman. Well, I love my mom and I can do this for her. I hope. David said and sighed. He was just drifting off to sleep when his cell phone rang. He raised his eyebrows and looked at the caller. It was Seth. He smiled and answered the phone.

"What if I had to work tomorrow?" David asked and Seth laughed on the other end.

"*With Alan down for a visit? Never happen.*" Seth said and David giggled. "*How did it go?*" He asked and David sighed. He turned the lamp on and lit a cigarette.

"Well, we decided to pretend we don't want to fuck and save my mom a world of hurt." David said and Seth laughed.

"*Ok, that's blunt.*"

"Well, that's the story." David said and took a drag of his cigarette.

"*Well, do you like this plan?*"

"Yea, it's the best thing I think. I can't deal with knowing Alan wants me and I don't do it cause of my mom. I bet he feels the same." David said. Seth sighed and cleared his throat.

"*If you guys are pretending, don't you still know?*" He asked. David sighed at the statement.

"Well, the idea is to eventually get over it." David explained.

"*Is that possible?*"

"It better be." David said and Seth laughed.

"*Well, good luck.*"

"Yea, thanks."

"*Ok so, I was wondering if Carman talked to you.*" Seth asked in a sexy sounding voice. David giggled and leaned back on the couch.

"Yea he did. What's the deal with this?"

"*Well, I thought that I was being especially cruel last week and thought I should make up for it.*"

"Uh, huh." David said and Seth laughed.

"*Look, I could be worse. I could walk around in my underwear all day*" Seth said. David laughed and shook his head.

"No, what did you have in mind?" David asked.

"*Well, I thought I would be nice and let you kiss me.*" Seth said and David giggled.

"Uh, huh."

"*What? You don't think I could live through a kiss?*"

"Well, that's a pretty gay thing to do Seth." David said and tapped the ash off his cigarette. Seth laughed.

"*Well, it's only gay if somebody hears about it. You wouldn't tell Carman or somebody would you?*"

"No. I could be quiet if I had to be." David said and smiled.

"*Uh, huh.*" Seth mocked David and David laughed.

"Look, half the shit you've done to me is a secret. You're a straight guy that finds fun in toying with a gay dude. What more could you do to me?"

"*Well, I could get you hard and walk away.*"

"To late to threaten that." David said and Seth laughed.

"*You wanna kiss me or what?*" Seth asked. David sighed and looked up at the ceiling.

"Well yea but I'm not going to." David said. He could hear Seth sigh a breath of relief and he giggled.

"*Remind me to punch Lance.*" Seth said and David giggled.

"Why?"

"*Well, he thinks that what I do with you is way too harsh and unfair and you should have to get something out of it.*"

"Thank him for me but really, I'm ok. I don't want you to do something that would freak you out." David said and took a puff from his cigarette.

"*That's what I told him but Lance is an idiot and thinks you can't be flirted with and not get laid or at least kissed.*"

"Well, I can. You're safe." David said thinking back to the way Alan had touched his jaw earlier that day. Seth sighed again and David smiled.

"*Well then on that note. How about something to think about before bed?*" Seth asked in a quiet seductive voice.

"Ok." David said quietly and Seth giggled.

"*How would you like to feel my hair run down your body while I slowly work my way down on you?*" Seth asked. David smiled and shook his head.

"Well," David said and giggled. Seth laughed and cleared his throat.

"*You could pull it while I gave you head.*"

"Uh, huh." David said trying to ignore the thought and Seth giggled.

"*I would push your cock as far down my throat as I could and suck it as hard as you wanted me to.*" Seth said. David closed his eyes and sighed. He felt the familiar tug in his groin of a growing erection as he pictured what Seth described.

"Uh, huh." David said again and Seth sighed.

"*I would run my tongue up and down your shaft till you came down my throat.*" Seth said in his overly seductive drawl. David giggled and shook his head.

"You're so cruel." David said and Seth laughed.

"*How will you sleep now?*" Seth asked.

"On my back. I'll break my cock off if I roll over." David said and readjusted his throbbing erection. Seth laughed.

"*Awesome.*" He said and David laughed. He took another drag from his cigarette and sighed.

"You certainly don't talk like your straight." David said as he rolled his cigarette in the ash tray.

"*It's a gift.*" Seth said and David laughed.

"It certainly is."

"*Well, I gatta go. Want me to come tuck you in?*" David laughed and looked up at the ceiling.

"Not if you wanna get out of here in one piece." David said and Seth giggled.

"*You know, you're a really good friend*"

"Why do you say that?" David asked

"*Well, you put up with my shit and never make me follow through. It's not something just ANYBODY would do.*" Seth said and David smiled.

"Well, Seth, I'm glad we're friends. I don't mind not making you follow through."

"*That's why I love ya.*"

"Uh, huh." David said and Seth giggled.

"*Good night, David.*"

"Good night." David said and hung up the phone. He shook his head and finished his cigarette. He turned the lamp off and lay back down on the couch.

It sure is strange to have a friend like Gabe used to be. Without the sex, of course. Speaking of sex, what the fuck is with all these hot guys and their constant flirting? None of them seem to want to put out. It would be nice to have a normal day. Those ass holes sure make it HARD for me. David giggled at the thought and concentrated on calming the erection Seth had given him.

At least Amanda takes care of that. I wonder what they would do if I quit flirting with them? I should try it and see what happens. David thought. He sighed again and closed his eyes. *It sure was nice to see Alan again. I didn't know how much I missed talking to him. I hope the plan of forgetting these feelings is going to work. I need to get on with my life.* David yawned and repositioned himself into a more comfortable position. It wasn't long before he fell asleep.

Chapter 12

David awoke the next morning to the sound of typing on the computer. He yawned and squinted his eyes open. His mother sat quietly at the computer with a steaming cup of coffee and a cigarette burning in the ashtray. She was wearing a pair of Amanda's pajamas and looked well rested.

"Alan is at Carman's and I need a new couch." David groaned as he rolled over. Nancy giggled and looked at her son.

"Oh, David. You should have got me up when he was leaving. I didn't mean to kick you out of your bed." She said and got up. She went into the kitchen and got David a cup of coffee. She brought it over to him and he smiled at her.

"Aren't I supposed to be waiting on you? You are the guest." David said and sipped his hot coffee. Nancy smiled and shook her head.

"I don't mind. Other than an uncomfortable couch, how was your sleep?" Nancy asked as she sat back down on the leather desk chair and turned it to face her son. She held her coffee in both hands and blew on it before she took a sip.

"Well, short." David said looking at the clock. It was 7:30 am which gave David a little less than six hours sleep. Nancy giggled and stared at her son.

"I'm glad you and Alan are talking again."

"Well, it's a slow start, but I think we'll work it all out." David said and lit a cigarette.

"I'm sure you will. I really like him David." Nancy said and took a drag from her burning cigarette. She put it out and looked back at David. He sighed and half smiled at his mom.

"What's not to like?" David asked and Nancy snickered.

"David, if I had known how you felt, I could have helped you rather than kept Alan from you."

"Mom, its fine. Water under the bridge or whatever. If Alan makes you happy, that's all that matters." David said and puffed at his cigarette. Nancy smiled and sipped her coffee.

"Well, I'm really happy." Nancy said. Just then the phone rang and David reached over to the side table to answer it.

"Hello." He said into the receiver through another morning yawn.

"Hi, I figured you would be up." It was Carman on the other end. David smiled and shook his head.

"Carman, for you, I'm always up." David said and Nancy shook her head. She turned back toward the computer and started typing again. David laughed and took another puff from his cigarette.

"I bet you are, anyway. I was calling because Alan and I thought it would be nice to take everybody out for a brunch thing. You wanna go?"

"Sure. What time?" David asked.

"How about around 10. Alan is just getting up and I have horses to move around this morning."

"Ok, ten it is then." David said. Carman yawned and David could hear his jaw click. "Have a long night or what?" David asked. Carman laughed on the other end.

"You're a pig." Carman said and David laughed.

"I know. Are we meeting up first or just going straight to the restaurant?"

"Well, your mom would probably like to change so why not come here in the next hour or so, so she can do that."

"Good idea." David said remembering that his mother and Alan never brought any suit cases in. "See you in a bit then." David said.

"Ok." Carman said and they both hung up.

"Looks like we're going out for breakfast." David said and stood up. Nancy looked at him and smiled. He went to the bathroom with his cigarette in hand and took a pee. He went into his bedroom and looked at Amanda. She looked so peaceful and David smiled. He put out his cigarette in the little ash tray on the bed side table and crawled in with her. She smiled and cuddled into his arms. "Good morning." David whispered and kissed her neck. Amanda smiled again and nodded.

"Did you sleep on the couch?" She asked in a groggy voice.

"Yea, about that. I love your taste but, next time. Go for comfort and not looks." David said. Amanda giggled and opened her eyes. David looked at her sleepy face and smiled. "I guess we're going out for breakfast so you better get up."

"Ok." She said and yawned. She stretched and David moved so she could get the most out of it.

"Wanna quickie before we go?" David asked running his hand across Amanda's breasts and down to her stomach. Amanda giggled and pushed his hand away.

"I would but I don't think your mom would appreciate it." David laughed and shook his head.

"Oh well. It's not like she doesn't know we do it."

"Well, I have to pee worse than I need sex." Amanda said and got out of bed. David smiled and stood up. Amanda went into the on suite bathroom and David went back into the kitchen. His mother was sitting at the table now looking at a magazine that she had found.

"Is she up?" Nancy asked and David nodded. She smiled as David sat down at the table.

"So, I'm going to take you to Carman's to get ready to go in about an hour."

"Well, that would be nice. I don't have any clothes here." She said and David giggled.

"You could always go like that." David said gesturing to the pajama's she wore. Nancy laughed and shook her head. They talked about the baby stuff in the magazine while Amanda got ready to go. When the shower shut off, David got up and went into Little Mike's room. He was playing with some trucks on his bed when David came in. "You're awake." David said and sat down with him.

"I want a play with my truck." Mike said and crashed it into David's leg.

"Well, you have to get dressed now so we can go have breakfast with Uncle Carman." David said and walked over to the little boy's dresser.

"I not hungry." Mike said with a pout and crossed his arms. David smiled and dug out some blue jeans and a t-shirt that said 'the devil is scared of me' on it. He walked back over to Mike and held up the shirt.

"This is perfect for today it looks like." Mike stared at David and stuck out his tongue. David giggled and tackled the little boy on his bed. Mike laughed and kicked as David tickled him. Finally he managed to talk Mike into getting dressed. When he was ready to go, they came out into the kitchen. Nancy had gotten dressed into the clothes she had worn the day before and Amanda was at the table with a coffee. Mike ran over to Nancy and jumped onto her lap.

"Oh, David. I hate that shirt." Amanda said and David giggled. He sat next to Amanda and rested his hand on her leg. She blushed and shook her head.

"I like it." Nancy said and tickled Little Mike. Mike squealed and squirmed on her lap. David, Amanda and Nancy all laughed at him. When they were finished their coffee, they got ready to go and headed down to the car. Nancy got into the back and sighed. "You know, anyone who would take out the bench in the front and put this stupid little seat back here should have their head examined." Nancy said as she tried to position herself so her knees didn't dig into Amanda's bucket seat. David giggled and started the car.

"Well, with a car like this, you don't need a back seat." David said recalling the night with Amanda in the front and the time with Gabe in the very back were a coffin once sat.

"I still think with a baby on the way, you should consider a different car." Nancy said as David pulled out of the parking lot. David rolled his eyes and looked at Amanda. She said nothing. She just ran her hand along the dash of her brother's once beloved vehicle. David smiled knowing she thought of Gabe.

"I might put in a bigger back seat, mom. But we're keeping the car." He said into the rear view mirror. Nancy rolled her eyes and looked at the reflection of David's eyes in the mirror.

"I just think that a sedan or something is more suitable for children." Nancy argued. David sighed and sped up the car. Amanda giggled but still said nothing.

"I like my car." Mike said in the back and David laughed. Nancy looked at the little boy and smiled.

"What about the baby?" Nancy asked. Mike looked around and then looked back at Nancy.

"Baby is small. He fit in here with me." Mike answered. All the adults smiled. David turned into Carman's drive way and felt his stomach jump when he saw Alan's sexy Mustang. He took a deep breath and Amanda rubbed the hand he had on the gear shift. Nancy didn't notice. They all got out and headed for the house. Nancy went in first and David shook his head.

"She is obviously not aware of the rules." David said and Amanda giggled.

"DEAD MAN WALKEN!" Mike yelled before David or Amanda got a chance to. They both laughed and followed him in.

"Even the kid knows the rules." Carman said as they entered. Nancy laughed and shook her head.

"I always forget." She said and quickly kissed Alan before she headed toward the bathroom with her bag. David seen it and sighed and Amanda squeezed his hand. They joined Alan and Carman at the table and David still hadn't looked at Alan.

"Good morning." Amanda said as Carman brought them both a coffee.

"Good morning." Alan and Carman said in unison. David stared out the window and Carman sighed. He leaned close to David and whispered in his ear.

"You know, not looking at him doesn't make him go away." He said. David sighed and nodded. He looked into Alan's eyes and they both smiled. Alan shook his head and took a sip of his coffee.

"So, where are we gonna go?" Amanda asked. Carman looked at her and smiled.

"Well, you know that place you said you always wanted to try? Apparently they have a pretty good breakfast menu that runs all day so I thought that's where we would go." Carman said. Amanda giggled and clapped her hands. Mike did the same and headed into the living room.

"What? No show?" Mike yelled from the other room and Carman laughed. He got up and went into the living room to turn the T.V. on for the little boy. David stared at Alan and Alan reciprocated.

"Get it all in guys, I bet a look like that would make Nancy uncomfortable." Amanda whispered and Alan and David both looked at her. She blinked and cleared her throat. "Well it's true." She said and took a sip of her coffee. Alan smiled and shook his head. David took a sip of his coffee and looked out the window. The two men's look away game was funny to her and she laughed. "Well, I didn't mean for you guys to pretend the other one doesn't exist." She said. David and Alan both laughed just as Carman walked into the room.

"I missed something didn't I?" He asked as he found his seat at the table. Alan, David and Amanda all looked at him and shook their heads. Carman rolled his eyes and sipped his coffee. David met Alan's gaze again and sighed. Alan smiled and looked at Carman.

"So, do you think the new pen will keep him in?" Alan asked.

"Well, if it doesn't I'm selling him." Carman said.

"What are you talking about?" Amanda asked and Alan looked at her craftily avoiding David's eyes.

"Diablo keeps jumping the fence so we put him in the round pen." He said. Amanda nodded and looked at Carman.

"Why is he doing it?" She asked. Carman leaned back in his chair and shook his head.

"Because he can I guess." Carman said and David laughed. They all looked at David and he was staring at Alan. Alan blinked.

"What?" Alan asked. David straightened his face and swallowed hard.

"I didn't mean to laugh out loud actually." David said and Amanda and Carman laughed. Alan held David's gaze and smiled.

"What are you thinking about?" He asked and David blushed.

"Never mind." David said and sipped his coffee. Soon, Nancy was ready to go and they left the house. Carman, Nancy and Alan road together in Carman's truck and Amanda, David and Little Mike road in their car.

"What was that about at the table?" Amanda asked as they followed Carman's truck out of the driveway. David sighed and looked at her.

"Alan said something to me yesterday in the elevator and it just seemed to strike me as funny." David said. Amanda smiled and stared at David.

"Are you gonna tell me or what?" She asked. David laughed and stared at the tail lights of Carman's truck.

"He said that if the circumstances were different and he had the guts, he would kiss me." David explained and Amanda giggled.

"Ok, so why is that funny? Isn't that the kind of thing you've been waiting to hear?"

"Well, it is. But it's funny to hear Alan talk like that." David said. Amanda thought about it and remembered all the times David had been confused by the things Alan would say. She thought about how David must feel hearing Alan be a little more candid and she laughed.

"I can imagine." She said. David smiled and shook his head.

"Amanda, I love you." He said and Amanda giggled.

"I know." She said and David laughed. They talked about Alan as they drove. It wasn't long before they were at the restaurant and getting out of the car. The waitress was very quick at finding them a suitable table and getting them their drinks. David spent most of the

223

meal looking at Little Mike or Amanda to keep himself from staring at Alan. They talked about the coming summer holidays and the next school year and what Amanda and David planned to do about finishing school.

"I think you guys should at least get your grade twelve's before the baby comes if you can. Collage can wait till the baby is older." Nancy said as she sipped at her after breakfast cup of tea.

"We will but I think we're going to do it at home. I don't want to be at school when I'm big and pregnant looking." Amanda said and smiled at David. Alan smiled and looked into David's eyes. David swallowed and tried to keep himself from getting lost in Alan's sexy gaze.

"Well, it's good to hear you have a plan." Alan said. David nodded and looked at his mom. She smiled at him and looked over at Amanda.

"We should take Mike to the bathroom before we leave." She said. Amanda agreed and they took Little Mike to the washroom. Carman leaned on the table and looked between Alan and David.

"How long are we going to play THIS game?" He asked referring to the deliberate no looking thing that Alan and David were trying to accomplish. Alan sighed and shook his head.

"Carman, there are some things that are left unsaid and undone. If it makes David more comfortable at a table, or in a room with his mom and me, then that's fine with me." Alan said. David smiled and looked into Alan's eyes. He let himself get lost in them and Alan sighed. Carman shook his head and leaned back in his chair.

"This is weird guys." Carman said under his breath and David laughed. He looked at Carman and winked. Alan laughed and shook his head. "That's better." Carman whispered and they all laughed. Alan and David continued their stare until Nancy and Amanda returned.

Amanda had beaten everyone to the bill and seemed to be pretty pleased with herself. Alan and Carman argued who would pay her for half of the meal but she just walked away from them. They eventually gave in with a laugh and a head shake. Alan had decided that he and Nancy would head for home right from the restaurant. Nancy hugged Amanda, Carman and little Mike before moving her attention to David. She held him tight and David smiled.

"Thank you for getting along with him." She whispered and David sighed.

"Mom, I wish you would stay a little longer." He whispered back and Nancy pulled away.

"Duty calls dear." She said and kissed his cheek. David smiled at her and looked at Alan. Alan walked up to him and David's palms began to sweat. Alan wrapped his arms around him in a close hug. David did the same and cleverly pulled Alan in close enough for their hips to rest right against each other. David could feel every line and curve in Alan's groin and he quietly whimpered. Alan sighed and, to his surprise and pleasure, he pushed himself against David. David quietly breathed out a small moan and whispered in Alan's ear.

"You're an ass hole." Alan giggled and nodded.

"I know." He said and pulled away. They looked at each other for a moment before Alan and Nancy got into Carman's truck.

"I'll be over later with your pay check." Carman said and David nodded. Amanda and David waved at them as they drove away.

"Nice hug." Amanda said and giggled.

"Yes it was." David said and they got into the car. They stopped at the store and picked up some groceries before going home. Amanda put them away while David laid Mike down for a nap.

"Does David miss Alan?" Mike asked in a sleepy voice. David smiled and covered the little boy up.

"Every day." David answered and left the room.

As the next couple of weeks went by, Seth was becoming more excited about graduation. David would talk to him almost every day and everyday Seth was as sexually cruel as he could be. Amanda continued the search for Beth and hit a snag. It seemed that with just using the birth certificate, Beth's age made it difficult to locate her. All Amanda would get was net nanny e-mails concerning Beth's age and dead ends with government sights. She switched her search to Beth's mother Lyn instead. David continued working with Carman and was becoming very good at his new job. On the day of Seth's graduation, Carman gave David the day off so he could take Seth suit shopping.

"Why isn't Lance or your dad taking you?" David asked as they drove through town looking for a men's dress store.

"Ok, Lance? I'm not dressing in drag for my grad. And my dad could care less. He thinks graduation is for the prom queen and the valedictorian. Besides, he would probably pick out something gay." Seth explained and David laughed.

"Ok, so what are you looking for?" David asked.

"Something sexy." Seth said and tossed his hair. David giggled and shook his head.

"Well, it won't matter *what* we find then." Seth laughed and looked out the windshield.

"It's gotta be good David. This girl from my English class is going with me and I want to impress her."

"Oh, do you like this girl a lot or what?" David asked. Seth nodded and David smiled. He pulled into a privately owned tuxedo shop and Seth raised his eyebrows.

"Why here?" Seth asked.

"Well, anyone else would have done this weeks before prom. But you being you, it's a last minute buy. I was in here once and you look to be the same build as the manikins." David said. Seth rolled his eyes and looked down at his body.

"I didn't know you paid such close attention." Seth said and David laughed. They went into the store and Seth tried on a few suits. It came down to a black three piece button up tux and a priest collared suite with a burgundy shirt.

"I like the last one." The suit maker said referring to the burgundy shirt and priest collared suit. David nodded and looked at Seth.

"Well, the collar is too tight on that one." Seth said and the man smiled. He brought Seth a bit larger sized jacket and Seth went in to put the suit on.

"It's nice of you to take your brother shopping for his suit." The tailor said putting the smaller jacket back on the hanger. David giggled and shook his head.

"He's not my brother. He's my friend." David said and sat down on one of the chairs waiting for Seth to finish changing. He could hear Seth giggling in the change room and shook his head.

"Well, it is a very important step in a young man's life. I think it's nice you're sharing it with him." The man said and walked away. David shook his head as Seth giggled again.

"If that was me, I would have told him you were my boyfriend just to see the reaction." Seth said from the change room. David laughed and stood up.

"Well, I'm not you." David said. Seth giggled again and stepped out. He looked amazing. The jacket fit him perfectly and the burgundy was the perfect touch under the jacket. The pants were a bit long but otherwise fit him nicely.

"Well?" Seth asked and David bit his bottom lip.

"Well, I wish I was the girl from your English class right now." David said and Seth laughed. He looked at himself in the full length mirror and smiled.

"You know, I think I like this." Seth said and David nodded. He walked up behind Seth and looked at the reflection of the young man.

"You look amazing." David whispered and Seth smiled.

"You want me don't you?" Seth whispered back and David giggled. Seth's hair hung down his back and reminded David of Gabe's hair against his leather trench coat. He smiled and stepped closer so his body was against Seth's. Seth laughed but held his ground. The tailor was coming so David cleverly rubbed his groin against Seth's backside and giggled.

"Oh, excuse me." David said and Seth rolled his eyes.

"Yea right." Seth said and David laughed. The tailor measured the pant legs and told David it would only take twenty minutes to hem them up for Seth. Seth took the suit off and they went to the counter to pay. The suit was just a little over two hundred dollars to buy so Seth decided he would like to own it. They sat in the waiting area while the tailor fixed the pant legs. When he was finished, he had Seth try them on again. They fit perfectly so the tailor packed them up with the rest of the suit and sent David and Seth on their way. They got into the car and David sighed.

"You look really good in that thing. That girl should be impressed." David said as he pulled the car on to the busy road.

"Well, if it impresses the guy that has a hard on for Alan Black, then it must be good." Seth said and David laughed.

"Nice Seth." Seth laughed and looked out the windshield. They discussed the graduation party afterward and David told Seth to call him if he needed a ride home. Seth agreed. They pulled up to Seth's house and David parked in front on the road.

"Thanks for taking me out to do this. You guys coming to the ceremony?" Seth asked.

"Yep, got the tickets on the fridge." David said. He had hung them next to the tickets he had received from his mother at Christmas time for the Gun's and Rose's concert in August. Seth smiled and grabbed the door handle.

"See you there." Seth said and opened the door. David smiled and shook his head. He watched Seth walk into the house with his new suit and was amazed at how sexy Seth's walk actually was. He sighed and pulled the car away. He got home and smiled to see Amanda and Carman at the table.

"So, is he all set?" Amanda asked as David kissed her and headed to the fridge for a pop.

"I think so. The suit looks amazing on him." David said in a stereotypical gay voice. Carman giggled and raised his eyebrows. David smirked and sat down at the table.

"What?" He asked Carman and Carman giggled.

"How does he look out of it?" Carman asked. Amanda and David both laughed. Amanda looked at David and waited for his answer.

"I don't know, he used a change room." David said in a mock pout. Carman and Amanda laughed. They talked about the ceremony as they drank their nice cool drinks. It was a very warm day for the end of June. It felt more like the middle of summer. Amanda made pork chops and fried potatoes for supper and made Carman stay for it. When they finished eating, Carman left to go get ready at his house. David showered first and then Amanda did. When she was finished, she bathed Little Mike while David finished getting ready. Carman arrived at their house at seven o'clock so David could follow him to the high school. They found a parking spot and went inside. They sat with Lance and Seth's mother.

"Where is the old man?" Carman asked Lance as they organized themselves into the chairs. Lance rolled his eyes and shook his head.

"He's working." Lance said and his mother sighed. Carman smiled at her and winked.

"At least we're here." He said to her and she smiled. Carman sat next to Lance and David sat next to Carman. Amanda sat next to David and kept Mike on her lap. The ceremony was long and Mike was asleep before it finally closed at some time after nine. David hugged Seth and congratulated him after he had gone through his family and Carman.

"Thanks for being here." Seth said and David smiled.

"I guess you owe me." David whispered and Seth laughed. He pointed out the girl he was taking to the after party and David smiled. "Yea, she's pretty easy on the eyes isn't she?" David asked. Amanda poked David in the ribs and Seth laughed. They said their good byes and headed home. Amanda was especially tired and David was worried for her. "Are you ok?" David asked. Amanda just smiled and nodded.

"Its hard work being pregnant you know. I think the chairs in there didn't help either." She said as she got out of her pretty blue dress and climbed into bed. David joined her and she rested her head on his chest. "I love you." She said and David smiled. He kissed her on the top of the head.

"I love you too." David whispered and Amanda sighed. David rubbed her back and they were soon fast asleep.

David was awoken by his cell phone ringing. He squinted his eyes at the clock. It was three thirty. Amanda stirred and rolled over. He grabbed the phone and looked at the caller. It was Seth.

"Hello?" David asked in a sleepy voice.

"*Can you come get me?*" Seth asked. David could hear in his voice that he was extremely inebriated. David smiled and sat up.

"Yea, where are you?" David asked and yawned.

"*Uh, I'll just meet you at that gas station by the diner.*" Seth slurred.

"Ok, give me ten minutes." David said. Seth hung up the phone and David sighed. He kissed Amanda and she looked at him.

"Who was that?" She asked still half asleep.

"It was Seth, he needs a ride home." David whispered and kissed her again. He got up and pulled on a pair of jeans and a gray t-shirt. He grabbed his jacket off the end of the bed and headed out of the house to his car. It took him about twenty minutes to get to the gas station. He could see Seth standing against the building smoking a cigarette. David pulled up beside him and he got into the car.

"Thanks David." Seth said. The fresh air seemed to have sobered him up slightly.

"No problem. Are we going to Lance's place or do you wanna go home?" David asked. Seth sighed and shook his head.

"Go to Lance's. My dad will just bitch if I come home at this time of night." Seth slurred and tossed the cigarette out the open window. David smiled and pulled out of the parking lot.

"So, how did it go with that girl?"

"Fuck, I was so sure she was into me but it turns out, she likes my friend and only went with me to try to hook up with him." Seth said and sighed.

"So I take it she did." David asked. Seth looked at him and nodded. David sighed and patted Seth's hand. "There will be other ones." He said and pulled his hand away. Seth giggled and shook his head. David looked at him with a confused gaze. "What?" He asked. Seth looked at him and shifted in his seat so he could face David.

"I graduated today and I never even got kissed." Seth said. David looked between Seth and the road.

"Ok, what can I do about that?" David asked. Seth shook his head and leaned closer to David.

"Well, you could do it." Seth said in a very seductive tone. David raised his eyebrows and found a place to park the car. He shut it off and looked at Seth.

"YOU want ME to kiss you?" David asked in disbelief and Seth nodded. David sighed and looked out the windshield. "Seth, your drunk. I can't kiss you right now. You'll hate yourself and me tomorrow if I did." David said remembering the conversation he had with Gabe about what sometimes happens when a guy does it with another guy for the first time. David figured a kiss would be no different. Especially if that kiss was with Seth.

"I thought you liked me. Don't you want to kiss me?" Seth asked. David sighed and looked into Seth's eyes. He was so attractive and seemed so willing.

"Seth, I do. But you're not thinking straight right now. You're not gay, remember?" David asked trying to get out of what was sure to be a huge mistake. Seth sighed and shook his head.

"So? I think you're really sexy, David. If I was ever gonna do anything with a dude, it would have to be you so why not just do it now?" David laughed and shifted in his seat.

"Well, why don't you proposition me when you're sober? I would be glad to do it then."

"But I want you right now." Seth said in a half whiny yet extremely sexy sounding voice and David could feel his stomach flip. Seth was so convincing that David almost changed his mind.

"Seth, it's not a good idea." David whispered and Seth groaned.

"You know, it's one thing to be shot down by some bitch at grad., but to be shot down by you on the same day is ridiculous." Seth said. David could tell he was becoming aggravated and he sighed.

"Seth, I promise to make up for it tenfold if you feel this way when you sober up." David said. Seth shook his head and looked back out the window.

"Whatever." Seth said. David sighed again and cleared his throat. Seth looked at him and David smiled.

"Do you think I'm lying to you?" David asked. Seth shrugged and looked down at the gearshift. "Seth, if you weren't so drunk and thinking a little clearer right now, I would have you in the back of this car doing a lot more than just kissing you." David whispered. Seth giggled and shook his head.

"So why wait?" Seth asked and rand his hand along David's jaw. David closed his eyes and sighed.

"Because you're drunk." David said and pulled his head out of Seth's hand.

"So what?" Seth asked. David laughed and shook his head.

"Seth, I'm taking you home now." David said and started the car.

"David, you should just take advantage of the situation. You'll like it, I promise." Seth said and put his hand on the inside of David's thigh. David looked down at Seth's hand and raised his eyebrows. He took Seth's hand off his leg and looked at him.

"You have got to cut it out Seth. This is stupid." David said. Seth shook his head and leaned back in his seat.

"I'm stupid now? I seem to remember that just a few hours ago; you were ready to bend me over in the suit place." Seth said.

"Seth, I was fucking around. What do you want me to do? Fuck you tonight so tomorrow not only do you hate me, but you'll be afraid of everything you've ever known." David scolded. Seth's eyes grew wide and he stared at David.

"Are you mad at me?" He asked. David rolled his eyes.

"Seth, its better I'm mad right now then what you could be tomorrow."

"What if I don't care? What if I just want you to do it no matter how I feel about it tomorrow?" Seth asked.

"I care." David said. He turned onto the street that Lance's house was on. Seth sighed and shook his head.

"Not even just a kiss?" Seth asked. David giggled and shook his head.

"Not even a peck on the cheek." David answered. Seth sighed and shook his head.

"You're mean." David laughed and parked the car in front of Lance's house. He got out and walked with Seth to the door. He opened the door for him and got him up to his room. Seth sat down on his bed and David staid standing at the door. "You could do it right now and no one would ever know." Seth said and stood up. David sighed and shook his head.

"I would know." David whispered. Seth stepped close to David and looked into his eyes.

"Just do it David. Just one kiss. I wouldn't hate you for that." Seth whispered and moved himself even closer. David put his hands on Seth's shoulders and stepped back. Seth staid where he stood and stared into David's eyes.

"Talk to me about it tomorrow." David said and took his hands off Seth's shoulders. Seth looked down at the floor and shook his head.

"This sucks man. Why doesn't anyone want me? You say you do but it's all a game to you isn't it?" Seth asked and looked up into David's eyes. David sighed and shook his head.

"Seth, you are amazing to look at. You're funny, and smart. You have a killer body and your hair is like foreplay. Trust me; it's not as much a game to me as it is for you." David whispered. Seth rolled his eyes and sat back down on his bed.

"You say that and yet you won't even kiss me." Seth whispered. David walked closer to Seth and looked into his eyes.

"I want to. Really bad, but I think it's better that I don't." David said and ran his hand through Seth's silky black hair. Seth closed his eyes and tilted his head back as David pulled his hand through his hair. David sighed and ran a finger along his jaw. Seth's breathing sped up and David closed his eyes. "Not today." David whispered and pulled his hand away. Seth sat still and slowly opened his eyes.

"I bet you'll hate your self tomorrow for not doing it." Seth said as David stepped out the door. He smiled and looked back at him.

"I already do." David said and left the room. He went out to his car and took a deep breath before starting it. It was after four when David crawled back into bed with Amanda.

"How is Seth?" Amanda asked in her sleep. David giggled and rubbed her back.

"Very, very drunk." David whispered and soon fell asleep next to Amanda.

Chapter 13

David was startled awake by his alarm clock just three hours later. He groaned and shut it off. Amanda was already out of bed and David could hear her making coffee. He sat up and looked around the room for his cigarettes. He remembered setting them on the table when he came in the night before and sighed.

"Fucking Seth." David whispered remembering the ordeal from the night before and got out of bed. He went out to the kitchen in his boxers and Amanda giggled.

"Is that what you're wearing to work today?" She asked and David laughed.

"Yea, I thought Carman would appreciate it." He said as he lit a cigarette. Amanda laughed and took two cups out of the cupboard.

"So, did Seth get home alright and everything last night?" She asked as she filled the sugar bowl. David thought to the night before and Seth's begging for a kiss.

"Well, I took him to Lance's place. He was pretty wrecked last night." David said.

"Well, it's his graduation; wouldn't you get nice and drunk if it were you?" Amanda asked.

"Well, probably, but I would watch who I hit on."

"Why? What happened?" Amanda asked probably thinking the worst. David giggled and told Amanda the whole story. She shook her head when he was finished and brought them both a coffee. She sat down across from him and sighed. "I think it was very good of you not to do it." Amanda said as she sipped at her hot coffee.

"Well, he was way too drunk to be himself last night. That's for sure."

"Are you going to talk about it with him?" She asked.

"I think I'll wait and see if he brings it up." David said and took a big sip of his coffee. He looked at the time and sighed. It was already 7:30 and Carman would be there to pick him up soon. He got up and kissed Amanda on his way to the bathroom. He showered and got ready for his day. When he finished, he came out to see Carman at the table talking with Amanda.

"Ready to go?" He asked.

"Yup." David said and kissed Amanda. She smiled and closed the door behind them. Their day was like most others. David was starting to get really good at the reprogramming and Carman would drop him off at some places so they could get two jobs done at the same time. When they were finished their day and Carman was taking David home, he turned and looked at him.

"David, what did Alan say about the whole helping me with the size issue thing?" David raised his eyebrows and looked at Carman.

"Well, he told me to use my own discretion." David said. Carman nodded and cleared his throat.

"What are you thinking then?" David looked at Carman with a confused gaze.

"I thought *you* had to decide if we were going to do this." David said. Carman sighed and shook his head.

"Will he be mad?" He asked sheepishly. David thought back to the conversation.

"Yes, but he said I should help you if I can." David answered. Carman nodded and stopped the truck at a red light.

"What would you do if you were me?"

"I have no idea." David said. Carman looked back out the windshield and seemed to fight with his mind to make a decision. "Why don't you give it more thought? It's up to you Carman."

"Jake and I have a date next weekend. I need to know I can get through it if anything happens." Carman said. David raised his eyebrows and scratched the side of his neck.

"Ok, well what if he isn't a big guy?" David asked. Carman rolled his eyes and swallowed hard.

"I was in the store the other day and ran into him. He was wearing these really tight pants and, trust me David, he is no little boy from what I can tell." Carman said. The light turned green and Carman started to drive again.

"Well, what says anything is going to happen on the first date?"

"Nothing. I just don't want to freak out again. I really like him." Carman said. They stopped at the last lights before David's apartment building.

"Carman, I will help you if you want me too." David said quietly and Carman nodded. They drove in silence to David's building.

"Well, I guess I have four days to get the guts to take you up on that offer." Carman said. David smiled and ran his hand through Carman's hair.

"I'm ready when you are." He whispered and kissed Carman on the temple. This coaxed a smile from Carman and David giggled. He got out of the truck and went around to the driver's side. Carman wheeled down the window and looked at him.

"What if I can't do it?" Carman asked.

"Then you can't. Besides, it's just to get over the size thing right?" Carman nodded. "Then we don't really have to do a lot, Carman. You just have to be in a situation where you're around one. We don't need to fuck or anything."

"I know. It's still the thought of it that freaks me out." David smiled and leaned close to Carman.

"Then don't think about it." David whispered and Carman laughed.

"Easy for you to say." David laughed and waved at Carman as he went into the building. He went up to his apartment and seen Seth sitting on the floor in the living room with Mike.

"Hi babe." Amanda said and kissed him. David smiled and grabbed her hips as she kissed him. He pulled her in close to him and breathed an exasperated moan. She laughed and pushed him away.

"Hey." David said to Seth and sat down on the couch. Amanda smiled at them and went back to making supper.

"Hi." Seth said and got up. He sat next to David and looked into his eyes. "I was a total ass hole last night. I'm really sorry." Seth said and David smiled surprised that he could even remember.

"You were drunk, it's ok."

"Thanks for not doing it." Seth said quietly and David smirked.

"It wasn't easy. You can be very persuasive." David said quietly. Seth smiled and shook his head.

"I feel like a real idiot."

"Don't." David said and stood up. He went to the fridge and got himself and Seth a beer. He came back to the couch and handed one to Seth. Seth thanked him and they both opened them at the same time. David watched as he took a big sip from his beer. David sighed as Seth slowly took the bottle away from his lips. "So, now that your sober, how about that kiss?" David asked. Seth laughed and shook his head.

"Nice David. I deserve that I guess."

"I'm serious." David said and Seth looked into his eyes.

"Right here in front of the kid?" Seth asked gesturing to Mike. David laughed and shook his head.

"Amanda uses him as an excuse too." David said. Amanda giggled but never looked away from what she was doing in the kitchen. David smiled and stared into Seth's eyes. 'I want you so bad.' David mouthed and Seth blushed. David giggled and looked at Amanda. She was at the sink washing vegetables for a salad. Seth cleared his throat and David looked at him. He smiled and bit his bottom lip.

"What would you do if I kissed you right now?" Seth whispered only loud enough for the two of them to hear. David raised his eyebrows and smiled.

"I would cum." David whispered back and Seth laughed. Amanda turned to look at them and shook her head.

"You guys are so weird." She said and went to the fridge for the carrots. David laughed and shook his head. "You staying for supper?" Amanda asked Seth. David looked at him and smiled.

"Uh, sure I guess." He answered and Amanda nodded. Seth looked into David's eyes and sighed. "I should kiss you just to see if you would." He whispered. David smiled and took a sip of his beer.

"Then do it." David whispered and Seth shook his head. David laughed and turned the T.V. on. They watched the news while Amanda finished dinner. When it was almost ready, David set the table and got Mike ready for the meal. They all sat down together and almost instantly, Seth ran his foot all the way up David's leg to his groin. He stopped his foot just short of touching it and David smiled. He reached across the table for the salad which pushed his genitals against Seth's foot. Seth laughed and took his foot away. Amanda looked at him with a puzzled gaze and shook her head.

"Half the time I think your trying to steal him from me." She said in a teasing voice to Seth and David laughed.

"No worry of that, you put out." David said and blew her a kiss. Seth and Amanda laughed. David looked across the table at Seth and winked. He frowned at him and tilted his head to one side. David did the same with his foot as Seth did to him but didn't hesitate going all the way. Seth cleared his throat and closed his eyes. David giggled and ate his meal not moving his foot. After a short time, Seth sighed and squeezed his legs together. David pushed with his foot and Seth laughed. David laughed too then moved his foot away. Amanda shook her head and looked at him.

"Do I want to know?" She asked and David and Seth laughed.

"He thinks he's smarter than me." David said and Seth shook his head.

"Is he?" She asked. David laughed and kissed her.

"I love you." He whispered and Amanda giggled. David smiled and went back to his meal. They talked about the girl that Seth had taken to the after party with him and came up with every dirty word they could to describe her that Little Mike may not repeat. Amanda wanted a bath after dinner so David made her go and told her that he and Seth could handle the dishes and Mike. She thanked him and went to the bathroom. David set Mike up with his before bed movie while Seth cleared the table.

"Does what that chick did really bother you that much?" David asked as he came to the kitchen to help Seth with the cleaning. Seth giggled and shook his head.

"No, I'm not hurting for attention or anything. I just thought she was the kind of girl I could date." Seth said. David smiled and nodded.

"I know what that's like." David said remembering what it was like first starting his relationship with Amanda. They had been friends their whole lives so seeing her as a girlfriend was weird. Now he felt like she always was.

"I don't think I want anything as serious as what you and Amanda have, but she seemed to have potential." Seth added and David smiled.

"Well, she's not worth the breath your using Seth. Girls are weird. Either they love you to death or they love you till something better comes along." David said and started the water in the sink. He rinsed a few dishes before he was surprised by Seth. He was standing right behind him. He turned around and faced him. They were almost exactly the same height. David cleared his throat and raised his eyebrows. "What?" He asked. Seth smiled and stared into David's eyes.

"Well, it's my move and after that shit at the table it's gonna have to be good to trump you." Seth whispered. David giggled and shook his head.

"Uh, huh." He said and Seth smiled. He closed his eyes and leaned close to David. He breathed in David's face and David swallowed hard.

The erotica of it was almost overwhelming. Seth smiled and pushed David against the counter. David looked into his eyes and whimpered. The excitement the young man caused him was definitely intense. Seth giggled and pressed his body against David's. He stared into David's eyes and quietly moaned. David closed his eyes and took a deep breath. It was all he could do to NOT kiss him. Seth sighed and whispered in David's ear,

"If I could get passed the fact that you're a guy, I WOULD kiss you." David giggled and shook his head. He smelled Seth's hair and whimpered again.

"You're so cruel." David whispered. Seth smiled and kissed David's neck making him shiver.

"I know." He said and stepped back. David opened his eyes and shook his head.

"How can I follow that?" David asked. Seth laughed and shrugged his shoulders.

"You'll come up with something." He said and put a dish in the dishwasher. David sighed and rolled his eyes.

"You would shit if I kissed you wouldn't you?" David asked. Seth smiled and raised his eyebrows.

"I don't think I would literally shit." Seth said. David laughed and went back to rinsing the dishes. When they were finished, Seth wiped the table and threw the cloth at David. He laughed and tossed it in the sink.

"You should kiss me and see how you like it." David said still half reeling from Seth's earlier production and Seth blinked at him.

"You think so?" He asked. David giggled and nodded. He figured he should try to get as much out of him now as he could manage. Seth raised his eyebrows and rubbed his chin with his hand.

"What if I told you I had already thought about that?" Seth asked.

"I would say I didn't believe you."

"Well, I did think about it. Actually I'm still thinking about it." Seth said and sat down at the table. David laughed and shook his head. He sat down across from Seth and looked into his eyes.

"You're so full of shit." David said and Seth laughed.

"I try." Amanda came out of the bathroom then and went into their bedroom. David smiled at her and looked back at Seth. He just yawned and winked at David.

"I think I'm going to propose to Amanda on her birthday." David whispered and Seth's eyebrows rose.

"Really?" He asked in an excited whisper. The subject was successfully changed from David's incredible desire and he was happy for that.

"Yea, but don't say anything to anybody. I don't want it getting back to her." David said. Seth smiled and nodded.

"That's so cool David." He said. David giggled and shook his head.

"Well, I should marry the only one that puts out after she turns me on." David teased. Seth laughed and shook his head.

"That's a good plan."

"I know." David said. Seth bit his bottom lip and leaned closer to David.

"Do I really turn you on that much?" Seth asked in a quiet whisper. David laughed and nodded. It seemed that Seth wasn't going to let David calm himself at all.

"Yea." He said and Seth smiled.

"What if I told you the feeling was mutual I'm just too straight to do anything about it?" Seth asked. David sighed and remembered back to the first time he had finally masturbated thinking of Alan. He smiled and shook his head.

"I would say that I know exactly what you mean." David whispered back. Seth sighed and shook his head.

"You're so funny." Seth said and David laughed. "Do you have a ring yet?" Seth asked switching the conversation again. David shook his head no and Seth smiled. "Can I help you pick it out?" David smiled and leaned back on his chair.

"I would love that." He said. Amanda came out and the three of them played a game of cards before Seth left. David walked him out to the elevator while Amanda put Mike to bed. Seth pushed the button and the elevator started its climb to the fifth floor.

"When are we ring shopping?" Seth whispered. David raised his eyebrows and thought for a second.

"Well, her birthday is on the 5th of July so we better start looking soon." David whispered back knowing that the date was a week and three days away. Seth smiled and looked into David's eyes.

"It's gonna be cool. I bet she'll say yes."

"I wouldn't be so sure. She hates the word girlfriend so I can't imagine what she thinks of wife." David said. Seth laughed and put his hand on David's shoulder.

"I bet she'll say yes." Seth repeated in a reassuring tone. David smiled and patted Seth's arm.

"I hope so." David said. The elevator doors opened and Seth stepped in.

"No kiss goodnight?" Seth asked and David laughed. He stepped toward Seth and he almost jumped backward. David burst out laughing and Seth shook his head. He stopped the door from closing and grabbed David's shirt. He pulled him into the elevator with him and pinned him against the wall. David looked into his eyes and Seth took a deep breath. David raised an eyebrow and stared at Seth's nervous face.

"Well? How brave are you?" David asked quietly. Seth closed his eyes for a second then backed away. "Uh, huh." David said and stopped the doors from closing again. Seth shook his head and sighed.

"I'm sorry David. You should have done it when I was drunk." Seth said. David rolled his eyes and looked into Seth's.

"And miss this struggle you have with being the one that does it? No way." David said. Seth giggled and David stepped out of the elevator. "That was pretty close though." David said and Seth laughed.

"Next time, you wait and see." Seth said as the doors closed. David laughed and went back into the apartment. He locked the door behind him and sat down on the couch next to Amanda.

"Did he do it?" Amanda asked. David laughed and shook his head.

"Nope. It was close though."

"What a pussy. It's easy to kiss you." She said and kissed him. He pulled her on top of him and kissed her deeply. She giggled and tugged at his shirt. He pulled it off and freed Amanda from the robe she was wearing. He took her right breast into his mouth and she moaned. She pressed her chest against David's powerful jaw. He grabbed her hips and pushed himself against her. She moaned again and leaned down to kiss him. His breathing picked up as Amanda slowly ran her hand down his chest and stomach and fought with the button on his jeans. He helped her with it and she pulled his pants off revealing the massive erection they had hidden from her. She straddled David again but he stood up with her and laid her on her back. Amanda giggled and kissed him as he positioned himself on top of her. He propped her right leg up on his arm and guided himself inside of her. She moaned and clawed at his hip with one hand and his arm with the other. David kissed her as he slowly moved his hips. She closed her eyes and breathed deeply against his face. He sped up his movements and Amanda moaned. He kissed her again and she bit his lip. He giggled and moved faster. "Oh God, David." Amanda moaned as she climaxed. David smiled and arched his back. He moaned as he felt his own orgasm building. "Cum for me David." Amanda whispered and David kissed her. She scratched his back as he brought her to climax again. He followed shortly after. He moaned fairly loud and Amanda giggled. She held him tightly on top of her when he finished and buried his head in her hair.

"God, I love fucking you." David whispered and Amanda giggled.

"Me too." She said and kissed his shoulder. She shifted slightly and David picked himself off of her. She smiled and ran her hand down his sweaty torso. "God you're sexy. How did I ever get so lucky?" She asked. David smiled and kissed her. He pulled himself out of her and handed her the robe he had tossed on the floor earlier.

"I was wondering the same thing." He said as she pulled it over her shoulders. She giggled and got up then kissed him and walked to the bathroom. David smiled and pulled his boxers on. He lit a cigarette and leaned his head against the back of the couch. He took a long drag from it and the phone rang. "Wow, talk about good timing." David said to himself and answered it. "Hello." He said.

"*Hi.*" Alan said on the other end.

"Oh, hi." David said and giggled.

"*How's it going with you guys today?*" Alan asked. David smiled and took a drag from his after sex cigarette.

"Good. And you?" He asked.

"*Oh, things are fine here. Listen, I wanted to know if you guys got a crib yet.*"

"Nope. Why?"

"*I was thinking about getting one for Amanda for her birthday. Is that lame?*" Alan asked. David laughed and shook his head.

"I think that's perfect." He said and took another puff off his smoke.

"*Oh good. I already bought it.*" Alan said in a relieved voice and David laughed.

"Well, I bet she'll like it."

"*Your mom wants to come down the day before to make a cake. She thinks you should help.*"

"Ok, I don't know much about that but I guess I could supervise." David said. Alan laughed and David could hear him light his own cigarette. He sighed and tapped the ash of his off into the tray.

"*I'm sure that's what she had in mind.*" Alan teased. David laughed and thought of the hug they had shared when he left the last time they were down.

"I miss you." David said quietly and Alan sighed.

"*Me too.*" Alan whispered and David closed his eyes.

"Can we do this?" David asked. Amanda came out of the bathroom and went to the kitchen for a glass of water.

'Good night.' She mouthed and David winked at her. She smiled and headed off to bed.

"*Do what?*" Alan asked quietly pulling David back into the conversation.

"Get over this thing." David said. Alan sighed and David could hear him take a drag off of his cigarette.

"*Well, I think we'll never be over it. I think we can get used to living with it though.*"

"What about when we see each other? Isn't it awkward for you?" David asked.

"*Yes. But I can live through it to see you and Amanda.*"

"Ok, what about that hug? Have you thought about it as much as I have?"

"*That depends. How often do you think about it?*" Alan asked. David laughed and shook his head. He took a drag of his cigarette and stared up at the ceiling.

"Often." Alan sighed.

"*Me too.*"

"It was way too good for just a hug Alan. We need to do something other than that from now on." David said and Alan giggled.

"*That's the point David.*" Alan said. David's eyes shot open and he looked at the phone. He put it back to his ear and cleared his throat.

"You hugged me like that on purpose?" David asked. Alan laughed and blew another drag of his cigarette out.

"*Well, yea.*" David was speechless. He put his cigarette out and stood up. He walked up to the sink and got himself a glass of water. "*David, are you ok?*" Alan asked finally and David sighed.

"Alan, you're telling me you held me that close on purpose." David repeated. Alan giggled.

"*Yes, David.*" David took a deep breath and set his cup down.

"Why?" He asked and Alan laughed.

"*David, do I really have to explain that to you?*"

"Yes." David said. He picked his cup up and went back to the couch. He sat down and took a sip.

"*Why would YOU want to hold ME like that?*" Alan asked. David sighed and shook his head.

"So I could be as close as possible to you without it hurting mom's feelings." David said quietly.

"*See, you're smarter than you look.*" David laughed.

"Alan, I feel like I'm in the middle of a really weird affair." David said.

"*An affair? David, one thing at a time here.*" Alan teased and David laughed.

"You're a dick. You know what I mean."

"*I'm sorry. You're right. It is weird. How about a hand shake next time?*" Alan offered. David thought about it for a second.

"Ok, but I'm really going to miss being hugged like that." David said. Alan giggled and took the last drag from his cigarette.

"*Then deal with the weird affair feeling.*" Alan said and David rolled his eyes.

"I guess we'll play it by ear when you get here."

"*Sounds good.*" Alan said. David put out his cigarette and took his cup to the kitchen.

"So, next Friday then?" David asked.

"*Yep. Next Friday.*"

"Ok, good night Alan."

"*Good night David.*" Alan said in his sexy seductive voice. David sighed and hung up the phone. He put it back on the receiver and shut the lights off. He went into his room and Amanda was sitting up reading her book.

"Was that Alan?" Amanda asked as David shut the door behind him.

"Yea, they'll be down next Friday." David said as he climbed in next to her.

"We need to do some grocery shopping before they get here." She said and set her book aside. David nodded and lifted his arm to get ready for Amanda to cuddle up with him. She rested her head on his chest and he rubbed her back with the arm she laid on.

"I love you." David whispered and Amanda kissed his chest.

"I love you too." Amanda said. David smiled and shut the lamp off. It wasn't long until they were both asleep.

Chapter 14

After work the next day, David picked up Seth so they could go ring shopping. Seth was dressed in a pair of black pants and a black t-shirt. He had on a black trench coat that reminded David of Gabe's. His hair waved in the slight breeze as he walked to the car. David sighed and shook his head at the beauty of it. Seth got into the car and smiled.

"Ready for ring shopping?" He asked and David smiled.

"Yep." David said and pulled away from the house.

"Do you have an idea where you want to start looking?" Seth asked. David sighed and thought for a second.

"A jewelry store." David said and Seth laughed. He looked at David and shook his head.

"Wow, how will you ever find the perfect ring in a jewelry store?" Seth asked in a sarcastic voice and David laughed. He looked at Seth and sighed again. It was uncanny how much Seth reminded him of Gabe. David bit his bottom lip and admired his long hair against the long black coat. He shook his head and looked away. "What's with you today?" Seth asked noticing David's odd behavior. David smiled and shook his head.

"Nothing." David said. He was so attracted Seth. It was always more intense when he wore his trench coat.

"It's not nothing. Tell me." Seth said. David looked at Seth and took a deep breath.

"There is only one thing that makes you sexier than usual and it's that coat." He answered. Seth smiled and shook his head.

"What is with you and the long hair and trench coats?"

"Well, Gabe wore a trench coat like that." David said. Seth rolled his eyes and it occurred to David that the statement seemed to bother him. "Are you ok?" He asked. Seth shook his head and looked into David's deep blue eyes. David stopped at a red light and was able to meet Seth's gaze.

"Sometimes I think your attraction to me is just because of this Gabe dude." Seth said. David was amazed at the honestly hurt sound in Seth's voice.

"If it was, why do you care? You're straight. It's not like we're dating or something." David said. Seth sighed and shook his head. He looked out the windshield at the cars driving by.

"David, I've never had a friend like you. I was serious when I said to you that if I was ever going to try anything with a guy, it would be with you. I just think that this Gabe guy is the only reason you have any interest in me at all." Seth said. David blinked and the light turned green. He started driving again and pulled into the parking lot at the mall. He shut off the car and looked at Seth.

"Seth, you were drunk when you said all that stuff." David said. Seth shook his head and rolled his eyes.

"Well, it was true." He said. David sighed and looked at the steering wheel.

"Seth, you do remind me of Gabe. But you're not him. There are just some things about you that remind me of him. That's all."

"So, if I remind you of him, then half of the attraction is how you felt about him. Wouldn't it?" Seth asked. David sighed and looked at him but he looked down at the floor of the car.

"Seth, are you jealous of a dead guy?" David asked. Seth giggled at the question and looked at David.

"No." Seth said and his face turned red. David laughed and shook his head.

"You have nothing to worry about. You are sexy because you're Seth. Not because you remind me of Gabe. And besides, what do you care? It's not like your available or anything."

"That's not the point." Seth said and sighed. David frowned and looked at Seth's face.

"Wanna explain to me what the point is then?" David asked. Seth sighed and looked at David. He looked as though he was really struggling with whatever he was going to say. David smiled and ran his hand through Seth's hair. Seth smiled and shook his head.

"That's the point David. Girls like me cause I have money and looks. They always want to be the ONE if you know what I mean. You're different. You don't care about my money or anything like that. You just like ME." Seth said. David smiled and shook his head. He took the key out of the ignition and put it in his pocket.

"Well, what's wrong with that?" David asked feeling like there was more to the story. Seth sighed and fidgeted with his hands.

"It's strange to be liked for me. I'm a trophy for most people." David laughed and shook his head.

"Seth, half the time I'm pissed with you. You're hardly a trophy."

"What? Why are you pissed with me?" Seth asked. David laughed again and looked into Seth's eyes.

"Half of the sex I have with Amanda is because I have to fix what YOU'VE done. You have no idea how sexy you are, and if you do, it's not nice what you do with your trophy looks and killer body." David said. Seth laughed and shook his head.

"Well, you're so easy David, how can I resist?" He asked. David laughed and they both got out of the car. David walked up beside Seth and smelled his hair. Seth closed his eyes and faced David. He giggled and looked into Seth's face. "What if I told you, I wasn't entirely NOT interested in you?" Seth asked. David raised his eyebrows and they started walking to the big glass doors of the mall.

"Well, I don't know what I would say." David said. Seth giggled and opened the door for David.

"What if I told you I would be willing to try it?" Seth asked. David sighed and looked at the jewelry store off to the right.

"I would say, 'incredible timing Seth'" David said as he stared at the shining jewels in the glass cases. Seth grabbed David's arm and drug him to the store.

"How about, I help you with the right ring and you talk to me about being with guys." Seth said as they looked down at the hundreds of rings in the first case.

"Look at all these." David said. Seth smiled and looked into David's eyes.

"Are you avoiding the conversation?" Seth asked quietly.

"Yes." David said. Seth giggled as the jeweler approached them.

"Can I help you?" She asked. David looked up at her and smiled.

"I'm looking for an engagement ring." David said. The lady raised her eyebrows and looked at Seth. Seth laughed and David rolled his eyes. "It's not for him." David said and looked into the case.

"What did you have in mind?" The woman asked. David perused the case and picked out a few to look at. Seth smiled as David looked the rings over.

"How much?" Seth asked as David kept going back to the same ring.

"Cost doesn't matter." David said. Seth smiled and shook his head. The action pushed the scent of Seth's shampoo and cologne into David's face. He closed his eyes and shook off the feeling it gave him.

"You don't want to buy a cheap ring." Seth said and checked the price on David's favorite. "See, anything less than a grand is like telling her you settle for what's easiest. If you have to work for it, it will be worth more to her. It will show her that you're willing to fight for her to have the best." Seth said. He put the ring back on the counter and led David out of the store.

"Won't it mean something to her just because I picked it out?" David asked. Seth smiled and shook his head.

"See, it's that romantic shit that adds to the glamour of ring shopping. Keep that crap in mind but don't cheap out. She has to ware it for the rest of her life you know." Seth said. David sighed and shook his head.

"Seth, I don't think you know Amanda that well. She wouldn't care if the ring came from a gumball machine." David said as they walked through the mall.

"Don't think like that. You want her to love it right?" Seth asked. David nodded and looked at the store they were approaching. "Then you get her the best. She's worth it isn't she?" Seth asked. David smiled and nodded. Seth smiled and gestured to the store. "Then we shop here." David stepped in and looked in the cases. The rings were beautiful and David couldn't see one under $999.

"So, you think the perfect ring is in here?" David asked. Seth smiled and led David to the display case with the engagement rings. David looked in and gasped. The rings in the case were breath taking.

"Anything you like?" A young woman said from behind the case.

"That one." David said pointing at the one that had really caught his eye. The woman smiled and opened the case. Seth looked at the ring David picked and smiled.

"Now you're talking." Seth said as David inspected the little ring. It had three small diamonds on it and was a mixture of pink and white gold. "That's an Amanda ring if I ever saw one." Seth whispered into David's ear. David smiled and nodded.

"I'll take it." David said to the woman without looking at the price. She smiled and took the ring to the counter. It rang through at $1599. David sighed and took out his credit card. Seth giggled and nonchalantly ran his hand across David's back. David shivered and the woman smiled.

"She's a lucky girl." The woman said and David smiled. She put the ring in a black velvet box then put it in a small pearl colored bag. David took the bag and the receipt and put them in the inside pocket of the jacket. They walked out of the store and Seth stopped him. David looked at him and smiled.

"Thanks for helping me Seth." He said. Seth smiled and moved close to David. David stood very still as Seth ran his hands along David's chest. He slid his hand into David's jacket pocket and took out the receipt.

"No evidence." Seth whispered and put the receipt in his pocket. David swallowed hard and Seth smiled. "You're stacked David." Seth said referring to the muscles adorned on David's chest and stomach and they both laughed. David shook his head and started to walk. Seth walked next to him and sighed. "Does it bother you that I randomly touch you like that?" Seth asked quietly as they walked.

"Yes." David said and Seth giggled.

"Aren't I supposed to be the one acting weird about physical contact?"

"Well, you're not the one who is restricted to the kind of rules that force you to behave yourself." David said. Seth nodded and stopped David again.

"If you had one minute of no restricted rules, what would you do with it?" Seth asked in a seductive voice. David looked into Seth's eyes.

"Make it count." David answered and started walking again. Seth giggled and walked with David to the food court. They got a drink and sat down at a table. David took out the ring and looked at it. Seth smiled and leaned back in his chair.

"Have any idea how you're going to ask?" Seth asked and sipped his drink. David shook his head and sighed.

"I thought I might just have my mom put it in her cake." David said. Seth smiled and nodded.

"Very romantic. She has to say yes to something like that." David giggled and put the ring back in his pocket. He looked across the table at Seth and sighed.

"Ok, so my side of the deal huh?" David asked.

"What do you mean?" Seth asked. David shook his head and looked around the food court. The mall was close to the collage so there were a lot of collage guys in the mall.

"You helped me find a ring so I have to explain the guy on guy thing remember?" David asked and Seth laughed.

"It's the bluntness about you I like so much I think." Seth said. David giggled and gestured to a guy at the smoothie stand with his head. Seth looked at him and then looked back at David.

"Ok, What?" Seth asked.

"Hot or not?" David asked and took a sip of his drink. Seth looked at the guy again. He was wearing a pair of slightly baggy blue jeans and a white hoody with some kind of skateboard logo on it. He had shaggy blond hair and a very attractive face.

"Not bad?" Seth asked not sure how to answer. David giggled and gestured to another guy standing by a pay phone. Seth looked over at him. He was in a business suit. He was an older guy than the one at the smoothie place but still young enough for the purposes of David's game. He was well built from the looks of it and had a bit of a tan. He had black hair that was wavy and combed to one side. He had a nicely shaped jaw and looked very impressive with his light collared sunglasses. "Um, hot?" Seth asked. David laughed and shook his head and Seth sighed. "I don't have good taste or what?" He asked. David giggled and gestured to one more guy. Seth looked at the third contestant. He had long black wavy hair. He was wearing a black leather jacket and blue jeans. He was also very well built and had a slight tan. He had a goatee that seemed to give him a rugged look. Seth looked back at David and shrugged. "Hot?" Seth asked. David shook his head.

"Seth which one is the hottest?" David asked. Seth took another look at each guy. He looked back at David. He had his hair slicked straight back like he always did. His strong jaw line and piercing blue eyes almost startled Seth.

"You." Seth said. David blinked at him and frowned.

"Me?" David said looking back at the guy in the hoody. Seth smiled and took a sip of his drink.

"You." He repeated. David shook his head and laughed.

"You're hopeless." David said and Seth rolled his eyes.

"Hoody guy is in no way built like you. Suit guy is way too into himself. You can tell by the shades and the hairdo. Leather coat guy only wishes he could pull it off like you do. Sorry, you win." Seth said. David laughed and looked at each of the guys. A collage guy walked passed his view. He was dressed in tight blue jeans and a jean jacket. His curly brown hair was pulled back in a ponytail which was mostly hidden by a cowboy hat. He wore a black leather belt with a medium sized collage rodeo buckle on it. He had long skinny but well-built looking legs that ended in a pair of aggressive looking black cowboy boots.

"What about him?" David asked. Seth looked at the cowboy and laughed.

"Yea David, he's a real stallion." Seth said. David laughed and the guy looked at them. Seth giggled and winked at the cowboy. David kicked him under the table and Seth laughed. The guy walked over to the table and spun a chair around. He straddled the chair and Seth smiled. "David, meet Kurt. Kurt, this is David." Seth said. David looked at Kurt and smiled.

"Hi." David said.

"Howdy." Kurt said and tipped his hat. Seth giggled and took a sip of his drink.

"How's collage?" Seth asked Kurt. Kurt looked at him and shook his head.

"Not as cool as it is in the movies." He said and Seth laughed. "How's Lance?"

"He's the same as always. Mom and dad finally moved into the big house so he has the place to himself. He sure likes it that way."

"What a world you guys live in. Parents move out instead of the kids. How does that even happen?" Kurt asked. David and Seth both laughed. Kurt looked back at David and smiled. "So what's your story?" He asked. David raised his eyebrows and took a deep breath.

"Nothing like Seth's." David said. A couple of guys waved at Kurt and he smiled at them.

"I gotta go. You should tell me about it sometime." Kurt said and winked at David. Seth giggled and said bye to Kurt as he walked from the table.

"You know him?" David asked. Seth giggled and stood up so David did the same.

"Yup." Seth said and started to walk again. David caught up and stopped him.

"And? How do you know him?" David asked. Seth giggled and tossed his hair. David sighed and closed his eyes to shake the reaction he always had to Seth's beautiful hair.

"We used to go to the same school. I'm a grade under him but let's just say, he would rather I WAS right under him." Seth said. David blinked and looked back at the gorgeous cowboy. Seth giggled and shook his head. David looked into Seth's eyes and swallowed hard. "So, who's hotter? Me or Kurt?" Seth asked. David rolled his eyes and leaned into Seth to whisper in his ear.

"You." David whispered. Seth smiled and closed his eyes. He put his hands on David's hips and pulled David closer to him.

"If I didn't know better, I would think you were just saying that because I was the one that asked." Seth said. David's breathing picked up a little and Seth licked his lips.

"It wouldn't matter who asked. The answer would have been you." David said. Seth bit his bottom lip and stared in David's eyes.

"Here's that moment again where one of us has to laugh and back away." Seth said quietly. David smiled and closed his eyes.

"Why do I get the feeling you're not the one backing down this time?" David whispered. Seth giggled and shook his head. David gave a defeated sigh and stepped back. Seth laughed and turned to walk toward the doors. David took one last look at Kurt. Kurt smiled at him and tipped his hat again. David sighed and followed Seth out to the car. They got in at the same time and David shook his head. "Why?" David asked turning to face Seth. Seth blinked and looked at David.

"Why what?" Seth asked. David shook his head and started the car.

"I am going to propose to Amanda in a little over a week. Carman needs my help with something before his date with Jake on Friday. You're introducing me to these hot guys that just seem too good to be true and YOUR always leading me on and then walking away. And Alan . . ." David sighed and pulled out of the parking lot.

"Stop the car." Seth said and David looked at him.

"Why?" David asked.

"Just stop the car." Seth said. He sounded almost angry. David rolled his eyes and turned the car around. He found another parking spot in the mall and forcefully put the vehicle in park.

"What?" David asked. Seth shook his head and stared into David's eyes.

"One minute starting now." Seth said in an even tone. David frowned at him and looked out the windshield.

"What are you talking about?" David asked.

"One minute, David. You're running out of time." Seth said in an angry tone. David realized that Seth was referring to the conversation they had about removing the rules for one minute and what David would do with the time he had. He looked at Seth and shook his head.

"Are you kidding? This is the kind of shit I'm talking about. So what? We make out or whatever for a minute and then you go back to thinking it's funny to torture me with your sexy stares and your hair tossing? How about the leg rubs under the table or the whispering and the closeness? Oh, and my personal favorite, the ONE MINUTE OF FREEDOM!" David yelled. He got out of the car and walked across the parking lot. Seth caught up with him and spun him around. He hit David with the post powerful kiss he had ever felt. David's eyes grew wide as Seth kissed him. Seth whimpered and David's breathing sped up. He wrapped his arms around him and closed his eyes. Seth pulled David close to him and held him there with his surprisingly strong arms. David moaned and wrapped his hands in Seth's long black hair. Seth whimpered again and slowed the kiss. He pulled his face away and looked into David's eyes. David's body shook and Seth smiled.

"I promise not to lead you on if I don't plan on ending your day like that." Seth whispered. David blinked and stared into Seth's eyes.

"Seth. You're straight." David breathed and Seth laughed.

"Yep, I am. I have to admit that kissing you was pretty cool but, it's not my bag. But I would like to kiss you whenever you wanted me to just to stay off that list." Seth said. David laughed and backed away from Seth.

"You're the coolest straight guy I've ever met. But I don't want you to kiss me just to stay off the hit list. You've got a free pass for being a dick now." David said. Seth laughed and they walked back to the car. They got in and David looked back over at him. "For the record, that was a better kiss than I thought you were capable of." He said and started the car. Seth laughed. They talked about the ring in the cake idea for the drive home. Seth thought that it was the most romantic thing that David will probably ever do. They laughed at Seth's teasing. David parked at the apartment building and they both went in. They stepped into the elevator and David was vibrating.

"What's up with you?" Seth asked quietly as the elevator made its climb.

"You kissed me." David said quietly and Seth laughed.

"We're not over that yet?" David shook his head and looked at Seth.

"No, I thought you would be off the list of bad timing and sexually frustrating situations but, you're not. Now you're on the top." David whispered. Seth smiled and cleared his throat.

"Do you wish now that I didn't do it?" Seth asked. David smiled at him.

"No, I'm glad you did. Just try to keep yourself from becoming a problem." David said. Seth laughed as the doors opened. They went into David's apartment and Amanda was putting chicken in the oven.

"How was your day?" Amanda asked as David came in and got himself and Seth a beer.

"Good, yours?" He asked and kissed her on his way to the table.

"Well, Mike has a tooth ache and Carman has been calling for you for the last two hours." She said and went to the sink. David sighed and looked at Seth.

"See, it never ends." David said. Seth giggled and took a sip of his beer.

"You should call him." Amanda said as she sat down at the table.

"Why wouldn't he call my cell phone?" David asked. Amanda shrugged and sipped at the water she had brought to the table with her. David rolled his eyes and took his cell phone out of his pocket and phoned Carman.

"*It's about time.*" Carman said when he answered the phone. David laughed and shook his head.

"Was I supposed to be in a hurry?" David asked.

"*Yes.*" Carman scolded. David laughed again and sipped his beer.

"Ok, what's the rush?"

"*Now David.*" Carman said. David frowned and got up. He walked into the bathroom and locked the door behind him.

"Now what?" David said quietly. Carman sighed and stayed silent for a moment.

"*It's Wednesday night. My date is on Friday. I happen to have the guts to do this now so let's do it.*" Carman said. David giggled and shook his head.

"Right now?" David asked. Carman seemed irritated on the other end of the phone.

"*Yes, right now.*" He said. David sighed and shook his head.

"I've been gone all day. What would Amanda think if I up and took off again?" David asked quietly and Carman sighed. "Carman I will do it if you think it can't wait for tomorrow." David said thinking of Seth's kiss and suddenly really wanting to have a few minutes with Carman. Seth was an alright kisser but Carman made kissing feel like sex.

"*No, you're right. It's too short of notice. It could probably wait for tomorrow.*" Carman said and sighed again. David smiled and shook his head.

"Carman, I can't believe I'm saying this but, I'll be there in twenty minutes." He said knowing that it really was now or never. Carman was quiet for a moment then cleared his throat again.

"*Ok.*" He said and hung up the phone. David hung his up too and rolled his eyes. He stepped out of the bathroom and smiled at Amanda.

"How long till supper is ready?" He asked.

"About an hour." Amanda said looking at the clock. David nodded and looked at Seth.

"I guess I'll take you home then. I gotta stop by and see Carman for a little bit. I'll be back in time for supper though." David said. Amanda smiled and nodded. Seth got up and took a long sip of his beer. David kissed Amanda and she giggled at the passion behind it. David smiled at her and he and Seth left the apartment.

"What's going on?" Seth asked. David rolled his eyes and rubbed his forehead with his fingers.

"Remember that list?" David asked. Seth nodded as they stepped into the elevator.

"It just got more complicated." David answered. Seth frowned and pushed the ground floor button.

"Ok, what's going on?"

"Well, he's ready for that thing I'm supposed to do." David said. Seth raised his eyebrows and looked at David.

"So, the size thing? What are you going to do?"

"No idea" David said as they stepped from the elevator. They walked out to the car and got in.

"You wanna talk about it?" David sighed and shook his head. He started the car and closed his eyes as it roared to life. He smiled and put it into gear. He pulled out of the parking lot and drove towards Lance's house. "You're not talking." Seth said and David giggled.

"No I'm not." David said and stared out the windshield. Seth seemed uncomfortable next to David and he sighed. "Look, Seth. This is a big deal. I'm not sure what I'm going to do. I think just going there and going with whatever happens. That's what I'm going to have to do." David said. Seth nodded and looked at David.

"Maybe I should have held off on that kiss." Seth said.

"What? No. It's not that at all. That kiss was perfectly timed. Carman isn't." David said. Seth nodded and smiled.

"Well, I wanna hear how it goes." He said. David laughed and shook his head. They drove the rest of the way to Lance's place in silence. David parked in front and Seth sighed. "Good luck." Seth said. He had that jealous sound in his voice again.

"Seth, are you ok?" David asked. Seth smiled at him and nodded.

"Yea, just a little jealous I guess."

"What? Why?" David asked. Seth sighed and shook his head.

"I promised my dad he wouldn't be the only straight guy in our family. You gotta help me keep that promise." Seth said and David blinked at him.

"You're faking straight?" David asked and Seth rolled his eyes.

"No, I just find it really easy to like YOU." Seth said. David laughed and shook his head.

"God. Not today Seth. Ok. We'll talk about this later." David said. Seth smiled and nodded. "Look, I need one normal friend ok."

"I know. You teach me to be." Seth said. David sighed and rolled his eyes.

"Ok." David said. Seth got out of the car and waved as he walked with his sexy swagger to the house. David shook his head and pulled away.

UN FUCKING BELEIVABLE! How can this be my life? I would give anything to be stuck in a room with Alan and my mom now. That's a way easier thing to deal with. If I have one more day like today, Gabe's tree is going to start looking pretty good again. Seth interested in me. Fuck what a turn. I wish now I had just grown some balls and told Alan how I felt. I would still be at home; Amanda would be the only thing interested in having sex with me. Well, Alan, but he would be easier to deal with than Seth and Carman. I could always just go home and not go to Carman.

David thought as he passed the apartment building turn off. He shook his head and stared out the windshield. He could see Carman's house and it looked as though every traffic light was green on the way. David sighed as the distance between him and Carman got smaller. He pulled into the yard and parked in front of the house. He stared at the door and took a deep breath. He got out of the car and slowly walked up the stairs onto the front deck. He took another deep breath and stepped in. He could see Carman standing at the counter. David threw his keys on the table as he walked by and, deciding to just get it over with, pushed Carman against the counter. He giggled and kissed David. David moaned as Carman kissed him. His tongue felt like silk and he tasted like mint and rum. David held Carman at the counter and pressed his body against his shaking torso. Carman whimpered and raked his hands through David's hair. David took his jacket off while he kissed Carman. He put his hands on the low of Carman's back and pulled him away from the counter. Carman moaned and his voice shook. David's breathing was heavy and his heart pounded in his chest. Carman ran his hands down David's back and around to his stomach. David pulled away and stared into his eyes. They were both breathing quite heavy. David looked down at Carman's hands and raised his eyebrows.

"Well, it's now or never." David whispered and pulled Carman into another deep powerful kiss. He pushed his throbbing erection against Carman and Carman sucked in a deep breath. David continued kissing and waited for Carman's reaction. He was shocked when Carman ran his hand down the bulge in his pants. David moaned and pushed himself against Carman's hand. Carman breathed heavy into David's face and closed his eyes.

"Oh my God David. You're huge." Carman whispered and David smiled.

"Are you scared?" David asked between kisses. He nodded and David kissed deeper. Carman moaned and squeezed David's large erection. David whimpered and pushed against his hand again. Carman stopped the kiss and pulled David over to the couch. David giggled as he pushed him down onto it and lay on top of him. Carman kissed him again and pushed his own erection against David's. David moaned and dug his fingernails into his back.

"This is about when I freak out and come up with a reason to stop." Carman whispered. David smiled and pulled Carman back into their kiss. Carman moaned and moved his hips in a mock sex action. David whimpered and moved his hips with Carman.

"Less scary?" David asked in a sleepy whisper. Carman smiled and trusted himself harder against David. David heaved at Carman's strength and they both giggled.

"Still scary." Carman whispered and kissed David again. David rolled Carman so he was now on top. Carman's body vibrated as David ran his hand down his side. He rested it on Carman's hip and looked into his eyes.

"So, what's it going to take?" David asked in a seductive whisper. His erection was almost painful against his jeans and Carman's sexy frame. Carman took a deep breath and ran his hand down David's chest. He slowly ran his hand down to his stomach and then down to his throbbing erection. David closed his eyes. He was so careful and seemed so nervous. David cleared his throat and undid the button and fly of his jeans. Carman's breathing turned panicked and David smiled. "Layers, Carman. I just don't know what else to do for you." David whispered. Carman sighed and pulled David down into another kiss. He pushed his hips against David's and quietly moaned. David pushed back and ran his erection against Carman's. He closed his eyes and put his hands back on David's hips.

"Take them off." Carman whispered and David raised his eyebrows. He pushed his jeans off but left his boxers on. Carman shook underneath of him. "We're down to three layers now." Carman said and swallowed hard. David giggled and nodded.

"Now what?" He asked. Carman sighed and undid the button and fly on his own jeans. David smiled and slowly pulled them off. Carman shook almost violently. David lay back on top of him and Carman moaned.

"Fuck you're really big." Carman whispered in an almost terrified voice. David kissed Carman and pushed their erections together again. Carman whimpered and shook even more. David stopped and looked into Carman's eyes.

"Carman, you're scared out of your mind. I think we should stop." He whispered and Carman sighed. He grabbed David and rolled them over again. But this time he lay David on his side and lay down facing him. They kissed again and Carman slowly reached down David's boxers and took him into his hand. David was vibrating now. He tightened his grip and David moaned. Carman moved his hand and kissed David again. David ran his hand down and took Carman into his hand as well. Carman shook and his heart raced. "Are you ok?" David asked. Carman tightened his grip again and David giggled. Carman moaned as David touched him and to David's surprise, Carman climaxed. He giggled again and kissed Carman.

"Sorry." Carman whispered with a face as red as a fire truck and David laughed.

"Are you kidding? You're apologizing for that? Don't." David said and pulled Carman's hand off of his erection.

"I can finish for you." Carman whispered. David smiled and shook his head. He figured stopping now would save him from more to explain to Alan.

"Save it for Jake. If you can go this far, you'll be too excited to stop with him." David said and kissed Carman again. Carman whimpered as David kissed him. "Think you'll survive?" David asked. Carman giggled and nodded so David smiled and sat up. He looked down at his erection and shook his head. He grabbed his jeans and pulled them on. Carman smiled at him and sat up too.

"Thank you David. That was very helpful." Carman whispered and kissed David's shoulder. David laughed and looked at him.

"Thank me when its Jake you're on the couch with." David said. Carman giggled and shook his head. "I hate to do this, but I have to go. I promised Amanda I wouldn't be late for supper." David said and kissed Carman again.

"Ok." Carman said and stood up. He pulled his own jeans on and handed David his jacket. "I owe you big time." Carman added. David laughed and readjusted his still erect penis.

"Next time. Finish the job." David said and smiled.

"I offered." Carman said and David laughed.

"I'm just fucking with you. See you tomorrow." David said and headed for the door.

"See you." Carman said.

Chapter 15

For the next few days, David managed to avoid Seth and keep the sexually frustrating chatter with Carman to a minimal. His date with Jake had been a success and he had another one planned for the Friday of Alan and Nancy's arrival.

"So, I thought that they should stay with you." Carman said as they drove back to David's apartment after work. David rolled his eyes and sighed.

"What? Why?" David asked suddenly a little nervous of the idea of having Alan in his home for a whole night.

"Well, Jake and I have another date on Friday and, just in case, I would like an empty house."

"Uh, huh. Can't you just explain to Jake that you have company coming down and you don't have time for your date?" David asked still reeling over the thought of Alan in his boxers or naked in his shower.

"What? Would you do that?" Carman asked. David sighed and shook his head. Carman laughed and lit a cigarette. "David, I'm going to bring the bed you and Amanda slept in at my place over tonight. Amanda wants them to have a nice room to stay in so she wants tomorrow morning to set it up."

"Ok. So Amanda already knew about this?" David asked. Carman giggled and shook his head.

"David, haven't you learned yet that you're the last to know anything?" David and Carman both laughed at this. Carman stopped at a red light and looked at David. "So, what did you get for her?" Carman asked.

"It's a surprise." David said and Carman sighed.

"Her birthday is on Saturday. What are the odds of it getting back to her in two days?"

"That's 48 hours for her to talk it out of you. Forget it." David teased. Carman giggled and shook his head. They talked about moving the bed over and Carman's coming date with Jake on the way home. When they arrived, Amanda was busy cleaning the bathroom.

"Hi babe!" David called as they walked in.

"*Hi!*" She called from down the hall. David smiled and got both him and Carman a beer from the fridge. They sat down at the table and Carman smiled at him.

"So, what are you making for supper on Saturday?" Carman asked.

"Whatever she wants I guess." David said and sipped his beer. Amanda came into the room. She looked as though she must have been doing house work all day. She had stray hair that come out of her pony tail and was hanging in her face. She wore David's Iron Maiden rock t-shirt and a pair of cute low rider jeans.

"So, I was thinking. What if we rented some movies and ordered Chinese food for supper tomorrow night?" Amanda asked as she walked passed David and quickly kissed him on her way to put the cleaning supplies under the sink.

"Ok. Whatever you like." David said and checked her out as she bent over at the sink. Carman giggled and took a sip of his beer. David looked at him and smiled.

"Are you ok with them staying here?" Amanda asked. David smiled at her as she got herself a glass of water and came to sit at the table with them.

"Sure. Why not?" David asked. Carman giggled again and shook his head.

"You should have heard him Amanda. He wanted me to cancel my date just because they were coming." Carman tattled. David glared at him and Amanda laughed.

"Oh, David. It will be fine." She said. When Carman and David finished their drinks, they headed to Carman's to get the bed.

"I can't believe their going to be here tomorrow already." David said as he and Carman carried the box spring out to the truck.

"Well, I think it's nice that their coming down for Amanda's birthday. It will be good for you to have to deal with them on your own for a night too." Carman said as they carefully set the heavy box spring in the bed of the truck. David rolled his eyes and got out of the truck to get the mattress. Carman followed him and they finished loading the truck. When they got back to David's house, they unloaded the bed and put it back together. Amanda asked David to take one of the end tables from the living room into the music room where they had set the bed. He did as he was told and when the furniture was set up how Amanda liked, Carman and David went back to the table for another beer while Amanda put sheets and blankets on the bed.

"God, I wish I was dead." David said and put his head down on the table. Carman laughed and shook his head.

"I thought things were going good with you and Alan. Why are you so panicky?" Carman asked.

"Well, it's one thing to talk on the phone with him but, when I have to be face to face with him, it's a different story." David said not lifting his head.

"What if I told you he is just as nervous?" Carman asked quietly. David looked up now and sighed.

"That would be better." Carman smiled and nodded.

"This isn't easy for him either you know. He wants you in his life but he's not sure how to act around you."

"That makes two of us."

"Why can't you guys just be cool like you and I are? It's not like it was you two on my couch the other day." Carman said and winked. David rolled his eyes and took a long sip of his beer.

"We lasted a whole week without talking about that. Why bring it up now?" David asked.

"Are you feeling bad for doing it?" Carman asked. David sighed and shook his head.

"Of course not. I just don't want sex on the brain when Alan gets here."

"No, it will just hit you when he walks through the door." David laughed and shook his head. They finished their beers and Carman went home for the night. David and Amanda ate a light meal and Amanda got Mike into the tub when they were finished. David went into the living room and turned the T.V. on. He sat down on the couch and lit a cigarette. He looked at the phone and almost expected it to ring when it did.

"Don't be Alan." David said to the receiver and picked it up. "Hello." David said.

"*HI. Doesn't it feel like we haven't talked in over a week?*" Seth asked on the other end of the line. David smiled and shook his head.

"Well, it feels like that because we haven't." David said.

"*Wanna tell me why I kiss you and then we don't talk again afterward?*" Seth asked. David sighed and took a puff from his cigarette.

"Ok, I'm sorry. It's like I told you that day. That list gets worse and worse every day. I feel like everybody I know wants to fuck me or at least acts like they do."

"*You are the only guy I know that can find a problem with that.*" David laughed.

"Well, I'm special." David said.

"*Yes you are. But I had a reason I was calling.*"

"Ok, what's going on?" David asked. Seth sighed and David could hear him move where he was sitting or maybe actually sit down. Seth was the type that would pace when he talked on the phone.

"*I don't want you to avoid me anymore. I miss hanging out with you. Can I make it up to you or something?*"

"Seth, you're really important to me. I'm cool with you liking me or having this weird straight dude crush or whatever but, I really need a non-sexual friend right now. I'm serious when I say; I can't deal with all this sexual tension all the time." David explained. Seth giggled on the other end and David smiled.

"*Sounds doable.*" Seth said. David laughed and shook his head.

"Are you coming on Saturday?"

"*Fuck yea! I'm not missing that. I can't wait to see her face when she sees that ring.*" Seth said. David laughed and tapped the ash off of his cigarette into the ash tray.

"Yea, I can't wait till it's over with actually." Seth laughed and David smiled.

"*Getting nervous?*"

"Well, kind of. I feel like I know she'll say yes but there's still this thing in the pit of my stomach that keeps me nervous." David explained.

"*Well, I think that happens for everybody. Are you still doing the cake thing?*"

"Yea, it saves me from asking." David said. Seth laughed and David joined him.

"*You know, the whole down on one knee thing is what all girls want to see.*"

"Well, Amanda is going to be embarrassed just to find it let alone me making a spectacle in front of a bunch of people." David said.

"*Maybe. But I would wait to get a feel for it before I didn't do it. I would have a proposal speech thought of beforehand.*"

"I do, but it's for just in case." David said. Seth and David laughed and talked about all the possible ways Amanda could react to finding the ring. Amanda was finished bathing Mike so he ended his conversation with Seth and helped her get him ready for bed. When Mike was all tucked in, they went back to the couch and sat down. Amanda leaned against David as they watched the end of a ninja movie David had been looking at.

"You should tell Carman to bring this new boyfriend of his on Saturday." Amanda said. David giggled and looked into Amanda's eyes.

"Why? I mean I can but aren't we having enough people over already?"

"Yea, but I want to meet him." Amanda said. David smiled and kissed her.

"I was thinking, there's only a couple days for me to have sex with a tight little sixteen year old. You wouldn't be mean and take that last time away from me would you?" David asked. Amanda giggled and took the remote from David's hand. She shut off the T.V. and pulled David into their bedroom.

David woke up before the alarm and rolled over to cuddle Amanda. When he reached for her she wasn't there. He groaned and sat up. He looked around the room and seen that her house coat was missing. He stretched and got out of bed. He went to the bathroom and got ready for his day. When he finished applying his cologne and deodorant, he came out into the kitchen and sat at the table. Amanda smiled at him and got him a coffee.

"Good morning." Amanda said quietly and David smiled.

"Hi." David answered and Amanda laughed. "What time DO you get up in the morning?" David asked. Amanda giggled and sat down with him.

"I've only been up for a little while. I always seem to have to pee right at 6:30."

"That sucks. I wanna wake up and cuddle in the morning sometimes you know." David said and sipped his hot coffee. Amanda giggled and passed him his cigarettes.

"Are you ready for today?" She asked. David sighed and nodded. Amanda reached out and held David's hand. He looked down at her little fingers and smiled.

"I love you." David whispered and Amanda giggled.

"I love you too." She said and kissed him. David smiled and put his hand on her stomach.

"I can't wait till it's bigger than a little ball in there." David said and Amanda smiled at him.

"It won't take long." She whispered. They talked about the baby and Amanda's worry about furniture. David reassured her that they had lots of time for that and he promised they would go shopping for baby things very soon. He kept the crib Alan was bringing in mind as he spoke. He wondered what kind of taste Alan had in baby furniture as he and Amanda discussed the colors she wanted in the baby's room. It wasn't long before they could hear Carman honking the horn in his truck from down in the parking lot. David and Amanda giggled and both stood up. David kissed her and they said their good byes. David went down to the truck and got in.

"Have I got a deal for you." Carman said as David shut the truck door. David looked at him and giggled.

"Ok, what?" He asked. Carman leaned close to David and smiled.

"How would you like to help pick out Amanda's birthday present today?" Carman asked.

"You still don't have anything for her?" David asked. Carman smiled and pulled away from the apartment building. He drove out of town and headed down the highway. "We have an out of town job today?" David asked. Carman giggled and shook his head.

"We have nothing until this afternoon. Amanda's present is out here."

"What are you getting her?" David asked. Carman giggled and turned down a little gravel road. They drove in silence and David looked around. He didn't recognize the area so he couldn't even guess what Carman was up to. He pulled the truck into a little farm yard and got out. David followed him and looked around. Carman smiled and led David up to the door. He knocked and they waited for an answer. To David's surprise, Kurt from the mall answered the door.

"Hi there." He said. David looked at Carman and raised his eyebrows.

"Hi Kurt." David said. Carman was surprised.

"You know each other?" Carman asked. Kurt smiled and grabbed his hat. He put it on his head and stepped out onto the deck with Carman and David.

"Not well enough." Kurt said and winked at David. Carman giggled and looked at David. He just rolled his eyes and looked at Carman's eyes.

"What are we doing here?" David asked. Kurt smiled and led David and Carman out to the little red barn. David looked in and saw a little collie and a litter of puppies. "A puppy?" David asked half surprised and half unsure.

"She once told me she could never have a dog because her mom was allergic. She said she always wanted a Sheltie." Carman said. David smiled and remembered the fights she used to have with her dad over getting a dog.

"All you gotta do is pick one." Kurt said and David looked at him.

"I have no idea. I don't know anything about dogs." He said. One little puppy with black spots on its face and a blue eye came over to David and lay down on his foot. David laughed and picked the little dog up.

"Well, that's a sign if I ever saw one." Carman said. David smiled and looked at the little dog. He reminded David of Lassie other than the funny black freckles on his little white face.

"Well Carman. It's your gift and you probably know more about these things than I do. I would pick this one though." David said and looked at Carman. Both Kurt and Carman smiled and Carman decided that the puppy in David's hands was the one. Kurt handed them a little bag of puppy food and the first shots paperwork from his vet.

"She's gonna love him." Kurt said and put the little pup in a box with a towel.

"Thanks a lot Kurt." Carman said and shook the cowboy's hand. Kurt smiled and then looked at David.

"It's nice to see you again." Kurt said quietly and David smiled.

"Yea, you too." David said. They said their good byes and loaded up the little puppy into the truck. They got in and waved at Kurt as they drove away. Carman pulled out onto the little gravel road and looked at David. He was playing with the puppy in the box. It was growling at him and David laughed.

"So, Kurt?" Carman asked. David rolled his eyes but didn't look up from the playful little puppy.

"I met him at the mall last week." David said and laughed as the puppy tried to pull his finger off.

"And?" Carman pried. David giggled and looked up at Carman.

"And nothing. He used to go to school with Seth. That's all I know." David said. Carman rolled his eyes and shook his head.

"Uh, huh." Carman said and David laughed. He looked back at the little puppy. It was sitting in its box staring at David. He smiled at him and shook his head.

"Amanda is gonna love this thing." David said. Carman smiled and looked down at the little puppy as he pulled onto the highway.

"He's almost cuter than you." Carman teased. David laughed and shook his head. They decided to hide the puppy out at Carman's place until Saturday. They stopped at Carman's ranch and set up the second bathroom as a place for the little guy to live for now. They headed back out to the truck and left for their work day. When the day was done, Carman took David home and dropped him off. David went up to his apartment and stepped inside.

"Hi." Amanda said. She looked a little tired but seemed to be in a good mood. David kissed her and she giggled. "So, I went out and rented that new action comedy you wanted to see and the Chinese place is going to deliver at 6:30." Amanda said.

"Oh that one with the guy from Crank?" David asked referring to the movie and walked over to the fridge to get a beer.

"That's the one." Amanda said. She sat down at the table with him and looked at the clock. It was 4:30. David looked up to and took a deep breath. "It will be fine." Amanda whispered. Little Mike came out of his room and came to the table.

"I hungry." He said and Amanda smiled.

"You can't wait till supper? Auntie Nancy will be here and I think she said she was bringing you a present." Amanda said. Mike squealed and hugged Amanda.

"Alan coming too?" He asked and Amanda nodded. Mike giggled and looked at David. "Now you don't miss Alan!" He said and ran around the table to hug David. David picked him up and laughed.

"You're getting heavy." David said. Amanda smiled at them and went to the sink. She opened the cupboard and took the full garbage bag out.

"Can you take this out for me?" She asked looking down at the heavy looking bag. David smiled and put Little Mike down.

"Of course babe." He said. She kissed him and got a Jell-O out of the fridge for Mike while David tied the garbage bag. He took it to the door and looked back at Amanda. "I'm gonna have to do this every day when the baby comes aren't I?" He asked. Amanda giggled and shook her head.

"Well, I could always just let the baby pee on the floor. Would that be easier?" David giggled and stepped out the door. He went to the elevator and pushed the button. He waited for the elevator doors to open and stepped in.

"Going down?" The young lady in the elevator asked.

"Yea, thanks." David answered. His elevator partner was cute. She had long curly red hair and light colored freckles under her green eyes. She was wearing a red button up shirt and a black skirt. She was also wearing fishnet stockings and an awesome pair of tall high heeled boots. David raised his eyebrows and watched the numbers fall to 1.

"Nice ride." The girl said and winked. David giggled and stepped out of the elevator. He opened the door for the red head and stepped out after her. He walked to the garbage can and watched her walk passed his long black 1985 Hearse. She slowly ran her hand down the side of it and smiled at the car. David raised his eyebrows again and shook his head. He turned to go back inside when he saw Alan's Mustang pulling in. His breath caught in his throat and he stared as the wine colored car as it pulled up beside him. Alan wheeled down the window and smiled at David.

"Hi." Alan said. David looked in and looked at his mom.

"Hi." David said to her and she giggled.

"Hello dear. We made it." She said. Alan smiled and shook his head.

"I'll wait for you; you can park behind my car." David said. Alan nodded and pulled away. David watched him park as close as he could to the back bumper of David's beloved car. Nancy came over to him as Alan opened the back hatch where their luggage was kept.

"Hi David." She said and hugged him. David laughed and swung his mother around in a circle before putting her down.

"How was your trip?" He asked.

"Long. Just between you and me, that car is in need of more comfortable seats." She said and headed for the glass doors. David giggled and looked back at Alan. "Can you help him?" Nancy asked as she opened the door. David nodded and walked toward him.

"Hi." David said and offered his hand. Alan giggled but shook his hand anyway.

"That's weird." Alan said. David laughed and picked up the two blue suitcases on the ground.

"Matching luggage?" David asked thinking that was something an old retired couple did and Alan laughed.

"Well, they came as a pair on sale and your mother wanted new ones." Alan said taking a large gift wrapped present out of the trunk. They took the things inside and Alan went back to his car for his guitar. He came into the building and they loaded their things into the elevator. The doors closed and Alan stopped the lift. David could feel his heart speed up. His hands were sweating instantly and he wanted to scream so the welling up feeling inside of him could escape. He looked at Alan and swallowed hard. Alan just stood there staring at him.

"What are you doing?" David asked in a barely audible voice. Alan smiled and shook his head.

"Just looking." He answered quietly. David giggled and shook his head.

"I thought we agreed to try to forget about this?" He asked. Alan sighed and looked into David's eyes.

"Yes, but it's a work in progress." David laughed and hugged Alan.

"I missed you." He whispered. Alan giggled and rubbed David's back.

"I know." Alan said. David laughed and smelled Alan's unmistakable cologne. Alan noticed and smiled. He buried his face in David's hair and hugged tighter. David shook in his arms and they both giggled. "Ok, let's get up stairs." Alan said and stepped away. David giggled and nodded.

"Cant hug or what?" David asked in a teasing voice. Alan raised his eyebrows and resumed their elevator ride.

"I can hug, it's the crap that could happen after the hug I'm trying to avoid." Alan said looking up at the climbing numbers. David laughed and picked up the two suit cases.

"You love being a dick, don't you?" David asked.

"Yes, yes I do." He said. They both laughed and stepped out of the elevator when the doors opened. David set the suitcases in the hall and took the guitar from Alan.

"What, no amp?" David asked.

"Don't you have one? I can't be expected to haul everything with me all the time." Alan answered. David giggled and shook his head.

"I just thought it was one of those things you don't leave home without." Alan laughed and took the large gift into the apartment. David followed with the guitar and a suitcase. Alan was hugging Amanda and Nancy passed David to get the other case.

"Oh, it's good to see you." Amanda said. Alan smiled and hugged her for a few seconds. He let her go and looked at her.

"You know, you're starting to look pregnant now." He said. Amanda blushed and looked at David.

"Isn't it great?" David asked.

"Next thing you know you'll be resting your dinner plate on there." Alan said. David and Amanda laughed. David led Alan to his room in the music room. He set the guitar down and got the suit case from his mom. He took it to the room and Alan smiled at him. "Looks nice in here." He said. David looked at the bed and back at Alan.

"Well, that's cause your bed is in here." David said without thinking. He instantly blushed and looked away. Alan giggled and patted David's back as they left the room.

"So I ordered Chinese food, I hope that's ok." Amanda said.

"Oh, that will be perfect dear." Nancy said and they all sat down at the table. Alan looked across the table at David and Amanda smiled.

"So, how's work?" Alan asked. David sighed and rolled his eyes.

"We're gonna talk about work?" David asked. Alan laughed and Amanda and Nancy gave each other confused looks.

"I was going to ask you Nancy, what was Lyn's parents' names? I've been having a really hard time finding them." Amanda said. Nancy rubbed her forehead with her fingers in thought.

"I think her dads name was John." She said. They got up and went right to the computer. David sighed and looked back at Alan.

"Beer?" He asked. Alan giggled and nodded. David got up and went to the fridge. He took out two beers and opened them both. He handed one to Alan and sat back down.

"So, where's Carman? I thought he would be here today." Alan asked taking a long sexy sip of his beer. David sighed at the sight of Alan and swallowed hard.

"Um, he has a date with Café Guy." David said and lit a cigarette.

"Oh yea. I forgot about that. That's why we're staying here right?" Alan asked. The question was more of a dig than anything else. David rolled his eyes and took a sip of his drink. It foamed up a bit when he set it down and Alan smiled. "Nice head." Alan said. David laughed and shook his head.

"Ass hole." David whispered and Alan smirked.

"Are you gonna play with me while I'm here?" Alan asked. David shot a look at him and then to his mother, then back to Alan.

"Am I gonna what?" David asked in a panicked whisper. Alan laughed and shook his head.

"Play guitar you walking hard on." Alan whispered. David laughed and took a drag from his cigarette.

"Oh, um maybe." David said. Alan laughed again and took another sip of his beer. All David could imagine was being attached to the long slender neck of the bottle in Alan's hand and mouth. He cleared his throat and looked away.

"Well, you better. I don't like bringing her along if she isn't going to get used." Alan said. David smiled and looked back at him.

"We'll see." David said. Just then Amanda squealed and Nancy clapped. David and Alan both looked over at the women at the computer.

"What?" Alan asked. Nancy and Amanda both looked at them.

"We found Lyn's parents. They're in Vegas." Amanda said. She smiled at David and he winked at her.

"So now what?" David asked.

"Now we call." Nancy said and got the phone. Amanda dialed the number with shaky fingers and waited.

"Answering machine." She said quietly to Nancy.

"Well, leave a message." Nancy whispered excitedly. Amanda was silent for a few seconds then said.

"Um, hi. My Name is Amanda Moore. I am Gabe's little sister, I mean, was Gabe's sister. Listen, I was wondering, if it's ok with you, would you get in touch with your daughter Lyn and tell her I called. I would love to speak with her. My number is 702-555-7798. Thank you." Amanda said and hung up. "Was that good?" She asked Nancy. Nancy hugged her and they both giggled. They got back to work on the computer.

"Think you'll inherit more kids?" Alan asked in a very quiet whisper. David looked at him and laughed.

"God, I hope not." David said and took the last drag from his cigarette and put it out.

"You look good." Alan whispered and David raised an eyebrow.

"Do I?" He asked in a far more seductive voice then he meant. Alan laughed and shook his head. David laughed too and took a sip from his drink.

"You should play with me." Alan said talking about the guitars again. David smiled and shook his head.

"I haven't played since before . . ." David stopped talking and looked at his beer bottle. There was condensation on the outside and it left a ring on the wooden table. Alan smiled at him and leaned on the table.

"You gotta get back on the horse, son." Alan said and David shot his eyes up to meet Alan's.

"Did you just call me *son*?" David asked in a whisper. Alan blinked and thought back to what he just said.

"I did. Didn't I?" Alan asked. David slowly nodded and took another sip of his beer.

"You know what, that's a total turn off." David said excitedly. Alan frowned and looked into David's eyes.

"This is a good thing because?" Alan asked in a whisper. David smiled and looked at his mom.

"Problem solved, pops." David said. Alan laughed and shook his head.

"Oh God. Can you call me something other than pops? It makes me sound old."

"Ok, how about, *dad*?" David asked. They both laughed and Nancy looked at them.

"What's so funny?" She asked. David and Alan where still laughing as David turned to look at her.

"Well, dad is a funny guy mom." He said and they both laughed again. Nancy and Amanda exchanged confused looks again and decided it was better not to comment.

"That does help, doesn't it?" Alan asked. David giggled and nodded.

"Yea, it's hard to wanna fuck when it's your dad you're talking to." David whispered and took a sip from his beer. Alan coughed and then laughed. David joined him. They discussed David's job and the color scheme they were thinking of for the baby's room. They hadn't decided on a color yet but they were working on it. It wasn't long before the food arrived. David paid the young Chinese guy at the door and brought the food to the table. Amanda and Nancy got plates and cutlery out and Alan got Mike ready to eat.

"Thanks Alan." Mike said very politely. Amanda smiled at him with a very maternal look in her eyes. David giggled and looked at Mike.

"It's grandpa to you little guy." He said. Alan laughed and looked at Nancy.

"Grandpa." She said under her breath. Mike clapped and looked up at Alan's face.

"I have new grandpa!" He yelled and Alan shot David a dirty look.

"It's on." He whispered and David laughed. They sat down at the table and dished out their plates. Mike referred to Alan as grandpa so many times at dinner that when they were finished and Amanda was getting the movie ready, Alan had actually started answering to it.

"It suits you." David said as he and Alan loaded the dishwasher and Nancy put the left over's in the fridge.

"I'm gonna fuck you up." Alan said teasingly. David and Nancy laughed.

"Promises, promises." David said and Nancy laughed.

"David!" She scolded and David and Alan laughed. They finished the dishes and joined Amanda and Mike in the living room. Amanda and David sat together on the couch with Little Mike and Alan sat on the floor in front of the chair that Nancy sat on.

"We all in our spots?" Amanda asked with the remote pointing at the T.V. Everyone said yes and she pressed play. David shut off the lamp and Amanda cuddled into the side of his chest. He stared at Alan. He was looking at the T.V. but didn't seem to be watching it. After a few seconds, he looked at David. David bit his bottom lip and Alan smiled. David looked back at the screen to see the previews ending. The beginning credits started and Mike cheered. Everyone laughed and David and Alan locked eyes again. Alan seemed to breathe a little heavier than usual as David stared at him. They both missed the first half of the movie. "What do you think is gonna happen?" Amanda whispered. Her question pulled David out of the trance Alan held him in.

"Um, I think he's actually the bad guy." David said not knowing what was actually happening in the movie.

"Me too." She said and David looked back at Alan. Alan was still staring at him. David smiled and Alan took a deep breath.

'This is weird.' Alan mouthed and David nodded.

'No shit.' David mouthed back. Alan smiled and finally turned toward the movie. David did the same and they managed to catch the end. David and Amanda had been right. The main character did end up being the bad guy and Mike cheered.

"Again!" He yelled and Amanda looked up at the time.

"What about bed?" She asked him as David turned on the lamp and she pressed stop on the movie.

"No. I wanna do it again." Mike pouted. Nancy smiled and stood up.

"What if grandma tucked you in? We can read a story." She said. David and Alan laughed.

"Grandma." David said. Nancy looked at him and smiled.

"It's not fair if HE gets grandpa and I have to stay Auntie." She said. Amanda laughed and they both took Mike to his room.

"Good movie huh?" Alan asked getting up off the floor. David laughed and stood up.

"Yea, I especially liked the part where the really hot guy bit his lip. That kind of shit drives me nuts." David said. Alan laughed and they went to the table. David got them both another beer and Alan looked toward the music room.

"So, how about them guitars?" Alan asked. David sighed and looked at the room.

"Yea, how about them guitars?" David repeated and Alan giggled.

"Are we gonna do it, or what?" Alan asked in a seductive voice. David closed his eyes and sighed.

"Dad, you're killing me." David whispered. Alan laughed and stood up. He went into his room and brought out his guitar, Susan and David's guitar, Abby. He handed Abby, the black guitar with the single red rose on it, to David and he smiled. He set Susan, the wood stained Stratocaster guitar, against his chair. He went back into the room and brought out David's big amplifier and set it on the floor out in front of them.

"Ok, *son*. Plug her in." Alan said and sat down on his chair. David sighed and did as he was told. Alan plugged his own guitar into the amp and turned the power on.

"What are we playing?" David asked. Alan raised his eyebrows and strummed his guitar strings. David smiled and stared into Alan's eyes. "You start." David said. Alan sighed and started to play Think About You by Gun's and Roses. David listened at first remembering the day Gabe had giving him the score to that song. Alan started to sing and David could feel a lump grow in his throat. Alan just smiled as he sang and David took a deep breath. He started playing with Alan and

Alan shut his eyes. He kept them closed until the song was over. David sighed at the end and took a sip of his beer.

"Now you pick." Alan said. David raised his eyebrows. He started to play Live and Let die. Alan smiled and played along. To Alan's surprise, David sang. Amanda and Nancy quietly walked out to the kitchen while David and Alan played. When the song was finished, Amanda and Nancy clapped and Alan smiled. "Very good, son." He said. David rolled his eyes and sipped his beer again.

"Copper Head Road." Nancy said and Alan laughed. David giggled and they started playing his mother's song together. They played all the songs the girls wanted to hear. When they were finished, Alan and David put the guitars away.

"Good job." Alan said as they put the guitars back into their stands. David smiled and shook his head.

"You too." He whispered and Alan smiled.

"Are you ok?" Alan asked. David sighed and looked into his eyes.

"I want to be happy for mom. I want to be happy for you too but, I'm unfortunately very selfish." David confessed. Alan giggled and shook his head.

"Well, what are we going to do about that?" He asked. David sighed and sat down on the bed in the music room. He looked down at the floor and shook his head.

"Piss and moan until I get over it I guess." Alan smiled and sat down next to David.

"I wish I could make it easier for you. I just don't know what to do."

"Me neither." David said and looked into Alan's eyes. Alan sighed and looked away.

"I have never been an unfaithful man, David." Alan said quietly. David blinked and couldn't help but giggle.

"Unfaithful? I don't expect you to be unfaithful to my mom. I just want to come up with a way to spent time with you without being a walking hard on, as you say." David said.

"I wasn't talking about an affair. I feel unfaithful already."

"Well, why?" David asked. "You haven't done anything wrong." David added. Alan smiled and stood up.

"Nothing you've seen." Alan said quietly and left the room. David blinked at the statement and left the room. Amanda and Nancy were already changed for bed and sitting at the table drinking tea.

"Get it all put away?" Amanda asked as David sat down at the table.

"Yup." David said staring at Alan. Alan giggled and looked at Nancy.

"Getting tired?" He asked. She smiled and nodded.

"Me too actually." Amanda said and looked at David. David smiled and got up. He walked passed Alan and went to his mom. She stood up and hugged her son.

"He's really into you, mom." David whispered. Nancy smiled and nodded.

"Same here." She said and kissed his cheek. "Good night dear." She said and hugged Amanda. David watched as Alan stood up and stretched. It seemed that every muscle in his torso and arms screamed at him to stare. He sighed and waited to see if Alan would hug him or shake his hand. Alan hugged him. David smiled and closed his eyes.

"Your evil." David said as Alan held him as close as possible.

"I know." Alan said. They stepped away from each other and Alan shook his head with a half-smile on his face. David smiled back and walked with Amada to their bedroom after shutting off all the lights. They climbed into bed and Amanda giggled.

"What?" David whispered.

"Dad." She said and David giggled.

"Would you rather I called him hunny or baby?" Amanda laughed and looked up at David.

"I dare you." She said and David laughed. She reminded him of when they were young, before Gabe's death and David's attempted at suicide. Before the pregnancy and moving away from their beloved small home town.

"You're on." David whispered and Amanda giggled.

"Just don't do it in front of your mom." She said quietly and giggled again.

"Do you think she knows how he feels?" He asked thinking about all the times she would look at them and either smile at Alan or laugh at the two of them. Amanda sighed and shook her head.

"She hasn't said anything to me." She answered and rested her head back on David's chest. He sighed and rubbed her back. It wasn't long before they were both asleep.

Chapter 16

The next day, Alan took Amanda into town for a birthday shopping spree so Nancy and David could get the apartment decorated for her party. Nancy had David blowing up balloons while she got out the supplies for baking Amanda's cake. She put out all the bowls and measuring cups.

"So, what did you get her?" Nancy asked as she went to the fridge and grabbed the eggs. David smirked and tied the balloon he had just finished blowing up. He tossed it behind him and went to his room. He grabbed his jacket and brought it out to the kitchen. He dug the velvet box out of the inside pocket and handed it to his mom. "What's this?" She asked and David smiled.

"Open it and guess." David said. He sat back down and took another balloon out of the bag. Nancy opened the box and gasped. She put her hand over her mouth and her eyes instantly filled with tears.

"Oh my God, David." She said staring at the ring. David smiled and blew up the balloon. "It's so beautiful." She whispered and took it out of the box. She admired the rose colored gold that wrapped around the little band and the three perfect diamonds on the top. "Oh David." She said again and looked at him. He had just tossed the last blown up balloon behind him.

"So, think she'll like it?" David asked casually. Nancy giggled and looked back at the ring.

"Well, if she doesn't want it, you could always give it to me." She joked. David laughed and shook his head.

"I don't think Alan would like that very much." David said. Nancy laughed and put the ring back into the little box. She set the box on the table and smiled at David.

"I'm so proud of you." She said and walked around the table to hug him. He smiled and rubbed his mother's back. She giggled and looked as though she might start jumping up and down.

"Can you put it in the cake?" David asked.

"How did you get so romantic? You must get that from me." She said. David giggled and she took the ring box to the counter. He hung the balloons around the room and on the chairs at the table. He hung the blue and pink streamers and the birthday banner Carman had found at a party store. It was huge. David laughed at it and Nancy turned from her work to look at it. "Wow, that's crazy big." She said. David and Nancy stood back to try to see the whole thing.

"What if I cut the balloons off the sides? That would make it a little narrower and less eye sore." David said. Nancy laughed and nodded.

"Good idea." She said. David did as he had planned and it certainly helped. The two layers of cake where finished and Nancy set them aside to cool. "So, how do you want me to decorate it?" She asked as her and her son sat down to drink coffee. David sighed and shook his head.

"Mom, do something she would like. Flowers and stuff maybe." Nancy smiled and shook her head.

"That's not helpful." She said and David giggled. They talked about the decorations and the cake with the ring in it. Nancy thought it was the most romantic thing she had ever heard. "We'll have to mark it somehow so she gets the piece with the ring in it." Nancy said and David nodded.

"So what do you think?" David asked. Nancy scratched her head and thought for a moment.

"What if I did put flowers on it and did one rose. The stem of that rose could hang down the cake where the ring is. That way we'll know where the ring is and where to cut a piece off for her." Nancy said excitedly. David smiled and nodded.

"See, that's why you're doing this and I'm not." He said. Nancy laughed and stood up to get to work on the cake. David checked the time and seen that people would start showing up soon. He got out Amanda's must have serving dishes and put them out with chips, dip, meat and cheese, pickles and Amanda's favorite, one large bowl full of chocolate covered almonds. When he was finished, he put out some small white plates and the ivory colored napkins Carman had picked up in the party store. When it was all set out, David raised his eyebrows and smiled. "Wow, if only I had a gay guy doing all my party shopping all the time." David said in the most feminine voice he could muster. Nancy laughed and looked at the table.

"Oh, it's so pretty David." She said and rubbed his arm. He smiled and looked down at himself.

"Yea, but I'm not." He said and Nancy giggled. He hurried into the bathroom and showered. He dug out his good pair of light colored blue jeans and the tight pearl white t-shirt Gabe had given him. He brushed his hair and applied his cologne and deodorant. When he was satisfied with how he looked, he rejoined his mother in the kitchen. She was finished the cake and had it set out in the middle of the table. "Wow mom. That looks awesome." David said. The cake was white and had a collection of beautifully colored flowers decorating it. He picked out the single red rose right away and took a deep breath. Nancy smiled at him and rubbed his back.

"She won't say no." She reassured him quietly and went to the bathroom to get herself ready. David sighed and looked around the room. He was expecting Seth and Little Mike first. He sat down on the couch and lit a cigarette. *Ok, don't say anything. Don't act weird. Just sit back and wait for her to find it in her cake. You can do this. Just relax. God I'm gonna panic! What if she swallows it? What if she breaks a tooth on it or something? What if she hates it? I don't even know if she likes rose gold. What if she thinks diamonds are corny? What if she's old fashioned and wants me to ask? Oh my god! What if she wants the whole down on one knee thing? Am I capable of that? IN FRONT OF PEOPLE? In front of Alan? Oh god Alan. Fuck, I hope my mom and him never break up or something after this. Would I have a chance with him if we were both single? Fuck, don't start thinking like that, David.* He scolded himself. He took the last drag from his cigarette and put it out. He got up and went to the fridge. His mother had made a few salads and cold meat finger sandwiches just like Amanda asked for. He reached in and got himself a beer. His mother went from the bathroom to her and Alan's room in a towel. She smiled at him while she went passed. Just then, there was a knock at the door. David raised his eyebrows and answered it. It was Seth and Little Mike.

"Hi there." David said and Mike ran into the house.

"Birthday!" Mike yelled and David laughed. Seth tossed his hair as he walked in and David grabbed his arm. Seth looked at him with wide eyes.

"What?" He asked. David giggled and shook his head.

"No hi or anything?" Seth smiled and leaned close to David. He smelled David hair and kissed his neck.

"Hi." He whispered into David's ear.

"Ass hole." David said with a giggle and they walked out to the kitchen. Mike was looking around at everything. "Don't touch till Amanda gets home." David said. Mike giggled and ran around hitting all the balloons.

"This looks awesome. Very girly." Seth said. David smiled and went to the fridge. He got out a beer for Seth and handed it to him. "Where is it?" Seth asked looking at the cake. David smiled and sipped his beer.

"Under the rose." He answered. Nancy came out of the bedroom and hugged Mike.

"I want cake." Mike said to her. She laughed and went to the fridge. She got the little boy a cupcake made from the same batter that the cake was made from. She had decorated the cupcakes with a single red rose. David smiled when he saw it.

"Subtle." David said and Nancy laughed.

"She won't get it until she finds that ring." Nancy said. Seth smiled and went back to the door. He brought two gift bags to the table.

"One from me and one from Mike." Seth said. David laughed and went to his room. He brought out a gift wrapped in pink paper.

"This one is from Mike too." David said and they both laughed. They piled all the gifts in front of the large gift from Alan and Nancy against the living room wall. They laughed and talked over their beer and cigarettes. Soon the door buzzer rang and David let whoever it was up.

He opened the door and waited for the elevator to open. It was Carman with a pink and white box in one hand and the lid in the other.

"Hi." Carman said and handed the box to David. The little puppy had a red bow around its neck and looked as though Carman had given him a bath.

"She is gonna shit." David said and Carman giggled.

"That's what I'm going for." Carman said and David laughed. They walked into the apartment and Nancy hugged Carman. "Good to see you again." Carman said as they hugged.

"Oh, it's good to be here. How was your date?" Nancy asked as she let him go. He smiled and winked at David then looked back at Nancy.

"Well, it was eventful." Carman said and David laughed and handed him a beer. Nancy saw the box with the puppy in it and squealed.

"Oh Carman! He's beautiful." She said and picked the puppy up. Carman giggled as she baby talked to the little dog.

"Think she'll like him?" Carman asked. Nancy smiled and nodded.

"She has always wanted her own dog." Nancy said and put the puppy back in the box. She looked at the clock. It was almost 6:00. "Ok, I told Alan six o'clock so, is there anything we're missing?" She said. Everyone looked around and couldn't see anything else that needed to be done. Mike was in the living room watching cartoons when Amanda walked in.

"HAPPY BIRTHDAY!" Everyone yelled. She jumped and put her hands over her mouth to suppress her little yelp.

"Oh my God guys!" She said and made her way around the room hugging everyone. Carman had craftily got the lid back on his gift just as Amanda walked through the door. Alan smiled at the decorations.

"Looks nice guys." He said and kissed Nancy as he got a beer out of the fridge.

"David decorated, I just sat around and made sure he didn't burn the place down." She said and sat down with Amanda and Carman.

"Well, it looks good David." Alan said. Seth smiled and elbowed Alan in the ribs. "Oh, Seth! I didn't even see you!" Alan exclaimed and gave the young man a very manly looking hug. Seth laughed and they chatted about school.

"Do present!" Mike yelled after everyone seemed to have their fill of the finger food David had put out. Nancy turned the living room chair around and sat Amanda down in it. Seth took his gift to her first. She smiled as she read the silly card. She took the paper out of the bag and giggled. Inside was a ten disk collection of all the songs from her favorite shows. She hugged Seth and thanked him. The first gift from Little Mike was next. He picked up the gift he had picked out with Seth and brought it to Amanda. She smiled at him and opened it up. Inside was a family board game that even Mike could play.

"Oh, what a good idea." Amanda said and hugged Mike. He ran over and got the other one. She laughed as he drug it across the living room floor. She patted his head and read the card. "To the Best Sister in the world." She read out loud and smiled at Mike. She opened the card. "Happy birthday. Love Mike." She read. Mike giggled and pushed the present closer to her. Amanda giggled and let him help her open it. Inside was a brand new wooden Jewelry box. "Oh my goodness. This is fabulous." She said and looked at David.

"He picked it out. I wanted to get you movies." David said and everyone laughed.

"Movie not nice for my Amanda." Mike said and hugged his sister.

"I'm next!" Carman said and David giggled. He carefully picked up the box and set it on Amanda's lap. She smiled at him and lifted the lid.

"HOLY SHIT!" Amanda yelled and everyone laughed again. She picked up the little dog and let the box fall off her lap. "Oh my God Carman! I love him." She said and hugged the little dog. Carman smiled and handed her an envelope that held all the vaccination information.

"Well I hope so. He's been living at my house for two days and I almost kept him." He said. Amanda giggled and kissed the little dog's nose.

"Oh my goodness." She whispered. The puppy licked her face and she giggled.

"Can I play with puppy?" Mike asked. Amanda smiled at him and put the puppy down.

"Keep him in the kitchen in case he pees." She said. David giggled as Mike got down on his knees and followed the little puppy around. "Ok, the big one." Amanda said still staring at the puppy. Alan and David carried the present over and Amanda stood up to open it. "I thought this was from David. What are you guys doing getting such big gifts for me?" She asked as she read the card. Alan and Nancy smiled. She peeled back the paper and gasped. "Oh my God." She said.

"Do you like it?" Nancy asked coming over to her. Amanda's eyes filled with tears as she looked at the picture of the red oak, sleigh bed crib.

"Oh, thank you." She said and hugged Nancy first then Alan. David moved the crib back against the wall and went into his room. He brought out one last gift. He handed it to Amanda and giggled. "Is this what I think it is?" She asked. David shrugged and she giggled. She sat down and quickly opened the wrap. Inside was the last remaining glass doll from Amanda's collection. "Oh, I love you!" She yelled and jumped into David's arms. David laughed and hugged her tight. Alan and Carman chatted about Carman's date and Seth and Mike played with the little puppy.

"What are you going to name him?" Nancy asked giving the pup a little dish of water. Amanda sighed still holding one arm around David's waist.

"I like Mack." Amanda said. David and Alan laughed.

"Mack." Alan said. David and Alan had a joke about truckers who drove Mack trucks and had to stare at the ass of a dog all day.

"Yea, Mack." She said and bent down to pet the little dog. He pulled at David's sock and everyone laughed.

"Shall we do cake?" Seth asked. David suddenly went stone still but Nancy deflected and pulled Amanda to the table.

"You sit here dear." She said. David turned away and took a deep breath. Alan noticed and went over to him.

"Are you ok?" He whispered in David's ear. David looked at him then looked at his mom. She smiled at him and he met Alan's eyes again.

"Yea, I just need a sec." David said. Alan frowned and looked at Nancy. She just smiled and went back to talking to Amanda.

"Thanks for ditching the candle thing. I hate candles." Amanda said.

"I know. I remembered from last year." Nancy said and handed Amanda the knife. "The piece with the rose has the most of your raspberry filling so that's your piece." Nancy whispered. David's stomach flipped and he closed his eyes. Amanda giggled and cut out her piece. She cut a piece for everyone else and each person thanked her as she went. David took his piece last and stared at Amanda.

"Happy Birthday." He squeaked out and Nancy giggled.

"Thank you." Amanda said and took a bite of her cake. David watched every bit she took. She excitedly talked about her gifts and giggled as the puppy went around begging for little tastes of peoples icing. David still hadn't touched his piece. Alan stood next to him again and leaned close to his ear.

"Either you've poisoned that cake or you're expecting something to jump out of it." Alan whispered. David looked at him and shook.

"Just watch." David said and looked back at the cake. Suddenly a little ring clanged against Amanda's plate. She looked down at it and David could feel Alan's arm go around him.

"Don't faint." Alan whispered. David never looked away as Amanda carefully picked up the ring and looked at it. He stared at her and waited. She looked around for a second and then back at the ring. Nancy giggled and put her hand on Amanda's shoulder.

"Look over there." Nancy said and gestured at David. David was as white as a ghost and Amanda giggled.

"Is this an engagement ring?" Amanda asked. Everyone was silent as they waited for David's answer. He stood there just staring at Amanda for a few minutes. "David?" Amanda said holding the ring and staring at him. He cleared his throat and stepped closer to her. Alan stood where he was and watched while David sank down to one knee. He stared into Amanda's eyes. She giggled and bit her bottom lip. He took a deep breath and took her hand. He stared at her hand and then looked back up at her. She was still smiling only now she had tears in her eyes. "Ask already." She whispered and David smiled.

"Amanda, would you put that on and pretend I was romantic enough to ask properly?" David said. Amanda laughed and kissed him.

"I love you." She said. She held the ring in her fingers and pulled David to his feet. "But you have to ask." She said as she stood and stared him in the face. David laughed and took the ring. Nancy was standing with Alan now crying. Seth and Carman waited silently. David cleared his throat again and smiled.

"Amanda, will you marry me?" He asked and Amanda squealed.

"Oh YES!" She yelled and jumped into his arms. David laughed and hugged her. Everyone clapped and Mack barked. David let Amanda go and put the ring on her finger. She giggled as the sticky raspberry filling came off on her finger.

"I love you." David whispered and kissed her. Amanda squealed again and hugging him. Nancy took Amanda to the bathroom to clean the ring and Alan stood in front of David. Seth and Carman watched as Alan stared into his eyes.

"Good job." Alan said quietly and hugged David. David smiled and hugged Alan.

"Thank you." David whispered. Alan cleared his throat and whispered into David's ear.

"I'm really proud of you." David could feel tears fill his eyes and he hugged Alan tighter.

"I love you." David whispered. Alan's heart seemed to jump in his chest and he took a deep breath. He held it for a second and then sighed as he exhaled.

"I know." He said. They stepped back from each other and Alan smiled at him. "Beer?" He asked and David laughed. They all sat down and talked about David's engagement. Alan would look at David and smile every once in a while and David would smile back. Amanda and Nancy giggled and discussed wedding plans and Amanda wanted Nancy to be her matron of honor. She also wanted Alan to walk her down the aisle. Alan smiled and agreed.

"So David, any ideas for a best man?" Nancy asked. David looked around at each of the men at the table.

"Um, how do I choose?" David asked. Amanda laughed and held his hand.

"Take your time dear." Nancy said. David sighed and looked at Alan. Alan smiled and shifted in his chair.

"I need a while to pick." He said. They all understood and discussed the best time of year for a wedding. Amanda wanted it outside and she didn't want to be pregnant so they decided to have it the next summer. Nancy put Mike to bed when it was about 9:30 and brought the guitars out for David and Alan. They giggled and Carman smiled.

"Right on." Seth said and got himself comfortable on his chair. David and Alan plugged in their guitars and stared at each other. David looked at Amanda and giggled. He started to play Amanda's favorite song Billy Jean. Alan laughed but played along with him. To everyone's surprise, Seth sang the song and sounded amazing. At the end, every one clapped and Carman cheered for Seth.

"Wow kid." Alan said taking a sip from his drink. Seth blushed and shrugged his shoulders.

"Well, what can I say?" He said and everyone laughed again.

"Can you play that whistling song?" Amanda asked. David smiled and started to play Patients by Guns and Roses. Carman sang as Alan and David played. Seth stared at David's hands and Alan smiled. David giggled and winked at Seth. When the song was over, Amanda and Nancy clapped. For the rest of the night they played whatever Amanda wanted. When she was tired, she said her good nights and went to bed.

"You should probably go with her." Alan whispered and David giggled.

"You're probably right." David said and all the guys giggled. Nancy rolled her eyes and put paper down for the puppy.

"Good night big boy." Seth said and Carman and Alan laughed.

"Yea, yea. Good night." David said and went to his room. Amanda was lying in their bed and smiling at her ring.

"Oh David, this is the best day of my life." Amanda said. David smiled and took his shirt off.

"Getting any better?" David asked flexing the muscles in his arms. Amanda giggled and shook her head. "No huh?" David asked and took his pants off. "How about now?" He asked and Amanda giggled.

"Um, getting better." She said and David laughed. He dropped his boxers and jumped into bed with her. She giggled and pulled him on top of her. He giggled and kissed her. She clawed at his hips and he playful bit her earlobe. Amanda giggled and pushed him off of her. She climbed on top of him and kissed him very deeply. David moaned and pushed his growing erection against her. He ran his hands down her back to her behind and gripped it tight in his strong hands. "God I want you." Amanda whispered and David smiled. He slowly guided himself inside her. She moaned and rocked her hips back and forth. David closed his eyes and gripped her hips tightly. She tossed her head back and sped up her movements. David's breathing sped up and he could feel her body clench around his erection. "Oh god David." Amanda whispered and bent down to muffle her moaning in the pillow next to David's head.

"I think they know what we're doing." David whispered through his giggling and heavy breathing. Amanda giggled too and pushed David farther inside her. He moaned fairly loud and Amanda laughed.

"Be quiet." She whispered and moved her hips quicker. David moaned again and clawed at Amanda's hips. "Uh, David." She moaned into the pillow and climaxed again. David could feel his own orgasm build as Amanda moved. His heavy breathing turned into light moaning and Amanda kept moving quickly. David's body shook and Amanda kissed him as he climaxed. She smiled as she sat herself up and looked down at him.

"You just kissed me to keep me quiet didn't you?" David asked. Amanda giggled and slowly got off of him. He smiled at her as she walked to the bathroom. When she returned, she rested her head on David's chest.

"I love you." She whispered as David rubbed her back.

"I love you too." David said. They were soon asleep.

Chapter 17

For the next few weeks following Amanda's birthday, David and Amanda shopped for the remainder of the furniture for the baby's room. They used Alan's crib as a starting point and decided to work around it. They picked out a change table and a dresser of the same red oak finish and a little white garbage can that had pink and blue stripes. Amanda had decided to wait till they knew what sex the baby was before they painted. With all the shopping and work, the count down for the Gun's and Roses concert had started and David was chomping at the bit to go. He and Alan talked about it every Friday night when Alan would call. Not only was the concert of David's favorite band, but it was also in Las Vegas which had them both pretty excited. Alan had a hotel room booked for them by the first of August. David was also getting used to the father son relationship that he and Alan managed to start building. Nancy thought it was wonderful that the awkward silences and strange glances had all but ended. She had mentioned to David that she was very happy to have him coming around to the idea of her and Alan. Amanda was also very happy with David and Alan's new relationship. She thought that the time had come that David's choice had been made as far as who he wanted to be with. She said such things while twirling the ring on her finger.

Carman and Jake were hitting it off quite well as well. Carman spent almost all his non work hours with him and David thought there were whispers of Jake moving in with him but Carman would never say. Seth, on the other hand, still kept David on his toes as far as the sexual frustration went. Although there hadn't been any more heavy physical contact between them, Seth still managed to keep David interested with his hair tossing and random touching. Seth insisted it was all in fun but David still thought there was a lot more to this kid than he was saying. Amanda thought it was funny and almost cute how irritated Seth's advances made David. She would say that as far as guys went, Seth was about as hot as they got. David would often take offence to the statement and Amanda would laugh.

As the final week before the concert approached, David could hardly sleep. His excitement made Amanda laugh and she was worried that he would be far too exhausted to enjoy the concert by the time he got there.

"What? It's G & R. You can never be too tired for them." David said over morning coffee before work.

"Well, how much sleep did you get last night?" Amanda asked setting a bowl of cereal down for Little Mike.

"A couple hours." David answered. Mike dug into his cereal and David smiled at him. "I can sleep when I'm dead, right?" He asked the little boy. Mike smiled and nodded.

"You know, you're a bad influence on him." Amanda said getting a cup of coffee and sitting down at the table.

"He needs to know these things Amanda."

"Uh, huh." She said and sipped the hot black liquid. David smiled and looked up at the time.

"I gotta go. Love you." He said and kissed Amanda as he got up.

"I love you to." Amanda said. David went over to Mike and gave him a high five. Mike squealed and clapped his hands.

"Love you!" Mike yelled from the table as David went to the door. He smiled at the boy and stepped out. The elevator was on his floor so he stepped in. He pressed the ground floor button and watched the numbers as they descended to one. When the doors opened, he stepped out and headed for the door. The office door was open to his left so he peeked his head in. Seth sat at the desk.

"You're in here today? Where's your dad?" David asked and sat down with his friend. Seth yawned and shrugged.

"Who knows? He just calls and says, 'Get up boy; I need you at the north end apartment'. So I get up and come over." Seth explained.

"That sucks. He can't tell you the day before?"

"You know my dad, does he really look like the plan ahead type?" Seth asked. David giggled and shook his head.

"No I guess not." Just then, he noticed Carman's truck out the big office window. "Well, I'll see you later." David said and got up.

"Yup." Seth said and winked at him. David giggled and walked out to Carman's truck.

"How is house training going?" Carman asked as they drove out of the parking lot.

"Well, I think it's going pretty good. Amanda says he's hardly having any accidents and I guess Mike is getting pretty good at the leash thing." David answered and Carman smiled.

"So, four days till the concert, are you shitting your pants yet?" Carman asked. David laughed and looked over the job list for the day.

"If I was any more excited, I would have a heart attack." David said.

"Well, I was talking to Alan last night and he said he was coming a day early so you guys could take his car."

"Yea well, he thought a Hearse in Vegas was way too weird so he talked me into the Mustang." David said. He set the list on the dash and looked at Carman. "It would be cool if you were coming." Carman smiled and shook his head.

"Well, I'm busy this weekend anyway." He said. David rolled his eyes knowing he spoke of Jake.

"You sure spend a lot of time with him." Carman smiled and blushed a little. David laughed and shook his head. "That's so Un-Carman of you." He added and Carman laughed now.

"Yes but, While your away with Alan wishing you could laid, I'll be fucking all week end." David laughed.

"I think we're passed that Carman." David said. Carman raised his eyebrows and looked at David with a sideways glance.

"Uh, huh. I'm supposed to believe that?" He asked as he pulled up to the first job sight.

"Sure, why not?" David asked. Carman shook his head and sighed.

"Well, you guys are both pulling out this crap about being passed it all the time. I think half of it is just trying to convince your selves you are. Take Alan, for instance. He insists on referring to you as son because when he says your name his mind wonders. And you, you can't even talk about him without your hands sweating and your dick getting hard, so I ask you, how over this thing are you?" Carman asked. David sighed and shook his head. They both got out of the truck

and went into the building. They did the job they were there for and
headed to the next one.

"You know something Carman, you don't make it any easier."
David said. Carman looked at him with a confused gaze.

"What do you mean?"

"Well, you point out that shit all the time. Can't you be a little
more supportive or something?" David asked. Carman sighed and
patted his leg.

"You're right. I'm sorry. I guess it's just strange to see you guys
more father and son than what you were before. It's hard to get used
to. I think I'm expecting a relapse or something." Carman explained.
David rolled his eyes and looked out the window.

"Well, I like the way it is now. We can talk and hang out together
and do all the things we used to without our feelings fucking it all
up."

"Ok, just don't try to be something you're not, David. The kind of
feelings you have for Alan don't just go away." Carman said pulling up
to the next building. David nodded and opened his door.

"You don't have to tell me that Carman. I know." David said.
Carman smiled and they went into the building. The reprogramming
of the computers at this job took the rest of the morning and by the
time they were finished, they were both hungry and ready for lunch.
They went to the little diner and Carman giggled when he saw Jake
at the counter. "God you're like a teenage girl." David said under his
breath. Carman laughed and they sat down at their regular table. Jake
smiled at them and brought the coffee pot with him.

"So, how are my two favorite guys today?" Jake asked pouring the
coffee. Carman smiled and stared into Jake's eyes. David sighed and
shook his head.

"Well, if you must know, I feel like I haven't slept in a week and Amanda has been having a hard time keeping up with my libido." David said and Carman laughed.

"Ah, that's right. The trip with Alan is this weekend. Carman said you've been getting a little randy over that." Jake snipped back. Carman laughed and David shook his head.

"Well, Carman has been known to exaggerate." David said. Jake giggled and went up to the counter to make them both a sandwich and French fries.

"Exaggerate? About what?" Carman asked. David laughed and shook his head.

"Everything." David answered and took a sip of his coffee. Carman giggled and watched as Jake made their meal. He leaned close to David and whispered in his ear,

"I think I'm falling in love with him." He said. David raised his eyebrows and looked at Carman.

"Really?" David asked. Carman giggled and nodded. "Well, I think that's great Carman. He's perfect for you."

"Isn't he?" Carman asked. Jake looked back at them and smiled. David sighed and shook his head.

"I bet he feels the same." David said.

"Oh God. I would never say if first. I'll wait for him." Carman said.

"Trust me, that doesn't always work out." David said. Carman sighed and watched as Jake walked over with their meal. He set the plates down and went to the counter to help another customer. Carman and David talked about Jake and Carman's new feelings as they ate. They would craftily change the subject when he was close which always prompted David to laugh. When they were finished, Carman paid and they left. They spent the rest of the day on small jobs and they seemed to make the day go by quickly. When they were finished, Carman dropped David off at home and told him that the morning was free for tomorrow. David smiled and waved at him as he drove away. He went up to his apartment to see Amanda hanging up the keys.

"Oh hi." Amanda said and kissed David.

"Just get back from a walk?" David asked taking her coat and hanging it up for her.

"Yea, Mike met a kid at the park the other day so me and his mom have agreed to meet there at the same time every day, weather permitting." She answered. They walked into the kitchen together and Amanda got herself a bottle of water and David a beer from the fridge. She sat down with him and sighed. "So, I was thinking, what if we took a drive out to your mom's one of these weekends?" Amanda asked. David smiled and nodded.

"That's a good idea. Did you want to hang out with her while me and Alan go to the concert?" David asked. Amanda's eyes lit up and she giggled.

"Oh yes! I'll call her right now!" Amanda said. David giggled as she practically ran to the phone. He got up and went to the bath room as she talked to Nancy. He took a pee and washed his hands. He stared at himself in the mirror and thought about what Carman had said.

God he's right. Who am I fooling? I will never shake the real feelings I have for Alan. The way it is now is easier but I wonder if he thinks the same way I do when he's not looking? I told him I loved him on Amanda's birthday. I wonder if he thinks about that? I wonder WHAT he thinks about that? He's never brought it up. Maybe he never will. I just wish there was a way to go back in time and change everything. If only he never knew how I felt. If only I never knew how he feels. I wonder if he still does. I wonder if it was just some kind of weird phase he went through. There's no way of really knowing unless I ask and I can't see that happening. David sighed and left the bathroom. Amanda was just hanging up the phone when he came into the living room.

"So, she says she would love to have me and Mike but she says you better call Alan and tell him we'll be coming there on Thursday." David blinked and looked at her.

"Thursday? Why a day earlier?" David asked.

"Oh, well that's when Alan was coming." Amanda said not knowing that David was not aware.

"I thought he was coming Friday."

"Oh, well I guess you got your lines crossed somewhere." Amanda said and headed into the kitchen to find something for supper.

"I gotta call him *and* Carman now. I hope he can live through a day without me." David said. Amanda giggled as David picked up the phone. He decided to call Carman first.

"*Hello.*" Carman said on the other end.

"Hi, we have a slight change of plans." David said and sat down on the couch.

"*What's that?*"

"Well, Amanda wants to go hang out with my mom so I'm going to take her down there but my mom is expecting us on Thursday." David explained. Carman giggled on the other end.

"*That doesn't change the plans David. Amanda and Nancy already planned this. You really need to talk to her more.*" Carman said. David looked at Amanda and shook his head. Amanda giggled and blew him a kiss.

"How does this happen? You always know what's going on in my own house before I do." David complained. Amanda and Carman both laughed.

"Don't be too mad at her. I make her leave it to the last minute. I love your reaction to it."

"Yea well. You guys are gonna get it one day." David said and Carman giggled.

"You say that but I know you love the attention."

"Whatever. So I'm leaving Thursday morning then." David said.

"Yep, no problem."

"Ok, I'll see you tomorrow." David said and sighed at the ridiculousness of the people he knew.

"Ok." Carman said and they both hung up the phone. David looked at Amanda and she giggled.

"Why?" David asked playfully and Amanda laughed.

"Well, cause its funny." She said. David laughed now and got up from the couch. He went up to Amanda and kissed her.

"I bet you're already packed aren't you?" David whispered. Amanda giggled and nodded. David shook his head and went back to his beer. "Am I packed?" David asked and Amanda laughed.

"Yes, actually. So is Mike." She confessed. David shook his head again and looked at the little dog Amanda named Mack. He was chewing on one of the little raw hide sticks Amanda had brought for him.

"Did you ever hear from Beth's mom or anything?" David asked.

"No, I was thinking about calling back but I've been too chicken." Amanda answered as she put a pot of water on the stove to boil. "I'm just going to wait. If Gabe didn't have anything to do with her, they might need time to think about it you know?" She added.

"Yea, maybe." David said and took a big sip from his beer. They talked about Gabe and his daughter as Amanda cooked. They ate dinner together and when they were finished, Amanda took Mike to the tub for a bath. David was cleaning up the kitchen when the phone rang. He dried his hands and answered it. "Hello."

"*Hi there, I hear you're coming down on Thursday.*" Alan's voice said on the other line.

"Yea, apparently this was already the plan." David said and sat down at the table.

"*That's what I hear, your mom just told me about it over supper.*"

"Well, at least I knew about it before you did." David joked. Alan giggled and cleared his throat.

"*Wanna hear something funny?*" Alan asked. David frowned and shook his head.

"Ok." He said.

"*Jake is moving in with Carman this weekend.*"

"What? I thought it was all a rumor." David said and giggled.

"*Guess not. I think it's good. A little fast but good.*"

"Yea, he's in love with Jake you know." David said.

"*So I hear.*"

"We sound like women." David said and Alan laughed.

"*We kind of do. How about we talk about a way more pressing issue.*" Alan proposed.

"Ok, like what?" David asked. He took a sip of his beer and heard Alan light a cigarette.

"*I want to get a tattoo.*" Alan said. David laughed and Alan giggled. "*What? I'm serious.*" Alan insisted.

"Ok, of what?"

"*I don't know. I thought you could help me pick.*" Alan said. David sighed and thought about it for a second.

"Where do you want it?" David asked. Alan giggled and David rolled his eyes. "I hope you're not thinking about tattooing something on your dick." David said and Alan laughed.

"Of course not! I was thinking on my back." David smiled.

"Ok, so like devil wings or something?" He asked.

"Nice." Alan said and he sounded almost serious.

"I bet you like that idea. You're so weird." David said. Alan laughed and David could hear his cell phone ringing in the back ground.

"Shit, it's my mom. I'll talk to you when you get here." Alan said.

"ok."

"By son." Alan said quietly and David laughed.

"By dad." He said and hung up the phone. He giggled and went back into the kitchen to finish with the supper dishes. He was surprised to look at the clock and realize that Amanda had been right. It was only seven o'clock and he was tired enough to sleep. He peeked his head into the bathroom to see Amanda drying off little Mike.

"Hi, was that Alan?" She asked.

"Yea, it's all set. You know something? I am really tired." David said. Amanda giggled and shook her head.

"Well, I told you this would happen. Why don't you go to bed?" She said. David smiled and kissed her on the top of her head.

"I think I will. Good night." He said. Amanda and Mike said their good nights and David went into the bed room. He took off his clothes and crawled into bed. He shut his eyes as he set his head down on the pillow and was quickly asleep.

David slept all the way through the night until 6:00 am. He stretched and rolled over onto his back. His never fail morning erection throbbed against the soft sheets of his and Amanda's bed. He sighed and rolled the rest of the way over to see Amanda sleeping next to him. He smiled and cuddled up to her.

"I have to pee." Amanda said sleepily and David giggled.

"You always have to pee." David whispered. Amanda yawned and sat up. David watched her walk into the bathroom and close the door. "God, I'm horny this morning." He said to himself and sat up. He could hear Amanda giggle at his comment from the bathroom and he smiled. "You know, I won't take no for an answer every morning." He said loud enough for Amanda to hear. She giggled again and David got up to go make coffee. He and Amanda discussed the trip over morning coffee. When Mike got up, they all went for a walk with Mack together. They went to the park and let Mike play on the equipment for about an hour. When they were ready to go, they took the long way around the park on their way home. Amanda seemed to be getting tired so David let her have a nap and watched a movie with Mike. After lunch, Carman showed up to pick David up for the afternoon work he had booked.

"We gotta go take a look at Lance's computer today but we're doing that last." Carman said. He seemed to be in a great mood.

"So, I hear you have a busy weekend coming up." David said. Carman giggled and looked at David.

"I do. Alan told you didn't he?" Carman asked.

"Yea, he did. Little fast isn't it?"

"Well, some people just click David. Jake is perfect, why wait?" Carman explained.

"I think it's great. At least it won't be such a big empty house anymore." David said. Carman smiled and pulled up to their first job of the afternoon. They worked together on it and then Carman dropped David off at a small job and headed to the next one alone. David walked into the little office in the collage and went up to the reception counter.

"Hi there. You're here to fix the lab computer, right?" The woman asked.

"That's me." David said. She smiled and stood up. She led him through the halls to the lab. He stepped in and went over to the computer. He sat down and seen the problem was an easy programming glitch. He was almost finished when he felt a tap on his shoulder. He looked over to see the red head from the elevator.

"Hi elevator boy." She said. She was holding her books under one arm. She was wearing a red plaid shirt that complimented her beautiful hair and ample breasts. She was also wearing a pair of blue jean shorts and a rope looking belt.

"Hi elevator girl." David said and she smiled.

"So, you're a computer geek." She said and sat in the chair next to him. David laughed and shook his head.

"No, I just do this because it's mindless work."

"I see. You're new to the building aren't you?" The red head asked referring to the apartment.

"Yea, my fiancée and I moved in there a couple months ago. We haven't really met anyone yet." David answered.

"You look a little young to be engaged." The red head said. David giggled and shook his head. He typed his program code in and pressed enter. The little bar at the bottom of the screen started to fill.

"Well, I also have a kid on the way and a four year old at home so I guess I'm not as young as you thought." David kidded. The red head raised her eyebrows and stared at David.

"Wow, I would have never guessed. Anyway, I guess now you've met someone so don't be a stranger, ok?" The red head said. David smiled and nodded.

"What's your name?" David asked as the girl stood up.

"Elevator girl." She answered and walked away. David giggled and shook his head. He finished with the computer and headed outside to wait for Carman. He lit a cigarette as he waited in the parking lot.

There were tons of young men and women going in and out of the three buildings that made up the collage. David watched them walk around and stop to talk to each other as he waited for Carman. When he arrived, David got into the truck and giggled.

"What?" Carman asked.

"Ever met someone who wouldn't tell you their name?" David asked as they drove out of the parking lot and headed toward Lance's house.

"No, not unless it was just in passing. Like a shopping line or something. Why?"

"Well, there's this girl that lives in my building. I met her once in the elevator and now I talked to her again at the collage today. I asked her name but she said it was elevator girl." David said. Carman laughed and shook his head.

"Ok, what does she call you?"

"Elevator boy." David answered. Carman laughed again and stopped at the last red light before Lance's street.

"Sounds like she's flirting with you or something." Carman said.

"Well, I told her I was engaged." David said defending his fidelity.

"That doesn't mean anything. The more you ask for her real name, the more interest you're exhibiting. It's like a mating ritual or something." David laughed and pointed at the light when it turned green. Carman drove on and parked out in front of Lance's house. They went up to the door and stood on the step.

"DEAD MAN WALKEN!" They both yelled. David still giggled when he had to yell it. He wondered how long it would take before he could say it with a straight face. Seth opened the door and David smiled.

"Hi." Seth said in his sexy voice. David sighed and followed Carman in.

"Where is your brother?" Carman asked.

"Actually, dad called him away so you'll have to get it done without him." Seth answered. They all walked downstairs and Carman went into the office. Seth stopped David and pulled him over to the big leather sofa. David laughed as Seth pushed him down to sit on it.

"Ok, now what?" David asked. Seth laughed and sat next to David.

"I want to ask you something." He said. David rolled his eyes and looked into Seth's handsome face. "It's serious." Seth said. David sighed and nodded.

"Ok, what is it?" He asked. Seth cleared his throat and stared into David's eyes.

"I wanted to know how you felt about that kiss a couple weeks ago." Seth said. David raised an eyebrow and sighed.

"Well, it wasn't what I expected." David answered. Seth shifted where he sat and cleared his throat again.

"Ok, like how? What do you mean?" Seth asked. David rolled his eyes.

"Seth, why do you ask?" Seth leaned back on the couch and sighed.

"Well, I kissed this girl the other day. We've been seeing each other for a couple weeks and she kissed me." Seth said.

"Ok, so what's the problem?" David asked not sure where he fit in.

"Well, she said I kissed like I was kissing a guy. To strong or something." Seth said. David laughed and shook his head.

"You are a powerful kisser Seth. Maybe some girls can't handle it."

"Well, the problem was, I was thinking of you when I kissed her." Seth said. David blinked and took a deep breath. He stared at Seth and then looked at the doorway that Carman had disappeared into.

"David, I just wanted to tell you cause I need help." Seth said pulling David back into the conversation.

"With what? I can't help you not think about me. And why are you thinking about me anyway?" David asked. Seth rolled his eyes and shook his head.

"You were the last person I kissed before her."

"So what? Do you think I thought about Amanda when you kissed me?" David asked. Seth shook his head. He looked very upset. "Seth, do you like this girl?" David asked and Seth nodded yes. "Ok, then why are you thinking about me?" David asked.

"I don't know." Seth answered quietly.

"*I don't mean to eavesdrop, but, could it be because you like David more than you say you do?*" Carman asked from the office. David giggled but Seth sat very still and his face was emotionless. David looked at him and sighed.

"You know, you're not going to get on with your live if you keep things from even yourself." David said quietly. Seth sighed and shook his head.

"I don't like guys though David. Just you." Seth said. David leaned close to him. Seth looked at him but didn't move.

"I think it's sexy. I just don't know what you want *me* to do about it." David whispered. Seth raised his eyebrows and cleared his throat.

"I don't know." Seth whispered staring at David's half parted lips. David leaned back again and looked at the office door.

"Well, you should think about it. It could just be because you're curious. It's not like you haven't been the only straight guy in a crowd of fags your whole life. Maybe you're just confused." David said. Seth sighed and shook his head.

"Maybe." He said quietly and David smiled.

"Seth, you're a gorgeous guy. Anybody would be lucky to have you. Don't think about it so much."

"That's easy for you to say. You practically have your pick as far as guys go. I just can't get passed you." Seth said. David laughed and they could hear Carman laugh from the office too.

"I don't want to have a choice. I want it to be easy like it used to be. There isn't anything harder than having a bunch of people wanting you at the same time." David said. Carman laughed in the office again and David shook his head.

"Well, I'm used to lots of girls wanting me. What I'm not used to is liking a guy." Seth said. David smiled and touched Seth's leg. Seth closed his eyes and David smiled.

"You'll get over it." David whispered and moved his hand away. Seth shook his head.

"What if I don't want to?" Seth asked in a whisper. David sighed and moved close to Seth. He lightly kissed him and backed away. Seth smiled and shook his head. "Is that supposed to be helpful?" Seth asked. David shook his head.

"No." David answered. They sat in silence as Carman finished with his work. They said their good byes and headed out to the truck. They both got in and Carman waved as they drove away.

"So, that's interesting." Carman said as he drove out onto the highway. David giggled and thought about the light kiss he had given Seth.

"I kissed him." David said. Carman raised his eyebrows and looked at David.

"When?" Carman asked.

"Once when I was shopping for Amanda's ring and once just before we left." David answered. Carman sighed and shook his head.

"I wish I was young again. I remember when I used to be able to just kiss random guys whenever I wanted to." David laughed and shook his head.

"Well, I don't like it. I only kissed him because I can't help myself sometimes."

"And yet, you've never kissed Alan." Carman said. David sighed and shot Carman an irritated gaze.

"Alan is different." David said. Carman laughed and waited for some passing cars before he turned into the apartment building parking lot.

"Yes he is." Carman said quietly and David smiled. He found it so easy to talk to Carman about Alan since he felt almost the same way about him as David did. "So, you're leaving tomorrow?" Carman asked. David nodded and his stomach flipped with excitement. "Well, drive safe and call me when you get there." Carman added as he stopped in front of the building to let David out.

"Yes mom." David said. Carman giggled and hugged David. David smiled and kissed Carman's neck. "I'll call you." David whispered and Carman smiled.

"Ok. Have fun." David got out of the truck and Carman waved as he drove away. David got into the elevator and saw the red head hurrying in.

"Hold the elevator!" She called. David did as he was told and held the doors open for her. She stepped in and smiled at him. "Hi elevator boy." She said as she pressed the seventh floor button. David smiled and pressed the fifth floor button.

"Hi, Elevator girl." David said. She laughed and leaned against the wall.

"So, you're engaged. What else?" She asked. David giggled and looked at the numbers.

"I play guitar." He said.

"Really? Me too." The red head said with an exited tone. The doors opened on David's floor and he stepped out.

"Nice ride." David said and the girl giggled.

"Always is." She answered as the doors closed. David rolled his eyes and went to his apartment. Amanda and Mike weren't back from their walk yet. David got himself a beer and looked at the time. It was 4:30 so they would be returning soon. He went to the fridge and took out the package of pork steaks and got them ready to go into the oven. He sat down at the table and stared at his cell phone.

Seth, Alan, Amanda and Carman. What choices. I wonder how Amanda feels now about me and men. I wonder if she's still ok with it or whatever. How do I even ask? Should I? Would it be a little weird to ask that now that we're engaged? It probably would be. Oh well. I'm happy with her. Seth can deal with his little crush on his own. Carman is with Jake and Alan is with mom so there's no problem with them anymore. I think my life is finally getting back to normal. David said to himself. His thoughts were ambushed by the sound of the door opening and Mack running into the house.

"Hi." David said when the little dog jumped onto his lap.

"Hi baby." Amanda said as she took Mikes coat and let him go and play.

"How was your walk?" David asked putting the little dog down and walking over to Amanda for his kiss. She complied and giggled when his kiss felt more like the kind that led to sex.

"It was fine. How was work?" Amanda asked.

"Well, good I think. Have you met the red head from upstairs yet?" David asked. Amanda frowned and shook her head.

"I don't think so, why?"

"Well, I run into her every once in a while and I was just curious to know if you had talked to her too." David said as they went into the kitchen together. They chatted about the red head and Mikes new little friend who was apparently going to spend the night one of these weekends soon. When dinner was ready, they ate together at the table and talked about the trip. Mike was very excited to take Mack for a car ride. David laughed as he talked about the little dog getting a turn to drive. Amanda and David did the dishes together as Mike watched T.V. on the floor with the dog. At 9:00, Amanda put Mike to bed and went over her checklist for the trip.

"Don't forget to put your tickets in your wallet." Amanda said as she looked at the tickets on the fridge. David smiled and put them in straight away.

"That would suck." David said and Amanda laughed. When she was satisfied that they were now ready to go, they went to bed. Amanda was very forceful in the bedroom that night and David was surprised at the short time it took for her to get him off. She giggled with pride as she cuddled up to him for the night.

"I love you, David." Amanda said. David smiled and rubbed her back.

"I love you too." He answered.

Chapter 18

Amanda had David wasted little time loading up the car and getting ready to go. She packed some snacks and a drink for Mike and made sure they both peed before they left. They talked excitedly about the trip as they drove. Mike played with the puppy in the back and giggled when he would fall off the seat. They reached Nancy's house in the early afternoon. She greeted them at the car and they talked as Mack took a pee in the front yard.

"I have such a great weekend planned for us." She said to Amanda as they headed into the house. It was exactly as David remembered. He smiled as they walked into the kitchen and sat down at the table. "I was thinking we would go into the city and get our hair done tomorrow. Alan said he had something planned for him and David so I thought we should do something."

"Oh, that sounds great." Amanda said and smiled at David. David smiled back and looked out the window. He could hear Mike playing with Mack in the living room over the cartoons Nancy had put on for him.

"Have you had lunch?" Nancy asked. They told her they hadn't and she got busy making some sandwiches for them.

"What's Alan got planned for tomorrow?" David asked as Nancy worked.

"I'm not sure, he didn't really say." Nancy answered. David grabbed the phone and dialed Alan's number.

"*Hello.*" Alan said and David smiled. His voice was still just as striking as it always was.

"Hi old man. We made it." David said. Alan giggled and it sounded like he sat down at his table.

"*How was your drive?*"

"Well, good. The highway wasn't too busy and Amanda only had to stop four times to pee." David said. Amanda giggled and shook her head.

"*When did you get here?*" Alan asked.

"About five minutes ago. I'm supposed to call Carman and let him know we made it but I was curious to hear what you had planned for tomorrow." David answered. Alan giggled and Nancy brought the sandwiches to the table.

"*Well, its tattoo day.*" Alan said. David laughed and shook his head.

"Really? What did you decide?" David asked. Nancy handed him a sandwich and he took a bite of it.

"*Well, my dagger down the center of my back with the handle and cross bars across my shoulders.*" Alan answered. David imagined Alan with his shirt off and the picture of his beautiful golden dagger on his back.

"Sounds awesome. When do we go?" Alan giggled.

"*Well, I'll pick you up at 10:00. We could go to the city for lunch first.*"

"Sounds good." David said taking another bite of his sandwich.

"*Ok, glad to have you down.*" Alan said in his sexy sounding voice. David smiled and nodded.

"It's good to be home." David said and Nancy smiled. David and Alan both hung up the phone. He called Carman next and had to leave a message on the answering machine. When he, Amanda and Mike finished their lunch, Nancy took them into the living room to watch a movie. David fell asleep half way through it but Amanda woke him up at the end.

"Are you not getting enough sleep dear?" Nancy asked. David giggled and rubbed Amanda's back.

"I am, its Amanda. She's up ten times a night and she's not nice getting out of bed." David mock complained. Amanda laughed and playfully slapped his leg.

"He's been too excited to sleep." She corrected and Nancy smiled.

"Alan too. This concert must be a pretty big deal." She said as they got up and went out to the kitchen. They talked about the concert until supper was ready. David and Amanda set the table while Nancy got Mike ready for his meal. They chatted about Nancy's surgeries and long hours at the hospital. She had managed to get the whole weekend off to spend it with Amanda and Mike. They played cards after dinner and Amanda won both games. Nancy took Little Mike up to bed with her and David, Amanda and Mack slept in his old room.

"It's weird to be in here huh?" Amanda said. David giggled and nodded. They got into bed and David leaned over to turn off the lamp. He saw the picture of Gabe that Amanda had given him. He picked it up and they both looked at it.

"God, I miss him Mandy." David whispered and Amanda nodded.

"Me too." She said and ran her finger along the hair that was pinned to the frame. David sighed and put the picture back. He shut off the lamp and held Amanda until they were both asleep.

Amanda and Nancy left before David did. Mike's old babysitter, Rita, almost jumped at the chance to spend some time with Little Mike so their first stop had been there to drop him off before they headed into the city. David was showered, shaved and ready for his day with Alan when he pulled up. He went out to the car and Alan got out.

"Hi." Alan said and hugged David tightly. David smiled and hugged back just as tight.

"Hi." He said as they held each other. Alan pulled away and smiled.

"You look good." He said as they got into the car. David giggled and sat down in the passenger seat.

"Thank you. So do you." David answered. Alan laughed and pulled away from the house.

"So, now that we have that out of the way. Are you gonna get a tat with me?" Alan asked. David raised his eyebrows and shivered at the thought of a hundred needles poking into his skin. Alan giggled and shook his head. "Or not." He said noticing David's shiver. David laughed and looked at his old History teacher. He was wearing a tight pair of light colored blue jeans and a black t-shirt that fit him perfectly. David sighed and looked away. He wanted to stay true to their 'father-son' deal and checking him out wasn't helping. Alan noticed this as well and smiled. "You know, it is possible to check me out and still be comfortable in the car with me." Alan said. David laughed and shook his head.

"What makes you think I was uncomfortable?" David asked. Alan smiled and looked over at David.

"Because I know you." Alan answered. They both laughed as Alan drove down the highway toward the city.

"So, why your dagger?" David asked referring to the tattoo.

"Well, I like those kinds of things and I thought my dagger was the perfect piece." Alan said. David smiled and nodded. They discussed the placement and colors that Alan wanted the artist to use. When they arrived, the artist took Alan right in. David sat in a chair at the head of the table like contraption Alan laid on.

"Your back is going to hurt for the concert you know." David whispered as the artist started working. Alan didn't even flinch. He just stared into David's eyes.

"I'll live." He said and David had to look away. He hated the way Alan was able to look right into his soul. "Why do you look away like that?" Alan whispered after a few seconds. David barely heard it over the buzzing of the artist's gun.

"Well, it's hard to see you as my dad when you look at me like that." David whispered back. Alan smiled and cleared his throat.

"I'm not your dad, David." Alan said and David nodded. The statement was true but he needed to keep Alan at a distance.

"You have to be." He said and looked around the room at the pictures of the artist's work. His eyes fell on one that was a single rose with a barbed wire stem. The petals were dark red with black around the edges. "That one is cool." David said pointing it out for the artist.

"It's a personal favorite of mine. The girl that designed it never actually got it done. It's really a great piece but she was too scared of the gun." He said. David nodded and looked at Alan. He was staring at David with very little expression on his face.

"What?" David asked. Alan smiled now and closed his eyes.

"I just think it's funny how young you are but how smart you are for your age." Alan said. David frowned and tilted his head.

"Why?" David asked. Alan giggled and the artist scolded him.

"Don't move sir." He said. Alan apologized and looked back at David.

"Well, you try to find ways to deflect how you feel around me. That makes you very young. You're smart because it's a good idea." Alan said explaining himself. David rolled his eyes and shook his head.

"If it's such a good idea, why don't you do it?" David asked.

"Well, I'm not uncomfortable around you. Why deflect the situation?" Alan asked. David sighed and looked away again. Alan giggled and the artist let out an irritated sigh. "Sorry." Alan said to the man with the gun. They were silent for the rest of the six hours it took for the artist to finish with Alan's back. When he was done, he took Alan to a mirror and held another one behind him so Alan could see his work. It was amazing. The cross bars where perfectly placed across Alan's shoulders and the blade went straight down his spine to the center of his back.

"Nice Alan." David said. Alan smiled and nodded. The artist took a picture of the piece and Alan paid him at the counter. They walked out to the car and Alan yawned.

"I almost fell asleep on that table." He said as he started the car. David giggled and lit both him and Alan a cigarette. Alan thanked him and pulled away from the building. They drove through the city in silence until they hit the highway. "You're pretty quiet." Alan said changing gears as the car climbed to highway speed.

"Sorry. I'm just thinking." David said. Alan smiled and looked between David and the road in front of him.

"Remember when we used to drive this highway and talk about everything? What's so different now?" He asked. David could remember those days and they seemed almost a lifetime ago. He sighed and looked over at Alan.

"That was before you read my journals and kicked the cat out of the bag." David blurted out. Alan sighed and stared out the windshield.

"I would never have found you if I didn't read them David." Alan said defending himself.

"I know, I just wish you could forget what they said." Alan smiled.

"I don't want to."

"Why not?" David asked quietly. Alan laughed and shook his head.

"David, you may not like it, but I prefer knowing how you feel instead of wondering. I was more uncomfortable around you not knowing what was going on in that head of yours than I am knowing. If my knowing makes you uncomfortable, I'm sorry but, think about the alternative. You could be dead." Alan explained.

"Sometimes I wish I was." David said quietly. Alan sighed and pulled the car into David's little home town.

"I don't. I like the world better with you in it." Alan said and winked at David. David rolled his eyes and looked out the window. "Don't be like that David. I'm trying to make this easier for you. I couldn't imagine going through what you have. But being dead doesn't mean it goes away. Think of the people you would have left behind. Amanda and your baby. Your mom, me." Alan said. David looked at him and sighed.

"Alan, I just wish things were different." He said.

"Ok, different how?"

"Well, I wish you would have told me you were seeing my mom right from the beginning. Then it wouldn't have been such a shock and I would have never ended up at that tree and you would have never read those journals." David answered. Alan pulled up in front of Nancy's house to see the girls were already back.

"David, I will never repeat what I read. Not even to your mom. Not even to you. I want things to be like they were just as much as you do. We're on the right track. Just forget you know that I know." Alan said.

"That doesn't change that I know how you felt." David said looking at the house. He could see Amanda and his mother in the kitchen window. They were working on dinner.

"Feel, David." Alan corrected. David sighed and shook his head.

"That's not helpful." David whispered. He knew he still felt the same for Alan as well but saying it in past tense was making it easier. He didn't wasn't to talk to this man about their feelings as if they still had them. Alan giggled and shook his head.

"Sure it is. It should make how you've been feeling a little easier knowing that I'm going through the same thing."

"I doubt it's the same." David said and got out of the car. Alan wheeled down the window and sighed.

"How would you know if you don't ask?" Alan called as David walked toward the house.

"You would never really tell me anyway. You're always too vague to satisfy my curiosity." David said back. Alan giggled and shook his head.

"Try me when we leave for Vegas tomorrow." Alan said. David smiled and waved as Alan drove away. He walked into the house and Mack jumped on him.

"Hi puppy." He said and pet the little dog. He walked into the kitchen to see Amanda and Nancy. Nancy's hair was trimmed and recolored. Amanda's looked a little shorter and layered.

"Hi babe." Amanda said and kissed him as he came in.

"Hi, your hair looks nice. You too mom." David said and sat down at the table.

"Thank you. How did Alan's tattoo turn out?" Nancy asked.

"It's pretty sweet mom. You got yourself a total badass. He didn't even flinch." David said. Amanda and Nancy giggled as they finished dishing out the meal. They all ate together at the table and David did the dishes when they were done. They watched a movie together before bed. Amanda was especially tired when bed time came and David gave her a well-deserved back rub before she fell asleep. He smiled at her and watched her sleep in the moon light. She looked so peaceful. David kissed her forehead and she smiled in her sleep. He stared at her until sleep took him as well.

Alan arrived to pick up David at eleven o'clock. After a quick visit and coffee, they kissed their women and went out to the car. Alan pulled away from the house and reached behind David's seat.

"Here is a drink for the road." Alan said as he handed David a bottle of pop. "And this," Alan said handing David an envelope. "Is to satisfy your curiosity. Since letters and journals seem to be the things that blows your hair back, I thought some reading material was fitting." He said and pulled onto the highway. David raised his eyebrows and tapped his fingers on the side of the envelope.

"How do you know what would satisfy my curiosity?" David asked. Alan giggled and shook his head.

"Just read it and see if it does. Anything else that you want to know should be easier to ask after you read that." Alan answered. David sighed and opened the envelope. He looked at Alan and then opened the letter.

David,

After our talk yesterday, I thought a lot about how I actually felt before your incident with the tree and then how I felt after. When you walked into my class room on September 5. I thought you were a cruel joke. Carman was the only one who knew the kind of guy that would do it for me so naturally I thought he sent you. When you sat down at the desk at the front of the room I was almost convinced. That was until I looked through the attendance sheet and found your name. I wasn't sure how to react to you. You were the most amazing thing I had ever laid my eyes on. When the opportunity came with the fishing trips and the Mid-Evil project came up, I have to admit that I planned to force you into them. When you were so easy to join I thought it was like a gift from heaven. (or hell, which ever place does these kinds of things to people.) Your love for the Iron Maiden and your willingness to play that game with Carman and I was just another thing that peaked my interest in you. It was so difficult because I had to keep reminding myself that I was a teacher, YOUR teacher and there was no way I could act on impulse with you. I wasn't sure how you felt either. One minute we could talk like old friends, then the next we would get locked together in these stares that seemed to last a life time but were never long enough.

After the shit with the tree and reading your journals, I realized that the feelings I had for you were much more than sexual. I never told your mother how I felt but I think she knew and still knows. When you told me you loved me at Amanda's birthday, I didn't react how I wanted to. I was scared to do anything but say I know. Your mother was standing there and Amanda and you were just engaged. The whole thing went by like a flash.

When you say you wish you could go back in time and change what happened, you say you would change knowing about me and your mom. If I could change what happened, I would have kissed you at Carman's and that time at Christmas when you hugged me and then backed away after a long awkward stare. I would have acted on impulse every time the opportunity presented its self. I know that knowing this sucks but I don't know how else to satisfy your curiosity other than to tell you that my interest in you runs deep into the pit of my stomach. I love you too David and I wish things could be different between us. That being said, I think it's cool how they ended up. I'm with your mom, which means we can come up with any excuse in the book to spend time together and no one would ever question it. Also, if things had been different between us, you wouldn't be engaged right now and expecting a baby. No, I think the way it is, is the way it's supposed to be regardless how much it sucks. I hope this answers some questions for you,

Alan.

David raised his eyebrows and folded the letter. He put it back into the envelope and looked at Alan.

"Your right, it doesn't help." David said and Alan laughed.

"I put a lot of thought into that letter." Alan said defending his question answering note. David smiled and shook his head.

"So, you're telling me that you felt something the moment you saw me?" David asked. Alan nodded but said nothing. "UH, huh." David said and Alan giggled.

"You know, you're not the only one who didn't want to stand up to quickly at the end of class. I just have better control than you do."

"Oh my God Alan." David said and Alan laughed. "That is *exactly* what I wanted to know. See how easy that was?" David said sarcastically. Alan laughed again and turned at the sign that guided him to Las Vegas.

"Well, now you know. Any questions?" Alan asked reverting to his 'teacher' voice. David sighed and looked at Alan.

"You were with mom from the beginning right?" David asked and Alan nodded. "Ok, so you still would have kissed me or whatever even though you guys were together?" Alan smiled and looked at David.

"No, I don't think so. The thought was there though." Alan said. David sighed and nodded.

"Ok, well then I guess if neither one of us had ever known anything, that would actually be better than knowing what we know then." David said. Alan thought about it for a second and looked at David.

"I still feel better knowing." He said. David sighed and shook his head. He had decided there was nothing left to discuss. They talked about the baby coming and the furniture they had found that matched the crib Alan had bought for them. When they got to Las Vegas, they both looked out at the lights and the people and pointed out their favorite things. "We don't have time to stop at the hotel before the concert, are you wearing what you wanted to?" Alan asked. David looked down at himself and then at Alan. He giggled and winked at Alan.

"I don't look as good as you do but it'll have to do." David said. Alan rolled his eyes and drove to the concert hall. He parked as close as he could to the doors and locked up the car. They went inside and the ticket taker tore his half from David and Alan's tickets and let them in. There were already hundreds of people there and it was fairly loud. They passed a t-shirt table and Alan bought them both a shirt. They quickly changed into them and headed into the large hall and found their spots. The concert started about an hour later. The lights and the music were amazing. By the time it was over, neither Alan nor David could barely talk from all the cheering they had done. They got into the car and talked excitedly about the concert as they made their way to the hotel. Alan went in to get the keys. It took him a little longer than usual but it gave David time to try to regain his hearing. He was almost deafened by the loud cheers and music that it seemed to not only hurt his ears, but it gave him a slight head ache as well. When Alan got back into the car he seemed to have a strange look on his face.

"What's the matter?" David asked. Alan sighed and pulled into a parking spot.

"Well, they double booked our room so we had to take a different one." Alan said. He got out of the car and opened the hatch. David got out and took his bag out of the back.

"So, what's the problem with that?" David asked. Alan cleared his throat and led the way to room number 106.

"Well, try to keep your stomach in one place. We have two choices." Alan said and put his hand on the door knob. "Either we sleep in the car, or we sleep in here." Alan said and pushed open the door. David looked in and laughed. There was one king sized bed in the center of the room. He stepped in and threw his bag on the floor.

"Well, it looks a lot more comfortable than sleeping in your car sounds." David said. Alan closed the door and set his bag down.

"Well, I expected you to freak out about having to sleep in the same bed together." Alan said. David rolled his eyes and sat on the end of the huge bed.

"Look at the size of this thing. You stay on your side, I'll stay on mine. There's enough room for ten people on this thing." David said jumping up and down where he sat. Alan laughed and shook his head.

"That's true." Alan said and took his bag to the far side of the bed. He yawned and went into the bathroom. David looked at the bed and shook his head.

Of course there would be only one bed. Why not? He thought to himself. He shook his head again and got undressed down to his boxers. He climbed under the covers and grabbed the remote. He found an action movie and got himself comfortable. Alan came out of the bathroom in his boxers and climbed into bed.

"My back is stinging." Alan said and David laughed.

"Let's see." David said. Alan rolled his shoulders to show David his back. The tattoo was red around the edges but the art work looked beautiful. "It's red but it looks cool." David said. Alan giggled and set himself back against the piled pillows behind him. They watched the movie until David's eyes felt heavy.

"Let's go to sleep." Alan said quietly and David nodded. He shut off the T.V. which made the room very dark. He moved his pillows down and closed his eyes. "Good night David." Alan said in his sexy pillow talk voice. David giggled at the sudden reaction his body had to Alan's voice.

"Good night." David whispered. He could feel Alan get comfortable on his side of the bed. It wasn't long before they were both asleep.

Chapter 19

D avid was startled awake by the sound of Alan clearing his throat. He lay where he was suddenly aware of his situation. Alan lay on his back still propped up slightly on his pillows. David had his head on Alan's chest with his left arm around his muscular waist. He could feel his never fail morning erection pressed up against Alan's hip and his left leg propped between Alan's legs. David's breath caught in his throat.

"Oh God." David said and quickly rolled away from Alan. Alan giggled and looked at David.

"Nope, not God. Alan, and I have to pee." He said and went into the bathroom. David breathed shallow and closed his eyes.

God I'm such an idiot. How could this happen? All this fucking talk about, you stay on your side and I'll stay on mine just to wake up like that. Fuck I can't believe it. Fucking hard on up against Alan. Alan! Oh

God I can't believe this. David said. He sat up and pulled his clothes on from the day before. He sat on the edge of the bed and lit a cigarette. *I cannot believe this.* David thought over and over in his head. The pit of his stomach was in a knot and it only tightened when Alan emerged from the bathroom. He said nothing to Alan as they put their things into the back of the car. Alan would smile at David which would just embarrass him more so he would look away. They stopped at a drive through window and Alan got them each a coffee. He made his way through the big city of Las Vegas in silence. David ran a thousand things through his head that he could say but nothing sounded good. Alan finally got to the high way and they started their long drive home. David looked at Alan finally and sighed. Alan looked back at him and raised his eyebrows. David just looked away and closed his eyes.

"God, Alan . . . I'm so sorry . . . I don't even know what to say . . . . I'm really, really sorry." David rambled. Alan giggled and shook his head.

"David, I would have laid there with you like that all day if I didn't have to pee so bad. What are you apologizing for?" Alan asked. David whimpered and looked out the window. "David, don't be embarrassed." Alan said quietly. David sighed but wouldn't look back at Alan. "In your defense, you were asleep. How can you be held accountable for what you do when you're sleeping?" Alan asked. David shook his head and looked at Alan.

"I'm really sorry." David said.

"For what?"

"I should have stayed on my side. That was the rules." David said. Alan laughed and shook his head.

"So what?" He asked. David whimpered again and took a sip of his coffee. "If you're apologizing for what I *think* you're apologizing for, don't. I had my own curiosity that needed satisfying. You did that in your sleep." Alan said. David looked at him and felt like he had just heard Alan confess to murder.

"What?" David asked as if they couldn't be talking about the same thing. Alan laughed and shook his head.

"I must be a lot more sexually driven than you are David." Alan said and turned toward home. David blinked at the statement and realized that Alan had been talking about his erection. He could feel his face turn red and he looked away. Alan giggled. "Oh to be so young again." Alan said. David sighed and shook his head.

"Alan, are we talking about my dick?" David asked. His stomach flipped so violently that he felt like he might get sick.

"Yea we are." Alan said almost way too excitedly. David closed his eyes and tried to wish his way out of the car. It didn't work. David groaned and lit a cigarette. Alan giggled and shook his head. "David, everything you ever ask me is based on how I feel. Nothing you've ever asked has been physical. Are you embarrassed by it or what?" Alan asked. David sighed and looked at him.

"Alan, I have just started to be able to sit in a room with you without that happening. There is no way I could talk to you about it." David said. He felt like he was choking on his words. Alan smiled and looked at David.

"Why not talk about it now?" Alan asked. David's eyes shot open and he stared at Alan.

"Are you kidding?!" David asked completely mortified. Alan laughed at David's outburst. He shook his head and waited to see what David would say. "I can't talk to you about that." David said and turned back toward the window.

"Why not?"

"Why not?" David repeated sarcastically in a low Alan mocking voice.

"Would you rather I went first?" Alan asked. David shot his head around to look at Alan again. The motion almost gave him whiplash.

"To do what? Ask sexual questions to me? No way." David said. Alan laughed again and shook his head.

"David, you're amazing, you know that?" He asked. David sighed and rolled his eyes.

"Why?" David dared to ask.

"Well, you can tell me you love me but you can't tell me you want me. I would think that want would be easier to say than love." Alan said. David rolled his eyes again and shook his head.

"Ok, I see your point. But that doesn't make it any easier." David said.

"Why not? It's not like you have to act on what you say." Alan said. David blinked and stared at Alan's face. He was so gorgeous in the morning sun.

"Ok, what do you want to hear then?" David asked then took a deep breath. His stomach was now a roller-coaster for his nerves. Alan giggled and thought for a second.

"Well," He said then lit a cigarette. "First things first. Have you talked to Amanda about how she feels about you with men since you put that ring on her finger?" Alan asked. David was taken aback by the question. It certainly wasn't what he expected.

"No, I doubt it changed." David said.

"I would ask if I were you." Alan said quietly. David frowned and shook his head.

"Ok, why?" He asked. He wasn't entirely sure he wanted to know why, but the curiosity of Alan's physical feeling for David was stronger than his embarrassment of the morning erection he had.

"Well, I love your mother to pieces, but I don't think I'll get out of bed so easily if that should ever happen again." Alan said. David could feel his heart pound in his chest and his hands sweat like they used to. He took a deep breath and looked out the window. Alan staid quiet as David absorbed the new information. They sat quietly for the next two hours. "David." Alan said and David looked at him.

"Yea." David said quietly. Alan cleared his throat and looked between David and the road.

"Don't think about it too much. I only told you that so you know that I have a physical attraction to you too. Like I said before, I prefer the way things are now. I just don't want you to get hurt. You should talk to Amanda. The next time something like that happens it might be with someone a little more willing to act on it." Alan said. David sighed and nodded. He knew what Alan was saying was right. Gabe certainly wouldn't have just got up and went to the bathroom. Especially if they had been laying like that for a long time. Alan suddenly giggled. "Don't get me wrong, I'm willing, just not able." Alan added. David rolled his eyes and shot Alan a dirty look.

"You are the biggest dick in the world Alan." He said jokingly.

"I think you have me beat in that department." Alan quickly answered as if it was choreographed. David giggled and shook his head. They changed the subject to the concert and talked about their favorite parts for the rest of the drive. When they got back to Nancy's, she and Amanda were outside on the grass with Little Mike and Mack.

"Alan, I had a really good time." David said as Alan slowed the car.

"Me too." Alan said and smiled at David as he shut off the car. They got out at the same time and the girls ran over to them and hugged them. They all walked into the house together and Alan and David told them about the concert. It turned out that they had a very eventful weekend as well. Rita took Mike and the other small group of children she had to the water park in the city while Amanda and

Nancy did clothes shopping for the baby. They also ran into some of Nancy's friends from work and ended up going out for a movie and supper. They all talked about their weekends until supper was ready. Alan would look at David and smiled every so often. David would smiled back and shake his head. When their meal was done, Amanda and Nancy took Mike up for a bath so Alan and David did the dishes.

"I'm going to tell Carman we slept together." David said as he started the water in the sink.

"Oh please let me tell him. You just play along with whatever I tell him." Alan said. David laughed and shook his head.

"But there's nothing to tell." David said. Alan giggled and stepped up close to David.

"From where I was, there's *a lot* to tell." He whispered and David shivered.

"I hate you." Alan laughed and finished clearing the table.

"You do not." He said as he got himself a dish towel and dried the dishes that David had washed. "You love me, remember?" Alan asked quietly. David shook his head and looked into Alan's eyes.

"And I get nothing out of it." Alan sighed and stared into the young man's eyes in front of him.

"Don't you?" Alan asked in his seductive voice. David could feel his penis react to Alan's seduction and he blushed. Alan giggled and dried a plate and put it away.

"There is no way you react the way I do." David said. Alan raised his eyebrows and smiled at David.

"Don't kid yourself, son." Alan said. David laughed and shook his head. They finished the dishes and Alan got them both a stiff drink of rum. They sat down at the table and both lit a cigarette. "Are you writing in your journals again yet?" Alan asked. David sighed and shook his head.

"I just don't think having a written history of my life is on the top of the list right now." David said. He took a sip of his drink and looked across the table at Alan. He looked so inviting that David had to look away. Alan noticed and shook his head.

"You used to stare at me for a lot longer than that. Why not do it now?" Alan asked quietly. David looked into Alan's eyes and he could feel his body reacting to him.

"Well, I don't want to tell you." David said and looked away. He took a drag of his cigarette and blew it over his shoulder. Alan smiled and tapped the ash off his own cigarette.

"Tight jeans hold it down you know." Alan whispered. David coughed and took a big sip of his drink.

"I really hate you." David said. Alan laughed and took a sip of his rum.

"Well, you don't have to hate me. I'm nice to you." Alan said. David mock laughed and shook his head.

"Oh yea, your Mother fucking Teresa." David said. Alan laughed again. Just then, Nancy and Amanda came down stairs with Mike.

"Time to say good night guys." Amanda said. Alan went first and hugged Mike.

"Good night buddy."

"Good night grandpa." Mike said and David snickered. Alan rolled his eyes and put Mike down. He ran over to David and hugged him. "Good night David." Mike said. David smiled and kissed the little boy on the cheek.

"Good night Mike." He said. Amanda took him upstairs and Nancy smiled at David.

"Why don't we have a game of cards before bed?" She asked.

"Sure mom." David said. She smiled and went up with Amanda. David got up and took out the cards. He set them on the table and Alan took them out of the box.

"We should talk them into a game of poker." Alan said as he shuffled the cards. David giggled and wondered what kind of poker face Amanda had.

"Ok, but what if they win?" David asked. Alan laughed and leaned on the table to get closer to David.

"Then we get laid." Alan whispered. David rolled his eyes and cringed at the thought of Alan and his mother having sex. "I don't know about you, but after a day like today, I certainly need it." Alan added. David blushed and Alan giggled. The women joined them at the table and Alan was successful in convincing them to play. David could see that Alan deliberately let good hands go and bet high on the worst pairs possible. In the end, Nancy and Amanda were victorious over all.

"Good game boys." Nancy said and Alan winked at David. He shook his head and looked at Amanda. She smiled at him and looked at Nancy and Alan.

"Good night guys." She said and stood up. Alan giggled and looked at David.

"Have a good night." Alan said. David laughed and shook his head as Amanda pulled him up the stairs by his hand. David had just closed the door when Amanda lunged at him. She kissed him hungrily and David giggled. He was quite easily aroused after the day he had with Alan and that was exactly what Amanda was looking for. She quickly stripped his clothes off of him and pushed him down on the bed. David helped her out of her clothes and rolled her over so he was on top of her. He pushed himself inside of her and she moaned. He moved his hips and felt her tighten around his penis.

"Ah, David." She moaned. David's breathing picked up and his mind sent him flashes of Alan. He shook them away and arched his back so he could push himself faster and deeper. Amanda clawed at his back and moaned quite loud. David giggled remembering her panic over making too much noise the last time Alan and Nancy where around to hear. He could feel her rake her finger nails down his back again with yet another orgasm. He moaned at the pain she caused him but didn't stop. He could feel his own climax building and she seemed to know it. "Cum for me David." She whispered. David pushed himself in deeper and Amanda dug her nails into his hips. His heavy breathing quickly changed into moans of ecstasy. He climaxed and Amanda pulled him down on top of her. "God, I love you." Amanda said quietly. David kissed her shoulder then looked into her eyes.

"I love you too." He said. He kissed her and ran his hand through her hair. She whimpered and gently ran her hands down his sides. He smiled at her and carefully rolled off. He lay next to her and panted. "That was awesome." He breathed and Amanda giggled.

"It always is right after you spend a bunch of time with Alan." She said. David looked at her and frowned.

"What?" David asked. Amanda rested her head on David's chest and sighed.

"It's like he warms you up for me or something." Amanda answered. David giggled and shook his head.

"Nice."

"Remind me to thank him." Amanda whispered. David laughed and Amanda joined him.

"You wouldn't." David said. Amanda shook her head.

"No. But it was funny wasn't it?" She asked. David smiled and nodded. He thought about his conversation about how Amanda felt about him and men with Alan. He thought this was the perfect time to ask.

"Hey, I was wondering." David said. Amanda looked up at him.

"What?" She asked in a sleepy voice.

"Well, now that we're getting married and the baby is coming, what are your views on me being with guys?" David asked. Amanda thought for a second and set her head back in its original position.

"Well, I don't know. Did something happen I should know about?" She asked.

"No, I just wanted to know so nothing does happen that shouldn't." David said. Amanda sighed and tapped David's stomach with her fingers.

"Am I allowed to be selfish?" She asked. David giggled and rubbed Amanda's back.

"Of course you are." He whispered. Amanda giggled and kissed David's chest.

"Well, I want you to myself, if that's ok. Like starting now. The flirting and whatever is ok, but could you save the kissing and sex for me?" Amanda asked. David smiled.

"That sounds perfect." He answered. Amanda sighed and kissed David's chest again. "I love you." David said and Amanda giggled.

"I love you too." She answered. David rubbed her back until she fell asleep. He was thankful that there was no noise coming from his mother's room.

Well, at least I know for sure where she stands on this. That should save me from any more awkward moments with Seth. But it certainly doesn't help the Alan situation. What if he wanted to kiss me or something? Am I capable of going against what Amanda wants just to kiss him? I'll have to tell him what she said so that never happens. David thought to himself. He closed his eyes and thought of his morning with Alan. He wondered how long Alan had lain there with him like that. He decided it was probably better not to know. It wasn't long after that, that he was asleep.

When David awoke the next day, Amanda was already up and out of bed. He yawned and stretched before sitting up.

"You're always up before me aren't you?" He asked his erection. He shook his head and stood up. He went to the bathroom and got into the shower. He washed his hair and his body and got out. He looked at himself in the full length mirror while he peed. He hadn't seemed to have changed too much with the time that had passed. He raised his eyebrows and washed his hands. He brushed his hair and applied his cologne and deodorant. He went down the stairs and sat down at the table with Nancy, Amanda and Alan.

"Good morning." Amanda said. She smiled at him and kissed him. David kissed her back and said his good mornings around the table. He rested his eyes on Alan's and sighed.

"So, what's the plan for today? You heading out early?" Alan asked. David raised his eyebrows but never looked away.

"I thought we would get a half decent start." David answered. Alan shifted in his chair careful not to break their gaze.

"When will you be down again?"

"Not sure. You coming to Carman's birthday next month?" David asked. He could feel his body reacting to Alan's gaze and wondered if he had the same problem.

"We will be." Alan said. David giggled when it was Alan that looked away.

"It will be fun to plan something." Amanda said cutting into the conversation. Nancy giggled and nodded.

"We would have to get Jake involved though." Nancy said. Alan and David laughed.

"You guys are such girls." David said. Everyone laughed. They discussed some ideas for Carman's birthday over their morning coffee. When David and Amanda decided it was about time to leave, Nancy got Mike ready while Alan helped David take the suit cases out to his car.

"Call me when you get home." Alan said.

"Yes dad." David said and closed the back door. Alan smiled and hugged David. David smelled his cologne and sighed.

"Did you talk to her?" Alan asked in a whisper.

"Yea, I let her be selfish." David answered. Alan hugged tighter and David giggled.

"That's too bad." Alan said with a slight moan in his voice. David giggled again and shook his head.

"I hate you." He said jokingly. Alan sighed and pulled away. He looked into David's eyes and he seemed to squint in thought.

"I love you, son." Alan said and David blinked. They stood there staring at each other for quite some time before David finally said,

"I know." Alan laughed and shook his head.

"You're a dick." Alan said playfully. David giggled and they walked back to the house together. When they approached David leaned close to Alan and whispered in his ear,

"I want you." Alan smiled and then sighed.

"Me too." Alan said. David smiled and hugged his mom when she came out with Amanda, Mike and Mack.

"Oh, have a good trip dear. Next time we need to spend some more time together." She said as they held each other.

"That would be great mom." David said and stepped away. He looked at Alan again and smiled.

"Call me ok." Alan said and offered out his hand. David giggled and shook Alan's hand.

"Will do." David said in the manliest voice he could muster up. They laughed and Alan walked them to the car.

"Be good." Alan said to Mike as he hugged him and got him into the car. He hugged Amanda and she giggled at Mack jumping up at them. Alan picked up the little dog and put him in the back with Mike.

"We'll see you next month." Amanda said and Alan nodded. She got into the long black Hearse next to David and Alan shut the door. He came around to David side and David wheeled down the window.

"Drive safe, son." He said. David smiled and Amanda giggled.

"I will. When are you talking to Carman?" David asked. Alan giggled and looked at his watch.

"Pretty soon." He said and patted David's arm. David looked into his eyes and smirked. Alan bit his lip and winked at him. "Get out of here so you can beat the traffic." He said. David nodded and started the roaring engine. He pulled away and Alan waved as he left.

"So, what's going on with you guys?" Amanda asked. David laughed and looked at her.

"As much as before." David answered. Amanda sighed and rubbed David's leg.

"My feelings about you with guys is stopping you two from doing something isn't it?" She asked.

"No, it isn't. I think it's sexy that you're being selfish. I like it." David said. Amanda giggled and shook her head.

"I see how you look at him." Amanda said quietly.

"I look at him the same way I always have."

"That's the problem David." She said. David sighed and shook his head.

"Amanda, I love you. I love having sex with you and kissing you and all the things you don't want me to do with someone else. Don't ever think for one minute that how I feel about Alan trumps how you feel about the situation, ok." David said. Amanda smiled and nodded.

"As long as I'm not hurting you."

"Is it possible? Nothing you do hurts me Amanda." David said. He looked at her and smiled. She giggled and shook her head.

"I love you David." Amanda said and David giggled.

"I love you too." He said. They chatted a bit about Carman's birthday and then had a deep discussion about writing their own vows. David wasn't sure if he liked the idea but Amanda insisted they wrote their own. When they arrived home, they were both very tired. They took Mack for a short walk and when they got home, Mike was sleepy enough for bed. It was 8:00 but Amanda and David thought bed wasn't a bad idea.

"Don't forget to call Alan." Amanda said as she sat on the edge of the bed putting lotion on her legs. David raised his eyebrows and sighed.

"Oh yea." He said and picked up the phone. He dialed Alan's number and waited through three rings.

"*Hello.*" Alan said on the other end.

"Hi, we made it." David said crawling into bed and leaning his head against the headboard. Amanda smiled and crawled in with him.

"*How was your drive?*" Alan asked. Amanda lay next to David and slowly ran her hand up his leg to his penis. David closed his eyes and shook his head.

"Good, hardly any traffic." David answered as casually as he could as Amanda stroked his growing erection. She smiled at him and started kissing his chest.

"*Well, that's good. Are you going to work tomorrow?*" Alan asked. David rolled his eyes and Amanda worked her way down his body with light kisses. She continued touching him and he was now fully erect. He sighed and remembered he was on the phone with Alan.

"Um, yea. Did you talk to Carman yet?" David asked. Amanda had made it down to his penis and took it into her mouth. David clenched his teeth and held his breath.

"*Yes I did. I told him we ended up having to sleep together and I made him think I was too anxious to talk about what happened.*" Alan said and laughed. David giggled and looked down at Amanda. She looked up at him and sucked harder. David closed his eyes and leaned his head back.

"So, what do you want me to say?" David asked. He couldn't help the shaking in his voice.

"*Well, you can say whatever you want just try to not say anything at the same time. You know what I mean?*" Alan asked.

"Yep." David said quickly and Amanda giggled. The vibration of her laugh made David clench the sheets in his fist.

"*Good, I think it's better to keep him guessing. At least for a little while.*" Alan said. David sighed and looked down at Amanda again. She had her eyes closed while she worked. David cleared his throat and she giggled again. His head shot back and she laughed. "*I was thinking about what we talked about.*" Alan said.

"Oh, and what did you come up with?" David asked wanting the conversation to end as soon as possible. Amanda still worked on him and he could feel his body start shaking.

"*Well, I felt bad about how uncomfortable you were with the physical stuff.*" Alan said. David rolled his eyes and cleared his throat again. He could feel his stomach tense with Amanda's movements and she noticed.

"Let me know." Amanda whispered and took David back into her mouth. David closed his eyes.

"And?" David asked Alan. Alan sighed and David could hear him light a cigarette.

"*Well, I thought if I told you how I felt, physically, it would be easier for you to talk about it.*" Alan said. David looked down at Amanda and held his breath.

"Are you thinking about doing this now?" David asked in a squeaky voice. Alan giggled on the other end and Amanda laughed at the sound of David's voice. She quickly got back to her oral sex and David closed his eyes.

"*Well, is it a bad time?*" Alan asked. David laughed and the movement pushed him into Amanda's throat. She pulled away and David mouthed, 'sorry'. She giggled and went back to work.

"There have been better times I bet." David said.

"*Well, I was feeling gutsy now so, could you live through it?*" Alan asked. David took a deep breath and looked down at Amanda again. He could already feel his climax starting to build.

"Ok." He said quickly and Alan giggled.

"*Ok, well. Remember the night at Carman's house when we first played that game?*" Alan asked.

"Yes." David said remembering the way Alan looked and sounded as he spoke to him. David clenched the sheets as Alan spoke.

"*Well, by the time we were ready to play guitar, I was so hard and wanted you so bad, I could have done you right there at Carman's bar.*" Alan said. David clenched his jaw and pushed Amanda off of him. She giggled quietly as David tried everything in his arsenal not to make a sound as he climaxed.

"Really?" David asked with a squeak in his voice. Amanda got up and went to the bathroom and got the tissue box.

"*Yea, does that satisfy your curiosity?*" Alan asked. David sighed and watched Amanda wipe up the semen from the sheets and David's stomach. He smiled at her and shook his head. She smiled back and tossed the tissue into the trash can.

"Like you wouldn't believe." David answered. Amanda climbed back into bed with him and rested her head on his chest.

"*Why didn't you just ask me if I wanted you like that?*" Alan asked. David sighed and rubbed Amanda's back.

"I was too chicken I guess." David answered. Amanda rubbed David's stomach as she fell asleep.

"*When will you learn that you can ask me or tell me anything?*" Alan asked.

"Alan, trust me. There are some things you don't want to hear." David said. Amanda giggled and David smiled.

"*I doubt that.*" Alan said in a very seductive voice. David closed his eyes and sighed.

"I wouldn't if I were you." David said quietly.

"*Try me.*" Alan said. David sighed and cleared his throat.

"Well, that night, I wouldn't have said no." David said. Amanda sighed and looked up at David. He smiled at her and she giggled.

"*I believe that. I should warn you though David before you think that way, I am not gentle.*" Alan said. David giggled and shook his head. He leaned his head down and kissed Amanda. She smiled and rested her head back where it was before.

"That's good. Neither am I if I don't have to be." David said seductively. Alan cleared his throat and giggled. David smiled and waited for his reply.

"*Oh, really?*" Alan asked. David giggled now and shook his head.

"Really." David said.

"*What are we talking about here? Whips and chains or clawing and biting?*" Alan asked. David laughed and thought about it.

"Whatever you like." David answered. Alan cleared his throat again and David smiled.

"*That's very interesting David. What do you like?*" Alan asked seductively. David sighed and shifted where he lay. Amanda lightly groaned in her sleep and David smiled.

"Big men." David answered. Alan laughed and took a deep breath.

"*Good to know.*" Alan said. David giggled and shook his head again.

"You're killing me old man." David said.

"*You should see what you're doing to me.*" Alan said. David closed his eyes and clenched his teeth.

"You're the cruelest person I know." David whispered. Alan giggled again and seemed to take a drag of a cigarette.

"*I know. I'm sorry. But seriously, you have triggered a very PHYSICAL reaction.*" Alan said. David sighed and shook his head.

"Well, you're welcome." David said and Alan laughed.

"*I wasn't thanking you.*"

"I know." David said and yawned.

"*I'm gonna let you go to bed. I have . . . something to take care of before I go to sleep.*" Alan said. David shook his head and clenched his teeth again.

"Ok, have fun with that." David whispered. Alan giggled and took a deep breath.

"*Uh, huh. Good night David.*" Alan said.

"Have a good night Alan." David answered. He hung up the phone and set it back on the receiver.

"Did he figure out what just happened?" Amanda asked in a very sleepy voice.

"No. He didn't." David answered. "You're not nice to me." David said. Amanda giggled and kissed David's chest.

"You just got sucked off while you were on the phone with Alan. What's not nice about that?" Amanda asked.

"Well, I'll let you know." David answered and Amanda laughed. They said their good nights and their I love you's before they both drifted off to sleep.

Chapter 20

As the weeks went by, Amanda came up with more ways to amaze and please David. As the pregnancy progressed, she seemed a lot more willing than she had ever been. They had seen ultrasound pictures and the technician said that the baby was a boy. They were both very excited and started picking out colors for his room and names for him. Amanda wanted to name him after Gabe but neither one of them could come up with a middle name. David reassured Amanda that they still had three months to come up with something.

Carman had given up trying to find out what had happened between Alan and David the night of the concert after three weeks. He decided that they had made the whole thing up just to bug him. David would just raise his eyebrows and say "Think what you want" whenever Carman would say that. He would just roll his eyes at David and David would laugh. Carman's more pressing issue was that of his mean black horse Diablo. He had already been hurt a couple times by him and was almost ready to sell. He had decided that breaking him was impossible without bringing in a professional but was too proud to admit he couldn't do it himself.

Alan was becoming more and more comfortable with talking about the whole sexual side of his feeling with David which to David's dismay and excitement, Amanda seemed to really like. She was becoming more and more excited for Alan and Nancy to arrive for Carman's birthday because, she had told David, the only thing better than having sex with him after he talked to Alan on the phone, was having sex with him after he actually saw Alan. David would just roll his eyes. He liked to have Amanda so willing all the time but listening to Alan talk to him like that was almost unbearable. He was not looking forward to their visit as much as Amanda was but he did miss his mom and he did miss Alan even though seeing him in person would no doubt be even harder to live through now more than ever.

It was the last Thursday before Carman's birthday weekend and Amanda was panicking because they still hadn't decided on what gift to get for him.

"What about computer stuff?" Amanda asked over dinner. David rolled his eyes and shook his head.

"He works with computers all day Amanda." David said. Amanda sighed and shook her head.

"Horsey stuff!" Mike yelled over the table and Amanda laughed. David smiled at him.

"You know, that's not a bad idea." David said. Amanda looked at him and sighed.

"He has all the tack and brushes and everything anyone would ever need for those horses. What could we possibly get him?" Amanda asked.

"What if we paid for Diablo to get broke? Like professionally." David said. Amanda's eyes lit up and she smiled.

"Oh, David. That's perfect!" She said and smiled. She looked at the clock and squinted. "How can we plan that so close to the day?" She asked.

"Well, we'll call around tomorrow and find the best person for the job. We could add to the gift and find a really good looking cowboy to do it." David said raising his eyebrows. Amanda laughed and nodded.

"Are you looking forward to Alan coming?" She asked with her sly, seductive voice. David shook his head and stared into her eyes.

"Not as much as you are." David said. Amanda giggled and took her plate to the sink.

"You like it." She said quietly and gathered up Mikes dishes.

"Can I watch Mr. Muddy?" Mike asked as Amanda wiped his face and got him out of his chair. David smiled.

"Come on." David said to him and took him out into the living room. He put the movie on for him and went back out to the kitchen to help Amanda clean up.

"Did Seth say if Lance was going to make it back in time?" Amanda asked. Lance had gone away on a business trip and was freaking out over missing Carman's party.

"It will be close but he'll be there." David said. Amanda smiled and rinsed dishes for David to set in the dish washer. He smiled when the baby would kick her away from the counter. "He's gonna be a football player." David said and rubbed Amanda's fat little tummy.

"I think you might be right." Amanda said and giggled. They finished the dishes and watched the rest of Mike's movie with him.

Amanda put him to bed when it was over and David took Mack out for a pee. On his way back in, he met up with Elevator girl at the door.

"Hi there." She said and opened the door for him. David smiled and walked in. She followed and pet Mack while they waited for the elevator to pick them up. "Can I ask you something?" She asked as they stepped into the lift.

"That depends on the question." David said. The red head laughed and shook her head.

"It's nothing bad, I just wondered if you guys had a balcony."

"Why? Looking to jump?" David asked. Elevator girl giggled and rolled her eyes.

"No." She said. The doors opened for David's floor and he held open the door.

"We don't have one. Do you?" David asked.

"No, I want to buy a barbeque but I need somewhere to put it. I was hoping you had space for it." She said and sighed.

"So, I've been promoted from elevator boy to storage dude?" David asked. The red head laughed and winked at David.

"Imagine what the possibilities for further advancement could be." She said. David laughed and let the doors close. He went back into his apartment to see Amanda sitting on the couch crying.

"Amanda, What's wrong?" David asked as he rushed to her side. She sobbed and buried her face in his chest.

"I talked to Lyn." She said between sobs.

"That's Beth's mom, right?" David asked. Amanda nodded and David rubbed her back. "Well, what did she say?" David asked quietly. Amanda looked up at him and shook her head.

"She said that, after careful consideration, they thought it was best that Beth didn't have contact with Gabe's family. They think that it would be too confusing for her." Amanda said and wiped the tears from her face.

"Why would it be confusing? Did she say?" David asked. Amanda shook her head and David sighed. "Can I do anything for you?" He asked.

"No, I think a lot of it has to do with her parents and the fact that Gabe was gay. She seemed really sorry for saying what she did. She sounded almost prompted." Amanda said. David shook his head and kissed Amanda's cheek.

"I'll find a way to fix this, ok." David said. Amanda nodded and wiped her face again. David hugged her and sighed. "I'm so sorry Amanda." He whispered. Amanda sniffed and nodded again. He smiled and picked her up. She cuddled his chest as he carried her into their bedroom and put her into bed. He went out of the room and turned all the lights off. He came back and crawled in with her. She cuddled up to him and sighed.

"Can I ask you something?" Amanda asked. David smiled and nodded. "Have you ever kissed Alan?" She asked and David giggled.

"I wish." David said without thinking but Amanda giggled and kissed David's chest.

"You're so hot." She said and David shook his head.

"I didn't mean that." He said.

"Yes you did. That's what makes you so hot." Amanda whispered. David sighed and rubbed Amanda's back.

"You're weird when you're pregnant."

"I'm not weird, I'm horny. There is a difference you know." She said. David laughed and kissed the top of her head. "I want to have sex now but I'm really tired. Would you take a rain check?" She asked and David smiled.

"Of course." He said. Amanda sighed and kissed David's chest again.

"I love you." She whispered.

"I love you too." David said and closed his eyes. It wasn't long before he fell asleep.

Carman and David started work early the next day so they would be finished when Alan and Nancy arrived in the early afternoon. Amanda got right down to the search for the perfect, sexy cowboy for Carman's birthday present.

"You know, Alan said he had some kind of surprise for you." Carman said as they headed to David's place to pick up Amanda and Little Mike.

"Really? And what's that?" David asked. Carman giggled and raised his eyebrows.

"I guess you'll have to wait and see." Carman teased. David laughed and shook his head.

"You're so full of shit Carman." David said. Carman laughed again and David playfully punched him in the arm.

"Easy tiger save it for Alan." Carman said.

"Fuck Carman. You have no idea how bad I want to kick your ass right now." David teased and Carman laughed.

"You say that but given the chance, I bet you could come up with better things to do with my ass than kick it."

"You're a dick." David said. They chatted about the so called surprise Alan had for David until they reached the apartment building. Amanda and Mike were waiting outside.

"Hi." Amanda said and kissed David as she got into the truck. David smiled and held Mike on his lap for the short drive to Carman's.

"I don't see any giant presents." Carman said. Amanda giggled and looked into Carman's eyes.

"What we got you can fit in your hand." She said in a surprisingly seductive voice. David giggled and Carman was shocked at Amanda's ability to speak like that with a straight face.

"Have you been playing that game with her?" Carman asked David as he pulled away from the building. David laughed and shook his head.

"No, but it looks like I should start." He said. Carman and Amanda both laughed. He pulled his truck into the yard and got out. He took Mike from David and put him down on the grass to play. Amanda slid out of the tall truck and David followed her. She smiled when he put his arms around her and rubbed her stomach.

"Have you been kicked yet?" Carman asked as they went up to the house.

"No, he quits as soon as I touch her." David said. Amanda giggled and put her hands over David's.

"You calm him, that's why." She whispered. David smiled and let her go up the stairs before him. They sat down at the patio table and watched Mike as he ran around the yard.

"When do you expect Alan and Nancy?" David asked Carman. Amanda smiled and twirled her hair in her fingers. Carman looked at her than at David.

"Um, in the next hour or so." Carman said still looking between Amanda and David with a totally wierded out look. David laughed and shook his head.

"Calm your hormones Mandy." David said and Amanda giggled.

"No." She said playfully and David and Carman laughed.

"Wow, pregnancy is weird." Carman said. Amanda giggled again and went into the house.

"Eating, fucking and peeing. That's all she does these days." David said. Carman laughed and shook his head.

"That's not too bad is it?" Carman asked.

"It is when she's getting off on Alan." David answered. Carman blinked and looked into David's eyes.

"What?" He asked and giggled.

"Well, she thinks it's hot that Alan and I talk about sex all the time. She gets all horny and then fucks the shit out me afterward, or during, depending on how she feels that day." David said and Carman laughed.

"You and Alan talk about sex?" Carman asked. David rolled his eyes.

"Not the conversation Carman." David said. Carman giggled and shook his head.

"So, she likes you talking about sex with Alan?" Carman asked.

"Not just Alan, any dude. God, if I was to say the six o'clock news guy was hot, she'd jump me right there on the couch." David said.

"Why are you complaining?" Carman asked leaning back in his chair. David sighed and shook his head.

"Carman, I'm scared I can't keep up with her." David confessed.

"I doubt that." Carman said and winked. David smiled and sighed. Amanda came back out and sat next to David.

"What did I miss?" Amanda asked. Carman smiled and looked at Amanda.

"We were discussing blow jobs." Carman said. David closed his eyes and shook his head.

"Really?" Amanda asked and leaned forward in her chair. Carman giggled and nodded.

"We have decided that deep throating is the only way to go." He said. Amanda giggled and ran her hand up David's leg. He cleared his throat and Carman laughed.

"What do you think Hun? Aren't I good at it?" She asked. David sighed and looked at her.

"Yes you are. Carman's just being an idiot." David said and Carman laughed again. Just then, they could see Alan's car pull into the yard.

"Oh look, David. It's Alan." Amanda said in a very seductive voice. David rolled his eyes and sighed. Carman laughed and stood up. He waved at Alan and Nancy as Alan parked the car. Amanda and David got up as well. Mike pulled Nancy out of the car and she laughed. She picked up the little boy and hugged him tightly. Carman, Amanda and David came down the steps to the car and greeted Nancy and Alan. David hugged his mom after Amanda and Carman had.

"Hi." David said as they hugged.

"Hello. You look wonderful." Nancy said. David smiled and shook his head. Nancy and Amanda walked up to the house together while David and Carman said their hello's to Alan. Carman went first and Alan made some wise cracks about Carman getting old. Carman rolled his eyes and stepped away so David could say hello. Alan smiled at him and took David into his arms. David giggled at the forcefulness of the hug.

"Hi." Alan said. David sighed and nodded. "Can't talk or what?" Alan asked. David giggled and hugged Alan so tightly that his arms shook.

"Hi." David said. Alan laughed and let David go. They got Alan and Nancy's things out of the car and brought them up to the house.

"Where is Jake?" Nancy asked.

"Still at work. He should be here around five." Carman said and sat down at the patio table. Alan brought another couple chairs over so there would be seating for a few more people. Amanda told Nancy about the talk with Lyn and how shifty it sounded. Alan and Carman talked about work but David just sat in his chair staring at Alan. Alan would smile at him through his discussion and David would feel his stomach flip every time. At about 4:00, Seth showed up and David went down to meet him.

"Hey." Seth said.

"Hi, I'm gonna kill somebody." David said and kept Seth at his car. Seth laughed and opened the back seat.

"Ok, you have my attention, what's going on?" Seth asked. David gestured over to Alan at the table and Seth looked. "Ok, Alan is here. And?" Seth asked holding his gift in his arms.

"And, we have been talking about sex for the last month and having him here now is killing me." David whispered. Seth giggled and shook his head.

"Well, that's what you get." David blinked at him and Seth laughed. "David, the only difference between now and before is, you know what you do for him. I would play with it if I were you." Seth said. They slowly started walking toward the house.

"What do you mean?" David asked quietly. Seth cleared his throat and stopped walking.

"Well, think about how uncomfortable you are right now." Seth said. David nodded so Seth continued. "Give him a taste of his own medicine then." He said in a quiet, devious voice. David giggled and shook his head.

"You're a genius." David said. Seth smiled and tossed his hair.

"I know." He said. They walked up to the deck and Seth set his gifts in the door. They both found a place to sit and Seth said his hello's to everyone. Alan looked at David and half smirked. David rolled his eyes and sat back in his chair. He shifted his hips up so he would slide down his chair a little letting his legs fall open and Alan almost blushed at the movement. Seth smiled at David and giggled. Alan had been beat this round. They all talked about the baby coming and Nancy and Amanda giggled through the whole conversation. When Jake arrived, they all went inside to eat. Jake had brought an arm load of pizza with him that seemed to peak Little Mikes interest more than anything else. They all talked over dinner and laughed as Mike sang Happy Birthday to Carman over and over. When supper was over, Alan and David agreed to do the dishes while Carman and Nancy got some drinks together and took them out to the patio table.

"It's good to see you." Alan said to David quietly as they loaded the dishwasher together. David sighed and looked at him.

"Alan, you're driving me nuts." David answered. Alan giggled and cleared his throat.

"Sorry." Alan said and David laughed.

"You are not." David said and grabbed a cloth to wash the table with. Alan laughed and kept loading the dish washer. "Why all the openness lately?" David asked. Alan giggled again and turned to face David.

"Well, you said it, since the cat was kicked out of the bag, why not talk about it?" Alan asked. David rolled his eyes. He walked up to Alan and tossed the rag into the sink. He stood inches from Alan and looked him right in the eyes. Alan swallowed hard but didn't move.

"Because, there's going to be a time when Amanda won't be enough to fix what you've done to me." David said and stepped away. Alan took a deep breath and rested his hands on the counter behind him.

"And?" Alan asked. David laughed and looked at him.

"Why do you always have to be the one to press the envelope?" David asked. Alan sighed and shrugged.

"Cause I'm good at it." He answered. David shook his head again and rinsed out the sink.

"Well, quit." David said. Alan laughed and shook his head.

"Why?"

"Because I hate it." David said louder than he meant to. Alan giggled again and David smiled.

"You liar." Alan whispered. They laughed now and finished with the cleaning. They went out and Carman pointed out their drinks for them. He had sat them right next to each other. When David stared at the drinks he could hear Amanda giggled next to him. He looked at her and shook his head.

"Nice." David said and Amanda giggled again. They talked about various things until Lance finally showed up. Every one cheered when he got out of his car. He laughed and came up to the deck with gift in hand. He hugged Carman and said happy birthday. He messed up David's hair and then hugged Alan. He found himself a drink and sat next to his brother.

"Presents now?" Mike asked from the yard. He was playing with some old tanker trucks Carman had found for him.

"Ok." Nancy said and went in. Alan helped her bring out the gifts and Amanda giggled as she watched David check out Alan. David looked at her and smiled. When all the gifts were out, Carman opened the one from Lance first. It was a wood carving set. Carman thanked him and they giggled. Apparently it was an inside joke. The next gift was the one from Alan and Nancy. They had got for him a new saddle that was far too big for any of his horses but Diablo.

"Like this will get used." Carman said and David and Amanda laughed. Carman hugged Alan and Nancy and thanked them.

"You better give him your gift next." Alan said to Amanda. David smiled as she took a card sized envelope out of the pocket. She handed it to Carman and he shook it. Everyone laughed and he opened it. He read the front of the card and opened it up. Inside was the receipt and paper work on the cowboy that they had paid for to break his big black horse. Carman giggled and looked at them.

"Are you serious?" Carman asked. Amanda nodded and David smiled.

"Looks like you'll ride him yet." David said. Carman laughed and hugged them both. Jake's gift was next. Carman giggled when he opened it up and saw two tickets to the sandals resort in Hawaii. Carman kissed him and Jake giggled. Nancy thought it was cute. Seth handed Carman his gift and Carman looked at him funny.

"Is this what I think it is?" Carman asked. Seth giggled and Carman tore into the gift. Inside was an antique war helmet. Carman laughed and Seth giggled.

"That's the one right?" Seth asked.

"Yup." Carman said and hugged Seth.

"Here's one!" Mike yelled and handed a box to Carman. Carman giggled and read the card. Amanda and David laughed. The card was from Little Mike and Mack. Carman giggled again and opened the present. Inside were things for his truck. Carman giggled and picked up the little boy. They went through the box and looked at all the air fresheners, there was a pair of pink fuzzy dice which made everyone laugh. There was a role of window tint, some window decals and new end for his gear shift. "I pick it all out." Mike said. Carman giggled and everyone at the table laughed. Carman put his gifts aside and thanked everyone again. Jake and Seth went in to get more drinks and Carman looked between David and Alan.

"So how long are you gonna make me wait before you pull out them guitars?" He asked. David and Alan both laughed. Alan went to his car and took out his guitar. Amanda giggled and reached back to knock on the door. Seth opened it and she smiled.

"Would you bring out Abby when you come?" She asked.

"My guitar is here?" David asked. Amanda giggled and nodded.

"I like it when you play." She whispered and kissed his cheek. David giggled and Alan smiled.

When everything was organized on the deck and Alan and David were ready to play, Jake requested Mama I'm Coming Home by Ozzy. David and Alan both laughed but played it for him. Alan stared at David while David sang the song. David met his gaze and Alan smiled. They played the song staring at each other like that. When it was over, everyone clapped and Carman stood up.

"I want to hear some G & R." Carman said. David smiled and started to play Welcome to the Jungle. Carman sang along and when they were done, Carman got a standing ovation. David and Alan laughed. Alan cleared his throat and started to play Who Wants To Live Forever by Queen. David played along and stared at Alan while he sang the song. He seemed to look right into David's soul while he sang. By the time it was over, David didn't know if he was sitting or standing but no one knew it but Alan. He smiled and leaned back in his chair. They both took a sip of their drinks and Seth started bugging David about lessons.

"Man, I gotta learn to play like that." Seth said. David smiled and looked at Alan.

"It takes a lot of time you know." He said.

"I know. I have a guitar already." Seth said. David and Alan laughed.

"He ran out and bought it after he heard you play at Amanda's birthday." Lance said and David giggled.

"Well, I guess we start next week." David said. Seth practically jumped out of his chair and everyone laughed. They played a few more songs for Carman and Copper Head Road for Nancy. After dark, it was starting to get cold so they moved the party inside. The guitars got put away and Carman put on the stereo. When Amanda started getting tired, Alan agreed to take them home. Mike had fallen asleep on the couch and Jake had told them it was fine to leave him there. They got into Alan's car and he drove them home. Amanda got out of the passenger seat and David followed her from out of the back.

"I'm fine. You visit for a minute." Amanda whispered. David rolled his eyes and Amanda giggled. "I mean it." Amanda said and kissed David. She waved at Alan and went inside. David sighed and sat down in the passenger seat next to Alan.

"Amanda thinks we need to visit." David said. Alan giggled and shook his head.

"Do we?" He asked in a voice that sent chills down David's spine. He sighed and looked at Alan.

"What are we doing?" He asked. Alan sighed and looked out the windshield.

"Being very counterproductive." Alan answered and David nodded.

"Alan, I want you *so bad*." David whispered. Alan sighed and looked at him.

"I know. That's not good. This is my fault. I thought we could talk about it without having any adverse effects. The plan was to get it off our chests so it was second nature and almost boring or something. It seems that was a bad idea. For both of us. I think we need to stick to the father son thing." Alan said. David laughed and ran his hand through his hair.

"Adverse effects." David repeated and Alan laughed. "Ok, Alan. Here's the deal, no more talk about sex. It's frustrating and it kills me." David said and Alan nodded. "And try to keep your voice as normal as possible. Normally your voice is bad enough, but when you break out that bedroom voice of yours, it wouldn't matter if we were talking about road kill, you would do it for me." Alan laughed.

"Ok, can I add something?" Alan asked. David nodded and looked into Alan's eyes. "Never tell me you're in bed when we talk on the phone." Alan said. David laughed and shook his head.

"Ok, why?" David asked. Alan sighed and cleared his throat.

"Well, if I told you it would break rule number one." Alan said. David remembered that rule number one was no talking about sex. David giggled and raised his eyebrows.

"Ok, fair enough." David said. Alan smiled and seemed uncomfortable all of a sudden. "Are you ok?" David asked noticing Alan's discomfort. Alan smiled and nodded his head.

"You know, I am I think." Alan answered. "It's been a very odd year. I'm kind of glad we got all our shit out in the open, that being said," Alan added and looked deep into David's eyes. "I want you to know, that I will always be here for you, even if it's not the way you want me to be." Alan said. David smiled and cleared his throat.

"I know Alan. I can't see my life without you in it. I need you." David said. His eyes filled with tears and Alan smiled.

"I know the feeling, son." He said and rubbed David's back. David smiled and took a deep breath.

"I don't have to call you dad, do I?" David asked. Alan laughed and shook his head.

"No, actually I would prefer it if you didn't." Alan answered. David laughed and they hugged. "Ok, you better get up there before the neighbors start talking." Alan said when they let each other go. David giggled and nodded.

"I love you Alan." David said and grabbed the door handle.

"I love you too, David." Alan said. David smiled and got out of the car. He waved at Alan as he drove away and then headed into his building. Amanda was sitting on the couch watching the news.

"So, how did it go?" She asked as David joined her. Mack jumped onto the couch with them and laid himself across their laps.

"Good. It went really good. How are you feeling?" David asked. Amanda smiled and rubbed her stomach.

"I'm pretty tired." She answered and David rubbed her stomach as well. He could feel his little son move inside her and he jumped. Amanda laughed and rubbed David's hand. "He's saying hi, Daddy." She said. David smiled and put his head down on Amanda's bulging stomach.

"Hi baby. I can't wait till you get here. You need to see the beautiful woman that has been growing you all this time." David whispered. Amanda giggled and the baby moved again. "God that's amazing." David said and Amanda smiled.

"Let's go to bed dear." She said and David nodded. He picked her up and cradled her in his arms. Amanda giggled as he carried her to their room. He laid her down on their bed and slowly pulled her shirt off. Amanda giggled as David stared at her breasts before helping her out of her skirt.

"God you're beautiful." David whispered as he looked over every inch of Amanda's naked body. She giggled and watched David undress. He crawled into bed with her and she immediately cuddled up to him.

"I love you David." She said and yawned. David smiled and rubbed her back.

"I love you too." David answered. It wasn't too long before they were both asleep.

David awoke to the sound of the phone ringing. He rolled over careful not to disturb Amanda. He reached for the receiver and put it up to his ear.

"Hello." He said in a groggy voice.

"*Hi, you're not up yet?*" It was Seth on the other end.

"You are?" David asked knowing there was no way they went to bed last night as early as he and Amanda had.

"*Well, you know what it's like around Carman's in the morning. Everybody's up with the chickens around here.*" Seth said. David giggled and sat up. He looked at the clock and read 9:30.

"Well, it is 9:30 so I guess they've slept in." David said. Seth laughed on the other end and David could hear talking in the back ground.

"*So, your mom and Alan want to see you guys before they head home. Are you awake enough for company?*" Seth asked. David looked back at Amanda and smiled.

"We will be." He said. Amanda opened her eyes and smiled at David. He smiled back and ran his hand through her hair.

"*Ok, I'll let them know. I think they want to leave soon.*" Seth warned.

"We're up." David said and Seth giggled.

"*Ok. Talk to you later. When is our first lesson?*" Seth asked. David sighed and stood up.

"How about tomorrow after work?" David asked.

"*Cool, ok. I'll be there.*" Seth said.

"Ok, talk to you later."

"*Yup, bye-bye.*" Seth said and David hung up the phone. He looked at Amanda and smiled.

"Looks like we're entertaining guests this morning." He said. Amanda groaned and rolled over. David giggled and walked to the bathroom. "You can stay in bed if you want, babe." He called from the toilet.

"No, I'm getting up." Amanda said sleepily. David finished and washed his hands. He went out into the kitchen and started coffee. He turned on the news and lit a cigarette. Mack walked out of Little Mikes room and yawned.

"You probably have to pee, don't you?" David asked the little dog. Mack wagged his tail and David smiled. He grabbed the leash and took the little dog out to the elevator. It stopped at his floor and the red head was standing in it.

"Well, good morning elevator boy." She said. David smiled and stepped in.

"Hello." David said and yawned. He took a drag from his cigarette and looked at the red head standing next to him. "Where are you off to on a Sunday?" David asked.

"Well, I have to study for a quiz in biology I have next week." She said and stuck out a pouty lip. David smiled and shook his head.

"What are you in collage for? Like, what do you want to be when you grow up?" David asked. The doors opened and they stepped out together.

"Well, I want to be a marine biologist. So far so good I guess." She said. David smiled and opened the door for her.

"That sounds like a lot of school." David said leading his little dog to the grass.

"I have found that, the longer the name of the career you want, the longer you have to spend in school to do it." She said. David laughed and nodded his head. Elevator girl smiled at him and waved as she headed toward the public library. David waited for Mack to pee then headed back up to his apartment. Amanda was at the table with a cup of coffee for both of them.

"You could have stayed in bed if you wanted to." David said as he took the leash of the dog and walked over to the table. Amanda smiled and shook her head. David sat down with her and sipped at his coffee.

"No, it's time to get up." David giggled. They talked about Amanda's house back home and how she was feeling a little panicked all of a sudden about selling.

"Well, we don't have to sell it." David said. Amanda sighed and shook her head.

"I'm locked into the sale until November First." Amanda said. David sighed and looked at the time. It was just after ten.

"Well, we haven't had any offers worth signing yet so maybe, it will stay like that until you can take it off the market." David offered. Amanda smiled and nodded. Just then, the door buzzer rang. They smiled at each other as David got up and pressed the door button. He went to the door and waited for the elevator to come up. When the doors opened, Mike ran out and was followed by Alan and Nancy. David laughed as Mike ran passed him and went into the apartment.

"Good morning." Nancy said and hugged David.

"Good Morning guys." David said to both of them. Alan and David smiled at each other and followed Nancy into the apartment. Amanda was getting cups out of the cupboard for them when they stepped in.

"Hi guys." Amanda said in a cheery voice. They said their hellos and everyone sat down at the table.

"So, I was thinking that you guys should come down around Halloween so Mike can trick or treat in his old neighborhood. I know Rita would love to see him again." Nancy said. Amanda smiled and looked at David.

"Has anyone noticed a pattern here? There is always a reason for us to go down or you guys to come up once a month." David said. Everyone laughed and Nancy and Amanda planned Halloween. Alan and David discussed the bench seat David was planning to put into the Hearse. They visited until after eleven and Nancy said it was time to go. They all said their good byes and Alan and Nancy were gone for another month.

For the next few weeks, David kept himself busy with work and Seth's guitar lessons. To David's surprise, Seth took to the guitar very easily and he even found himself looking forward to the lessons. Amanda, on the other hand, was becoming more and more fatigued and harder to live with as her pregnancy progressed. With only six weeks left to go, she was looking forward to having her baby.

"Have you thought of any good middle names yet?" Amanda asked David over morning coffee. David looked at her and sighed.

"Amanda, it's hard to think of one. I mean, we said we didn't want to name him after anyone we knew but Gabe. What was his middle name?"

"I hate Gabe's middle name." Amanda said. David sighed knowing that not only would she not tell him what Gabe's middle name was, but it would soon turn into an argument over how she seems to be the only one who cares.

"Ok, well why not name him after a Greek god or a rock star or something then?" David asked. Amanda rolled her eyes and shook her head.

"Why would we do that? We aren't Greek. And I'm not naming my son after a cracked out rock star." Amanda said. David could see that the conversation was upsetting her.

"Why don't I get you one of those baby names books? Bigger than the one you already have. You and mom went through it with a fine toothed comb already and didn't find anything. Maybe a new book would help." David offered. Amanda sighed and bit the inside of her cheek.

"Why are you always trying to get out of it? This is your kid too you know!" She snapped. David sighed and took a sip of his coffee.

"Baby, no offence but, you hate every name I come up with." David said. Amanda's eyes filled with tears.

"So now it's my fault that our son has no middle name?" She asked. The tears started to fall and David winced.

"No, of course not. I just think this would go a lot easier if you were a little more open minded." David said trying to sooth the situation. Amanda started to cry harder now and David shifted in his chair. "Now what did I say?" He asked quietly.

"You think this is easy for me? It's the name he has to have for the rest of his life. I'm not going to settle with ridiculous middle names like my parents did. I mean, Amanda Ingrid Moore. Give me a break." She said. She wiped the tears from her cheek and stared across the table at David. He looked at the time and was thankful to see that Carman would be there to pick him up soon.

"Ok, we won't settle Mandy, the right name will come along. We just need to be patient." David said.

"Patient! We have six weeks David, maybe less! The room isn't painted yet, we don't have a car seat and little Gabriel has no middle name! The time for being patient is over." She snapped. She stood up and got a glass of water from the sink. David stood up and went over

to her. He carefully put his hands on her shoulders. She started to cry
very hard and spun around to hold him. "Oh David. This *is* all my
fault! You've come up with beautiful names. I'm going crazy I think.
How do you put up with me?" She asked through her violent tears.
David sighed and rubbed her back.

"Babe. I love you. I love our little baby. I am not putting up with
you. I am so happy it's you I have to do this with." David said quietly.
Amanda stopped crying and looked at him. She was red with anger.

"You're glad it's me you *have* to do this with? If you don't want to
do this, David, no one is forcing you. Please God, don't do it because
you *have to!*" She yelled and stormed off to the bedroom. David sighed
again and tried to follow her. She slammed the door in his face and the
door buzzer rang.

"Amanda, I have to go. I didn't mean that. I am happy to be doing
this *with* you and I *want* to be doing this *with* you. Please don't be mad
at me." David begged at the door. Amanda opened the door a crack
and looked at him.

"You do?" She asked. David smiled at her and she opened the door
farther.

"Of course." He said gently. The door buzzer rang again and
Amanda rolled her eyes.

"Guess you have to go." She said and stepped out to hug and kiss
David.

"I love you." David said and stepped away.

"I love you too." Amanda said in a cheery voice. David sighed
again and headed for the door. "Have a good day hunny!" Amanda
called as he left the apartment.

"You too!" He called back and stepped into the elevator.

Holy God! Six weeks left. Only six weeks left. David said to himself as he watched the numbers descend to one. The doors opened and David could see Carman standing in the foyer.

"Good morning." Carman said and David put his head against Carman's chest. "Are you ok?" Carman asked as he put his arms around David and rubbed his back.

"Six *more* weeks." David complained. Carman giggled and kissed the top of David's head.

"It will be over before you know it and we'll be watching him Graduate. You can do this." Carman said quietly. David sighed and nodded his head.

"I know." David said and they headed out to the truck. They both got in and David lit himself a cigarette.

"So, two weeks till Halloween. Looking forward to your trip?" Carman asked. David giggled and rolled his eyes. He was looking forward to it but the last time he had brought it up to Amanda, she had decided that he was only looking forward to it so he could cheat on her with Alan.

"I'm almost considering cancelling if I could get a feel for what kind of shit I would be in for that." David said as Carman drove to the first job. Carman giggled and shook his head.

"Well, why don't you ask her what she wants to do?" Carman asked.

"Her mind changes every ten minutes. How could I get a real answer? She's got crazy Carman." David said and Carman laughed. David joined him and then after the laughing, they sat silent for the rest of the drive. The day went relatively fast and soon David was back at home with Amanda. She had a pot of coffee made and was sitting at the table waiting for him.

"So, Lance phoned. He wants us to go over for supper." Amanda said. She had said it in such a way that David didn't know if it was a good thing or not.

"Ok, what would you like to do?" David asked. Amanda sighed and shrugged. "We can stay home if you want." David offered.

"Why? So I can slave in the kitchen while you sit on your ass waiting for me to feed you?" Amanda asked. David sighed and shook his head.

"Amanda, we can go or we can stay. If we stay, I'll make supper." David said as evenly as he could.

"What? You worked all day. And now you're going to stand in the kitchen? Yea, right David." Amanda said and stood up. David grabbed her hand and smiled.

"Then let's go to Lance's." David said again trying not to get upset.

"Ok, I'll just go get ready." Amanda said in a cheery voice. David sighed and shook his head.

I cannot believe this. David thought as he got himself and Little Mike ready to go.

Chapter 21

L ance had prepared a wonderful meal and to David's relief, Amanda managed to eat it without a single complaint. When their meal was finished and David and Lance had finished cleaning up. Amanda, David, Lance and Seth all sat down at the table with a coffee.

"So, did you sell that house of yours yet?" Lance asked Amanda. David was waiting for a snappy remark.

"Are you kidding, I couldn't dump that pile if I was giving it away." Amanda said and sipped her coffee. Seth giggled and David shot him a look as if to say, 'Watch what you laugh at.' Lance rolled his eyes and smiled at Amanda.

"You haven't considered lowering the price have you?" He asked. Amanda shook her head and seemed to be thinking.

"Do you think that would help?" She asked.

"It wouldn't hurt. Even a couple thousand dollars can be the difference between a sale or not." Amanda nodded and looked a David.

"What do you think babe?" She asked. David searched his mind for the right thing to say.

"Um, I trust your judgment dear. I think your asking price is good but, if you want to lower it, I'm behind you 100 percent." David said. Amanda smiled and patted David's hand.

"Oh hunny. We always think alike." She said. She looked at Lance and giggled. He smiled at her and then looked between Seth and David. They both shrugged and Lance giggled.

"So, what will you do than Amanda?" Lance asked.

"Well, lower the price a bit of course. You really should pay closer attention to the conversation if you want to be in it." Amanda said. She got up to go to the bathroom and everyone seemed to take a relieved breath.

"Wow, I'm so glad I can't knock up a dude." Lance said quietly.

"Careful, she has super human hearing." David warned and looked toward the bathroom. Seth laughed and shook his head.

"It can't be that bad." He said and Lance and David both shot him a devastating look.

"Are you kidding? I can't believe she's lasted so long without crying." David said.

"Or yelling." Lance added and David nodded. Seth rolled his eyes and shook his head.

"You guys are over reacting. She's never mean or anything like that." Seth said. Just then Amanda came out and Lance and David said nothing.

"So, we should deal with that when we go down at the end of the moth David." Amanda said and sat down next to him.

"Of course." David said. She smiled and took a sip of her coffee. They discussed the coming trip and the new price of the house. She was willing to come down by ten thousand just to be able to sell it. Lance thought it was a good idea and after she was satisfied with her decision, she decided it was time to go. David packed up little Mike and got him into the car while Amanda said her good byes. David walked over and thanked Lance for supper and said a quick good bye to Seth. He hurried to the car and got on the road to home.

"So, you're sure you want to lower the price?" David asked trying to make conversation.

"What? You think I'm not capable of making a decision like this?" Amanda asked. David sighed and shook his head.

"Look, I just want you to be happy Amanda. Why do you have to take everything I say the wrong way?" David asked. Amanda blinked at him and tears filled her eyes.

"Wow, it's not like I don't have enough to worry about without having to try to interpret what you're saying. I'm so sorry that you talk like an uneducated moron and you don't explain yourself properly!" She snapped. David rolled his eyes and stared out the windshield. "You're ignoring me now?" She asked. David looked at her and shook his head.

"No, I'm not." He said.

"See, I'm wrong again!" Amanda barked. David gripped the steering wheel and drove as quickly as he could the rest of the way home. He got out of the car after it was parked and got Mike out. He opened Amanda's door for her and she shook her head. "I'm pregnant, not disabled. I think I can open my own door." She snipped. David sighed and looked into her eyes.

"For fuck sakes, Amanda! Give it a rest. What the hell did I do to you to deserve this?" David asked. Mike plugged his ears with his hands and David rubbed his back.

"What did you do? What did you do?" She asked and got out of the car. She pointed to her stomach and raised her eyebrows. "You did this!" Amanda yelled and stalked toward the building.

"Amanda!" David called but she went in. He quickly locked up the car and went in still carrying Mike.

"Amanda doesn't like us anymore." Mike whispered and David hugged him.

"Yes she does. She's just not feeling good right now buddy. The baby makes her a little bit sad sometimes." David said as the elevator doors opened. He stepped in and held Mike in his arms.

"The baby doesn't like us?" He asked. David smiled and shook his head.

"He doesn't know us yet. He will love us when he comes." David said. Mike nodded and David put him down when the doors opened. They went in together and David seen that Amanda had gone to bed. He got Mike ready for bed and laid him down. He peeked his head into his room to see Amanda lying on the bed. She was uncovered and seemed to be shivering. He stepped in and gently covered her up. She staid asleep and he stepped out of the room. He walked out into the living room and sat down on the couch. He lit himself a cigarette and leaned his head back on the soft cushions that made up the back of the sofa.

Six more weeks? How do guys make it through this? What can I say or do to keep her happy? It's like she's been drugged or something. How can her mood change so rapidly like that? David's thoughts were cut short by the phone ringing.

"Hello." He said quietly.

"Hi, how was your week?" Alan asked on the other end. David sighed and closed his eyes.

"Hell on earth. How was yours?" David asked. Alan giggled and cleared his throat.

"Better than yours I guess. I am in school every day so it's like a suburb of hell." Alan said. David laughed and took a drag from his cigarette.

"There is still six weeks of this Alan." David said.

"I know. It's only a short time David. It will pass and then there will be a little baby there to make up for it."

"Yea, but SIX WEEKS." David repeated and Alan giggled.

"It will be over soon, David. Tell her she's beautiful and smart and powerful and all those kinds of things." Alan offered.

"I do, sometimes it works. Other times she thinks I'm trying to get laid or something and gives me shit that sex is uncomfortable and I shouldn't even be thinking of stuff like that. God it's ridiculous." David explained. Alan giggled again and David rolled his eyes. "I'm glad you're finding humor in this." David added.

"I'm sorry. You'll look back and laugh about it too someday." Alan said.

"Sure, just like the Jews that survived the holocaust." David said. Alan laughed and David added. "I bet their laughing it up now." Alan laughed again and David smiled.

"Ok, it seems bad now but it will just be a distant memory soon." Alan said still giggling. David rolled his eyes and looked at the time. It was 8:30.

"It will be nice to come home for a few days." David said changing the subject.

"Oh yes. Your mother and I are really looking forward to it." Alan said. David smiled and wondered what Alan was wearing. He thought

it was better not to ask. *"Will you guys come on the Friday or the Saturday?"* Alan asked.

"That depends on Amanda. Whenever she decides we're going. I've learned not to plan anything." David said. Alan laughed again and David shook his head.

"So, it will be a surprise then?" Alan asked.

"Yea, that's the deal I guess." David answered. "For all I know, she could decide we're leaving a day early." David added. Alan giggled and David could hear him light a cigarette.

"Well, an extra day with you guys would be nice too."

"Tell that to Amanda. She's convinced we're having an affair." David said taking the last puff from his cigarette and putting it out in the tray.

"Why?" Alan asked.

"Because I told her I was looking forward to going."

"Well, tell her you don't want to come then and see what that gets you." Alan said and David laughed.

"She'll think of some reason to give me shit for that too."

"Oh, David. I don't have the answers for you. I was never a father so I have no advice." Alan said.

"You would have made a good father, Alan." David said. Alan sighed and took a drag from his cigarette.

"Well, I'm sure you will too. And thank you."

"You're doing a good job with me." David said and Alan laughed.

"Shut up you tit." Alan said. David laughed and shook his head.

"I should go. I have shit to do before I go to bed. Maybe if I set up coffee and stuff I'll be in the good books for tomorrow morning at least." Alan giggled.

"Ok, have a good night David."

"Good night Alan." David said and hung up the phone. He set up coffee like he said he would and turned off all the lights. He looked in on Mike one last time before turning in for the night. He undressed and got into bed with Amanda. She cuddled up with him and He smiled. "I love you." He whispered and kissed the top of her head. She squirmed a bit but didn't wake up. He rubbed her back until he fell asleep.

The next two weeks were about the same. Amanda was very back and forth about when she wanted to head down to see Nancy. But as David had predicted, she wanted to leave Thursday when he got home from work. She already had the house cleaned and everyone packed to go. He called Carman and let him know what was happening. They had already planned around it so Carman was cool with it. They left at 4:00 sharp and David called Alan to let him know they would be in by 9:00pm or so. They rode most of the way in silence. They were already in Nevada before Amanda spoke.

"So, I've been really cranky lately and I'm sorry." She said quietly. David raised his eyebrows and looked at her.

"Oh babe. You're an angel." David said trying to sound convincing.

"You're so good to me David. I just hope I haven't been so unbearable that you would rather have Alan over me." She said. David sighed and shook his head.

"Amanda, I love you. I want to marry you and raise our baby together. Why are you so threatened by Alan all of a sudden?" He asked. Amanda took a deep breath and looked out the window.

"It's not all of a sudden David. I've always felt like you would rather have him than me. I feel like you're only marrying me because I'm pregnant and it's the right thing to do."

"What? Amanda, I love you so much. I don't think you know how much. I wish I could make you understand but I can't. Alan and I are close but that's it. I mean, he has mom. I have you and we're happy with that." David explained.

"So, you guys are settling?" Amanda asked. David rolled his eyes and shook his head.

"No. We are not. There is no *we*, Amanda. There is Alan and mom and you and me. No me and Alan, ok?" David asked. He knew the conversation would have to change soon or there would be a fight.

"I just wish I wasn't standing in your way. I know how you feel about him." Amanda said. She sounded very sincere.

"Amanda, if I have you, that's all that matters. You are everything I need. There could be a million Alan's in this world and I would still choose you."

"Yea, because I'm pregnant." Amanda said. David scratched his head.

"Actually, I wish we could skip the pregnancy part." David said. Amanda gasped and David cringed.

"What? You don't want this baby?" Amanda asked.

"Yes, yes I do Amanda. I'm sorry I said it wrong. I want this baby so bad. I wish it was here already is all I meant. I hate waiting for him." David said. It almost sounded as though he was begging for forgiveness.

"Really?" Amanda asked. David smiled and nodded. Amanda smiled back and rested her head against the window. David sighed a breath of quiet relief. They traveled for the last of the drive in relative silence. Amanda would ask questions about the surrounding area once in a while but never really opened up into a full discussion. They arrived at Nancy's house at 9:45. David pulled up in front and seen Alan's car parked there as well.

"Hi." David said as he opened the door and seen Alan standing there waiting for him to get out.

"Hi there." Alan said and hugged David. David smiled at the warm feeling being held by Alan gave him but pulled away quickly in order to avoid Amanda's insane ranting. Nancy and Amanda got Mike out of the car and they all said their hello's as they went inside. David staid out with Mack so he could pee. Alan stepped out after a few minutes and lit a cigarette. "So, how was your drive?" Alan asked. David laughed and shook his head.

"Not bad actually. Very quiet." David said. Alan smiled and watched the little dog play with a stick.

"You look really tired." Alan said as he puffed on his cigarette. David smiled and nodded.

"I am kind of tired." David said. He looked at Alan and sighed. He was wearing a pair of light colored blue jeans and a white sweater that looked to be two sizes too big for him. He was so amazing to look at. David smiled and looked away. Alan noticed and giggled.

"You're so cute when you're caught." Alan said quietly. David laughed and shook his head.

"No rule breaking Alan." David said and they both laughed. They watched the little dog play in the grass until Alan was finished his cigarette. They went inside and joined Amanda and Nancy in the kitchen.

"So, Mike tells me that he's going to be a ghost for Halloween." Nancy said. Mike giggled and clapped his hands.

"David said it's a scary one!" Mike said excitedly. Amanda and Nancy laughed at his excitement and then Amanda grabbed her stomach. David was next to her in a flash.

"Are you ok?" David asked. Amanda smiled and nodded.

"The doctor calls it Braxton Hicks contractions. There fake contractions or something. They don't stay long." She said reassuring David. David sighed and rubbed Amanda's stomach. Alan and Nancy smiled.

"Do you need to lay down or anything?" Nancy asked. Amanda smiled and nodded. David helped her up and took her up to his old room.

"Oh David, I can't wait until this is over." She said as she lay down on the bed.

"I know." David said quietly and helped her get comfortable and covered up.

"Don't stay up too late. I sleep better when you're with me." She whispered. David smiled and kissed her forehead.

"Ok, I'll just get Mike to bed and then I'll be here." David said. Amanda nodded. He smiled again and left the room. He went downstairs to see only Alan at the table. "Where's mom?" He asked as he sat down with Alan.

"She took Little Mike up to bed with her. How is Amanda?"

"Sleeping." David answered and ran his hand through his hair. Alan smiled and leaned forward in his chair.

"You look like you're expecting a baby." He whispered. David laughed and shook his head. He looked into Alan's eyes and sighed.

"You're so good looking." David blurted out and Alan laughed. "Sorry." David said and Alan shook his head.

"Don't be. You're allowed to compliment me. It doesn't bother me at all." Alan said.

"Well, Amanda feels differently." David said and stood up. Alan sighed and stood up as well.

"This too shall pass, son." He said. David smiled and hugged Alan.

"It's so good to see you again." David whispered. Alan smiled and breathed in David's sent.

"Like wise." He said and let David go. David smiled and headed up stairs to bed. He looked in on his mom and Mike. She was reading him a story and David smiled at them.

"Good night mom." David whispered.

"Good night dear." Nancy whispered back and went back to Mike's story. David smiled again and went into his room where Amanda lay sleeping. He got undressed and crawled carefully in with her.

"Is Mike in with Nancy?" Amanda asked in her sleep.

"Yup, she's reading to him." David whispered. Amanda smiled and went back to sleep. David sighed and stared up at the ceiling.

God Alan looks just as good as he always did. How long will it take before I don't see him as a walking billboard for sex? This is a lot harder than I thought it would be. Maybe it's harder because of how Amanda has been lately. Maybe it will get easier once the baby is born. David thought. He sighed again and closed his eyes. *I wish I had guts enough to just kiss him or something before I was a married man. I wish I was the cheating type just for two seconds. But, I can't hurt Amanda. She really is the most important thing to me.* David thought to himself as he slowly fell asleep.

The next day was a little slow. Both Nancy and Alan had to work so David and Amanda spent a lot of the day playing cards or Amanda would nap. At 3:30, Alan arrived. Amanda was sleeping so David met him outside.

"Hi." David said. Alan smiled and sat down on the front step with David.

"Hi. How was your day?"

"Quiet."

"Well, that's better than really busy or really boring." Alan offered. David smiled and shook his head.

"How was your day?" David asked. Alan looked at David and smiled.

"Slower than molasses. At noon it felt like I had been there for three days." Alan said and stretched. The movement caught David's attention and he watched as Alan's body tightened and moved with the stretch. The muscles in his chest and back flexed with his stretch and David groaned. Alan laughed and David blushed.

"Sorry." David whispered and looked away.

"You're always apologizing." Alan said and patted David's back.

"The least you could do would be ignoring me when that happens." David said. Alan laughed and shook his head.

"Well, the least you could do would be returning the favor." Alan said and stood up. David shook his head and stood up with him. They went inside and David made a pot of fresh coffee while Alan waited for it at the table. Little Mike had fallen asleep on the floor in the living room. David sat down at the table across from Alan and stared at him. Alan shifted in his seat but met David's gaze.

"When does mom get home?" David asked never looking away from Alan's luring light green eyes.

"About five today I think. How long does Amanda nap for?" Alan asked. David smiled and shook his head. Alan laughed and lit a cigarette. "Sorry, I thought you wanted to know how much alone time we had." Alan added. David laughed and met Alan's gaze again.

"Alone time?" David asked.

"Yea, did you need a man to man talk or something?" Alan asked. David smiled and got up to get coffee cups ready for him and Alan.

"Man to man talk. I don't know if *that's* what I need." David said as he put cream and sugar in each cup. Alan giggled and shook his head.

"Ok, then what do you *need?*"

"Oh, a holiday." David said. Alan laughed and took a drag from his cigarette. "That wasn't the answer you were expecting was it?" David asked.

"Well, no. But I'm glad you're sticking to the rules." Alan said. David giggled and shook his head. The coffee was ready so he poured them each a cup and took them to the table.

"So, speaking of the rules. How is it working for you?" David asked sitting down at the table taking a sip from his cup.

"Well, work keeps me busy during the day and, as much as you don't want to hear this, your mom keeps me busy at night. It's the time in between that's the hardest." Alan said. David nodded and took another sip from his coffee.

"Well, nothing keeps me busy enough so, good on ya." David said. Alan laughed and shook his head.

"You're such a dick." Alan said. David laughed and Alan joined him. They discussed putting the seat into the Hearse while they were down since the new bench seat was in Nancy's garage. They had agreed to do it the next day since it was Saturday and Alan had the day off. It wasn't long before Amanda was awake and seemed to be in a very good mood. She had decided that she was going to make supper for when Nancy got home. She talked David and Alan into taking the dog for a walk and let Mike play at the park. They did what they were told and when they got back, Nancy was home and supper was ready. David quickly got Mike cleaned up for dinner and dished him up a plate.

"So, I was thinking that I might take Amanda to my book club tonight. Would you two be ok with Mike?" Nancy asked over dinner.

"Yea, why not?" Alan asked. Amanda smiled and looked at David.

"I don't have to go if you don't want me too." She said. David smiled and shook his head.

"If you wanna go, than you should go babe." David answered. Amanda giggled and kissed him on the cheek. David sighed and smiled at her. They finished their dinner and Amanda and Nancy got ready to go while Alan and David did the dishes. They left at 7:00 and David gave Mike a bath. When he was done, he brought Mike downstairs with him and saw Alan asleep on the couch. David smiled at him and put a movie on for Mike. He sat down in his father's old chair and stared at Alan. His muscular chest lifted and fell with his breathing. He had one arm behind his head and the other hand resting on his stomach. His feet were crossed on the arm of the couch and David thought he had never seen Alan look so sexy before. He could feel his body starting to react so he thought it was better to look away. He stared at the T.V. but the image of Alan was burned into his mind. He shut his eyes and concentrated on his growing erection. He tried to think of anything that would make it go away. When he thought he had it beat, he heard Alan moan in his sleep.

"Damn it." David whispered to himself as he could feel all his hard work go right down the toilet. He opened his eyes and looked at Alan again. He was still asleep. David sighed and shook his head. He looked at the clock and seen it was almost 8:30. "Come on buddy. Time for bed." He said to Little Mike.

"But, I watching my show." Mike said. David smiled and shut it off.

"And now it's gone." He said. Mike sighed and stood up. David smiled at him as he followed the little boy up the stairs.

"Is trick or treat tomorrow?" Mike asked as David tucked him into bed.

"Yes sir." David said and Mike giggled.

"Can I eat all my candy I find?"

"Well, you can have some but, you should save some for later." David said. Mike smiled and nodded. David pet the little boys hair and kissed his forehead. He left the room and went back downstairs. Alan was still asleep on the couch so he decided to sit at the kitchen table and play solitaire. He had just shuffled his second hand when his cell phone rang. "Hello." He said.

"Hey, how is your visit going?" Seth asked on the other end. David smiled and dealt out his next hand.

"Good, Mom and Amanda are at a book club thing and Alan and Mike are sleeping." David said. Seth giggled and David could hear him take a sip of something.

"So, you're all alone for a little while then?"

"Yea, why?" David asked.

"Well, you've been so busy with Amanda and Mike. You have some time for yourself. What are you doing with it?" Seth asked. David looked down at the cards and giggled.

"Well, I'm playing solitaire." David said and Seth laughed.

"Wow, that is really sad, dude."

"What would you do?" David asked. Seth sighed and seemed to be thinking.

"Well, that would depend on what my surroundings were."

"Ok, well, Mike is upstairs, Amanda and Mom won't be home for a half hour and Alan is asleep on the couch." David answered.

"So, you have Alan asleep on a couch and you aren't out there taking advantage of this situation?" Seth asked. David frowned and looked out into the living room at Alan.

"What?" David asked. Seth giggled and took another sip of his drink.

"*David, you could be out there looking and, I don't know, if he's a deep enough sleeper, touching if you dare.*" Seth said. David laughed and shook his head.

"You're an idiot, Seth. And then he wakes up and freaks out right." Seth laughed.

"*Sorry I have a twisted imagination. What can I say?*" Seth asked. David shook his head again and made a few moves on his solitaire game.

"Try not saying anything." David joked and Seth giggled.

"*Touchy, touchy. Come on. Like you didn't think of it. He might like it you know.*"

"Seth, I really don't want to talk about this." David said.

"*You're such a prude in your old age David.*"

"Yes well, it keeps me out of jail." David said. Seth laughed and David laughed with him.

"*Well, be good then if you must. I would keep it in mind though. You never know. He may have done the same thing.*" Seth offered. David laughed and looked at the couch again. Alan had moved and was on his side now.

"Well, if the opportunity is ever to present itself, I'll let *him* do it then." David said and lit a cigarette.

"*Chicken.*" Seth said and they both laughed. David took a drag of his cigarette and sighed.

"Well, are you done being a bad influence yet or do you need more time?" David asked.

"*No, I get it. I'll let you go. Have a good time.*" Seth said.

"Ok, bye Seth."

"*Bye.*" Seth said and David hung up the phone. He shook his head and piled the cards back up. He put them back into their box and set them back in the top drawer of the china cabinet. He went back to the table and caught movement in the corner of his eye. Alan had sat up. He came out into the kitchen and smiled at David.

"You know, you could have woke me up." He said and grabbed a bottle of water out of the fridge.

"And miss your rendition of sleeping beauty? Never happen." David said as Alan sat down with him. Alan giggled and shook his head.

"So, what did I miss?" Alan asked.

"Well, Mike had a bath and I just kicked my ass in three hands of solitaire. You missed a hell of a party." David answered. Alan laughed and looked into David's eyes.

"You really should have woke me up. I would have liked the couple of hours of alone time." Alan said and took a sip of his water. David smiled and shook his head.

"And what would you do with that time Alan?" David asked. Alan sighed and shook his head.

"Nothing I would *like* to do." Alan answered. David shook his head and stared into Alan's eyes.

"You don't make this easy you know."

"And you do?" Alan asked. David blinked at him and he could feel confusion spread across his face.

"What did I do?" David asked. Alan sighed and shook his head.

"You got here." Alan said. David sighed and looked down at his cigarette burning away in the ash tray. "I'm sorry David. I guess I'm just having a more difficult time with this than I thought I would." Alan confessed.

"Well, you and me both. What do we do about it?" David asked. Alan shook his head and crossed his hands on the table.

"I don't know. Shock therapy?" David laughed and nodded.

"Yea, that would work." He said. Alan giggled and sat back in his chair.

"Ok, seriously. We can go back to not talking about it at all." Alan suggested. David smiled and nodded.

"Sure. That sounds doable." David said and bit his bottom lip and tapped his thumb on the table. Alan shook his head and looked away.

"That doesn't help." Alan said quietly. David sighed and got up. He went to the fridge and got a water bottle for himself.

"Sorry." David said as he sat back down. Just then, they could see the lights of Nancy's car pull into the driveway.

"You should have woke me up." Alan whispered and winked at David. David giggled and shook his head.

"Why? So we could have made out for the last three hours?" David asked sarcastically. Alan smiled and watched the ladies walk passed the window.

"Or whatever." Alan whispered. David could feel his stomach flip and his penis react almost violently. He cleared his throat and Alan giggled.

"You're a dick." David whispered.

"I know." Alan said. The girls walked in and told Alan and David all about the discussion they had at their book club. Amanda was fairly tired so David took little time getting her upstairs to bed. He kissed her when they were both lying down.

"Are you horny tonight, David?" Amanda asked in a half whisper.

"Very." David answered and tightly gripped Amanda's back side. Amanda giggled and climbed on top of him. She could feel that he was fully erect already and she smiled.

"Are you ever." She said in a seductive voice and started grinding herself against David's large erection. David closed his eyes and quietly moaned at her movements. She bent down and kissed him as he pulled her underwear off. She ran her hand down his body and took David tightly into her grasp. David moaned again and pushed his hips up moving his penis in her hold. Amanda smiled and carefully guided him inside of her. She moaned and tightly gripped David's arms as they both moved. David watched her breasts move with every deep thrust he made. Amanda moaned and scratched his chest as she climaxed. David's orgasm came right after hers and Amanda giggled. "You were pretty horny for it to happen that fast." She whispered. David smiled and shook his head.

"You have no idea." He said and Amanda carefully rolled off of him. She lay down next to him and rested her hand on his chest.

"Aren't you used to how he looks by now?" She asked quietly. David sighed and looked at her pretty face.

"You know me so well." David said. Amanda smiled and rubbed David's chest.

"Well, at least I'm the one that gets to fix it." She said and closed her eyes. David smiled and put his hand on Amanda's. He stared up at the ceiling as sleep took Amanda first.

Why does he have to be like that? One minute he wants to make this whole stupid thing easier, the next he's hitting on me so hard it's amazing I stay upright. I can't keep doing this. I should have woke him up. Doesn't he know what he does to me after twenty minutes let alone three hours? Like really Alan. David said to himself. He closed his eyes and tried to shake the vision of Alan asleep on the couch. Soon the innocent vision turned into a rigorous make out session in David's over active mind. He sighed and tried to shake the thought. When that didn't work he rolled over and tried to think of something else.

Come on sleep. He's with your mom which technically makes him your new dad. What kind of sick twisted weirdo would you have to be to want to fuck your dad? David scolded himself in his mind. The kissing turned quickly into sex and David sat up.

"That's it." David said out loud and got his robe on. He went downstairs and got a shot glass and a bottle of Scotch out of the cupboard. "I'll drink myself to sleep." David said and sat down at the table. He poured the first shot and drank it down quickly. He slammed the shot glass down on the table and refilled it. He stared at the glass and took the next shot just as fast. He slammed the little glass down again and refilled it. He lit a cigarette and sat back in his chair. He let his head rest on the back of the chair and closed his eyes. He could still see the epic sex story he had manifested in his head and opened his eyes. He lifted his head back up and seen Alan standing on the bottom stair. He was wearing a pair of jeans but no shirt.

"What are you doing?" Alan asked quietly.

"Trying to sleep." David answered and took his new shot. Alan sighed and got two drink sized cups out of the cupboard. He brought them to the table and sat down with David. He filled each cup and handed one to David.

"Well, let's talk." Alan said and sipped at his drink. David sighed and rolled his eyes.

"Really, Alan. No thank you." David said and took a long sip from the cup Alan had handed him.

"Why not? Who else are you going to talk to? I told you I would be here for you no matter what. So, spill your guts." Alan said. David sighed and shook his head.

"What if the problem is you? Then who do I talk to?"

"You talk to me. I happen to know a bit about the subject." Alan said and David giggled.

"I don't want to." David said and took a sip from his drink. He rolled his cigarette in his ash tray then took a long drag.

"Ok, well who do I talk to then?" Alan asked. David looked at him and shrugged. "If I talk to Carman, he calls me an idiot because he really doesn't know the whole story. I can't talk to your mom because, well . . . It's your mom." Alan said. David smiled and nodded.

"Ok Alan. You win again. What do you want to talk about?" David asked. Alan sighed and looked at the Scotch bottle.

"Tell me why you're using Scotch as a sleeping aid." Alan said. David sighed and looked down at his cigarette.

"I can't sleep. Scotch helps." David answered quietly. Alan shook his head.

"Yea, but why can't you sleep?"

"Why can't you sleep?" David asked back trying to deflect the question.

"Well, I had a two and a half hour sleep after supper. What's your excuse?" David sighed and shook his head.

"I have an over active imagination." David answered. Alan raised his eyebrows.

"Ok, so night mares? Boogie man, Tooth Fairy? What are we talking about?" Alan asked. David rolled his eyes and looked at Alan.

"I would give anything for a night mare right now." David answered quietly.

"Ok, what's going on?" Alan asked and took a sip of his drink. David looked out the window at his long black Hearse and sighed.

"Remember when I said, what you were going through was nothing like what I was going through?" David asked. Alan nodded and David took a long sip of his strong drink. "Well, I lose sleep at night, Alan. Just thinking about you. I can't help it either. It's so intense and vivid and real. A nightmare with that kind of clarity would give a person a heart attack." David said never looking at Alan's handsome face. Alan shifted in his chair and cleared his throat.

"Well, what if I told you I know what you're going through?" Alan asked. David sighed and looked at him. He raised his eyebrows and shook his head.

"Somehow I doubt it." David said and looked away again.

"Ok, why?" Alan asked. David mock laughed and shook his head.

"Well, somehow I think, given your age, you have a little more control over your body and your mind than I do."

"Really? You think so?" Alan asked. David nodded and Alan sighed. "Do you know how long it was, before your mother, since I had sex?" David looked at Alan and shook his head. "Two years David. That's a long time. When you walked into that class room, those two years hit me so hard that I couldn't even take care of it myself." Alan said. David swallowed hard and tried not to imagine Alan jacking off. It didn't work. David shut his eyes and drank the last of the scotch out of his cup.

"Ok, so?" David asked as Alan refilled his glass.

"So, I get it. Ok. I do." Alan said.

"Why tell me this?" David asked. Alan rolled his eyes and his shoulders fell.

"David, you don't tell me anything. I can only guess what's going on with you. I try to interpret the situation and try to relate to you. What else can I do? Was I wrong?" Alan asked. David swallowed again and looked back out the window. "David, were you, or were you not, thinking about having sex with me and that's why you're sitting here now?" Alan asked. David's stomach flipped and his hands began to sweat. He closed his eyes and slightly nodded. "Well, then I guess my interpretation wasn't wrong." Alan said. David sighed and shook his head.

"I don't want to think about you like that anymore. I want to be able to spend time with you and talk to you with out all that other shit." David said. He could feel his stomach relaxing and Alan sighed.

"I want that too David. More than anything in the world. We can't change how we look or walk or whatever, so what do you think will work?" Alan asked. David shrugged and took a long sip from his glass. Alan sighed and shook his head. "You see, that's where I'm at with this whole mess too. I guess we *are* on the same page David." He added. David looked at him and sighed.

"I want to sleep at night, Alan. I want to have sex with Amanda because *she* made me horny, not you. I want to come out here and play that game with you without feeling sick afterward." David said. Alan raised his eyebrows and then frowned.

"Sick? Why do you feel sick?" Alan asked. David rolled his eyes and took another sip of his drink.

"I get so . . . riled up Alan that I almost feel sick." David said trying to explain. Alan sighed and shook his head.

"Ok. I'm sorry." Alan said. David looked out the window at his car again.

"It's not your fault Alan. You can't help it. I just want things back to normal." David said. Alan nodded and took a sip of his small glass of Scotch.

"Maybe we need a little more time apart? Maybe less time on the phone might help too." Alan suggested. David shot his eyes to meet Alan's.

"Are you kidding? It's worse when there's more time between visits."

"Well, ok then. God David, I don't know what to do." Alan said and looked down at his drink.

"Marry my mom." David said and Alan shot his head up to look into David's eyes.

"What?" Alan asked.

"Marry my mom. Adopt me. If we're related, it's harder to think this way about you." David insisted. Alan sighed and shook his head.

"David, I can't just marry your mom. It doesn't work that way. Besides, would it help you if you knew I had sex with her before I came down here?" Alan asked. David shivered then remembered he had done the same.

"No, would it help you knowing I had sex with Amanda before coming down here?" David asked and Alan giggled.

"No." He said. David rolled his eyes and sat back in his chair. "David, we can do this. We just have to quit pushing the envelope. We have to stop talking about it and speaking our minds. We need to convince ourselves that the other one isn't available."

"But we aren't Alan. You're with mom, I'm with Amanda. Neither one of us is available." David said. Alan rolled his eyes.

"If I tried to kiss you, would you stop me?" Alan asked. David took a deep breath and thought of Amanda. He thought about her pregnant stomach and her engagement ring. He thought about his mother and the promise he made Alan make about not hurting her. He tried to convince himself that kissing Alan wasn't the most pressing thing on his mind. Not only just kissing him, but anything that might follow. He looked into Alan's light green eyes and sighed.

"No, I wouldn't." David whispered. He shook his head and looked down at his glass.

"Then I guess what we need to do is remember that." Alan said. David looked at Alan with a confused gaze.

"Why?" David asked.

"I would stop you. If you can't stop me then, we make sure that never happens. I promise never to put you in a situation where you would feel the need to have to stop me. Ok?" Alan asked and David nodded.

"Isn't that what we're doing now?" David asked. Alan sighed and took the last sip out of his glass.

"David, what is one thing I do that turns you on?" Alan asked. David raised his eyebrows and thought.

"Well, everything. But I guess those long stares are the worst." David said.

"Well, that's the same for me. We just make sure that doesn't happen." Alan said. David nodded. He finished his drink and got up. He took Alan's glass and took them both to the sink. Alan got up and put the bottle of Scotch in the cupboard.

"Ok, well. I guess we try that huh?" David asked. Alan smiled and nodded.

"David I can only think of one other thing and I won't let either one of us do it." Alan said. They walked to the stairs and David stopped him.

"What's that Alan?" David whispered. Alan sighed and looked into David's eyes.

"Do it and get it over with." Alan said and headed up the stairs. David blinked and watched him go up. Alan stopped at the top and looked down at David. "It can't be an option David." Alan said. David nodded and ran his hand through his hair.

"Yea, I know that. I was just wondering how the hell I was supposed to sleep after you said that." David answered. Alan giggled and shook his head.

"With your eyes closed." Alan said and headed for Nancy's room. David sighed and went up to his room. He lay down with Amanda and shut his eyes. He was soon asleep but not without a full erection.

Chapter 22

Mike had a very good haul from trick or treating and he seemed very proud of himself. He had fallen asleep before they got home so, he wasn't able to enjoy his haul until the next day. Amanda put a few of his treats together for snacks for the road. The plan was to stop and see the real estate agent on their way home. David and Alan's plan seemed to be working. They only looked at each other if they absolutely needed to and the ladies never noticed the difference. David and Alan spent the morning putting the new bench seat into the Hearse. It fit perfectly and looked like it had always been there. After saying their good byes and getting everything put into the car, they were off to the real estate agents office.

"That was a great weekend hey?" Amanda asked as David pulled out onto the highway.

"Yea, it was good." David said. Amanda smiled and held his hand.

"Did you get a chance to have a good visit with Alan while we were gone?" She asked.

"Actually, he slept until 8:30 so our visit was short. But it was still good." David said. He stared out the windshield trying to think about anything but Alan.

"Well, your mom and I may have come up with a good middle name." Amanda said. David raised his eyebrows and looked at Amanda.

"What did you come up with?" David asked.

"Why don't we call him, Gabriel Alan Smith." Amanda said. The names ran together so smoothly it was like he had heard it before.

"That sounds really good Amanda." David said. Amanda giggled and clapped. She rubbed her stomach and whispered the name to the baby. David smiled and drove on. When they reached the real estate office, they were right on time for their appointment. They went in with Mike and sat in the waiting room. It wasn't long before their agent was ready for them. They went in and Amanda explained what she wanted to do. The agent wrote it all down and thought he might have people in mind now at the new price. David and Amanda waited quietly while he talked on the phone with his perspective buyers. When he hung up the phone, he looked at them and smiled.

"Well, you can sell it right now at that price if you want." The agent said. Amanda looked at David and he raised his eyebrows at her.

"What do you think?" David asked her. Amanda chewed the inside of her cheek and then smiled.

"Where do I sign?" She asked. The agent smiled and told them he would have to write up the new deal and everything. He told them it would take a few days to have it all signed and finished and asked if they would stay close for that. David and Amanda agreed and they all stood up. The agent shook both their hands and on their way out, David phoned Alan.

"*Hello.*" He said on the other end. Amanda had decided to go to the bathroom with Mike before they headed back. David sat down in the waiting room and talked to Alan on the phone.

"Hi, it looks like we're hanging out for a little while longer." David said.

"*Oh, what's going on?*" Alan asked.

"Well, Amanda sold her house."

"*That's great news David. One less thing to worry about, right?*" Alan asked. David smiled and suddenly pictured Alan asleep on the couch again.

"Yea." David said and Alan laughed.

"*You don't sound so happy.*" Alan said. David sighed and shook his head.

"I am. I just have a wondering mind today, that's all." David confessed.

"*Oh, I see.*" Alan said. They were both silent for a second then Alan finally spoke. "*Are you heading back then?*"

"Yes, Amanda is just in the bathroom and then we'll be back." David said. He looked out the window at his car and seen Mack staring in at him. He smiled at the little dog and he could see that Mack had started barking.

"*Ok, I'll let your mom know then.*" Alan said.

"Thanks Alan." David said.

"*Your welcome.*" Alan said and they hung up the phone. Amanda came out of the bathroom and smiled at David.

"Are we ready to go?" She asked.

"Ready if you are." David said. Amanda giggled and they headed out to the car. David headed back to his mother's house and when they arrived. He called Carman and filled him in. He was ok with David taking the time off. Amanda talked excitedly to Nancy about the sale of the house and when David decided it was time to take Mack out, Alan and Little Mike joined him.

"So, how did you sleep?" Alan asked. David took a deep breath and looked at Alan.

"Do I have to answer that?" David asked. Alan laughed and shook his head.

"As well as I did I assume then." Alan said. David smirked and watched Little Mike play with Mack on the grass. "I want you to know something David." Alan said and David looked at him.

"Ok, what's that?" David asked. Alan sighed and put his hands in his pockets.

"Your mom has been asking me questions about you and me. I'm not really sure what to tell her." Alan said.

"What's there to say?" David asked sitting down on the front step. Alan joined him and they both lit a cigarette.

"Well, lots but nothing." Alan said. David giggled and nodded.

"What have you said so far?" David asked.

"Well, I told her that I talk to you about your feelings about men. And I told her that I had an interest as well back in collage. I'm just not sure I should tell her about my interest in you." Alan said. Alan's words made David's stomach jump.

"Jesus." David said to his stomach. Alan smiled and looked at David.

"Jesus what?" Alan asked.

"Uh. It's stupid. My stomach does this flippy thing around you all the time. I wish it would quit." David said quietly. Alan smiled and nodded.

"Me too." Alan said. David looked at him and smiled.

"I think it's a good idea not to tell mom any more than you have to." David said. Alan nodded again and leaned back on his hands. David looked down his strong looking body and shook his head. "Is it ok to be selfish for a second?" David asked quietly.

"Does it go against the rules?" Alan asked. David giggled and nodded. "Well, as long as it isn't too bad." Alan said.

"It's not fair." David said and Alan laughed.

"Are you pouting?" Alan asked. David laughed and nodded. Alan shook his head and took a drag from his cigarette. "That's classic David." He said. David laughed again and looked back at Mike and Mack.

"You know, it won't be long until there will be two kids playing in the yard with the dog." David said. Alan smiled and sat forward resting his arms on his legs.

"Two boys. How unlucky." Alan said. David giggled and looked at Alan.

"Why do you say that?" David asked.

"Picture this, a perfect mixture of you and Gabe. You're gonna have your hands full my boy." Alan joked. David laughed and checked Alan with his shoulder. Alan giggled and shook his head. "How far did you go with him?" Alan asked quietly. "I mean, your journal said you had sex with him, but, what counts as sex these days?" Alan asked. David's stomach flipped again and he shook his head.

"Well, sex, Alan." David said. He tried to keep his voice steady but he was not successful. Alan giggled at the sound he made.

"Ok, I guess my question really is, did you do him or the other way around?" Alan asked. David swallowed hard and he cleared his throat. Alan smiled and looked at David. "You don't have to answer me, I was just curious." Alan said. David closed his eyes and took a deep breath.

"I did him but, he sucked me off." David answered quietly. Alan raised his eyebrows but said nothing. David wasn't sure how he felt about the silence but he was too afraid to say anything else. They watched the two little monsters play in the yard until Nancy called them in for dinner. They got the dog and Mike in and David cleaned up Mike for his meal. They talked about getting the rest of Amanda's family's things out of the house. Alan agreed to store her things in his shop until they could find a different place for them. Nancy and Amanda made a plan to start packing her things up on Monday and Tuesday as Nancy had those days off. David would be in charge of the dog and Mike and carrying out the boxes once they were full. When dinner was finished, David and Alan did up the dishes while Amanda and Nancy took Mike down to the corner store with the dog for ice cream. David looked across the kitchen at Alan while he wiped the table. Alan looked at him and smiled.

"What?" Alan asked noticing David staring at him.

"Why did you ask me that stuff about Gabe earlier?" David asked. His stomach flipped again but he ignored it. Alan sighed and seemed to put his hand on his own stomach for a second. David smiled but didn't say anything about it.

"Well, I was just curious as to how much you had done with a guy, that's all." Alan said. David giggled and shook his head.

"How much have you done?" Alan laughed and shook his head. He brought the cloth back to the sink and hung it over the side.

"You mean other than the kiss with Carman in collage?" Alan asked. David nodded and Alan sighed. "Nothing." Alan said. David shook his head and giggled.

"You don't know what you're missing old man." David said. Alan laughed and went to sit at the table.

"And, what am I missing?" Alan asked. David took a deep breath and sat down at the table with him.

"Nothing I can explain." David said and looked out the window. Alan shook his head and lit a cigarette.

"Sorry, I shouldn't have asked. It's not helpful to talk about this stuff." Alan said. He reached behind him and grabbed the cards out of the china cabinet. David sighed and looked at Alan.

"It's ok. I had someone to ask this shit to. It's rude not to answer." David said. Alan shook his head again.

"I could always ask Carman. I just don't care how much experience he has." Alan said. He dealt out a hand of crib and David looked at his cards.

"Why do you care how much experience I have?" David asked. Alan giggled and looked across the table at David.

"I don't know. I just like to know I guess." Alan said. They played their game and Alan won by a land slide. The girls and Mike were home soon after and Alan dealt them in. Amanda won and really rubbed it in. Everyone just laughed. They played a few more games until they were all ready for bed. Nancy took Mike up with her and Amanda went ahead of David.

"Hey, Alan." David said as they shut the lights off and started heading to their rooms.

"Yes?" Alan said. David smiled at him and shook his head. He loved the way Alan answered him.

"How did you guys have sex with Mike in bed with you?" David asked. Alan laughed and shook his head.

"In the shower you tit." Alan said.

"Oh." David said and Alan giggled.

"Good night David." Alan said as they got to the top of the stairs.

"Good night Alan." David said and went into his room. He got undressed and laid down with Amanda.

"I love you." She whispered. David giggled and cuddled up behind her.

"I love you too." David said and Amanda smiled. He hugged her tightly and she giggled. She rubbed David's arm and He smiled. "You're beautiful." David whispered.

"I'm tired." Amanda said and David laughed. Amanda giggled and David thought it was a good idea to let her sleep instead of try to get laid.

The next two days were very busy but they all managed to get the house sell worthy by the time the prospective buyers came to see it one last time. The real estate agent came over to Nancy's just as dinner was put on the table on Tuesday night.

"So, they have decided to buy it for the price we talked about." He said. Amanda clapped and David smiled.

"The whole 310 thousand?" Amanda asked.

"Yes ma'am." The agent said. Amanda giggled and signed all the papers. Nancy had bought a bottle of non-alcoholic wine so Amanda could celebrate after dinner. They all talked and listened to Amanda's excited giggling through dinner. Alan and David did dishes again while Amanda and Nancy played cards at the table and drank their funny wine. When Alan and David were finished with the cleanup, they took the dog outside for a pee. When they stepped out, they both lit a cigarette. David leaned against the hand rail that went up the little step and Alan walked down to the grass with the dog.

"So I was thinking." Alan said and David rolled his eyes.

"That can't be good." David said. Alan giggled and shook his head.

"Amanda's gonna have that baby this month right?" Alan asked and David nodded.

"Yea, she's due on the 20th or so." David said. He took a drag of his cigarette and looked at Alan.

"Ok, so I guess that gives us almost a month apart, right?"

"Yea, what are you getting at here Alan?" David asked. Alan looked down at his feet and took a drag of his cigarette.

"What if we didn't talk until then? Hopefully we would have a shit load of stuff to talk about by then and all this other crap might not come up. At least not at first." Alan offered. David thought about it for a second.

"Ok, but what if there's nothing to talk about?" David asked.

"Well, by the time the baby comes, your mother will be planning Christmas and mid-term exams will be starting. Not to mention, your work and Amanda's delivery and Seth's guitar lessons. There should be quite a bit to talk about." Alan said. David raised his eyebrows and nodded.

"You know something, that might actually work." David said.

"Ok, so when we come up when Amanda is having the baby, no tight, show off everything t-shirts and no tight, leave nothing to the imagination jeans. Sound good?" Alan asked. David giggled and nodded.

"That's also a good idea. Why didn't you ever come up with any of this before?"

"Well, in my defense, you *are* the brains in this outfit." Alan said. David laughed and shook his head.

"You have life experience Alan."

"Not as much as you have." Alan said and winked. David's stomach flipped and he sighed.

"Nice." David said and they both laughed. Mack was soon finished so they went back into the house with the little dog. They joined Amanda and Nancy at the table and watched them finish their game. They dealt the boys in and they played one more hand of crib before bed. Amanda cuddled up to David like usual but seemed especially uncomfortable. "Are you ok?" David asked as she seemed to squirm around where she lay.

"Yea, the baby is laying funny. Nancy said he has dropped and that's why I can't get comfortable anymore." Amanda explained. David sighed and rubbed Amanda's back.

"It sure went by fast huh?" David asked. Amanda giggled and shook her head.

"Not fast enough. I wish it was over. My back hurts and my boobs are always leaking. I feel like a cow, David."

"You're not a cow Amanda. You're beautiful." David said trying to sooth Amanda's obvious mild depression.

"You're such a liar." She said and giggled. David sighed again but continued rubbing Amanda's back. They lay silent for a while and just as David was starting to fall asleep, Amanda spoke. "Are you scared?" She asked in a whisper. David smiled and kissed Amanda's hair.

"A little maybe. Other than Mike, I've never been around a baby before. I guess it's kind of scary. Are you?" David answered and asked. Amanda nodded. She seemed too quiet lately as far as David was concerned. "What scares you the most?" David asked. Amanda sighed and rubbed her stomach.

"What if I'm not a good mom?" She asked. David laughed at the thought of Amanda being anything other than the perfect mom.

"Amanda, you have so much practice from raising Little Mike. You already know everything you ever needed to as far as raising a baby go's. That's a lot more than other mom's your age can say. You're perfect for this. I wish I was that kid. You're gonna be the best mom in the whole world." David said. Amanda giggled and kissed David's chest.

"You really think so?" She asked. David giggled and nodded.

"Of course." He said. Amanda hugged him and seemed to calm a little. The baby kicked David's hip and he laughed. "Look, he hates me." David whispered. Amanda laughed and shook her head.

"He loves you. He has to because I do." She said. David smiled and kissed the top of Amanda's head.

"Well, I love you guys too." David said. He could feel the baby kick a few more times before it finally settled down and let David and Amanda go to sleep.

"Good Morning." David said as he came down to the table to sit with Nancy and Little Mike.

"Well, you beet Amanda out of bed. That doesn't happen very often." Nancy said. David smiled and got himself a coffee. He messed up Little Mikes hair on his way to his chair at the table.

"Hey, you mess my do." Mike said. David laughed at him and took a sip of his coffee.

"How was your sleep?" David asked. Nancy smiled at him and looked out the window at Alan's car. David met her gaze and rolled his eyes. "I didn't ask how your night was, I asked about your sleep." David corrected. Nancy laughed and shook her head.

"I slept fine David." She said and David giggled. He could hear the shower turn on upstairs and smiled.

"Does he stay here a lot?" He asked.

"Well, sometimes more than others. He never stays for this many days at one time but, I think he stayed because you guys are here." Nancy said. David nodded and smiled at his mom.

"Do you like it when he stays?" David asked. Nancy smiled and blushed a little. "Oh God mom. Do you really think that's what I meant?" David asked. Nancy giggled and shook her head again.

"Sorry. But yes, David. I do like it when he's here. It's pretty lonely around here since you guys are gone. It's nice to have someone to have supper with and stuff." She said.

"Well, that's good mom." David said and took another sip of his coffee.

"How are things at home?" Nancy asked. David sighed and looked up the stairs.

"Well, it will be better when the baby comes and all the hormone stuff is over." David said. Nancy laughed and took a sip of her own coffee.

"Amanda needs to sleep. I sleep when I cranky." Mike said. Nancy and David laughed and Mike giggled.

"It *will* get better, right mom?" David asked. Nancy laughed and nodded.

"Of course it will David. It doesn't stay forever." She said. David sighed a breath of relief and Nancy giggled. "You know, I always thought that I would be so angry with you if you got a girl pregnant so young. But you and Amanda are a lot more mature than some grownups I know. I'm really proud of you, son." She said. Tears filled her eyes and David smiled.

"Mom, don't get all weepy. Growing up fast has its disadvantages you know." David said. Nancy smiled and nodded. She wiped the tears from her eyes and sighed.

"Don't cry grandma. It's a happy day!" Mike said. Nancy giggled and pet the little boy's hair.

"You're right Mike. It *is* a happy day today, isn't it?" Nancy said. Mike nodded and took the last bite from the toast Nancy had made for him. David smiled and took another sip from his coffee. The shower turned off and someone came out of the bathroom. David looked at his mom and smiled.

"Would you ever marry Alan?" He asked. Nancy looked at him with shock in her eyes.

"Oh, David. I don't know. I never thought about it." Nancy said. She tapped her coffee cup nervously and David raised an eyebrow.

"Really? He's perfect mom. Why wouldn't you think about it?" David asked. Nancy shifted in her chair and David giggled. "You have thought about it, haven't you?" David asked in a half excited voice. He giggled again and shook his head. "Geeze mom. I thought we were passed the whole replacing dad crap." David added. Nancy sighed and looked at her son.

"Well, we are. I just don't think I'm at a place in my life right now to think about getting married." Nancy said. She took the last sip of her coffee and got up to refill it.

"Why not? I mean, you love him don't you?" David asked. The question was almost as painful as his expected answer was.

"David, I can't answer that."

"Why?" David asked. Nancy poured her coffee and shook her head.

"Because I can't. It's hard to explain. I just think that taking our time is the best course of action for both of us." Nancy said. Just then Alan came down the stairs and smiled at them both. He said his good mornings and Nancy brought him a coffee. The subject was swiftly changed. They chatted about work and the baby until Amanda woke up. She remembered an appointment she had for the next day and thought it would be a good idea to get home and so they would get a good night's rest beforehand. They finished their coffees and got ready to go. The people who had bought the house were going through it with a contractor and Amanda seemed to get a little choked up. She didn't want to talk about it. She just wanted to go home. They said their good byes and hit the road as quickly as Amanda could push them.

"What's the rush?" David asked once he hit the highway. Amanda sighed and looked at him.

"I could see them out your bedroom window. I just had to get out of there before they started ripping walls out or something." Amanda said. David smiled and nodded.

"Ok babe. Do you want to talk about it?" David asked. Amanda shook her head and looked out the window.

"That was my home David. It's just hard to see someone else in it." She said. David sighed and held Amanda's hand. They were fairly quiet for the rest of the trip. When they got home, Amanda went to lay down so Mike and David took Mack for a quick walk. When they got home, Amanda was still sleeping so David made supper. He woke her up for their meal and she seemed to be in a happier mood. They talked about where they would like to buy a home. David wasn't as eager to spend the money as Amanda was. She felt it was important to own instead of rent when it came to raising children. Carman had called just after dinner to see if David would be at work. He said he would as Amanda's appointment was fairly routine. Amanda bathed Mike before bed and her and David watched the rest of a T.V. movie before they too went to bed.

"Why don't we move home David?" Amanda asked as they got into bed.

"Well, if you wanted to do that, we shouldn't have sold your house." David whispered. Amanda sighed.

"You and I both know that living in the house that Gabe used to live in would never work." Amanda said. David nodded and hugged her.

"Ok, well. We could start looking after the baby comes I guess if you want." David said. Amanda smiled.

"Are you sure? Wouldn't you miss working with Carman or hanging out with Seth?"

"Well, yea but, I would rather you be happy than me be selfish." David said. Amanda sighed and David giggled.

"I love you David." She whispered.

"I love you, Amanda." David said. He lay there for some time wondering what life would be like living so close to Alan and his mom again. He wondered what kind of crap he would get himself into having to spend so much time with Alan. To his dismay, his G rated thoughts quickly changed to a very sexual manner. He imagined Alan taking the place of Gabe in the Hearse. He tried to shake the thought but his mind fought him. He tried to think of anything else but his mind would wonder back to he and Alan in the throes of love. These thoughts plagued his brain until he finally fell asleep.

Chapter 23

For the next week, Amanda did a lot of sleeping. Her Braxton Hicks contractions seem to keep her up a lot during the night so she did a lot of her sleeping during the day. David had found a sitter in the building for Little Mike so Amanda wouldn't have to worry about him. David went to work every morning with Carman still and every day, Carman thought that it would be the day that David would call Alan.

"I can't believe you haven't given in and talked to each other yet." Carman said as they drove towards David's house on the tenth of November.

"Look, Carman. It works ok. By the time we see each other the next time, we'll have a shit load to talk about and it should keep our minds off of the sex stuff." David defended. Carman laughed and shook his head.

"Well, the way he talks is the longer it takes to talk to you the worse it gets for him." Carman said.

"Aren't you supposed to keep your conversations with him to yourself?"

"Look, I'm just saying." Carman said. David laughed and shook his head.

"I like it better this way." Carman sighed and pulled into the apartment parking lot.

"Whatever you say dude. How many days left anyway?" Carman asked.

"Well, remember when the doctor said it would be the 20th of November?" David asked. Carman nodded and parked the truck in front of the building. "Well, I guess they were wrong. She isn't due until December first."

"Wow, well at least it's not like a whole month off or something." Carman said. David giggled and opened the truck door.

"Well, even ten days is long Carman. We're ready for this to be over. Amanda especially." David said. Carman smiled and nodded.

"See you tomorrow." Carman said as David got out of the truck.

"See you." David said and headed up to his floor. He walked all the way down to room 516 to pick up Mike. He was excited to go home and play with his cars. David smiled at him as they walked. "Be quiet going in just in case Amanda's sleeping, ok?" David said as they got to the door. Mike nodded and put his hand over his mouth. David giggled and opened the door for him.

"Hi." Amanda said from the kitchen table. David raised his eyebrows when he saw Lance and Seth at the table with her.

"Hey guys." David said. Mike ran into his room and they could hear him dump his toy box. David smiled and sat down at the table with a beer.

"So, guess what." Amanda said. David smiled and opened his beer.

"What?" He asked.

"We can buy this place if we want it." Amanda said and giggled. David looked at Lance and frowned.

"What is she talking about?" David asked and took a sip of his beer.

"Well, these places are rent or own single level condos, David. I talked to my dad and I think I worked out a pretty sweet deal if you're interested." Lance said and winked at him. David looked at Amanda and she was smiling.

"Are we interested?" David asked. Amanda laughed and nodded. David sighed and looked at Lance again. "So what's this sweet deal then?" David asked.

"105 thousand." Amanda said excitedly. David giggled and looked at her.

"Do you want to buy it?" He asked.

"Oh David, I love it here."

"I thought you wanted to go home."

"I did. But I thought about it and, I really do like it here David. I think we could build a life here. And the price is right." Amanda said. David smiled and held Amanda's hand.

"It's your money babe. Do with it what you will." David said and Amanda squealed. She hugged David and he laughed.

"Ok, I'll get the paper work for you tomorrow and then it's a done deal." Lance said.

"Oh, thank you Lance." Amanda said. She went over and hugged him and David looked at Seth.

"Looks like you won't be losing your guitar teacher." David said. Seth giggled and tapped the case next to his chair. "Uh, huh." David said and Amanda giggled.

"Please, stay for supper. I'm making spaghetti." Amanda said to Lance and Seth.

"Well, I could never say no to a meal." Lance said and Amanda giggled. David and Seth headed into the guitar room to have their lesson. Lance helped Amanda in the kitchen.

"So, you're giving up a yard to keep her happy?" Seth asked as they got their guitars ready.

"Well, yea. I'm happy if she's happy Seth." David said. Seth smiled and turned the amplifier on. David went through the scales first like they always did then they started on learning the songs from David's list that Seth wanted to learn. Their lesson was ended with Amanda calling them out for supper. They all ate together and Amanda and Lance went into the living room and watched a movie with Little Mike while Seth and David cleaned up.

"Do you ever think about that kiss?" Seth whispered as they filled the dish washer. David raised his eyebrows and looked at Seth.

"Which one?" David asked.

"That time on my couch." Seth said. David sighed and set a plate in the washer.

"I don't know. Sometimes I guess. Not as much as the one at the mall. Why do you ask?"

"Well, I liked the one on the couch better. I want to do it again." Seth whispered. David hardly heard what he had said.

"Why?" David asked. Seth shook his head and handed David another plate.

"Because I liked it." Seth said. David swallowed hard and looked at Lance and Amanda in the living room. They were laughing at Mike who was doing all the same actions as the little characters on his movie were doing.

"I can't Seth. I would but I promised Amanda I wouldn't." David said. Seth nodded.

"I know, I just wanted to tell you."

"Why though? If I can't do it, why would you tell me you wanted me to?" David asked. He grabbed a cloth and wiped off the table while he waited for Seth's answer.

"Well, because. You don't react to me like you used to. I guess I kind of miss it." Seth said. David giggled and took the cloth back to the sink. He tossed it in and leaned in close to Seth.

"There is still a reaction, Seth. I just don't make it as obvious as I used to." David whispered. Seth smiled and looked into David's eyes.

"Could you start doing it again?" Seth asked. David laughed and nodded.

"If it will keep you happy, sure." David said and blew into Seth's hair. Seth closed his eyes and quietly moaned. David laughed and went out into the living room to sit next to Amanda.

"All done?" Amanda asked and leaned on him. She rubbed her tight stomach and groaned. David smiled and put his hand on hers.

"Are you ok?" David asked.

"Yea, just those stupid Braxton Hicks." Amanda answered. David sighed again and rubbed her stomach for her. She shifted where she laid and moaned a bit louder. "God, there really bad tonight." She said and sat up. Everyone looked at her and waited. Another one hit and this time much more powerful. Amanda groaned and hit the floor on her knees.

"Ok, get Mike ready, we're going to the hospital." David said to Seth. Seth and Lance got Little Mike ready and David carried Amanda down to the car.

"We'll follow you." Lance said. David nodded and set Amanda in the car. He started the car and pealed out of the parking lot. He sped all the way to the hospital with Lance right on his bumper. They reached the hospital in just under seven minutes. Amanda's contractions hadn't gotten any stronger but they seemed to be fairly close together. David carried her in and the nurses had her in a room and put on a drip right away.

"God, David. What if this is it?" Amanda asked. David sat in the chair next to her bed.

"Then we'll be parents when it's over." David whispered. Amanda smiled and then squeezed his hand with another contraction.

"It's too early David. There is still almost a month left." Amanda said in a worried voice.

"The doctor will know what to do." David said. Amanda nodded and rested her head back on her pillow. David sat quietly with her as the contractions subsided. After a few minutes, Amanda's doctor came in.

"Ok, well let's get you comfortable and get an ultrasound done ok?" He asked. Amanda nodded and a nurse came in with a gown. David helped Amanda get changed and called the nurse when she was back in her bed. The nurse came in with a mobile ultrasound machine and took some pictures of Amanda and David's little baby. She cleaned the green goop off of Amanda's stomach and told them that a doctor would be in shortly.

"Did you see him?" Amanda asked. David smiled and nodded. "He looks like you." Amanda said. David giggled and shook his head.

"He looks like a baby to me." David said.

"I haven't had another contraction for a while." Amanda said.

"Well, that's good. I think it has to do with the stuff in your I.V."

"Yea, I think so too. Do you think they'll let me go home?" Amanda asked. David shrugged.

"I guess they will if you're not having a baby tonight." David said. They talked about the pictures of their baby they saw as they waited for the doctor to return. Lance came in after a while and smiled at Amanda.

"How you doing Baby mama?" Lance asked. Amanda giggled and then yawned.

"I'm good. Still waiting for the doctor." She answered.

"Ok, that's cool. Mike is getting a little cranky. I thought Seth and I would take him to our house for the night. You can come get him tomorrow sometime if you like." Lance offered.

"Thank you Lance." Amanda said.

"Yea, thanks Lance." David added. Lance smiled at David and winked.

"Anything for you good looking." Lance said and left the room. Amanda giggled and shook her head.

"I can't believe I even considered moving away from these people." Amanda said. David looked at her and smiled.

"Why? I get it Amanda. You wanted to raise our baby in a place you recognized. I mean, we have family there and all that." David said. Amanda sighed and shook her head.

"We have your mom and Alan there. Our family is here. Look at them, David. They just take Mike like it's expected or something. It's like having a collection of little daddy's." David and Amanda both laughed. She yawned again and David rubbed her arm. Just then, the doctor came in.

"Well Amanda." He said and sat down on the stool on the other side of the bed. "Looks like you're moving in for a while." He said.

"What? Why?" Amanda asked. David frowned and looked at the doctor.

"Well, the lining of your uterus is very thin. We don't want to risk you having that baby for at least the next week or so. We just want to see the baby's lungs develop a little more." He said. Amanda nodded but her eyes were quickly filling with tears.

"So, what happens if she has the baby too soon?" David asked.

"She could have the baby now. The problem with that is, the lungs will be small and it would take some time in an incubator and stuff. Amanda here is the best thing for him until he comes." He said and stood up. "You're welcome to stay with her if you want. She does need to rest though. It's been a stressful few hours for her and the baby." The doctor said and left the room.

"Oh David. What did I do wrong?" Amanda asked and started to cry. David hugged her and kissed her neck.

"Nothing baby. My mom told me about this. It happens sometimes with first time moms. You just need to grow the baby for a little while longer so he's healthy when he comes out." David whispered into her hair. Amanda nodded and lay back on her pillow. "Are you tired?" Amanda nodded.

"I am." She said and closed her eyes. David smiled and took out his cell phone. He stared at the time it read. It was 1:45 in the morning. He sighed and dialed his mother's number. It rang four times before Alan answered.

"*Hello?*" He answered in a sleepy voice. David smiled at the sound of his tired voice.

"Hi Alan." David said.

"*David, is everything ok?*" Alan asked. He suddenly sounded a lot more awake.

"Well, Amanda is in the hospital." David answered.

"*Is it time already? Should we come?*" Alan asked.

"No, No it's not time. They put her on some kind of drip thing and they want to keep her pregnant for as long as they can. Something about the baby's lungs. She'll be in here until he comes."

"Do you want us to come?"

"Um, you don't have to but, I have no idea how long this drip stuff lasts or what. If you want to come you can." David answered and Alan sighed.

"Ok, we'll be there tomorrow. I don't know what time but we'll have to work it out with work and stuff." Alan said.

"Ok Alan." David said. Amanda seemed to have fallen asleep and David smiled at her.

"Hang in there. You're not alone ok." Alan said. David smiled at him and closed his eyes.

"I know." He whispered.

"So, did it work?" Alan asked quietly. David giggled knowing Alan talked about the no contact plan.

"No, you?" David asked. Alan sighed and staid quiet on the other end for a while. "Are you still there?" David asked.

"Yes, I'm here. No it didn't work." Alan answered. David giggled and shook his head.

"Well, that's ok. I like flirting with you anyway." Alan laughed on the other end.

"I bet you do." Alan said. David giggled again and leaned back in his chair.

"You better get some sleep if you're coming out here tomorrow."

"Yea, good luck sleeping in those chairs. It's no fun." Alan said quietly. David remembered back to his time in the hospital and all the time Alan stayed with him and slept in the chair in his room.

"I miss you Alan." David whispered.

"Me too." Alan said.

"Good night."

"*See you tomorrow.*" Alan said and they both hung up the phone. David stared at Amanda while she slept. He smiled at the way she held her stomach like she was already holding their baby. A nurse came in shortly after and woke Amanda long enough to administer a steroid for the baby's lungs. When she was finished she left the room and Amanda went back to sleep. David's phone suddenly beeped and he looked down at it. He had a text message from Alan.

Wanna know what I'm thinking about? The text message read. David giggled and shook his head. He typed back.

I don't know. Do I? David typed. He pressed send and waited for Alan's reply. It came and David read it.

That depends on how many rules you're willing to break in a text message. David laughed and typed back.

Well, do your worst. He pressed send and felt his stomach flip. He watched his phone and when it beeped at him he jumped. He stared at the phone for a second before opening the message.

Well, I was thinking about what you told me about you and Gabe. The message said. David took a deep breath and tapped the edge of his phone.

And? He typed back. He closed his eyes and waited. He thought about what Alan would be thinking about when it came to him and Gabe. After a few minutes, his phone beeped again. He opened it and read the message.

What was it like? David took a deep breath and stared at the message. He tapped the phone again and looked over at Amanda. She was still asleep and he smiled. He looked back down at the message and he could feel his stomach flip again.

Well, it was different. David typed and sent the message. He wondered what Alan's face must look like right then. A nurse came in with a pillow for David and he thanked her. He propped it up behind him and put his feet op on the bar under Amanda's bed. He stared at his phone until his eyes grew heavy. It beeped at him and he jumped. He shook his head and turned the volume down before reading the text.

Did you like it better than being with Amanda? David thought about the question and sighed.

I don't think I liked it more. It was really different. It's not comparable really. You'd have to do it to know I guess. David typed. He read over the message and giggled. He sent it even though it seemed to open up for a very sexual conversation he wasn't sure he was ready for but, didn't want to miss either. He yawned and waited for Alan's reply. When it came, David smiled and opened his phone.

Lol. Well, when do you see that happening? David giggled and shook his head.

Aren't you supposed to be sleeping? David typed. He sent the message and giggled to himself again. He rested his head back on this pillow and shook his head. He closed his eyes and waited for his next text. His phone quietly buzzed and David looked down at it.

Are you deflecting? David read the message and sighed.

Yes. Sorry. David typed and pressed send. He sighed and stared at the phone. He wished for a second that he could openly tell Alan everything he wanted to know. He wished he could just show him. He shook off the thought as his next text message came in.

It's ok. I was only curious. And your right, I should be sleeping. I'll see you tomorrow. David read the text and shook his head. He knew even from reading the text that Alan must have felt like an idiot or something. He smiled to himself and typed,

It was like a normal orgasm only ten times better. If that makes sense. I'll see you tomorrow. David typed and sent off the message. He smiled to himself and closed his eyes. He could feel sleep coming when another text message came in. He sighed and opened his phone.

That's very interesting David. Thanks for telling me. I'm sorry I asked I just really wanted to know for some reason. David smiled at the message and wondered if he should send back. He giggled and decided to play the game for just a second.

I wish I could just show you. David typed and sent. He giggled wondering what kind of look Alan had on his face after that message. It wasn't long before the next message came. He laughed and opened the phone.

You're not nice David. The message read. David laughed quietly and shook his head.

Sorry, I couldn't help it. Good night Alan. David typed. He yawned again and pocketed his phone. He closed his eyes and got as comfortable as he could. He thought about Carman and thought to himself that he had better remember to call him in the morning. He was almost asleep when his phone buzzed again. He sighed and took it out of his pocket.

Good night David. For the record, I would let you if the circumstances were different. I would have let you a long time ago. David read the message twice and put the phone in his pocket. He shook his head and smiled.

Oh Alan. How is it you always have to have the last word? It's so unfair. I should text him back and tell him the circumstances don't matter or something. David thought to himself. He decided not to when he took one last look at Amanda before he fell asleep.

Chapter 24

David was awoke the next morning by the sound of Carman's voice.

"Hey, David." He said. David opened his eyes and met Carman's.

"Hey, what are you doing here?" David asked in a sleepy voice. Carman smiled and held up a coffee cup.

"Coffee delivery service." Carman said and handed David the cup. David looked over to see Amanda reading a book.

"Good morning babe. How are you feeling?" David asked. Amanda looked at him and smiled.

"Oh, I'm ok I guess. Did you sleep ok?" Amanda asked. David rolled his eyes and patted the arm of the chair he sat in.

"I had such a good sleep I may even take this sucker home with me." He said. Amanda and Carman laughed. Carman sat down on the edge of the bed and looked at David.

"So, I talked to Alan this morning. He said he tried to call you but you didn't answer your cell phone." Carman said. David took it out of his pocket and seen that the battery had died.

"Well, that's why." David said. Carman smiled and dug a charger out of his pocket.

"I figured." He said and handed the charger to David. David plugged it into his phone then plugged the other end into an outlet on the wall. "Anyway, your mom has a doctor's appointment to hear some test results or something so, they will be later than they thought." Carman finished.

"Oh, did he say what tests she had?" David asked. Carman shook his head.

"Not really. I guess she's been having headaches or something?" Carman asked. David nodded and took a sip of his coffee. "Yea, something about that I guess." Carman said.

"Well it's about time. She's been having those headaches for a few years." Amanda said looking up from her book. Carman and David both sipped at their coffees.

"So, are you going to live here or are you going to ever go home?" Carman asked David. David sighed and looked at Amanda.

"I really should stay with her." David said. Amanda smiled and shook her head.

"That's what doctors are for, David." She said not looking up from her book.

"And not to mention, you should probably save Little Mike from Seth. Nothing good can come from Seth taking care of him for long periods of time. You want him to grow up sane don't you?" Carman asked. David laughed and nodded.

"Yea, I guess a shower wouldn't kill me either." David said. Amanda giggled and looked at David.

"This is true." She said and winked. Carman and David both laughed. A nurse came in the room and changed Amanda's I.V. bag.

"Are you comfortable dear?" The nurse asked in a very friendly sounding voice.

"Well, I could use another pillow." Amanda said. David quickly handed the nurse his pillow and Amanda smiled. The nurse put it behind Amanda and patted the sides.

"Is that better?" She asked.

"Yes, thank you." Amanda answered. The nurse smiled at everyone and left the room.

"Why didn't you tell me you wanted another pillow?" David asked. Amanda giggled and shook her head.

"Well, I didn't know I wanted one until she asked." Carman giggled and Amanda smiled at David. "I will remember to ask *you* for stuff from now on, ok?" She asked. David smiled and shook his head. He took another sip of his coffee and looked at Carman.

"So, are Lance and Seth coming here today?" David asked and Carman nodded sipping at his hot coffee again.

"Yea, Lance said they would come just after lunch or something." Carman said. David looked around the room for a clock. It was 7:45.

"Are you hanging out with us or are you going to work?" David asked.

"Well, I have a couple jobs today that can't wait. I need to do them this morning but after that, I'll come by and see how things are going." Carman said.

"You know, I bet I would be fine without you guys looking after me all the time." Amanda said. David looked at her and smiled.

"We know that. I just feel better knowing you're not by yourself." David said. Amanda smiled at him and nodded.

"I understand that. I seem to remember not too long ago I was in your shoes." Amanda said and smiled. David smiled and looked down at his feet.

"Thank god it's not for the same reason." David whispered. Amanda nodded and pet David's hair. Carman took another sip of his coffee and smiled at the two young parents in the room.

"So, what color hair do you think he has?" Carman asked and Amanda giggled.

"Well, I think it will be dark like his dads." She said and David smiled.

"I bet he'll be blonde. It's supposed to be a prominent gene or something." David said. Amanda giggled and Carman smiled.

"Well, my money is on black." Carman said. David and Amanda looked at him and frowned.

"Why?" Amanda asked. Carman giggled and shook his head.

"Well, the way I see it is, this little guy is the reincarnation of Gabe. Why wouldn't his hair be black?" Carman asked. Amanda and David both laughed.

"Gabe was a blonde, Carman. He dyed his hair." Amanda said. Carman smiled and shrugged. David and Amanda both laughed.

"God, I could never picture Gabe blonde." David said. Amanda giggled and shook her head.

"Me neither actually. I don't think I was old enough to remember when he started coloring it." She said. They all smiled at the memory of Gabe and David and Carman sipped at their coffee. At eight o'clock, Amanda decided to have a nap so David went out with Carman for a cigarette before he left for work. They stepped outside and went to the designated smoking area. There were two round picnic tables and a few tall stand-up ash trays. They sat down at one of the tables and both lit a cigarette.

"So, enough with the tough guy shit. Aren't you scared or something?" Carman asked. David looked at him and shrugged.

"I'm not really sure how to feel right now. I think I'm worried and excited at the same time." David answered. Carman smiled and took a drag from his cigarette.

"Well, if I was you, I would be scared just because she's in here and not at home."

"I am a little scared about that. But the doctor hasn't said anything is really wrong or nothing so, I guess I'm just more worried that the baby will try to come earlier than he's supposed to." David said. Carman smiled and they both took a drag of their cigarettes.

"You know, David. If you need to take some time off or whatever through all this, you know you can right?" Carman asked. David sighed and nodded.

"I know, I'll go nuts just sitting around and not doing anything though." David said.

"Well, if you need something to do, you could always clean my house." Carman said. David laughed and shook his head.

"No, I'm sure I'll have plenty to clean up when I get home today. We left Mack there all alone."

"Poor guy, want me to stop by and take him out quickly before I go to work?" Carman asked. David smiled and shook his head.

"Nah, I'll get there soon enough. But thanks anyway Carman."

"Well, if you change your mind, you let me know. I mean about work or if you need anything or whatever." Carman said. David nodded and took another drag from his cigarette. "David, can I ask you something?" Carman said quietly. David looked at him and was puzzled by Carman's sudden change in tone.

"Yea, of course." David said. Carman sighed and looked into David's eyes.

"Are you aware of Seth's little dilemma?" Carman asked. David frowned and shook his head. "Well, he's really messed up over some stuff and I was wondering if you wouldn't talk to him about it." Carman said.

"Yea, I can. What's going on?" David asked.

"Well, I don't know if I should really say. Lance was talking to me about it the other day and I think the best person for him to talk to is you." Carman said. David sighed and shook his head.

"Can't I at least have a heads up?" David asked. Carman giggled and took the last puff from his cigarette.

"Alan didn't get one." Carman said and stood up. He walked over to the closest ash tray and put his cigarette in to it.

"This is about him liking me?" David asked. Carman looked at him and nodded.

"You know?" Carman asked. "I thought those two times you guys kissed were just bugging each other or something." He added. David put his own cigarette out and walked with Carman to his truck.

"That's what I thought at first too, until he started talking about it. Remember when we were at Lances place?" David asked. Carman's eyes lit up and he nodded.

"Oh yea, you guys were having that talk on the couch." Carman said and David nodded.

"I've already told him how Amanda feels about it and stuff. I thought he was cool with it. I mean, we just talked about it again yesterday." David said. Carman sighed and shook his head. He opened the door of his truck and got in.

"Trust me David, he is not cool with it." Carman said. David raised his eyebrows and closed Carman's truck door for him. Carman wheeled down his window and looked into David's eyes. "Talk to him about it. With no one else around to keep him from saying what he means to." Carman said.

"Ok, tonight or something maybe." David said and Carman smiled.

"Don't forget you have Alan and your mom coming down too." Carman reminded him and started the truck.

"I'll do it soon, Carman." David said. They said their good byes and David headed back into the hospital. He walked past the counter and went into Amanda's room.

"Hi." She said.

"I thought you were going to sleep." David said as he sat down on the chair next to Amanda's bed.

"I was but I wanted to ask you to do something first." Amanda said.

"Ok, what can I do?" David asked. Amanda smiled at him.

"Well, can you phone Lance and tell him to bring the paper work on the condo with him? I want all this done before the baby comes." Amanda said.

"It can't wait till you're out of here? I mean, do you want to be dealing with paperwork and real estate right now?" David asked. Amanda smiled and nodded.

"Might as well, David. I'm not doing anything else." She said. David giggled and shook his head.

"Ok, I'll call." He said and picked his phone up from where he had set it to charge. He turned it on and dialed Lance's number.

"*Hello?*" Lance said on the other end.

"Hey Lance." David answered.

"*Hey man. Are we parents yet or what?*"

"No, not yet. Amanda wanted something from you though." David said and Lance giggled.

"*Not doing a good enough job in the bedroom David?*" Lance asked. David laughed and shook his head.

"Oh Lance, wouldn't you like to know."

"*I would actually. Does she need me to keep you happy while she's in the hospital?*" David laughed again.

"No, she does not. She wants the paper work on the condo when you come." David said still giggling about Lance's last comment.

"*Oh, I see. I guess I can do that. You're sure you don't need any company in that big bed of yours?*" Lance asked. David laughed again and shook his head.

"If I did, I would ask Seth." David said. Lance giggled on the other end.

"*I only laugh cause, well, it's funny you should say that.*"

"Yea, I know all about it. I'll talk to him about it as soon as I can." David said. Lance sighed.

"*David, let me tell you something you need to promise never to repeat.*"

"Ok." David said.

"*Well, this isn't just some silly crush. He's really beating himself up about it. Please be gentle.*" Lance said quietly. David sighed and nodded.

"Yea, I know how *that* feels."

"*I figured you would understand. Just ease into it and see what he says. I know Seth and it takes a bit to get information from him. He might talk to you a little easier but if he doesn't, know this, he is a hurting unit.*" Lance explained. David sighed and ran his hand through his hair.

"Ok, Lance. I'll do my best."

"*I know you will. Anyway, Mike is hungry and Seth is coming down so I'll let you go for now ok?*" Lance asked.

"Ok, see you later." David said. They both hung up and David smiled at Amanda. "Well, your paper work is coming." David said. Amanda smiled and nodded.

"What's going on with Seth?" She asked. David sighed and shook his head.

"I finally understand Alan a little better I think." David said. Amanda looked at him with a confused gaze.

"What do you mean?"

"Well, remember when I told you about Seth and his kiss at the mall?" David asked. Amanda nodded. "Well, it wasn't just because. I guess he's really torn up inside about the whole thing. Lance and Carman want me to talk to him about it." David said and Amanda smiled.

"Well, I think you should. Remember how messed up you were in the beginning?" Amanda asked. David nodded and Amanda sighed. "I don't envy him at all. I wouldn't want to go through this kind of thing." She said. David laughed and shook his head.

"You're so cute." He said. Amanda smiled and winked at him.

"Why don't you talk to him while Lance and I go through the paper work on the condo?" She offered. David sighed and nodded.

"Sooner rather than later, huh?" David asked.

"Wouldn't you have rather had that then what you got?" David smiled and nodded. He got up and leaned over to kiss Amanda. She smiled and ran her hand through his hair as they kissed. He sat back down and stared into Amanda's eyes.

"Are you feeling ok?" He asked.

"Yes David. If I wasn't I would tell you." She said and rolled her eyes. David smiled and sat back in his chair. Amanda closed her eyes and it wasn't long before she had fallen asleep.

Lance and Seth showed up right at noon. Amanda was still asleep so they decided to go out for a cigarette. They sat down at the same table Carman and David had sat at that morning.

"Ok, what's happening?" Seth asked. David took a deep breath and looked at Lance.

"First things first. Where's Mike?" He asked. Lance smiled and shook his head.

"With Carman. He wanted to have a donkey ride so Carman decided he would bring him to you later." Lance said. David shook his head and smiled.

"So, what's happening?" Seth asked. David smiled and looked at Seth. His long raven black hair moved slightly in the light breeze. He was wearing his black trench coat and a pair of black pants that had silver buckles on the legs.

"Well, Amanda was in labor but they stopped it with some drip thing. Now she has to stay here until the baby comes because they did an ultrasound and, I guess it said that her uterus is to thin or something. Anyway, they want her to stay here to monitor her." David answered. Seth nodded and tossed his hair. David smiled at him and Seth blushed.

"Jesus." Lance said under his breath. David giggled and looked at Lance. "You know Seth, if you were any more obvious, I could swear you were a lot gayer than you think you are." Lance said to his brother. Seth squinted his eyes and shook his head.

"You're just jealous cause I got the looks." Seth said. David giggled and shook his head.

"Yes well, I have the cock." Lance said and grabbed himself. David and Seth both laughed.

"Fight nice kids." David said and Lance giggled.

"So, when is daddy showing up?" Lance asked referring to Alan. Seth giggled but David's face didn't crack.

"Well, mommy has a doctor's appointment so they will leave after that." He answered. Seth giggled and Lance raised his eyebrows.

"Are you guys fucking yet?" Lance asked. David laughed and shook his head.

"Are you talking about Alan?" David asked. Lance nodded and David sighed. "Oh, Lance. If only we could all live in your world." David replied. Seth giggled and shook his head.

"You guys are so mean to each other." Seth said and put out his cigarette. Lance and David both laughed.

"You wanna know what mean is?" Lance asked. Seth nodded and David laughed. "Mean is this kid with half a bottle of Scotch in him and still not drunk enough to say yes." Lance said. David laughed remembering Lance's advances when he and Alan had come up to Carman's for spring break.

"Wow, that's harsh bro." Seth said. "He'll kiss me when he's sober AND shopping for his engagement ring." Seth added. David laughed and Lance shook his head.

"Touché." Lance said. David and Seth both laughed while David and Lance put out their cigarettes.

"Are we going in?" Seth asked.

"Lance is, you're staying out here with me." David said and Lance stood up.

"Good luck." Lance said quietly and David giggled. Seth and David watched as Lance went into the hospital. When the doors shut behind him, Seth looked at David and sighed.

"Ok, what?" Seth asked. David smiled and moved a strand of hair from Seth's face. Seth swallowed hard and closed his eyes.

"What's going on with you?" David asked pulling his hand away. Seth took in a shaky breath and stared into David's eyes.

"You know." Seth said and looked down. David smiled and shook his head.

"Actually, I don't." David said. Seth sighed again and shook his head.

"I don't want to like you, but I do."

"We can't be friends?" David asked. Seth rolled his eyes.

"That's not what I mean." Seth said. David sighed and lit another cigarette.

"Seth, I know what you're going through. It does get easier you know."

"Yea right. When was the last time you had a conversation with Alan and the thought of kissing him or having sex with him or something like that didn't go through your head?" Seth asked. David raised his eyebrows and thought about the question.

"Well, never. But I can't have a conversation with you without thinking the same way." David answered. Seth laughed and shook his head.

"Nice David."

"What? It's true. Look Seth, I meant what I said in the kitchen yesterday. I would love to do anything you would let me if it wasn't for a promise I made to Amanda." David said quietly. Seth sighed and nodded. "I know it sucks. Believe me, Seth, I know. The same thing is happening with Alan and me right now. We both want to but we're stopped by promises we made to the women in our lives." David added.

"But why does it have to be this way?" Seth asked. David shrugged and took a drag from his cigarette.

"I don't know. Unwritten rules or something."

"What would happen if it was *Me* that kissed *you*? You wouldn't be breaking any rules then." Seth said. David giggled and shook his head.

"Seth, I would kiss back. There is where the problem is at. I like the way you kiss. It's like a prelude to sex or something." David said. Seth blushed and looked away. David giggled and flicked the ash off of his cigarette. "Any other guys make you feel like this?" David asked. Seth sighed and shook his head.

"Just you."

"So far. It was only Alan for me for a long time until I saw Gabe after four years." David said. Seth looked back at David and sighed.

"I don't want anybody else." Seth whispered. David sighed and nodded.

"Neither did I. But then there was Gabe, and you." David said. Seth smiled and the red came back in his face a little. David smiled and shook his head. "It's not fair, or easy. But it is what it is." David said. Seth sighed again and looked across the hospital parking lot.

"What did you do? I mean in the beginning before you found Gabe?" Seth asked. David sighed and thought back to his journal.

"Well, I wrote it all down in a journal and read it over to myself sometimes. I also did a lot of jacking off." David said. Seth laughed and shook his head.

"Well, naturally." David laughed and put his cigarette out.

"Are you jacking off already? God it took quite a while before I did." David said. Seth blushed again and David giggled. "Look, just because you like guys doesn't change who you are. It just means you have more selection." David said and winked. Seth giggled and they both stood up. "Do you feel any better?" David asked.

"Not really." Seth said. David sighed and hugged Seth.

"Seth, you can tell me anything and I promise I will never keep anything from you. Just promise me you won't keep beating yourself up about this." David whispered in Seth's ear. Seth sighed and nodded.

"I promise. Can I ask you something though?" Seth whispered. David nodded. "Did the first time you jacked off about Alan seem really different than usual?" Seth asked. David giggled and pulled away from Seth. He kept his hands on Seth's shoulders and looked into his eyes.

"Very, very different." David said and kissed Seth's forehead. Seth sighed and they headed into the hospital together. They stepped into Amanda's room and seen that she was finishing up with the signing and what not.

"You need to sign this too." Amanda said and handed David her pen.

"Ok." David said and signed where Amanda was pointing. When he finished, Lance smiled and put the paperwork back into his briefcase.

"Well, your home owners." Lance said. Amanda giggled and hugged David. David smiled and sat back down in his chair. He looked at Seth and realized he was staring at him. David smiled and Seth blushed. Lance noticed and rolled his eyes. "Do you see this shit?" Lance asked Amanda. She giggled and nodded.

"It seems you're getting a taste of your own medicine, David." She said and Seth's face went even redder. He turned away and David smiled.

"Shhhh." He said to Amanda and stood up. He walked over to Seth and pulled him out of the room. He pulled him down the hall a little ways and stopped him just in front of the elevators. "Hey, it's ok. Just ignore them." David said. Seth sighed and shook his head.

"Lance thinks it's hilarious because he told dad it would happen. Now that it has, he wants so bad to rub it in dad's face. He thinks it would be the perfect punishment or something for him." Seth said. He shook his head then and walked away from David. David caught up to him and stopped him again.

"Punishment for what?" David asked. Seth sighed and shook his head.

"Dad cheated on mom and the lady landed him with the kid." Seth said. David frowned.

"Ok, I thought there was just you and Lance." David said. Seth rolled his eyes.

"Yea, I'm the kid David." Seth said. David blinked and let Seth go. Seth shook his head and looked away. "See, dad always said that the 'Gay Gene' was on mom's side. That's what he used to say to Lance all the time. It was the kind of thing that managed to hurt both Lance and mom at the same time. Lance has been waiting for a way to save both him and mom from the kind of shit that dad says about them. He thinks this is perfect." Seth explained. David sighed and put his hands in his pockets. "So now, not only am I the illegitimate son of a married millionaire but, I am also gay. That's just another thing for them two to fight about." Seth added. David stepped close to Seth and looked into his eyes.

"So you promised your dad you would stay straight just to save your brother the fight?" David asked. Seth sighed and nodded.

"And mom too." Seth said. David sighed and shook his head.

"Wow, that really sucks Seth. I don't know how to help you." David said. Seth smiled and shook his head.

"I didn't tell you so you could help me David. I told you so you know what the story is with Lance and this whole, 'I might be gay thing'." Seth said. David shook his head again and ran his hand through his hair.

"So what if I had a little talk with Lance?" David asked. Seth mocked a laugh and shook his head.

"Good luck. He's been waiting for this his whole life. He's gonna use it eventually."

"Oh, I think I can talk him out of using it for a while." David said and winked. Seth frowned and tried to figure out what was going through David's head.

"How?" Seth asked. David giggled and guided Seth back toward Amanda's room.

"I happen to know something he would like even more than getting even with your dad. I could dangle it in front of him for a while. At least long enough for you to figure some of this out." David proposed. Seth sighed and shook his head.

"That sounds great, but what is this thing?" Seth asked. David giggled and leaned close to Seth.

"Me." David whispered and Seth's eyes went wide. He looked at David with a puzzled gaze.

"What?"

"He's been trying since we met on Alan's last birthday. He wasn't joking when he said he couldn't get me drunk enough. I'll just tell him to back off for a while with the promise of him getting something out of it."

"It would really piss him off if you don't do anything though." Seth said. David giggled and shook his head.

"I'll make sure he doesn't. All you need to worry about is figuring this stuff out. Trust me, it's nice to have the time. No one can do it for you. But I would be happy to buy you some time." David said. Seth sighed and shook his head.

"Well, if this works I guess I owe you big time." Seth said. David smiled and blew in Seth's hair. Seth shivered and David smiled. He loved to see Seth react to him like he used to react to Seth.

"Payment accepted." David whispered. Seth laughed and they headed to Amanda's room.

Chapter 25

Alan, Nancy, Carman and Little Mike arrived just after supper time. David met them out in the hallway and hugged his mother first.

"Oh, is she doing ok?" Nancy asked into David's shoulder.

"Yea, mom. She's in there." David said pointing out Amanda's room. Carman led Mike and Nancy to see Amanda and Alan stayed in the hall with David.

"Hi." Alan said. David smiled and hugged Alan.

"Hi. You have no idea how freaked I am right now." David whispered and Alan rubbed his back.

"It's ok. She's in good hands, son." Alan whispered. David nodded and hugged Alan tighter. Alan smiled and continued to rub David's back. "Things like this happen all the time." Alan added and David nodded again.

"Thanks for coming." David said and let him go. Alan grabbed David and pulled him back in. David giggled and shook his head.

"I was enjoying that." Alan said and they both laughed. Alan let go and they went into the room with everyone else.

"David, will you sit here with Amanda, I want to talk to you guys about something." Nancy said. Carman sighed and picked up Little Mike.

"Let's go get ice cream hay?" Carman asked.

"Ice Cream!" Mike cheered and they left the room. Alan stood next to David's chair and rested his hand on David's shoulder.

"What's going on mom?" David asked. Nancy looked up at Alan then back at David.

"I had some tests done on those headaches I've been getting." Nancy said.

"Yes, Carman said something about that. What did the doctor say?" Amanda asked. Nancy took a deep breath and closed her eyes. David leaned forward a little and he could feel Alan's grip tighten a little.

"Mom?" David said it like a question. Nancy opened her eyes and a single tear ran down her face. "Mom, what is it?" David asked. His heart pounded in his chest and he could feel Alan rubbing his shoulder blade with his thumb. Nancy sighed and looked between David and Amanda.

"Well, I have a tumor." Nancy said.

"A what? Like a brain tumor? They can take it out right?" Amanda asked in a frantic voice. David sat very still under Alan's hand. He stared at his mother's face and waited for her to speak. She shook her head and smiled at David.

"It's inoperable." She whispered. David closed his eyes and Amanda started to cry. Alan kept his hand on David's shoulder. "We caught it too late." She added.

"What does 'we caught it too late.' mean?" David asked quietly through clenched teeth with his eyes still closed. Alan squeezed his shoulder and David swallowed hard. Nancy took another deep breath and held Amanda's hand.

"It means, they can't take it out, so it will kill me." Nancy answered. David took a shaky breath and Alan rubbed his shoulder blade with his thumb again.

"Oh my God." Amanda said and squeezed Nancy's hand. She wiped the tears from her face with the other hand. David still hadn't opened his eyes. He tried to pay attention to Alan's thumb. He could hear his heart pounding in his ears.

"How long?" David asked through clenched teeth again. Alan cleared his throat and David looked up at him. He looked down at David and took a deep breath. David looked at his mother's face and waited for her answer.

"How long Nancy?" Amanda asked in her quiet frightened little voice. Nancy looked at Alan and He nodded.

"David, let's go." Alan said. David shook his head.

"No way, How long mom?" He asked again. Nancy's breathing shook and she looked at him.

"About a year." Nancy said. Amanda started to wail and David closed his eyes again. Alan squeezed his shoulder and David whimpered.

"A year?" David asked through his painfully clenched jaw.

"Yes." Nancy said. He tried to stand up but Alan held him down.

"Alan, come with me." David said and Alan let him up. David kissed his mother and hugged her. "I need to get out of here for a second." He whispered to her. Nancy nodded and he and Alan left the room. David led the way out to his long black Hearse and he got into the driver's seat. Alan got in with him and David started the roaring engine. "A year?" David yelled. He backed out of his parking stall and drove out to the highway.

"David, please don't do anything stupid." Alan said. David laughed and shook his head. He looked at Alan as he brought the car to high way speed.

"I would never take you with me if I planned on killing myself." David said. Alan nodded and David gripped the steering wheel with white knuckles. "How long have you known about this tumor thing?" David asked.

"We just found out today at the doctor's office." Alan answered. David nodded and turned down a little gravel road. Alan lit them both a cigarette and stared out the windshield. "I wish I knew what to say to you." Alan whispered. David shook his head and took a long drag from his smoke.

"How do you miss something growing in your head?" David asked.

"It was only ever a head ache, David. I guess she always meant to go but life got in the way. If it was even a year ago, they might have been able to do something but when these things get going, it speeds up the bigger it gets." Alan explained. David shook his head and thought of the last year his mother had gone through.

"Well, I guess my suicide attempt will kill someone after all." David said and hit the steering wheel with both hands. Alan sighed and took a drag from his cigarette.

"This isn't your fault, David. She has had that thing growing in her head for years."

"Yea? Well if she didn't have all my bull shit to deal with, she would have went a year ago wouldn't she have?" David yelled. Alan shook his head.

"David. She would have come up with some other reason not to go. The only reason she went now was because I made the appointment. I was worried about how frequent her head aches were getting."

"So, no treatments or something? There's absolutely nothing they can do?" David asked. Alan shook his head no.

"She gets a year on the treatments. It would be only months without it."

"Great!" David yelled and tossed his cigarette out the window. Alan ran his hand through his hair. "Why is this happening?" David asked. He could feel tears burning his eyes. Alan cleared his throat and put his hand on the hand that David had on the shifter.

"I don't know. These things just happen I guess." Alan said quietly. David shook his head and looked at Alan.

"They just happen? What kind of horse shit is that, Alan?" David asked. Alan rolled his eyes and shook his head.

"David, I don't know what else to say." David sighed and took his hand out from under Alan's. Alan went to move his hand away but David grabbed it. He put Alan's hand on the shifter and put his on top of Alan's.

"I like to be on top." David said through his tears and Alan laughed.

"Ok, have it your way." Alan said. David smiled and shook his head. Tears rolled down his face and he took a few deep breaths.

"What do we do for her?" He asked. Alan sighed and shrugged.

"Keep her comfortable and happy I guess." Alan answered and David nodded.

"So, pulling over and ripping your clothes off is out of the question then, huh?" David asked. Alan laughed and looked at David with a puzzled gaze.

"You have a very odd way of dealing with this kind of news." Alan said. David shook his head and looked at Alan.

"Well, I have no Scotch, don't do drugs anymore, so naturally sex is next on the list." David explained. Alan rolled his eyes and smiled.

"Are you gonna be ok?" He asked in a serious voice. David nodded and slowed the car. He pulled into a driveway and turned the car around. Alan took his hand back and lit David another cigarette. "Your mom wants to stay here with you guys for a while. Will you be ok with that?" Alan asked.

"Yea, of course. What are you gonna do?" David asked.

"Well, I have to finish with the final exams then I'll be down for Christmas. I will, however, try to come up on the weekends until then." Alan said. David nodded and took a drag of his cigarette.

"I can't believe this is happening." David said as he stared out the windshield.

"I know." Alan said. They traveled in silence back to the hospital. They walked in together and went into Amanda's room.

"Hi." David said and hugged his mom.

"I'm sorry." Nancy whispered and David shook his head.

"Don't be. You didn't do this. I love you." David said. Nancy rubbed his back and then let him go. He sat down on the chair and Alan stood next to him.

"I was just telling Amanda that I would like to see you guys get married." Nancy said. David cleared his throat and nodded.

"I said we would move it up to March or April." Amanda said. David nodded again and Nancy smiled.

"That sounds good mom." David said. Nancy and Amanda smiled. Alan set his hand down on David's shoulder again. David sighed and looked up at him. Alan smiled and David shook his head. "So, you're gonna hang with us for a while I hear." David said looking back at his mom. Nancy nodded and Amanda smiled.

"It will be nice to have you around to help when Gabriel comes." Amanda said. Nancy giggled and held Amanda's hand.

"I am so excited to see this little grandson of mine." She said. Amanda giggled too and put Nancy's hand on her stomach. Nancy smiled when the baby kicked her. David sighed and Alan bent down to whisper in his ear.

"We'll grab Scotch on the way home tonight, ok?" Alan asked in his sexy whisper. David nodded and leaned his head against Alan's for a second. Alan smiled and stood back up. Nancy and Amanda giggled and talked about the baby.

"Can I ask you something mom?" David said breaking into their conversation. Nancy looked at him and nodded. "Does it hurt all the time?" He asked. Nancy sighed and shook her head.

"It only hurts sometimes, like a head ache or a migraine. The doctor said it will get worse as time goes on though." She answered. David nodded and Alan rubbed David's shoulder with his thumb. Just then, Carman and Mike returned to the room. Carman smiled at Alan as he came in and then at David.

"Are we all doing ok?" Carman asked. He put Mike down and he ran to sit with Nancy.

"Yes, Carman. Thank you." Nancy said. Carman nodded and David looked at him.

"You knew about this?"

"No, not until about five minutes before you did. I only got told first so I could get Mike out of here before you guys were told." Carman said. David nodded and looked at Little Mike. Mike smiled at him and reached his arms out. David giggled and took the little boy from his mother.

"Hi." Mike said and David hugged him.

"Hi. How was your ice cream?" David asked.

"Cold and yummy." Mike said and giggled. Nancy and David looked at each other and smiled. That was what David used to say about ice cream.

"Well, that means it was really good ice cream." Alan said. Mike giggled and clapped his hands. Everyone laughed and Mike went back to Nancy.

"What time is it?" Nancy asked. David looked at his phone.

"Its 8:47." David answered. Nancy nodded and kissed Mike on the forehead.

"That sounds like bed time doesn't it?" She asked him. Mike shook his head and Amanda giggled.

"Yes sir. You better kiss everybody before you go." Amanda said. Mike sighed and hugged and kissed Nancy.

"I'm coming with you buddy." She said but hugged and kissed him anyway. He went to David next and David smiled.

"I love you Mikey." David said as they hugged.

"I love David." Mike said. He went to Amanda next and kissed her stomach as well. Everyone giggled. He went to Carman and Carman picked him up.

"It's your job to make sure grandma gets a good night's sleep ok." Carman said as he hugged the little boy. Mike giggled and nodded.

"I will." He said as Carman put him down. Alan was last and Mike jumped into his arms. "Are you coming home with me?" Mike asked.

"Yep, you bet. I'm on babysitting detail tonight." Alan said and winked at David. Mike laughed and kissed Alan. Alan laughed and tickled the little boy. He held on to him as David and Nancy said their good byes to Amanda.

"I love you." Amanda said to David.

"I love you too. I'll be back in the morning ok. But call if you need anything." David said. Amanda smiled and nodded. David went over to Carman and smiled.

"Thanks for staying with her." David said.

"Well, I'm not gonna stay all night but I will stay for a while." Carman said. David nodded and hugged Carman before they left the room. They walked out to David's car and Alan smiled.

"I'm gonna take my car so we can come back in it tomorrow. I can just imagine what a Hearse does for the moral of the patients around here." Alan said. David and Nancy laughed.

"I'll ride with David." Nancy said. Alan smiled and nodded. He walked to his car and pulled away as David and Nancy loaded up Mike and got into the car.

"Are you ok?" Nancy asked as David started the car.

"Shouldn't I be asking you that?" David asked as he pulled away. Nancy sighed and held her son's hand.

"I will be ok." Nancy said. David shook his head and looked at his mother.

"No, mom. You won't. That's the kicker in the whole thing. You won't be ok. You won't survive or get out alive or any of those retarded clichés." David said. Nancy leaned back in her seat and watched the lights go passed them as they headed to David's condo.

"David, it would be a lot easier for me if you would look forward to the year I have left and not what happens at the end." She said quietly. David sighed and shook his head.

"I'm sorry mom. I just can't believe this happening."

"I know. But it's not a bad dream or a sick joke. It's real. I wish it wasn't, believe me." Nancy said and shook her head. She closed her eyes and David could see tears fall down her cheeks. He gripped the steering wheel and clenched his teeth. He drove in complete silence all the way to his home. He parked the car and carried a sleeping Mike into the building. They waited for the elevator and stepped in.

"It's like death row mom." David whispered. Nancy nodded and rubbed Little Mike's back. David smiled at her and readjusted Mike in his arms. The elevator doors opened and they stepped in. Nancy pushed the fifth floor button and the elevator went up. They went into the condo to see it had been cleaned. There was a note on the table. David frowned at his mom and she picked up the note.

Hey David,

   I have Mack and I cleaned up his mess for you.
Hope Amanda is doing well. Talk to you soon.
                                           Lance and Seth.

Nancy read the note aloud and David smiled.

"That was nice of them." Nancy said. David nodded and took Mike to his room. He carefully changed him into his pajamas and got him into bed. He came out to see his mom sitting at the table.

"You look tired." David said.

"I am, I'm just waiting on Alan so I can change and go to bed." She said and smiled at her son. David sighed and rubbed his mother's hand.

"God, mom. I wish I knew what to say." He said and his voice cracked. Nancy shook her head and stared into David's eyes.

"There is nothing to say, David. Just tell me you love me and you'll love Alan when I'm gone." She said. David raised his eyebrows and cleared his throat.

"Well, I do love you mom. And you being gone will never change how I feel about Alan." David said and Nancy smiled.

"That's all I need to know." She said. Just then the door buzzer rang and David got up. He walked over to the controls and pushed the talk button.

"Yes?" David asked in a dorky sounding voice. Nancy giggled and waited.

"DEAD MAN WALKEN!" Alan yelled into the machine. David laughed and shook his head. He pushed the button again.

"You know how wrong that is? It's just me and my mom up here you weirdo." David said. He pushed the listen button and he could hear Alan laughing.

"Just let me in you tit." Alan said. Nancy laughed as David pushed the door button.

"Why do I get the feeling that's fairly mild for you two?" Nancy asked. David laughed and looked at his mom.

"You have no idea." He said and went to the door. He opened it up and waited for the elevator doors to open. When they did, Alan stepped out with a large suit case in each hand and a large brown paper bag in his mouth. David giggled and took the bag from him. "You're so cute when your mouth is full." David whispered. Alan laughed and shook his head.

"I don't even know what to say to that." Alan responded and David laughed. They went into the apartment and Alan took the suit cases into the spare room. Nancy got up and followed him. David put the paper bag on the counter and took out the two bottles of rum and a bottle of Scotch. David raised his eyebrows and shook his head. He set the bottles aside and found two glasses. He poured a straight scotch for both him and Alan and set them on the table. He sat down with his drink and lit a cigarette. It wasn't long before Alan stepped out of the room. He turned off the light and shut the door behind him.

"Is she ok?" David asked. Alan smiled and joined David at the table.

"Same as always David. She's ok." Alan said and took a sip of his drink. David looked behind him at the bottles on the counter then back at Alan.

"Are you looking to get me drunk and take advantage of me?" David asked. Alan giggled and shook his head.

"Like I'd need the booze." Alan said. David laughed and took a drag from his cigarette. Alan smiled and looked toward the spare room door. "It's really nice of you to have the wedding early so your mom can be there." Alan said. David sighed and took a long sip of his drink.

"Well, I agree with her. I couldn't do it without her there. I need her there just as badly if not worse than she wants to be there for it." David said. Alan smiled and looked at David.

"You know, I was never close like that with my mom. Me and my dad were close but my mom and I, we never really got along."

"That's weird. Don't boys usually cling to their mothers and girls to their fathers?" David asked. Alan smiled and shook his head.

"I guess I'm an oddity." Alan said and took a sip of his drink. David giggled and shook his head.

"Yes you are." David said in a seductive sounding voice. Alan looked at him and took a deep breath.

"You're really not being nice today." Alan said. David rolled his eyes and dug his phone out of his pocket. He tossed it onto the table and raised his eyebrows.

"Revenge." David said. Alan laughed remembering the text messaging from the night before.

"I was nice."

"Yea, Mother fucking Teresa again." David said. Alan giggled and raised his eyebrows. He took another sip from his drink and set his cup down.

"You know, David." Alan said and paused. He leaned on his elbows on the table and looked into David's eyes. David sighed and met Alan's gaze. It wasn't long before they were locked together in the same kind of stare they used to get locked into. Alan continued to speak. "I find it very difficult to imagine what sex with a man would be like." Alan said. David could feel his heart pound in his chest and his palms start to sweat. He could feel his stomach tie up in a knot like it always did around Alan. He cleared his throat and looked away from Alan's light green eyes.

"It's like sex with a woman only better." David answered and took a sip from his drink. Alan laughed and shook his head.

"I remember a time when you used to be able to hold a straight face a lot longer than that." Alan said. David sighed and shook his head.

"That was before I knew you were thinking the same thing I was."

"How do you know what I'm thinking?" Alan asked.

"Well, I bet I could guess." David said and locked Alan back into his stare. Alan smiled and leaned closer to David. David leaned in as well and parted his lips for a moment. Alan's breathing sped up a little and David smiled. "I bet right now, you're thinking, 'kiss me David'." David said. Alan giggled and nodded.

"Ok, so you do know what I'm thinking." Alan said. David smiled and shook his head but didn't pull away.

"Wanna know how I know that?" David asked.

"How?" Alan whispered. David moved a little closer and Alan swallowed hard.

"Cause my mind is screaming it." David whispered. Alan closed his eyes and leaned back in his chair. David laughed and leaned back in his own chair. "I win." David said and Alan laughed.

"Well, I wasn't ready." Alan said. David and Alan both laughed. "I could win you know." Alan said. David laughed and shook his head.

"No you can't old man. You don't have the guts." David said. Alan smiled and stood up. He walked over to David and pulled his chair away from the table. David looked up at him with an arrow straight face. Alan straddled David's lap and looked deep into David's eyes. Alan slowly lowered himself onto David. Hes wallowed hard but didn't look away. Alan smiled and blew lightly on David's neck. David closed his eyes and whimpered. Alan giggled and looked back into David's eyes.

"Am I winning yet?" Alan asked in a seductive whisper. David kept his straight face and lifted his hips so his erection pressed up against Alan. Alan's eyes grew wide and his breath shook. He stared into David's eyes and David's breathing sped up. Alan started to quiver with excitement and David closed his eyes.

"Tie?" David asked in an almost inaudible whisper. Alan stood up and took a deep breath.

"Tie." Alan said and sat back down in his chair. David took the last large gulp from his glass and poured another one. Alan did the same. They stared at each other for a second and David started to giggled. "What?" Alan asked. David shook his head and took another long sip from his glass.

"Alan, I'm speechless. I need a second." David whispered and Alan laughed. He lit himself and David a cigarette and waited for David to gather his thoughts. David took a couple drags from his cigarette before finally looking back up at Alan. "Ok, here's the thing." David said and Alan giggled again. "There is no way I would have any kind of stamina with you." David said. Alan laughed and shook his head.

"Yea right David." Alan said. David raised his eyebrows and shook his head.

"Look Alan. You win." David said and took another drag from his cigarette thinking about how close he had been to cumming. Alan smiled and shook his head.

"No, it was certainly a tie David." Alan said. David shook his head and sighed.

"Why do you say that?" David asked.

"Do you think I can shake like that on purpose?" Alan asked. David laughed and shook his head.

"No, I guess not." David said. They both laughed and soon switched the conversation back to the baby and the wedding.

"Have you decided on a best man yet?" Alan asked. David sighed and nodded.

"I wanted to use you, but you're giving Amanda away." David said and Alan smiled. "I think it's gonna be Carman." David said. Alan smiled again and nodded.

"That's a good choice David. When will you tell him?" Alan asked.

"Um, soon I guess. I'm going to have to now that the wedding is only a few months away."

"That's true. Can I be there when you do it?" Alan asked. David smiled.

"Sure. Why?" Alan giggled and shook his head.

"Carman cries over stuff like this. I like to be there so I can make his life a living hell after words." Alan said. David laughed and shook his head.

"Wow, am I ever glad I'm not your best friend."

"OH, you're different." Alan said and winked. David giggled and shook his head.

"You're mean." David said in a pouty voice. Alan laughed and shook his head.

"You like it." They both laughed. David looked up at the clock and seen it was already after midnight. He looked back at Alan and Alan smiled. "Tired?" He asked. David nodded and took the last sip from his glass. Alan did the same and they both stood up. "I got the lights and stuff. You just go to bed." Alan said. David smiled and nodded. He stretched and Alan walked over to him. David giggled and looked at Alan's handsome face.

"I hate the rules." David whispered. Alan smiled and hugged David.

"I know." Alan whispered. They both took in the scent of the other and stepped away from each other.

"Good night Alan." David said. Alan smiled and ran his hand through David's hair. David whimpered and closed his eyes.

"Good night, David." Alan whispered and pulled his hand away. David opened his eyes and smiled at Alan.

"I really hate the rules." David wined. Alan laughed and shook his head. He led David to his room and opened the door.

"Try to sleep. We'll go to the hospital together tomorrow, ok?" Alan said. David nodded and stepped into his room. Alan shut the door and David could hear him walk away.

"Holy shit." David whispered to himself and leaned against the door.

That was the coolest thing he has ever done. David thought to himself as he remembered how it felt to have Alan on top of him at the table. His stomach flipped and he smiled. He went to the bathroom and then got ready for bed. He climbed in and stared up at the dark ceiling.

I wish the only thing I could think about was him. But I can't help but wonder what life is going to be like with mom gone. How can she be dying? Just like that. Just out of the blue. I don't get it. Why is this happening? How can I raise a baby and be married and do all these things without my mom to tell it all to? God mom! David could feel tears fill his eyes and he rolled over onto his side. He shut his eyes and prayed for sleep. He lay crying for half the night before he finally fell asleep at 4:00 am.

Chapter 26

Alan woke David at ten o'clock on November 12.

"If you want to go, we should head over there soon." Alan said from the door. David opened his eyes and looked at Alan. He smiled and winked at David. "I would come cuddle with you but your mom is awake." Alan whispered. David laughed and threw a pillow at Alan. He easily dodged it by shutting the door. David shook his head and sat up.

"God, what a night." David said and went into the bathroom. He took his morning pee and washed his hands when he was done. He turned on the shower and stepped in. He let the water pound against his chest for a few minutes before turning around and washing his hair. He washed his body next and stepped out of the tub. He dried himself off and applied his cologne and deodorant. He brushed his hair and his teeth and left the room. He went out to the kitchen and sat down at the table with Alan and his mom.

"Good Morning." Nancy said and smiled.

"Good morning mom. How did you sleep?" David asked as Alan got him a coffee.

"Oh, actually, I like this bed better than mine. I may never leave." Nancy said and David giggled. Alan smiled and put cream and sugar into the coffee he prepared for David.

"Well, that would be just fine mom." David said. She giggled and shook her head.

"You would get sick of me."

"Well, the way I see it is, I owe you eighteen years of rent free living don't I?" David asked. Nancy and Alan laughed. He handed David his coffee and rubbed his fingers across David's when he did it. David cleared his throat and Alan smiled. "Thank you." David said. Alan nodded and went to his seat.

"So when would you like to go see Amanda?" Nancy asked.

"As soon as I'm done my coffee." David said and took a big sip of the hot liquid.

"Ok, I'll come a little later. Seth is coming to get Mike and I after Mike's nap." Nancy said. David nodded and smiled at Little Mike. He was sitting on the living room floor watching a cartoon of a dog.

"Don't let him sleep longer than two hours or he doesn't sleep at night." David said.

"I remember." Nancy said. David smiled and then sighed.

"Mom, you could go if you wanted. You shouldn't baby-sit or anything like that." David said. Nancy frowned at him and shook her head.

"Do you think I'm not capable of dealing with him?" Nancy asked. Alan and David looked at each other before looking back at Nancy.

"No, of course not mom. I just thought you might want to rest or something." David said. Nancy laughed and shook her head.

"I'm fine son. You need to be with Amanda right now." Nancy said. David nodded and Alan took a sip of his coffee.

"Did you notice if you need anything around here? I could bring some stuff back with me later." Alan said to Nancy. She raised her eyebrows and looked around the tidy kitchen.

"I'm not sure." She said and looked at David. David shrugged.

"I wouldn't know. Amanda does most of the cooking and stuff. I would have to look around." David said.

"No, no. I'll do that this morning after you guys go. I'll put a list together and bring it with me to the hospital when I come." Nancy said and smiled at David. David smiled back and took another sip of his coffee.

"Thanks mom." David said. Nancy smiled and got up to go to the bathroom. Alan cleared his throat and David looked at him.

"How did you sleep?" Alan asked quietly. David sighed and shook his head.

"Well, I was hoping to not get you out of my head but, all I could think about was mom's fucking tumor. I didn't fall asleep until around four." David answered. Alan smiled and nodded.

"Me too. I managed to get to sleep sooner than you though." Alan said. David smiled and took another sip of his coffee.

"You were the first thing I thought about when I woke up though." David said. Alan laughed and shook his head.

"That's because I woke you up." Alan answered. David smiled and looked down the hall to the bathroom door. He looked back at Alan and giggled.

"Wanna know what I'm thinking about?" David asked in a whisper. Alan smirked and nodded.

"I bet I can guess." Alan said.

"I bet you can't." David whispered.

"What are your terms for this little bet?" Alan asked leaning closer to David. David giggled and rolled his eyes.

"Well, how about, if I win, you have to answer whatever question I can come up with without hesitation." David said. Alan giggled and shook his head.

"Ok, and if I win?" Alan asked. David thought for a second.

"Whatever you want. Pick your own terms." David said. Alan laughed and tapped the table.

"If I win, you have to answer any question *I* can think of without hesitation." Alan said. David laughed and nodded.

"Ok, guess what I'm thinking about then." David said. They could hear the toilet flush and David raised his eyebrows.

"You're thinking about how I straddled you last night." Alan whispered. David giggled and shook his head.

"Nope, I was thinking about straddling you." David said. Alan laughed and shook his head. "It seems I have won." David said.

"Ok, next time though, you should have to write it down so I know you're not cheating." Alan said. David laughed and Nancy came back into the room.

"What did I miss?" Nancy asked.

"I lost a bet." Alan said. Nancy laughed and shook her head.

"Did you cheat?" She asked David. Alan laughed and David shook his head.

"No I did not." David said.

"Did you pay up?" Nancy asked. David giggled and waited to see what Alan would say. Alan cleared his throat and shifted in his chair.

"Not yet." Alan said. Nancy giggled and looked at David.

"What does he owe you?" Nancy asked David. Alan laughed and looked at David. David scowled at him and then smiled at his mom.

"Ask him." David said. Nancy laughed and looked at Alan. Alan shook his head and met Nancy's eyes.

"I have to answer any question he can come up with without hesitation." Alan said. Nancy looked at him and frowned. She looked back at David and shrugged her shoulders.

"What kind of terms are those?" She asked. David laughed and took the last sip out of his cup.

"Awesome ones." David said and kissed his mom. "Let's go old man." David said and put his cup in the sink. Alan smiled and kissed Nancy.

"Looks like you've been told." She whispered and Alan smiled.

"Yep." He said and took his cup to the sink.

"Bye Mike." David said. Mike waved and went back to his show. Alan and David left the apartment and waited for the elevator to come up.

"So, what's your question?" Alan asked as they waited for the lift. David giggled and shook his head.

"Just a minute." David said. Alan rolled his eyes and the doors opened. They stepped in and when the doors closed David looked at Alan. Alan stared at him and smiled.

"Well?" Alan asked in his seductive voice. David chewed on the inside of his cheek but held his gaze on Alan. Alan bit his bottom lip and squinted his eyes. David giggled and the elevator stopped. They had already reached the main floor and the doors opened. David smiled and they stepped out. They went out to Alan's car and both got in. Alan started it and looked at David. "Are you going to ask your question or what?" Alan asked and David smiled.

"Ok fine." He said and Alan stared into his eyes.

"Well, go ahead then."

"You can't hesitate." David said. Alan laughed and nodded.

"I know." He said. David cleared his throat and his stomach flipped. He leaned close to Alan and Alan did the same. David blew across Alan's neck and Alan shivered. David smiled.

"Remember, you can't hesitate." David whispered. Alan nodded and shut his eyes. He gripped the steering wheel and held his breath. David smiled and shook his head. "Are you ready?" David asked. Alan exhaled his breath and nodded again. "Have you ever considered breaking the rules?" David asked.

"Yes." Alan answered without hesitating. David giggled and Alan opened his eyes.

"That's very interesting Alan." David whispered. Alan turned his head and they were almost close enough for their noses to touch. David blinked and held his breath.

"Not today though." Alan said. David closed his eyes and sat back in his seat. Alan smiled and shook his head. "I would have come up with something a lot better than that." Alan said and pulled out onto the road. David rolled his eyes and Alan giggled. "What? I would have." Alan said.

"Like what?" David asked. Alan sighed and tapped the steering wheel.

"Oh I don't know. Maybe something like, do you *want* to break the rules?" Alan asked. David smiled and shook his head.

"I'll remember that next time." David said.

"I don't plan on losing any more bets with you so there will be no 'next time'" Alan said. David giggled and looked out the window. He could see the hospital in the distance and he sighed. "Are you ok?" Alan asked. David smiled and looked at him.

"I wish I could be normal." David said. Alan frowned and looked at David with a puzzled look.

"What do you mean?" Alan asked. David sighed and shook his head. He looked back out the window at the hospital.

"She's in there trying to save our baby's life and I'm here with you. And trust me, there's nothing faithful about the way I think about you." David said. Alan smiled and shook his head.

"Your right David. I don't make it any easier for you either. I'm sorry." Alan said. David looked at him and smiled.

"That's ok Alan. Like I said, I *wish* I was normal. I'm not though, am I?" David asked. Alan laughed and shook his head.

"I think you're perfectly normal. I think you've been handed a stress load far beyond your years and your mind doesn't know how to deal with it." Alan said. David sighed and nodded. Alan pulled up to the hospital and parked the car. "Listen David." He said and shut off the car. David looked at him and raised his eyebrows. "I don't think there has ever been a day that you didn't strike me as a normal kid. You're doing fine and you will get through this. You'll get through the stuff with your mom too." David smiled.

"Thanks Alan. I don't think I could without you though." David said. Alan smiled and ran his hand through David's hair and patted his cheek.

"How could I stay away?" Alan asked in a whisper. David giggled and shook his head.

"You're so *mean*." David said. Alan laughed and they both got out. They went into the hospital together and went to Amanda's room. She was sitting up doing a cross word puzzle. She looked up at them and smiled.

"Hi guys." She said and set her book aside.

"Hi." David said and kissed her. Alan sat on the side of the bed and David sat down in the chair.

"How was your night?" Amanda asked. Alan smiled and looked at David.

"Well, it was good. Alan tried to rape me, but it was good." David said. Alan and Amanda both laughed. Alan shook his head and rolled his eyes.

"Well, that sounds like fun." Amanda said. David and Alan both giggled.

"That's not exactly how it went down." Alan said. David laughed and Amanda turned her attention to Alan. Alan smiled and batted his eye lashes. Both Amanda and David laughed. "You see, "Alan said. "He thought he was better at the game I invented so I had to prove him wrong." Alan explained. Amanda rolled her eyes and looked at David.

"Is this true?" Amanda asked as though he and Alan were brothers and she was trying to dig the truth out of her two badly behaved children. David laughed and shook his head.

"Not really. We tied. So I guess we're about the same." David said. Alan smiled and looked at Amanda.

"That is true." Alan said. Amanda giggled and shook her head.

"You guys are so weird." She said and David and Alan laughed.

"I was going to ask if you wanted your T.V. hooked up in here." Alan asked. Amanda raised her eyebrows.

"Yea, that's a great idea." She said. David smiled and got up.

"Where do I go?" David asked Alan. Alan sighed and looked out into the hall.

"I would guess the nurses' station." Alan said. David nodded and left the room. He went to the nurses' station and got the T.V. and the phone hooked up in Amanda's room. When he returned, Alan was helping Amanda with her cross word puzzle.

"Ok, so you have T.V. and phone." David said and sat down in his chair.

"Thank you babe." Amanda said. Alan smiled and read over the cross word puzzle.

"Lecture." Alan said and pointed at the page. Amanda smiled and wrote it in.

"What would I do without you?" Amanda asked Alan. Alan giggled and shrugged. David smiled and watched Alan as he read the page. His eyes quickly read the questions and he bit his lip while he thought. David smiled and stared at the muscles in Alan's jaw. Alan looked at him and smirked. Amanda studied the questions and paid no attention to Alan and David. David raised an eyebrow and Alan bit his bottom lip. David sighed and shifted in his seat. Alan smiled and went back to the puzzle. David giggled and dug out his phone. "Who are you calling?" Amanda asked. David looked up at her.

"No body. I was going to text Seth and find out when they planned on coming." David said as he sent his text. He shut the phone and smiled at Amanda.

"Sick of our company already?" Alan asked. David smiled and shook his head.

"No, but I'm interested in seeing Lance. I have some things to talk to him about." David said. Alan raised an eyebrow and looked at David with a questioning gaze.

"You sure get around." Amanda said and Alan burst out laughing. David and Amanda joined him.

"It's not like that. Boy you have little faith in me." David said. Amanda giggled and blew David a kiss.

"I love you." She said. David smiled and nodded.

"Uh, huh." David said. His phone buzzed and he opened it.

We will be there when ever Mike wakes up. It looks like it will be another hour or so your mom says. The text message read. David read it aloud for Alan and Amanda.

"Tell him not to rush. We're having an orgy." Amanda said. David and Alan laughed. David typed the message and sent it.

"You're picking up way to much from hanging out with us." Alan said. David giggled and shook his head.

"Do you feel corrupted?" David asked her. Amanda giggled and shook her head.

"You should hear what your mom and I talk about. Corrupted. HA!" Amanda said. Alan and David laughed again. David's phone buzzed and Amanda and Alan fell silent and waited to hear.

In your wildest dreams. David read the message aloud and they all laughed. Alan winked at David and David giggled. Amanda shook her head and Alan and David laughed again. They talked about the baby and told Alan what they had decided for a name. He smiled and thought it was cool that they were naming their son after him. It wasn't too long before Seth, Nancy and Little Mike showed up. They all said their hello's and Nancy took over the chair David was sitting in.

"So, I talked to the hospital. They are willing to let me go with a six month severance check and a year of medical coverage." Nancy said. Alan smiled and nodded.

"That's good right?" Amanda asked. Nancy smiled and nodded.

"It's good for a government job." David said. Nancy giggled and patted her son's arm.

"When is your last day?" Alan asked.

"Um, today. I have to go back and sign some paperwork and stuff." Nancy said. Alan and David both raised their eyebrows.

"Ok, when will the paperwork be ready?" Alan asked.

"Tomorrow." She answered.

"Well, I guess we should go then and get this done so we can get back before little Gabriel gets here." Alan said.

"Actually, I'm going to take her." Seth said. Nancy smiled and David raised his eyebrows again.

"Oh, why?" David asked. Nancy smiled and patted David's arm again.

"I would rather one of us was here just in case he comes. I will be back in two days." Nancy said.

"Are you sure?" Alan asked.

"Of course. I would send you to deal with it if they would accept a forged signature." Nancy said. Everyone laughed and Nancy looked at Amanda. "Please hold him in until I get back." Nancy said. Amanda giggled and nodded.

"Of course Nancy." Amanda said. Nancy smiled and said her good byes to everyone. Alan walked her out to the car with Seth. David smiled at Amanda and kissed her.

"What was that for?" Amanda asked. David giggled and shrugged.

"I just really wanted a kiss." David said. Amanda giggled and Mike jumped up onto the bed with her.

"Is baby coming yet?" Mike asked. Amanda giggled and shook her head.

"Not yet." She said quietly and rubbed her stomach.

"But why you here den?" Mike asked. David smiled and rubbed Mikes back.

"Well, the baby wanted to come too soon. If he comes out early, he'll be sick. So, the doctors are giving me special medicine so he stays in a little while longer." Amanda explained. Mike sighed and shook his head.

"Don't he know better?" Mike asked. David and Amanda laughed.

"He's just a baby, Buddy. He doesn't know anything yet." David said. Mike sighed and rubbed Amanda's stomach.

"Stay in dare little Gabey Baby. You have to be big to play with me." Mike said. Amanda and David looked at each other and smiled. Mike talked to the baby until Alan came back. He sat on Alan's lap and leaned his head against his shoulder. "Baby is gonna get bigger and come out and play, Grandpa." Mike said. Alan smiled and rubbed the little boy's leg.

"That's right Mike. And then Amanda can go home and won't have to stay here anymore." Alan said. Mike nodded and looked at Amanda.

"How does baby get out of dare?" He asked. David and Alan giggled and Amanda sighed.

"Well, Mike. The doctors might have to cut Amanda open and take him out." She said. Mike shot up arrow straight.

"No they can't! Is dare another way?" He yelled. Alan rubbed his back and cradled the boys head against his chest.

"You know what?" Alan asked him. Mike looked up into Alan's face with the beginning of tears in his eyes. Alan smiled at him and kissed his forehead. "Amanda can always push him out like a big poop." Alan said. Mike laughed and looked at Amanda. David and Amanda giggled at the little boy's reaction.

"Is that for real?" Mike asked Amanda. Amanda smiled and nodded. Mike laughed again and shook his head. "Mandy, you have to poop out the baby?" He asked. Amanda sighed and rubbed her stomach.

"If the doctors say I can." Amanda said.

"How does a baby fit out your bum? Won't there be poop on him?" Mike asked. David and Alan burst out laughing and Amanda giggled at her little brother.

"He won't come out my bum. He would come from where I pee." Amanda tried to explain. Mike made a pain noise and grabbed his genitals. David and Alan laughed again and Amanda just shook her head.

"That doesn't sound good." Mike said still in his pained voice.

"No it doesn't, does it?' Alan asked. David laughed and shook his head.

"Amanda doesn't have the same stuff we do buddy. She is built for this." David said. Mike looked at Amanda with amazement.

"Really?" He asked in a profound sounding voice. Amanda nodded and Mike sighed. "That's good cause a baby would never come out of a doodle." Mike said. Everyone was laughing now. Mike giggled and clapped his hands. "I funny right?" Mike asked.

"Yes you are." Alan said and hugged the little boy again. Just then Amanda's hand shot to her stomach and everyone was silent.

"Mike, feel." She whispered. Mike put his hand on Amanda's stomach and he giggled.

"He kicking me." Mike whispered. Amanda grabbed Alan's hand and put it on her stomach as well. Alan closed his eyes and smiled. David smiled at him and he felt warmth come over his body.

"Can you feel him?" Amanda asked Alan. Alan nodded and rubbed his thumb on her stomach. David watched Alan. He saw a smiled slowly come across his face and David sighed. Alan slowly opened his eyes and looked at David.

"That's amazing." He whispered. David nodded and they smiled at each other. Amanda giggled as Mike laid his head on her stomach.

"Hi baby. I your uncle Mike. I gonna play with you all day long." Mike said. David and Amanda giggled.

"It's funny he knows who he is." Alan said.

"Well, Seth has been explaining it to him for the last little while." David said. Alan smiled and nodded. Amanda yawned and David looked up at the clock. "Is it after two already?" David asked. Alan nodded and stretched his back. Amanda smiled at Mike and pet his hair.

"Can Amanda sleep for little while?" She whispered. Mike sighed and nodded.

"I had a nap too, Amanda." Mike said.

"That's good. Now it's my turn. Why don't you take David and grandpa for a coffee and ice cream?" She asked. Mike smiled and nodded. He hugged her and jumped off the bed.

"Come on boy's. Uncle Mike's buying." He said. Alan and David laughed. They both hugged Amanda and David kissed her.

"We'll be back later." David whispered. Amanda smiled and nodded. They stepped out of the room and headed toward Alan's car. They got Mike into the back and got into their own seats.

"Where to Uncle Mike?" Alan asked as he started the car.

"Coffee and ice cream!" Mike yelled. David and Alan smiled and Alan pulled out of the parking lot. David sighed and looked out the window.

"What are you thinking about?" Alan asked. David giggled and shook his head.

"Sex." David said. Alan laughed and stopped at a red light.

"Really?" Alan asked. David looked at him and nodded.

"Yea, what else do I ever think about?" David asked. Alan shrugged and giggled.

"So, two days of alone time. What are we gonna do with it?" Alan asked. David giggled and stared into Alan's eyes.

"Like I said. I was thinking about sex." David said. Alan laughed again and continued down the road to a little café. He parked in the front and David got Mike out of the car. They walked in together and ordered two coffees and a small cup of ice cream. They sat at a little round table by the window that David and Alan were almost too tall for. They laughed when their knees touched under the table.

"So, Gabriel Alan Smith, huh? Sounds like a rich guy's name." Alan said. David giggled and nodded his head.

"I think it sounds cool." He said. Mike giggled and shook his head. David and Alan both looked at him. He looked up from his ice cream and smiled.

"It sounds like my brother's name." Mike said. David smiled and nodded.

"It is your brother's name."

"Everything but the middle." Mike said. David looked at Alan and smiled. He looked back at little Mike and sighed.

"What was Gabe's middle name?" David asked. Mike smiled and thought for a second.

"Gabriel Adrian Hawkeye Moore." Mike said. Alan and David both laughed.

"Hawkeye?" David asked. Mike nodded but failed to see the humor in the name. "What's your middle name?" David asked. Mike smiled and sat up tall in his chair.

"Michael Tucker Steven Moore." He said proudly.

"Well, that's not so bad." Alan said. David giggled and shook his head.

"Hawkeye. No wonder he never told anyone." David said. Alan giggled and shook his head.

"No wonder Amanda didn't want to use it. Adrian is ok though." Alan said. David nodded and Mike laughed.

"Adrian is Grandma's name." Mike said. Alan and David laughed again. Mike giggled and went back to his ice cream.

"Wow." Alan said. David giggled and looked at Alan.

"What's your middle name?" David asked. Alan smiled and sipped his coffee.

"If I tell you mine, will you tell me yours?" Alan asked. David nodded and sipped his own coffee.

"Clifford." Alan said. David giggled and Alan shook his head. "It was my Grandfathers name. What's yours?" Alan asked. David leaned back in his chair and smiled.

"I have a ton of them." David said. Alan raised his eyebrows and waited. "David Elvis Jonathan Ringo Smith." David said. Alan burst out laughing and shook his head.

"Wow, you must love your parents." Alan said.

"Ringo." Mike said and laughed. David, Alan and Mike all laughed.

"What's your mom's?

"She doesn't have one." David said. Alan laughed and shook his head.

"Are you serious?" He asked. David nodded and took a sip of his coffee. Alan giggled and sipped his own coffee.

"I like David's all names." Mike said. David smiled and ruffled up the boys hair.

"Thank you Michael Tucker Steven Moore." David said. Mike laughed and went back to his ice cream.

"David Elvis Jonathan Ringo Smith. That's a hell of a name boy." Alan said. David rolled his eyes and smiled.

"Alan Clifford Black. Actually sounds kind of cool when you say it all together." David said. Alan laughed and shook his head.

"Well, I'm kind of a cool guy." Alan said. They talked about strange names and where they came from. Mike finished his ice cream around the same time David and Alan finished their second cups of coffee. They cleaned Mike up with some napkins and took him out to the car. They both got in and lit a cigarette.

"Think she's up yet?" David asked. Alan looked at his watch and shrugged.

"We've only been gone an hour." Alan said. David took a drag from his cigarette and looked back at Mike.

"Wanna go see Lance?" David asked. Mike clapped and Alan smiled.

"Ok, Lance it is." Alan said. He drove down the road to Lance's house and parked in the front. They went up to the door and Mike yelled.

"DEAD MAN WALKEN!" David and Alan laughed and waited for Lance to answer. He opened the door and smiled at Mike.

"Well hello there." He said and picked the little boy up. Alan and David smiled and Lance smiled back. "How you doing old boy?" Lance asked Alan.

"Still younger than you." Alan said and patted Lance's shoulder.

"Why do those couple of hours even count?" Lance asked. David and Alan laughed. "And you good looking. How are you?" Lance asked.

"Alive." David said and winked. Lance giggled and they followed him into the house. He took them downstairs and turned the huge T.V. on for Mike. There was a football game on and Mike begged Lance to leave it on. He did as he was told and went up to the bar with David and Alan.

"Looks like you have a sports fan there." Alan said. David and Lance laughed.

"He only watches it for the cheer leaders." David said. Lance and Alan laughed.

"It's true. You should have seen him when Dallas was playing. He lost his mind over them ones." Lance said. Alan laughed and shook his head.

"Well, I guess so far, you have to worry about *him* knocking somebody up." Alan said. David laughed and Lance shook his head.

"It doesn't always last forever." Lance said referring to Seth. David looked at him and shook his head.

"Lance, I've been meaning to talk to you about that." David said. Lance smiled and met David's gaze.

"Really? Start talking." Lance said as he mixed three weak drinks.

"Well, I was wondering, what would it take to get you to hold this bit of information in for a little while?" David asked in an almost seductive voice. Alan giggled and waited to see what Lance would say.

"Well, that depends. Define while." Lance said. Alan smiled and took a sip of the drink Lance had put in front of him. David sighed and looked around the room.

"Oh, a couple months." David said. Lance rubbed his chin with his long fingers.

"Hmmm, a couple months, huh?" Lance asked. Alan giggled and David smiled at him. Lance sighed and raised his eyebrows. "Do I get paid in advance or do I have to wait those couple of months?" Lance asked. Alan laughed and shook his head. David cleared his throat and looked deep into Lance's eyes.

"You have to wait." David said. Lance nodded and tapped the bar with his fingers.

"So, if I have to wait for it, I better decide something pretty good, huh?" Lance asked. David nodded and Alan giggled again. Lance giggled now too and David smiled. Lance moved close to David across the bar and David met him in the middle. "I wanna fuck you." Lance whispered. David smiled and looked into Lances eyes.

"Ok, well. Hold your tongue for three months and you can have it." David whispered. Lance giggled and held out his hand.

"You have yourself a deal good looking." Lance said. David smiled and shook Lance's hand. He sat back in his chair and looked at Alan.

"So, what does he want?" Alan asked. Lance shook his head.

"You can't say." Lance said. David laughed and looked back at Alan.

"Nothing." David said and winked at Alan. Alan giggled and shook his head. They talked about Nancy and the brain tumor. When they finished nursing their drinks, they got Mike ready to go. Lance walked them up to the door and hugged Mike before they left.

"Be good." He said to the little boy.

"I will." He said and headed for the car. Lance and Alan hugged and then Lance hugged David.

"You hang in there. She'll do great." Lance whispered. David smiled and nodded. They said their good byes and joined Mike at the car. They got him in and took their own seats.

"What did he ask for?" Alan asked as he pulled away. David laughed and shook his head.

"He said he wants to fuck me." David said. Alan's breath caught in his throat and he looked at David.

"And you said you would do it?" Alan asked. David laughed and shook his head.

"I don't expect to have to pay up. He'll never keep his mouth shut for three months Alan." David said. Alan thought for a second then he laughed.

"That is a long time for him not to say anything." Alan said. David sighed and nodded.

"Especially if I start making it impossible for him not to." David said. Alan laughed and shook his head.

"That's all fine and good. Just make sure Seth doesn't get hurt in the cross fire. I know that man and he's not the kindest kitten in the basket."

"Where do you hear this shit? You must be old." David said referring to the 'Kitten in the basket' saying. Alan laughed and turned onto the hospital street. "Besides. I plan on having Seth all figured out by the end of those three months so he can tell his dad about it first." David said and Alan sighed.

"Do you think you could have told your dad?" Alan asked.

"That's different. This guy already has a gay son. And they work together and he gave him the house and everything else. Seth has it easy. Their dad is already desensitized to it." David said. Alan raised his eyebrows and nodded.

"You've thought about this haven't you?"

"Yup, I have so." David said. Alan smiled and shook his head.

"See, you *are* the brains of this outfit." Alan said. David laughed and shook his head. Alan soon pulled into the hospital parking lot and they both got out. Alan carried Mike in and they went into Amanda's room. They visited with her until seven o'clock when they thought it was about time to get Mike home for supper. They said their good byes and took Mike home. David made him a grilled cheese sandwich and he and Alan decided to have chips and dip after he went to bed. David bathed Mike and got him into bed by 9:00. He came out to see Alan had poured him a rum and coke.

"So, tired tonight?" Alan asked. David smiled and nodded.

"I am. I should sleep pretty well tonight." David said and took a sip of his drink. Alan smiled and did the same.

"So, I was wondering. What happens if Lance keeps his word and Seth doesn't say anything to his dad?" Alan asked. David took a deep breath and shrugged.

"We smuggle me out of the country." David said. Alan laughed and shook his head. He looked at his phone and sighed. "Think their home yet?" David asked wondering why they hadn't heard from Seth and his mother. Alan looked at him and smiled.

"I was just wondering that myself." Alan said and dialed the number. There was no answer so he left a message.

"You know, she really likes you." David said and sighed. Alan smiled and nodded.

"I know. I like her too." Alan said. David leaned back in his chair and stared into Alan's green eyes.

"I'm glad she has you. You make her happy." David said quietly. Alan tilted his head to one side and stared into David's eyes.

"She makes me happy too. And her kid is like a total bonus." Alan said. David giggled and shook his head.

"Well, he likes you too." David said. Alan smiled and took a sip of his drink.

"That's good cause, I wanna fuck him." Alan said. David coughed on his drink and Alan laughed. David shook his head and stared at Alan's face.

"You're such a dick." David said laughing. Alan giggled and nodded.

"I know." David and Alan both laughed and finished their drinks.

"I'll see you tomorrow." David said standing up and putting his glass in the sink.

"Good night, David." Alan said and winked at him. David smiled and shook his head. He went into his room and closed the door. He smiled to himself and got into bed.

Wow, I don't think I can stand having Alan being this open with me. I'm glad I love Amanda so much or I wouldn't be sleeping alone tonight and definitely hurting my mom with every thrust into Alan I could make. David thought to himself and sighed. He closed his eyes and soon fell asleep.

Chapter 27

David awoke the next day, November 13th, at 7:30. He had a shower and got ready for his day before going out to the kitchen and making coffee. He could hear Alan turn the shower on in the main bathroom and smiled. He went into Mike's room and turned the light on. Mike groaned and rolled over.

"Come on Mike. Gotta get up and have breakfast." David said quietly. Mike sighed but stayed in bed. David smiled and went back out into the kitchen. He unplugged his phone and noticed he had a text message. He opened his phone and read,

Hey, what kind of puppy food does Mack eat? We grabbed the container but it's almost empty. David smiled and shook his head at Lance's message. He typed back.

It's the puppy food in the green bag. I don't remember what it's called but I know its $11. David typed back and pressed send. He put his phone in his pocket and lit a cigarette. He watched as the coffee pot slowly filled. He rolled his cigarette in his ash tray while he waited. Mike came out of his room and climbed into his chair.

"Ready for breakfast?" David asked. Mike yawned and nodded. David smiled and got a bowl of cereal for him. He put milk in the bowl and set it in front of Mike with a spoon. Mike smiled and dug right in. David got two cups down for coffee and put cream and sugar in both. When the shower shut off, he poured the hot black liquid into the cups. He took the cups to the table and set them down. He then took the last puff from his cigarette and put it out. He sat down on his chair and took a sip of his coffee.

"Are we going to see Amanda today?" Mike asked.

"We sure are." David said. Mike smiled and took another big spoonful of cereal. David smiled and sipped at his coffee again. There was a pile of mail on the table so he sifted through it. On the bottom of the pile was a letter to Amanda and the return address said it was from Gabe's daughter, Beth. "Holy shit." David said and Mike looked at him.

"What wrong?" Mike asked. David looked up at him and smiled.

"Nothing is wrong buddy. Amanda got a letter from someone really special." David said and waved the letter in the air.

"Read it." Mike said and put another spoonful of cereal into his mouth. David smiled and shook his head.

"I can't. It's for Amanda. We'll take it with us, ok?" David said. Mike smiled and nodded. Just then, Alan came out to the kitchen and sat down at the table.

"Good Morning." Alan said.

"Hi Grandpa. Amanda has a special paper." Mike said. Alan smiled and looked at David.

"Yea, it's from Beth." David said and handed it to Alan. Alan took the letter and read the return address. He raised his eyebrows and took a sip of his coffee.

"Well, that's a little unexpected." Alan said handing the letter back to David.

"I know." David said and reached around himself to put the letter into the inside pocket of his leather jacket he had hung on the back of the chair.

"What do you think it says?" Alan said. David shrugged and sighed.

"Something good I hope. She doesn't need more stress right now."

"No kidding." Alan said and took another sip of his coffee. He lit a cigarette and leaned back in his chair. "So, I'm wondering if you shouldn't give it to her until she has the baby." Alan said. David looked at him funny.

"Why?" David asked.

"Well, what if its bad news or something. She might be better prepared to read it after words." Alan said. David sighed and took a sip of his coffee. He tapped the table with his finger and thought about it for a second.

"What if its good news?" David asked and Alan smiled.

"Then it will make her feel good after hours of long painful labor." Alan said. David smiled and nodded.

"I still think she should get it now." David said. Alan shrugged and took a sip of his coffee.

"It's up to you. Her last contact with them wasn't so pleasant so, I don't know. It's your call."

"Yea." David said and took another sip of his coffee. Mike was finished eating so David told him he could watch cartoons for a few minutes before he got dressed and ready to go. "Did mom ever call you back?" David asked.

"Yes, I had my ringer off and missed it. I thought I would call her a little later. After nine or so." Alan said. David looked up at the clock and seen it was almost 8:30.

"Ok." He stared at Alan and sighed. Alan giggled and shook his head.

"What?" Alan asked through his giggled. David laughed and took another sip of his coffee.

"What he asks." David said. Alan giggled and stood up. He went into his bed room and came out with his phone.

"Did you charge yours up?" Alan asked.

"Yup." David answered. Alan nodded and put his in the holder on his hip. Mike was giggling at a show he was watching and Alan and David both smiled at him. Alan sat back down and took another sip of his coffee. "It's gonna be weird to have a baby here too." David said.

"Well, from what I know about kids, once you have them, you wonder how you lived your life without them." Alan said. David smiled and stared at Mike.

"You know, I feel like that with Mike."

"See, and then there will be two." Alan said. David and Alan both smiled at each other and finished their coffees. David got Mike dressed and ready to go while Alan went through the freezer deciding what to make for supper. When they were all ready, they headed down to Alan's car and got in. Alan started it and headed to the hospital.

"What do you get for a dying person for Christmas?" David asked as Alan drove. Alan sighed and shook his head.

"You know, I was wondering that this morning too." Alan said. They both sighed. "Maybe we should send her somewhere nice." Alan suggested. David smiled and nodded.

"That's an idea, like where though?" David asked. Alan sighed and shook his head.

"We'll have to think about it I guess." He said. He came up to the hospital parking lot and pulled in.

"What do *you* want for Christmas?" David asked. Alan laughed and shook his head.

"I don't know." Alan said. David rolled his eyes and looked out the window. "What do you want?" Alan asked. David giggled and looked at Alan.

"A blow job." David said. Alan burst out laughing and parked the car.

"Uh, huh." Alan said and they both laughed. They got out of the car and David held Mike's hand as they walked up to the doors of the hospital. Alan opened the door for them and they all walked in together. They went into Amanda's room and she was just finishing her breakfast.

"Hi guys." She said in a cheery voice. Mike laughed and jumped on the bed with her.

"Hi Amanda. I had cereal too." Mike said.

"That's good." Amanda said. David came over to her and kissed her. She smiled and held his hand as he sat down on the bed with her. Alan said good morning and sat down in the chair.

"How are you feeling?" David asked.

"Really good today actually." Amanda said. She turned her T.V. on to cartoons for Mike and he clapped. He sat on the end of the bed and stared up at the T.V. Amanda smiled at him. David pulled the letter out of his pocket and handed it to Amanda. She frowned and read the address. "Oh my God." She said and looked at David.

"I told him to wait but I guess he couldn't." Alan said. Amanda giggled and leaned forward to kiss David. David smiled and crossed his legs on the bed.

"Are you gonna open it or what?" David asked. Amanda giggled and looked between Alan and David. Alan smiled and they both watched as she pulled the letter out. She unfolded it and read aloud.

"Dear Amanda, I know you don't know me but I'm your niece." Amanda read and smiled. She continued. "My mom doesn't know I'm writing to you. She thinks that my grandma and grandpa would get mad if I have anything to do with you." Amanda read. She looked up at David. "See I told you." Amanda said. David smiled and nodded. "Anyway," Amanda said and went back to the letter. "I want to get to know you weather she likes it or not. I've only ever seen pictures of my dad and I don't think it's fair. My mom will never take me there so you'll have to do it. I know I could get in big trouble and maybe you could too. I wish things were different. My grandparents never liked my dad I guess, but I don't care." Amanda read. She looked up at David and Alan. Alan raised his eyebrows.

"Does it say anything else?" Alan asked. Amanda nodded and went back to reading.

"I hope you'll write back. If you send it to the address on the envelope, my mom will never know. It's my friends address and she said I could use it to write to you." Amanda read. She sniffed and smiled. David squeezed her hand and she giggled.

"Anything else?" David asked. Amanda swallowed hard and nodded. Alan smiled and he and David waited quietly. She took a few seconds for herself and then continued to read.

"I really hope you write back. I want to know all about you and my dad. All I know so far is that he was gay and him and my mom were best friends before. I have two pictures. One of just him and then one with you in it too. I know you'll be older now but I bet you're just as pretty now as you were then. I can't wait to hear from you. Love Beth." Amanda finished reading and sighed. "Oh David." She said and cried. David smiled and hugged her.

"What do you want to do?" David whispered. Amanda cleared her throat and shook off her tears.

"I need paper." Amanda said and Alan stood up.

"I'll get you some." Alan said and left the room. Amanda smiled and kissed David.

"Can you believe this?" She asked looking at the letter again.

"How did she get our address?" David asked. Amanda thought for a second and shrugged.

"I don't know. Who cares though?" She said and giggled. Mike turned around and looked at them.

"If Gabe has a kids, does that mean I their uncle too?" Mike asked. David and Amanda laughed.

"That's what it means Mike." David said. Mike smiled and went back to his television show. David and Amanda looked at each other and Amanda giggled. David rubbed her stomach and smiled. "Is he sleeping?" David whispered and Amanda shrugged.

"I don't know. I guess so. I haven't felt him for a while." Amanda said and put her hand on David's. They both rubbed her stomach until Alan came in.

"So, I had to get this from the gift shop but at least it comes with an envelope." Alan said. Amanda smiled and took the stationary kit from Alan. It was off white paper with fall colored leaves along one side. The envelopes looked the same.

"Thank you." Amanda said and Alan smiled. He sat back down in the chair and Amanda opened her kit. She looked at the paper and smiled. "This is perfect." She said. David smiled and looked at Alan.

"Suck up." David said and Amanda and Alan laughed. They talked about what Amanda should tell Beth in her first letter until almost noon. When both Amanda and Mike were getting tired, Alan and David decided to go do some shopping and stuff to let Amanda rest. They got Mike into the car and headed to the store. They picked up a few things and headed back to David's apartment. Alan put the groceries away while David put Mike down for his nap. They watched the news and made fun of the anchors while Mike slept. When he woke up, Alan made some soup for lunch and they all ate together at the table. Mike told them about how he dreamed he was an astronaut and he found people on the moon. Alan and David giggled as he told his story. When they were all finished and the dishes were tucked away into the dishwasher, they headed down to the car to go back to the hospital.

"So, I was thinking about your mom's Christmas present. Why don't we all go to California? We could go in February or March just before the wedding." Alan said. David raised his eyebrows and nodded.

"That's a good idea, we could drive there too. It would be like a family road trip." David said and Alan giggled.

"We'll have to rent a van or something but, it would work." Alan said looking in his rear view mirror at his tiny back seat. David giggled and nodded.

"Mom would love that. She loves California." David said and sighed.

"I know, that's why I thought of it. She told me she hasn't been there for a holiday since you were ten or something like that."

"Yea, that's about when we last went." David said. Alan giggled and shook his head. "I think it's funny that it's been so long. I mean it's not like it's that far to the coast." Alan nodded and pulled into the hospital parking lot. Mike clapped in the back.

"Amanda!" He yelled and David giggled. They got him out and he ran to the doors. They were too heavy for him so it gave Alan and David time to catch up. They opened the door for him and he ran into Amanda's room. As they got closer, they could hear Amanda laughing at Mike.

"Hi." David and Alan said in unison. They giggled and Amanda laughed.

"Hi guys. Did you have a good nap?" She asked Mike. He nodded and looked up at the T.V. Amanda sighed and turned the T.V. on for him. Alan sat down in the chair and David sat on the edge of the bed.

"So, what did you guys have for lunch?" Amanda asked.

"Soup." David answered and Amanda giggled.

"You guys are such bachelors." She said. Alan and David smiled. "I had roast beef and mashed potatoes with hospital gravy and green beans." Amanda said. Then made a gross face. "I would have preferred your soup I bet." She added. David and Alan laughed.

"Did you get a nap?" Alan asked.

"A little one. I started my letter but I don't really know what to tell her." Amanda answered.

"Well, what did you write so far?" David asked.

"Well, I told her about you and the baby. I told her about your mom and Alan. I left out the brain thing though." Amanda said and David nodded. "I told her about Mike too. I just wasn't sure if she knows Gabe is dead. I mean, she did talk about him in past tense so I'm guessing she knows." Amanda explained.

"She probably does. I mean, if she knows that her grandparents have something to do with her not seeing her dad, it's probably safe to assume that she knows he's dead too." Alan said. Amanda sighed and nodded.

"I'm not going to mention it. I'll tell her a bit about him and talk about him in past tense too and see if she asks I think." David smiled.

"Sounds very smart, babe." David said and rubbed her stomach. She smiled and watched his hand.

"I bet she'll be very excited to get a letter back. I think it was very brave of her to write to me." Amanda said.

"That's for sure, especially if she has people not wanting her to." Alan added. Amanda nodded and David looked at Alan. He smiled and winked at him. David giggled and looked back at Amanda.

"We were thinking about going into California for a gift to mom." Amanda smiled.

"She would love that. Like go for Christmas?" Amanda asked. David and Alan raised their eyebrows and looked at each other.

"Exactly." Alan said. David laughed and looked back at Amanda.

"Oh, California at Christmas. That sounds so nice." She said and smiled. They talked about the trip for quite a while. Alan remembered a place that rented out seven passenger vans and said he would look into it when he got home. Amanda talked excitedly about all the places she wanted to see. Soon, Carman walked into the room.

"Hi, how was your day?" Alan asked. Carman sighed and sat down on the bed with Amanda and David.

"Fricking long. I miss you." Carman said with a pouty voice to David. David giggled and shook his head.

"Poor Carman." Mike said and hugged Carman. Every one giggled as Carman hugged the little boy. Amanda shifted on her bed to make more room for Carman to sit there.

"Well, to be honest, I'm getting a little stir crazy myself." David said.

"Well, you need to be with Amanda." Carman said. Amanda smiled and winked at David. David smiled back at her and sighed.

"Yea, I know." He said. Alan yawned and David looked at him. Alan bit the inside of his cheek and David smiled. Amanda explained the California trip to Carman while Alan and David stared at each other. Alan took a deep breath and stood up.

"Carman, let's go smoke." Alan said and Carman looked at him.

"Good idea." Carman said and sat Mike on the bed with Amanda. They stepped out of the room and David turned himself around so he could lie next to Amanda.

"I miss our bed." Amanda said and rested her head on David's chest. David smiled and rubbed her back.

"I miss having you in it." David said back. Amanda giggled and shook her head.

"I bet Alan would cuddle with you if you asked really nicely." She teased. David laughed and kissed the top of her head.

"I don't think so, Amanda." He said. She giggled again and rubbed David's muscular stomach with her warm hand.

"I wish I could go home. I'm sick of it here." She said.

"I know babe. But just think, soon we will have our little baby and he can come home with us too." David whispered. Amanda sighed and nodded.

"I wish I could have him now and get it over with."

"Oh, baby. I know." David said. He cradled her in his arms and hummed her favorite song by Guns and Roses, Patients. She smiled and closed her eyes while he quietly sang the words to her. By the time he was finished, she had fallen asleep. He lay there holding her and watching Mikes T.V. show until Carman and Alan came back in.

"Hey, is she sleeping?" Carman asked in a whisper. David nodded and Alan and Carman took their seats as quiet as possible.

"It's going on to 4:30, we should start thinking about taking Mike home to feed him." Alan said. Carman smiled and tapped Mike on the shoulder. Mike turned around and looked at him.

"Wanna come have supper at my house?" Carman asked. Mike nodded and giggled.

"And a sleep over?" Mike whispered. Carman looked at David and David shrugged.

"If you want to." Carman said quietly to the boy.

"Yes!" Mike yelled. Amanda stirred and all three men said 'shhhh' to the little boy. Mike put his hand over his mouth and giggled. "Yes." He said in a whisper. Carman smiled and nodded his head.

"Ok, you can come with me then." Carman said.

"Thanks Carman." David said. Carman smiled at him and picked up Mike. Mike giggled as he threw him over his shoulder.

"See you tomorrow." Alan said.

"You bet." Carman said. David could see them exchange some kind of knowing glance to each other before Carman left the room. David looked at Alan and sighed.

"Just you and me, huh?" David asked. Alan nodded and sat forward on his chair.

"Wanna go out for supper then?" Alan asked and David shrugged.

"Sure if you want? Are you wanting to go now?" David asked. Alan shook his head.

"No, we'll go when you're ready." Alan said. David smiled and handed Alan the remote. He closed his eyes and rested his head against Amanda's. He listened as Alan searched through the channels before leaving it on a Cold War documentary.

"Trying to put yourself to sleep?" David asked with his eyes closed and Alan giggled.

"I love this stuff." He said. David sighed and shook his head.

"You love the Cold War? Those have to be the worst documentaries ever made." David said. Alan giggled again and David looked at him. "Well, they are." He said.

"That may be but, I like the old guns." Alan said. David looked at the T.V. and rolled his eyes. The film was in black and white and all he could make out was clouds of dust. Alan watched the program while David lay with Amanda. At 6:30, a nurse came in with Amanda's dinner. David carefully woke her and she smiled at him. They visited with her until she was finished eating. David kissed her and hugged her before they left. They got into Alan's car and David lit a cigarette.

"So, what did you and Carman talk about?" David asked as Alan drove around trying to decide where to eat. Alan giggled and shook his head.

"Nothing." He said. David rolled his eyes and took a drag of his cigarette.

"I bet." David said. Alan sighed and tapped the steering wheel.

"You wanna know what I'm thinking." Alan asked. David smirked and looked at Alan.

"I bet I can guess." David said. Alan laughed and shook his head.

"Ok, you're on. Same terms as before?" Alan asked. David nodded and Alan smiled. "Ok then, guess." Alan said. David took a deep breath and looked out the windshield.

"I thought you had to write it down." David said.

"That's only you." Alan said. David laughed and shook his head.

"Nope, it's a rule."

"Well, I'm driving. I swear on my unmolested virgin soul that I will not cheat." Alan said. David laughed and shook his head.

"Ok, well I think you're thinking about your talk with Carman." David said. Alan giggled.

"Nope. I was thinking about that blow job you wanted for Christmas." Alan said. David laughed and shook his head. Alan laughed with him and pulled into a bar and grill. They went inside and the waitress found a table for them. They both ordered a beer and she handed them menus.

"So, what's your question?" David asked. Alan looked over his menu and took a sip of his beer.

"I'm thinking." Alan answered and went back to his menu. David giggled and shook his head. He found what he wanted and set his menu aside. "Boy you pick fast." Alan said still looking his over.

"Well, I know what I like. I'm very rarely confused." David said. Alan giggled and shook his head.

"Uh, huh." Alan said. He finally picked out what he wanted and set his menu aside as well. They both took a sip of their beer at the same time and Alan locked his eyes on David. David giggled and waited for his question. Alan squinted and leaned closer on the table. David did the same and deepened his stare into Alan's eyes. "Remember, you can't hesitate." Alan said. David nodded. Alan took a deep breath and put his mouth close to David's ear. David's breathing sped up and Alan giggled.

"Just ask already." David whispered. Alan blew on David's neck and David shivered. Alan giggled and blew on David's neck again. David sighed and shut his eyes.

"The waitress is coming." Alan whispered and slowly sat back in his chair. David sighed and looked up at her. She was very pleasant and quickly took their orders. When she left the table, David took a sip of his beer and looked at Alan.

"Don't you even have a question?" David asked. Alan shook his head.

"I want it to be a good one." Alan replied and David laughed.

"Ok, well don't work on it too hard." David said. Alan sighed and looked around the restaurant. David watched as Alan seemed to study every person in the room before his eyes came back to David's. David smiled at him and he took a sip of his drink.

"Did you sleep with Carman?" Alan asked. David was shocked.

"No." He answered with very little hesitation. "Is that what you guys were talking about?" He asked. Alan nodded and looked down at the cutlery on the table.

"He won't tell me what happened. I know you didn't just go in there and show off your stuff. He isn't talking. Will you?" Alan asked. David sighed and looked at Alan. He was having a hard time figuring out if it was concern or jealousy on his face.

"Well, what did he tell you?" David asked. Alan sighed and rolled his eyes.

"He said you helped him in a very unique way. What does that even mean?" David sighed and shook his head.

"Alan, I just got him to the place where he usually freaks out and then went just a bit farther. We didn't have sex or anything. Why does it even matter? I thought you said you wanted me to use my own discretion?" David explained tacking on questions as he spoke. Alan sighed and shook his head.

"I did. I just . . ." Alan stopped talking and looked away. He watched a waitress clean off a table. David sighed and leaned closer to Alan.

"Are you mad?" David asked. Alan shook his head. David sighed and kicked Alan under the table. Alan looked at him and frowned.

"Owe." He said. David giggled and rubbed Alan's shin gently with his foot.

"Sorry." David said and pulled his foot away. Alan sighed and stared into David's eyes.

"I don't know how I feel about it, ok." Alan said. David smiled and shook his head.

"Alan, I only wanted to help Carman. By the time he was ready to do it, I didn't even want to anymore. After the talk with you and all the stuff with Amanda and Seth and stuff. God, I felt like a tool or something. I only did what I did because I promised Carman I would. And when I talked to you about it, I seem to remember you saying that if I could help him, I should." David said. Alan sighed and nodded.

"I know what I said David. I guess I'm just feeling a little jealous or something." Alan said. David giggled and Alan scowled at him. "So, you're gonna laugh at me?" Alan asked.

"No, I'm not. I just find it funny that *you* would be jealous of Carman." David said.

"Why? Carman is a good looking, readily available guy. Why wouldn't I be jealous?" Alan asked. David sighed and shook his head.

"Alan, you have nothing to be jealous about. Trust me." David said and sipped his beer.

"Sure I do." Alan said still staring into David's eyes.

"Ok, like what?" David asked. Alan rolled his eyes and shook his head.

"I really like your mom, David. And I know I made a promise to you not to hurt her. And I know you promised Amanda you wouldn't be with a guy or whatever. But the truth is, I'm jealous that Carman was the last guy you were with when is some cases, I feel like, I should have been." Alan explained. David raised his eyebrows and stared at Alan.

"Alan, why do you do this shit?" David asked. Alan blinked at him and looked away. "Don't look away. We're supposed to be trying to get over this shit. All we've been doing these past few days has been making it worse. Why would you say something like that? Don't you think at that moment with Carman when I made him cum, I didn't wish it was you?" David asked in a quiet but stern voice. Alan blinked at him but said nothing. David continued, "Don't you think that every time you blow on my neck or hug me so I can feel your entire body against mine, that I don't wish I could set aside mom and Amanda's feelings for just one second? What makes you always feel like you have to ask me this shit?" David asked. Alan stared into David's eyes.

"David, I . . ." Alan started but David cut him off.

"Alan, I don't want to hear your excuses anymore. I have my own too, and right now I wish I didn't but, it is what it is. I will never get over you completely, I know that. But I have to try. I have to try for Amanda and for mom. I love how you look at me and the things you say to me. But, Alan, I need things to even out. I really do." David said and looked down at the water ring his beer had formed on the table. Alan sighed and leaned closer to David.

"I'm sorry." Alan said. David shook his head.

"Alan, don't apologize. I'm the one that usually starts it. I think I'm madder at myself than you. But please, don't ever say you're jealous of Carman. Or anyone else for that matter. When it comes to you Alan, God. No one holds a candle." David said. Alan sighed and kicked David under the table. David looked up at him and Alan smiled.

"Can you shut up now?" Alan said. David giggled and gave Alan a funny look.

"What?" David asked.

"Shut up for just a second." Alan said. David smiled and shook his head. He sat silently staring at Alan. "If you say you want some normalcy, I'll give it to you. If you want me to continue flirting with you and playing our silly games, I will. I would do anything you asked of me David. Within reason, of course. But, please don't tell me not to be jealous. I'm not normally a jealous guy. I like the feeling. It's exciting to me. I always tell you that I know how you feel and you always argue with me. Don't argue David. I'm not the type of guy that wears their heart out on their sleeve or anything but, you've made me change in a lot of ways. I'm not mad that you helped Carman, I just thought you wouldn't. It's hard to explain." Alan said. David smiled and leaned close to Alan.

"I wouldn't have if you told me not to." David whispered. Alan rolled his eyes and shook his head.

"I couldn't do that." Alan said. David sighed and sat back in his chair. He could see the waitress coming with their meals. She set them down in front of them and Alan asked for two more beers. She smiled sweetly at them and hurried away. David smiled at Alan and Alan looked at him funny. "What?" Alan asked.

"I was thinking about the other night." David said. Alan giggled and cut into his steak.

"Ok, what about it?" Alan asked. David sighed and twirled his pasta on his fork. Alan waited as David neatly tied it to his fork and stuck it in his mouth. He chewed it and tapped his fork against his lips.

"Well," David said after he swallowed his bite. "Do you have any idea how close you were to getting laid?" David asked. Alan laughed and thanked the waitress who had come back with their beers.

"Why do you say that?" Alan asked. David rolled his eyes and shook his head. Alan giggled and took a sip from his beer. "Are we talking about the neck blowing and the straddling?" Alan asked. David giggled with a mouth full of pasta. He nodded and Alan smiled. "Well, I guess if the opportunity is ever to present its self to you like that again, you had better do something about it." Alan said. David smiled and pushed his chair back. Alan laughed and shook his head. "You're so bad." Alan said. David pulled his chair back in and looked at Alan.

"Your loss." He said. They talked and laughed over their meals and neither one of them brought up Carman and David's evening together again. When they were finished with their food and beer. David took the check from the waitress and Alan laughed.

"You know, if memory serves me correctly, you paid last time." Alan said. David shrugged.

"So? I'm paying again." David said and went up to the counter. Alan shook his head and went up with David. David paid and they went out to the car. They both lit a cigarette once they were inside.

"Hey, you said you wanted things to even out for you, what do you mean?" Alan asked as he started the car. David sighed and picked at his teeth with a tooth pick he had taken from the restaurant.

"Well, what I mean is not feeling torn between a bunch of people." David said. Alan nodded and turned onto David's street.

"Ok, how can I help to fix that?" Alan asked. David sighed and shook his head.

"Actually, you are the one person who shouldn't have to do anything."

"How come?" Alan asked. David looked at Alan and smiled.

"Because, you and Amanda were here first. It's everybody else that makes it hard." David said. Alan nodded and stopped the car at a red light.

"So, this is what I think." Alan said as he stared out at the light. "When we get to your place, I would like for you to explain how this all turned into a problem. I'll see what kind of insight I can shed on the whole thing after that." Alan said. The light turned green so he continued on. David nodded and sighed.

"You can't repeat anything." David said.

"I cross my heart." Alan answered.

Chapter 28

Alan and David walked into the apartment together and David sat down at the table while Alan poured them both a drink.

"Ok, you tell the story." Alan said. David took a deep breath and thought for a second. Alan finished pouring two tall drinks of rum and coke and sat down at the table with him. "So, why don't you start with moving to Portland? I know what happened before then." Alan said.

"Ok." David said and took a sip of his drink. "Well, I guess it started right away. I mean, ever since the time Carman and I had that kiss out at his place on spring break, there was always this weird sexual tension or something." David explained. Alan nodded and sipped his drink. David continued, "So, Amanda found this place after like, the first week we were here. When we went to go see it was when I first saw Seth. He was so hot. He reminded me of Gabe like almost instantly. So there was that. Plus I was working with Carman and that's when we started talking more about his fear of big men." David said. Alan lit a cigarette and handed it to David. David smiled and continued with his story. "Anyway, I felt bad for him because he told me about the guys that he had ended relationships with or whatever because they didn't fall into the seven inches or smaller rule." David said and took a puff of his cigarette. Alan nodded and took another sip of his drink. "That's about when we first started talking to Jake. Well, I guess he like, literally ran into him at the store and they got talking. Carman, being Carman, was checking him out like the whole time and decided he had to be bigger than seven inches or something. That's when we started talking about it more and we ended up kissing and stuff a lot more than usual." David said and raised an eyebrow. Alan smiled but said nothing. David continued, "So, while all this is going on, I'm getting to know Seth a little better. He was like a breath of fresh sir at first until his graduation. He called me to come pick him up cause he was too drunk to get himself home. I went and picked him up and took him to Lance's place. Well, all the way there and until I left, he was begging me to kiss him or something. He was fairly convincing too but I never gave in. Shortly after that he told me there was a little truth in what he was saying that night. Well that kind of changed everything because I was in the process of deciding if I wanted to propose to Amanda before or after the baby was born. I decided to do it for her birthday, as you know, and Seth asked to come help me pick out a ring. Well, he did and that day after I bought her ring and we were leaving, I kind of tried to explain how I was feeling about you, Amanda, Carman and him. Well, he didn't like being on the list of people who string me along and don't do anything about it so he kissed me." David said. Alan sighed and rolled his eyes.

"I string you along?" Alan asked. David sighed and raised his eyebrows. "You made me promise." Alan said in his defense.

"Just listen." David said. Alan nodded and took another sip from his drink. "Anyway, so this kiss was really cool but it seemed to make things worse cause his playful, desensitizing flirting now had something to back it up. And on top of all this stuff, Amanda was pregnant and I was trying to rebuild something with you. Now it feels like it's really fucked up because you're really laying it on thick, I have a pretty good idea that Seth isn't going to lay off. Amanda and I are getting married and Lance now thinks we're gonna fuck. I'm telling you, I feel really strung apart." David said. Alan nodded and thought for a second.

"Well," He said, "Carman has Jake now so that should be off the list." He said. David nodded and sipped at his drink. "Ok, Seth well, I think we'll have to just see how that plays out. Lance is your fault but I think your plan around it should work. Me, well . . ." Alan stopped and David looked into his eyes. "I hate to say this but, I wouldn't just string you along if I didn't have to." Alan said.

"Why do you hate to say that?" David asked.

"Well, I would like to take myself off the list. I just don't know how to." Alan said. David sighed and shook his head.

"You are off the list in a sense Alan. You're with mom. I'm with Amanda, in all in tense of purposes, you should be off the list." David said.

"Then why aren't I?" Alan asked. David sighed and shook his head.

"I like you there I think." David said quietly. Alan sighed and tapped the side of his glass with his fingernails.

"Well, you shouldn't keep me there David. As much as I love being there, it's too hard on you. And I guess what I do does string you along and that's not fair." Alan said. David sighed and shook his head.

"I'm used to *you* doing it. You did it before you even knew you were doing it. The problem is, god, I don't even know what the problem is." David said and looked down at his glass.

"I think I know what it is." Alan said. David looked up at him and sighed.

"Ok, what is it?" David asked.

"I think you never worried about it when Amanda was ok with you being with guys. I think that now she doesn't want you to be, you feel like it's worse. Because you can't, you know?" Alan asked. David thought about it for a second. "And, all these guys you're mentioning know you promised Amanda you wouldn't so that's what the real kicker is. Their almost doing it on purpose." Alan said and smiled. David rolled his eyes and shook his head.

"Why would they do that?" David asked.

"Cause it's easier to get a reaction from someone who has guilt backing them then someone who doesn't." Alan answered. David sighed again and took another sip from his drink. Alan did the same and smiled at David. "You're a good looking kid David, it would be a lot stranger if they didn't hit on you like they do." Alan added. David smiled and shook his head.

"Nice Alan."

"What? I'm serious." Alan said. David sighed and itched the side of his neck.

"Can I ask you something?"

"Shoot." Alan said.

"Well, if you liked guys back in collage and you had that kiss with Carman, why not do anything else with him?" David asked. Alan sighed and shook his head.

"He was too scared to. I didn't ever press the issue like you did, but after that, I just never really thought about it I guess."

"Why not?" David asked.

"Well, I think it was because I thought I would never find anyone else that did for me what Carman did. I always told him that it would take a pretty special guy to turn my head again. I mean, he always said he wanted me and all that but, when it came down to brass tax, he was too afraid." Alan said. David cleared his throat and took a sip of his drink.

"Are you jealous not because I was with Carman but, maybe because he was with me instead of you?" David asked. Alan thought about it.

"I think it's a little of both. Mostly because of you but I think there might be a little of the other in there as well." Alan said. David smiled and shook his head.

"That's weird Alan." They both laughed and finished their drinks. Alan talked to Nancy on the phone while David put their glasses in the sink and put the pop and booze away. She had said that all the paper work had been signed and she and Seth would head out in the morning. Alan updated her on Amanda and then they said their good byes. David smiled as Alan stood up and his knees cracked. "You're getting old." David teased and Alan laughed.

"I still got it where it counts." Alan said and smiled. David laughed and shook his head.

"I bet you do." He said. Alan smiled and walked over to stand close to David. He stopped right in front of him and sighed.

"Wouldn't you like to know." Alan whispered. David smiled and put his hands on Alan's hips. Alan giggled and hugged David. "You're so funny." Alan whispered. David sighed and rested his head on Alan's shoulder.

"Will you still be with me when mom is gone?" David asked quietly. Alan rubbed David's back.

"Of course I will. I'm not ever going anywhere David." Alan whispered. David nodded and closed his eyes.

"That's good, I can't lose both of you." David said. Alan hugged David tighter and took a deep breath.

"You won't. I promise." Alan whispered. David rubbed Alan's back and smelled his cologne.

"I wish I could sleep standing up." David said. Alan laughed and let David go. He looked into his eyes and sighed.

"Well, I would love to sleep with you but I think that would be a bad idea." Alan said. David giggled and nodded.

"It certainly is." David said and stepped back from Alan. Alan smiled and shook his head. "Hey, by the way, how long *did* you lay there that morning in Vegas?" David asked. Alan giggled and led David to the master bedroom door.

"Well, a while." Alan said. David sighed and shook his head.

"I thought we were passed vague." David said. Alan smiled and scratched the back of his head.

"You would yell at me if I told you." Alan said.

"I promise I won't."

"Ok, well. I would say about . . . two hours." Alan guessed. David blushed and Alan smiled. "It was a learning experience I'll tell you that." Alan added. David shook his head and opened his bedroom door.

"You have no idea how embarrassing that whole thing was." David said. Alan smiled and patted David's back.

"Not for me it wasn't." He said. David rolled his eyes and Alan laughed. "For the record, it was really nice to lay there with you all horny and stuff." Alan said. David sighed and blushed a little deeper red.

"Good night Alan." He said and Alan smiled.

"Good night David."

David woke up on November 14th to the feel of a hand on his side. He opened his eyes and saw Alan sitting on the side of his bed. He was already showered and dressed. He was wearing a light colored pair of blue jeans and a shirt that clung to his beautiful frame. David smiled and stretched. He rolled over onto his back and Alan let his hand slide on David's side to his chest. David looked at Alan's hand and sighed.

"Good Morning." Alan said. He took his hand away and David giggled.

"Good morning. How long have you been sitting there?" David asked and propped himself up of his elbows.

"About two minutes." Alan said. David smiled and looked at the clock. It was 8:45. David yawned and looked back at Alan.

"So, just out of curiosity, how do you feel about morning sex?" David asked. Alan giggled and shook his head.

"I like it I guess." Alan said. David nodded and sat up.

"Good to know." David said. Alan smiled and stood up.

"Well, I like it better when it's my idea." Alan said. David swung his legs over the edge of the bed and brushed his hands through his hair.

"Me too." David said. Alan walked over to the door and stopped. He turned to David and smiled.

"Who's idea is it this morning?" Alan asked. David giggled and looked down.

"Mine." He said. Alan laughed and left the room. David got up and went to the bathroom. He got ready for his day and when he felt that he was satisfied with how he looked, he went out to the kitchen and joined Alan at the table. Mike was on the living room floor watching T.V. "When did he get here?" David asked.

"Um, 7:00 or so. Carman dropped him off on his way to work."

"When did you get up?" David asked.

"6:30." Alan answered. David raised his eyebrows and sighed. Alan smiled and got them both a cup of coffee. They sat drinking their coffee and talking about cars and Alan's plan to start looking for another one to restore. When they finished their coffees, they loaded Mike into the car and headed to the hospital. Alan stopped by a coffee shop and got himself and David a coffee and grabbed one for Amanda too. They got to the hospital at ten o'clock. They went into Amanda's room and she looked up at them and smiled.

"Good morning guys." She said and Mike got on to the bed with her.

"Good Morning." David and Alan said at the same time. Amanda giggled at them. Alan sat in the chair and David sat on the bed with Amanda and Mike.

"I talked to Nancy and she said they will be here by noon or one." Amanda said excitedly. David smiled and rubbed her stomach.

"How did she talk him into leaving so soon?" Alan asked. David laughed and looked at Alan.

"She can be very convincing." David said. Alan and Amanda laughed. Suddenly she took in a deep breath and both her hands went to her stomach. "Amanda, what's wrong?" David asked. Alan stood and went to her side as well.

"Uh, this started yesterday. It just feels so tight." Amanda said.

"Why didn't you tell me this yesterday?" David asked.

"Oh, David. It's nothing. The doctor said its normal when their stopping a pregnancy for so long. But he thinks I won't keep him in for much longer." Amanda explained.

"Do you need anything?" Alan asked. Amanda shook her head and smiled. David smiled at Alan and Alan rested his hand on David's shoulder.

"Did the doctor give you a time limit or anything?" David asked. Amanda giggled and ran her hand along the side of David's face.

"No, there's no time limit babe." Amanda said and smiled. David closed his eyes and kissed her hand as it went passed his mouth. Amanda giggled and put her hand back on her stomach.

"Are you sure you're ok?" David asked. He could feel Alan rub his thumb on his shoulder. David smiled to himself but Amanda smiled at him.

"Yes, I'm ok." Amanda said. David sighed and leaned over to kiss her. She giggled when he pulled away and he smiled. Alan sat back down in his chair and Mike poked David's ribs. David jumped and looked at him making Mike laugh.

"Cartoons?" Mike asked. David giggled and grabbed the remote. He found the cartoon with the little dog on it and Mike cheered. Everyone laughed and Mike clapped.

"So, I noticed in the car that there wasn't an infant car seat." Alan said. Amanda giggled and looked at David.

"Yea, I know. I better get one of those." David said. Alan smiled and shook his head.

"For a couple of fairly responsible kids, no car seat is kind of a surprise." Alan said. David sighed and looked at Alan.

"I'll get one today." David said. Alan giggled and shook his head.

"You answered me like I was giving you shit." Alan said. David and Amanda laughed. "I don't do the daddy thing very well, huh?" Alan asked. David and Amanda laughed again.

"Oh dad, you're doing great." David said. Alan rolled his eyes and Amanda laughed. They all laughed and talked until noon. Amanda's lunch came so David and Alan decided to take Mike down stairs to the cafeteria to find something to eat. They picked out a couple sandwiches and some muffins. Alan paid for them and they took their meal up to Amanda's room and ate with her.

"Did you bring a muffin up for me?" Amanda asked. Mike giggled and handed her a chocolate chip muffin and chocolate milk. "Oh, chocolate. I love you." Amanda said and kissed Mike. David and Alan laughed.

"You know, they say that chocolate is an aphrodisiac." Alan said. David giggled and looked at him. Amanda laughed at the look on David's face and hid her muffin under her crossword puzzle book.

"I don't think you need any." Amanda said. David and Alan laughed. They finished their meals and David put Amanda's dishes and all the little pieces of plastic wrap that their sandwiches had come in on the cart in the hall way. While he was out, he saw Seth and his mom come in. She smiled at him and he quickly walked over to them. He hugged his mom and she laughed.

"I think you barley made it. The doctor says they can't keep him in there for long." David said as they hugged. Nancy giggled and kissed David on the cheek. She rushed into the room and David grabbed Seth. Seth laughed as David hugged him. "Thanks for helping my mom." He said. Seth smiled and tightened his hold on David.

"It was my pleasure, David." Seth said. David pulled away and smiled at his friend. Seth giggled and shook his head. "Did you miss me or what?" Seth asked. David laughed and led Seth to the room. They all talked with Amanda and Nancy giggled and cried when Amanda told her about the letter from Beth. Mike started getting cranky at around 2:00, so Seth took him back to David's for a nap.

"He was so helpful." Nancy said talking about Seth. David smiled and shook his head.

"He is a good kid, isn't he?" Alan asked. David looked at Alan and smiled. Alan winked at him and turned his attention back to the puzzle he was helping Amanda with. "Do they get harder as the book go's on or what?" Alan asked. Nancy giggled and took the book from him. She read over the question he pointed out and rolled her eyes. She handed the book back and sighed.

"Professor." She said and David laughed. Alan rolled his eyes and wrote it in. They talked about the baby and the condo and everything Amanda felt like Nancy missed. When Alan got frustrated with the crossword puzzle he was working on, he tossed it aside and looked at David.

"Let's go have a smoke." David smiled and stood up. He kissed Amanda and his mom and followed Alan out. They went out to the picnic table and sat down. They both lit a cigarette at the same time and Alan looked deep into David's eyes. It kind of surprised David and he giggled.

"What?" David asked. Alan sighed and shook his head.

"Your gonna have a baby and get married and all that stuff." Alan said. David smiled and nodded.

"That's the plan. Are you ok?" David asked. Alan shook his head and took a long drag from his cigarette.

"Yea, I'm just freaking out all of a sudden." Alan said. David giggled and patted the hand Alan had on the table.

"That's kind of funny Alan."

"Why?" Alan asked. David laughed and shook his head.

"Well, you're supposed to be the adult in this outfit, remember?"

"Oh, well I had a momentary fit of immaturity. I think I'm ok now." Alan said. David laughed and leaned back in his chair.

"Wanna explain it to me better?" David asked. Alan sighed and tapped the table with his fingers.

"Well, it just hit me. You are going to be even *more* unavailable than you are now." Alan said. David laughed again and shook his head.

"Oh my God Alan. Are you kidding?" David asked. Alan nodded and started laughing. They talked about Nancy and how she wasn't going to be working anymore so she would have all kinds of time to spend with David, Amanda and the new baby. When they finished, they went in and rejoined Amanda and Nancy. They were watching a talk show on Amanda's T.V.

"What did we miss?" Alan asked as he sat down on the chair. David climbed up on the bed and lay between Amanda and the wall. She smiled at him and cradled his head against her chest. Nancy giggled and looked at Alan.

"Well, they are interviewing this lady who used to be a truck driver and, I guess, she was abducted by aliens right out of her truck. She says the truck killed like, eight people or something while the aliens had her." Nancy explained. Alan shook his head and giggled.

"I miss you when you're gone." Amanda whispered in David's ear.

"Me too." David said and kissed her neck. Amanda giggled and held his hand.

"He hasn't moved for a while." She said. David sighed and rubbed her stomach. They lay silently with their hands holding Amanda's tummy while Nancy and Alan watched T.V. It was around 4:00 when Carman showed up.

"Hi guys." He said when he came in. David and Alan both said hello and Nancy hugged him. "How's the little mommy?" Carman asked. Amanda giggled and shook her head.

"I'm good. The doctor says it will be any day now." Amanda answered.

"Well, that's good. I hate waiting." Carman said and Everyone laughed. He came over and sat on the arm of Alan's chair. "Will you be delivering in here?" He asked.

"I don't think so. I think their gonna move me to some other delivery room thing."

"Well, they will probably want to have you in more sterile conditions, that's for sure." Nancy said looking at Carman's dirty shoes. Carman looked down at them and laughed.

"Yea, that's probably true." He said. David looked over at Alan and then at Carman. He thought it was funny that he had only known these two for just over a year. He felt like he had known them his whole life.

"What do you think Seth and Mike are up to?" Nancy asked. David giggled and shook his head.

"No good, I bet." He said. Carman and Alan laughed.

"He said he was taking him to our house. Why don't you call him? I would like to see Mike before he goes to bed." Amanda said to David. David smiled and took out his cell phone.

Are you ever coming back? He typed. He pressed send and smiled at Amanda.

"If he doesn't answer right away, I'll call the house." David said. Amanda nodded and smiled at Nancy.

"Did anyone tell you what we have decided to name him?" She asked. Nancy smiled and nodded.

"Gabriel Alan right?" Nancy asked. Amanda and Nancy giggled. David sighed and looked at Alan and Carman again.

"We should go have a smoke." David said. Carman and Alan looked at each other.

"Sure." Alan said. They got up and David carefully got off the bed.

"Don't forget to get hold of Seth for me." Amanda said.

"I won't, Babe." David kissed her and smiled at his mom. She smiled back and he joined Alan and Carman out in the hall way. They went out to their picnic table and all lit a cigarette. David took a drag from his just as his cell phone buzzed at him. He took it out and read the message.

Tell Alan to phone me. The message read. David giggled and showed the message to Alan.

"Wonder what he wants." Alan said. He took out his phone and dialed Seth's cell phone number. "Hi, what's up? . . . Oh, um. No you don't have to. Just bring it the way it is . . . well, she will soon . . . . Ok . . . No she wants to see Mike before bed time . . . I'm sure that will be fine . . . ok Seth . . . yup, bye." Alan hung up his phone and smiled at David. "He's on his way." Alan announced.

"Well, that's good." Carman said. David sighed and took another drag of his cigarette. "Did you have your talk with him yet?" Carman asked. David giggled and looked at Alan. Alan smiled and rolled his eyes.

"Well, I did. And I think the more pressing matter is the fact that Lance insists on being a dick. So I have managed to buy Seth some time to get all this figured out." David answered. Carman frowned and looked between Alan and David.

"I have known Lance for 100 years. How did you ever buy time with him?" Carman asked. Alan laughed and nudged David.

"Yea, David. How did you do that?" Alan asked. David laughed and looked at Carman.

"I told him that if he keeps his mouth shut for three whole months, I would fuck him." David said. Carman laughed and shook his head.

"Well, it's a pretty safe bet that Lance won't last that long." Carman said and laughed. Alan laughed now too and they all thought about the bet. They all made a guess at how long Lance would last before talking. When they were finished their cigarettes, they started heading back into the building. They reached the door when David heard Mike calling him. He stopped and seen Little Mike running up to him and Seth walking behind with a large box.

"They come in a box?" Alan asked. Seth giggled and nodded. Alan took the gift wrapped box and they all went in. "I said you didn't have to wrap it." Alan said to Seth as they walked to Amanda's room. Mike had already run ahead.

"I know, but presents are fun." Seth said. Alan smiled and shook his head. When they all got into Amanda's room, Seth set the box on the bed and handed Amanda a card.

"What's this?" She asked and opened the card. She read it out loud. "Dear Amanda, David and Baby." She read and giggled. "We are so proud of you and we love you very much. We hope we got the right color for you. Love Grandma and Grandpa." Amanda said. David giggled and brought the gift closer so Amanda could open it. "Help me open it." Amanda said to Mike. He squealed and tore at the paper. Amanda smiled and ran her fingers along the side of the box when she could see what was inside. She turned the box so David could see. Alan and Nancy had gotten them a car seat.

"Wow, cool Mom. Thanks Alan." David said. Nancy giggled and Alan smiled. He pulled a pocket knife out of his jacket and cut the tape off the top for Amanda. David put the box on the floor and pulled the seat out. It was mostly black with red seems. David raised his eyebrows and looked at Amanda.

"I love it." She said and Nancy sighed.

"Good, I was afraid it was too dark or something." Nancy said. David pulled out the instruction booklet and he, Carman and Alan looked it over. They all talked about the baby and how well the car seat matched the Hearse. When Amanda's supper arrived, they stayed and visited with her until she was finished and ready to sleep. It was about

7:30 when they all left. Seth had decided to take Mike to Lance's place so he could play with Mack. Carman decided to follow Alan, Nancy and David back to David's place for a drink. When they got there, Nancy put a frozen pizza in the oven and Carman poured all four of them a drink.

"So, mom. Did you bring more stuff with you? You are staying for a while right?" David asked.

"It's still in the car I think." Nancy said. Carman giggled and looked at David.

"Come on, we'll go down and get it." Carman said to David. David nodded and took a quick sip of his drink before getting up and following Carman down to the car. They managed to get all of Nancy's things up in one load. They set it all neatly in the music/Alan and Nancy's room. They rejoined Alan and Nancy and they visited through diner and a few hours afterward. When Nancy started yawning, they all decided it was time for bed. Carman told them he would be at the hospital after lunch the next day before he left. Nancy hugged David before going to bed.

"Good night." Nancy whispered and David smiled.

"Good night mom. Have a good sleep." He said. She let him go and smiled at him. Alan hugged David next.

"Good night." Alan said. David could smell Alan's cologne and it made his knees buckle. Alan noticed and giggled. "Easy tiger." Alan whispered. David laughed and stepped back from Alan.

"Good night." David said and they all went to their rooms. David undressed and got himself comfortable in bed. After the past week he had had, it didn't take long for him to fall asleep.

Chapter 29

November 15, 2006. 8:35 am. David woke up to the sound of the main bathroom shower. He sighed and sat up. He felt like he had hardly slept which was practically true.

Fucking nightmares. Wonder why I'm having them again? Nothing bad is happening or anything. Except for mom of course. David thought. He stretched and went into his bathroom. He took a look at himself in the mirror while he peed. When he finished, he washed his hands and shaved. He dug through his closet and found a nice pair of blue jeans and a gray t-shirt that said, 'If it's too loud, your too old.' He smiled at it and wondered what Alan would think of it. He hung them over his arm and went out to the kitchen in his robe. Carman and Nancy were sitting at the table drinking coffee.

"I thought you were going to see us at the hospital today." David said as he joined them.

"Well, the job I had for today cancelled on me so I thought I would come over and have coffee with your beautiful mother. Is that ok with you?" Carman asked. David giggled and nodded. He could hear the shower turn off and he looked down the hall.

"He still has to get dressed." Nancy said.

"Why?" David asked looking at her. Nancy and Carman laughed.

"You're so weird son." She said. David giggled and chatted with Nancy and Carman until Alan was finished with the bathroom. He walked out and David passed him in the hallway. He could smell Alan's cologne. It filled the air around him and the air in the bathroom.

"God, you smell good." David whispered. Alan smiled and winked at him. David quickly had his shower and finished getting ready for the day. When he was finished, he went out to the kitchen to rejoin with Nancy, Alan and Carman. Alan looked at him as he walked passed him to get a coffee.

"You smell good too." Alan whispered. David smiled and shook his head. He poured himself a coffee and sat at the table between Alan and Carman.

"So, I was thinking. Have you and Amanda talked about breast feeding?" Nancy asked. David looked at her with the straightest face he could muster up.

"Well, we have. And we have concluded that she is much better suited for it than I am." David answered. Everyone laughed and Nancy shook her head.

"That's not what I mean. Is she going to, or not?" Nancy asked. Alan and Carman were still both laughing.

"She said if she can, she will." David said. Nancy looked between Alan and Carman who were still giggling over David's comment.

"You know, it's no wonder he says the things he does. He has you two for role models." She said. Now David started laughing with them.

Nancy kept it together for quite some time before she started laughing too. "Ok, I was trying to be serious." Nancy said. The boys tried to stop laughing but they couldn't. She just shook her head and drank her coffee. It took them about ten minutes to finally settle down.

"Ok, are we going soon?" Alan asked. Nancy looked at him and raised an eyebrow.

"Do you think you can behave long enough to have a visit in the hospital with Amanda?" She asked. They all started laughing again but this time it didn't last as long. When they finished their coffees, they all went downstairs together. Alan and Nancy rode together in Alan's car and David and Carman rode together in Carman's truck.

"So, are you ready for this daddy thing?" Carman asked. David sighed and looked out the windshield at Alan's mustang.

"I better be. The doctor said he's coming." David answered. Carman smiled and nodded.

"I was thinking David. Have things changed with us?" Carman asked. David looked at him and frowned.

"What do you mean?"

"Well, you used to talk to me more than you do and we used to laugh and have fun together. I was wondering what happened."

"Carman. I still have fun with you. I didn't notice any big change except, now you're with Jake so there isn't any more kissing and stuff. Which, by the way, I do miss but completely understand." David said. Carman giggled and looked at him.

"You miss kissing me?" Carman asked.

"Oh yes." David said without hesitation. Carman smiled and seemed to cheer up a whole lot.

"Well, that's very nice of you to say David. Come to think of it, I kind of miss kissing you too." Carman said. David smirked and looked back out the windshield.

"Do you think things are better this way? I mean like, no contact with each other?" David asked. Carman sighed and turned the corner to head toward the hospital.

"Well, I think we are ok either way. Was it hard for you before?" Carman asked. David nodded and looked at Carman.

"I don't know why. But it was." David said. Carman smiled and patted David's leg.

"You'll see that it is better this way David. I'm too old for you anyway." Carman said teasingly. David laughed and shook his head.

"You certainly are." David said. They both laughed and talked about Jake for the few minutes that were left in their drive to the hospital. Carman parked right next to Alan's car and they all went in together. Amanda was watching a cooking show when they came in.

"Hi." Amanda said.

"Hi baby. How was your night?" David asked and went over to kiss her. She shook her head.

"Not good. I hardly slept at all. My stomach kept doing that tightening thing and my legs wouldn't quit cramping up. God I can't wait till this is over." She said. David winced and hugged her. Alan sat down in the chair and Carman brought two chairs into the room from the hall. Both Nancy and Carman sat in one of them. David sat on the bed and studied Amanda's face. She looked very tired and pale.

"Can I get you anything? You don't look very good." David asked. Amanda sighed and shook her head.

"The nurse took the drip off. The doctor says it's up to the baby now. If he doesn't come by next Friday, he said their going to induce me." Amanda said.

"Would you like a cup of coffee?" Nancy asked. Amanda's face lit up a little.

"Oh, Nancy if you don't mind. That would be great." Amanda said. Carman smiled and stood up.

"I'll come help you." He said. Nancy thanked him and they left the room.

"Would a couple more pillows help?" Alan asked and Amanda shrugged.

"I don't know." She said. He got up and went out of the room. "I like this." Amanda said. David giggled and shook his head.

"You don't look like your enjoying yourself." He said.

"No, I'm not. But I like everyone fussing over me." She said. David smiled and kissed her forehead.

"I love you." He said.

"I love you too baby. Are you getting along ok at home with your company?" She asked.

"Oh yea, it's been really good." David said. Amanda smiled and shut her eyes. "Are you tired?" David asked. Amanda nodded and David held her hand. Alan came in with another pillow and put it under Amanda's legs.

"OH, that's lots better." Amanda said. Alan smiled and sat back down in his chair.

"You look tired girl." Alan said. David smiled at him.

"I am." She said. Alan leaned forward in his chair and patted David's leg. David looked at him and he pointed to the hall way. David nodded and kissed Amanda. She smiled as he stood up.

"I'll be right back." David said. Amanda nodded and he followed Alan out of the room. Alan sat in a chair in the waiting room and David sat next to him. "What's up?" David asked. Alan sighed and leaned on the arm of the chair so he was closer to David.

"Your mom said something strange to me last night and I wanted to talk to you about it." Alan whispered. David frowned and looked at him.

"Ok, what?" David asked.

"She said you were having night mares a while back and she was concerned that you hadn't had any follow up sessions with a therapist." Alan said. David rolled his eyes and shook his head.

"It was nothing Alan. And as far as the follow up sessions, I didn't think I needed them. I'm fine. Back to my old self again." David said. Alan nodded and tapped the arm of the chair with his fingers.

"Are you sure?" Alan asked. David smiled and looked into Alan's eyes. He was leaned over so close that all David would have to do was tilt his head just right and Alan would be able to lean in and kiss him.

"I'm sure." David whispered. Alan smiled and closed his eyes for a second. He seemed to be wrestling with his mind. He leaned back and took a deep breath. David giggled and shook his head. "Are you ok?" David asked.

"I almost kissed you." Alan whispered. David could feel his stomach flip and his heart speed up.

"Really?" David asked with a squeak in his voice. Alan smiled and stood up.

"Really." Alan said. David could see Carman and his mom coming down the hall way with the coffees they had hunted down.

"She might be sleeping." David said. Nancy nodded and quietly stepped into her room. Carman joined David and Alan in the waiting room. They drank their coffees and talked about the cowboy that was breaking Carman's big mean horse Diablo. David laughed as Carman went on and on about the guys butt in the jeans he would wear. Alan thought it was funny too but had mentioned that they should have all the guys over to Carman's when he was there. Carman seemed horrified but agreed. Nancy had come out about a half hour later.

"She's asleep now. I think we should go and let her rest. I guess she didn't sleep well last night. I told her to phone David's cell when she woke up." Nancy said. They all agreed and headed out to their vehicles. They had decided to go to the little coffee shop and have a small breakfast. When they arrived they were happy to see that it wasn't busy. The waitress sat them down and they all ordered a coffee and a cinnamon bun. They talked about various things for the hour they were there. When they hadn't heard from Amanda yet, they decided to just go back to David's house and wait there. Nancy decided to lie down when they got there and David, Alan and Carman sat down and played crib for a while. It was 12:35 when David's cell phone rang.

"Hello?" David said.

"*Hello, Mr. Smith. This is Doctor Crowley. Its time son.*" The doctor said on the other end. David could feel all the color leave his face. He sat silent for a second until the doctor woke him up. "*David, are you there?*" He asked. David blinked his eyes and nodded.

"Yes, we're on our way." David said and hung up the phone. Alan and Carman were staring at him both ready to jump into action.

"Ok, its time." David said. Carman and Alan both smiled. Alan got up and went to get Nancy. She was ready to go before the guys were. They rushed down to their vehicles and hurried to the hospital. David was the first in the room. Amanda wasn't there. Nancy stopped at the nursing station and found out where she had been taken. Nancy led the way to delivery room 3. Amanda was lying on the bed and David rushed to her side.

"What's happening?" David asked. Amanda giggled and shook her head.

"Not too much yet, My water broke when I was sleeping so they brought me in here." She said. David pulled a tall stool type chair over to sit on. He sat down and held Amanda's hand.

"What do I do?" David asked. Carman and Alan giggled but Nancy just smiled.

"I don't think *you* do anything. Just stay right there." Amanda said. Nancy came over to her and kissed her forehead.

"Are you having contractions?" Nancy asked quietly.

"Yea, there not that bad though. Kind of like period cramps." Amanda answered. David sighed thinking of how bad Amanda's period cramps had sometime gotten.

"It will get worse." Nancy said and Amanda giggled.

"I know." She said. Alan and Carman went to stand next to David.

"Should we go get cigars or something?" Carman whispered to Alan. Everyone heard it though and laughed. Carman giggled and winked at Amanda. She smiled at him and then her eyes slammed shut and she moaned. She squeezed David's hand and he cringed but made no sound. It soon passed and she took a few deep breaths.

"You have to remember to breath hunny." Nancy said. Amanda nodded and looked at David.

"Are you ok?" David asked and Amanda nodded.

"It was more fun making him than it is having him." She said. Everyone giggled. Nancy smiled at Amanda and David. Carman cleared his throat and leaned in close to Amanda.

"You're the bravest person I've ever met." He said. Amanda laughed and kissed Carman on the cheek.

"Tell me that when my contractions are a minute apart." She said. Carman laughed and stepped back.

"I won't be here for that. Well, not in the room anyway. It's almost too much for me already." Carman said. Just then, Amanda had another contraction.

"Breath Amanda." Nancy said quietly. Amanda did as she was told and soon the contraction was over. David took his hand away and opened and closed his fist a few times. Alan laughed and Carman shivered. David took Amanda's hand back and she smiled. Carman took a couple deep breaths and Alan patted his back.

"You can always sit in the waiting room." Alan said. Carman nodded and smiled at Amanda.

"It's ok, Carman. I have a job for you anyway." She said.

"Ok." Carman said sheepishly. Amanda smiled and shook her head.

"I need you to call Seth and let him know what's happening. He still has Mike, doesn't he?" She asked. Carman nodded and stepped out of the room.

"What a marshmallow." David said. Alan laughed and shook his head.

"He doesn't do well with pain." Alan said. Amanda giggled and looked at Nancy.

"How long did it take for you to have David?" She asked and Nancy smiled.

"Fifteen hours."

"Oh my god." Amanda said and closed her eyes. David and Alan giggled.

"You were built for this babe. You can do it." David said. Amanda laughed and looked at him.

"Next time, you get to do it." She said. Nancy and Alan laughed. David leaned in and kissed her.

"I would love to." He whispered. Carman peeked his head in with his cell phone up to his ear.

"Do you want him to bring Mike to see you before any real labor starts?" He asked. Amanda giggled and nodded.

"That's a good idea." She said. He disappeared out the door again and Alan smiled.

"I'm gonna go make sure he's ok. I'll be back in a bit." Alan said. Nancy smiled at him and he left the room. David stared at Amanda's face.

"You're so pretty right now." He said. Amanda rolled her eyes and squeezed his hand.

"Thanks." She said sarcastically. Nancy giggled and rubbed Amanda's arm.

"Have they checked your dilation yet?" Nancy asked.

"Yea, when I first got in here they did. They said I was 2 ½. Centimeters." Amanda answered. Nancy nodded and looked at the fetal monitor.

"He looks good." Nancy said sweetly. Amanda nodded and smiled at David.

"What's that noise?" David asked. Nancy smiled and turned the volume up on the monitor.

"That's your baby's heart." Nancy said. David closed his eyes and listened to the thump, thump, thump the monitor made. He smiled and squeezed Amanda's hand and she giggled.

"I love you." She said. David opened his eyes and looked at her.

"I love you to." He said. Amanda was struck by another contraction and Nancy checked the time. She coached Amanda's breathing until the contraction was over.

"Eight minutes." Nancy said. Amanda nodded and took a few deep breaths.

"Are you ok?" David asked quietly. Amanda smiled and nodded. They all sat quietly and Nancy seemed to stare at the clock counting the minutes. She did this for every contraction until they were five minutes apart. It took about two hours. Amanda took a few deep breaths and looked at David.

"Where are Seth and Mike?" She asked. David shrugged and looked at his Mom.

"I'll go find out." She said and left the room. Amanda looked at David and tears fell from her eyes.

"This hurts so bad." She said. David kissed her forehead and nodded.

"What can I do?" David asked. Amanda shook her head and closed her eyes.

"I don't know." Just then, Alan came in with Mike. He seemed a little scared when he saw Amanda in her current state. "Hi Mikey." She said as sweetly as she could manage.

"HI." He said. Alan picked him up and brought him over to the bed. "Is he coming out?" Mike asked.

"He's trying to." Amanda whispered.

"Does it hurt?" Mike asked. Amanda smiled and nodded.

"It hurts a lot." She answered. Just then another contraction hit and Alan stepped back. Amanda clenched her fists on the bed sheets and concentrated on her breathing. When it was over, she fell back on her pillow and heaved. "God this is terrible." She said. Mike had tears in his eyes.

"Amanda, are you ok?" He asked. Amanda looked at him and smiled.

"I would be if I got a kiss." She said. Alan brought him close to her and he kissed her on the cheek.

"All better?" He asked.

"All better." Amanda answered. Nancy came in and told Alan that the nurses had found Mike some toys to play with. He took Mike out of the room and Nancy took his place next to the bed.

"How are you doing?" Nancy asked. Amanda nodded and stared at David. Soon, another contraction came. Amanda sat straight up and moaned in pain. She pulled on the sheets as beads of sweat poured from her face. When it was over she fell back on the bed again. She took a few deep breaths and then looked at David.

"How long was that?" She asked. David looked up at the clock.

"Like 4 ½ minutes." He said. Amanda nodded and closed her eyes. A nurse came in and put on some gloves.

"Let's have a look at that cervix ok." She said. Amanda nodded and the woman lifted the sheet that covered Amanda up to her knees. "Ok, a little pressure." The nurse said as she felt the inside of Amanda. She smiled and pulled her fingers out and took the gloves off. "You were born to do this sweet heart. You're already 6 centimeters dilated." She said. Amanda nodded and the nurse left the room.

"Good for you dear." Nancy said and rubbed Amanda's arm.

"How far does it have to go?" David asked. Nancy smiled at him.

"It has to dilate to ten centimeters before she can start pushing." She said. David raised his eyebrows.

"Think it will go back after?" He asked. Amanda laughed and slapped his shoulder.

"You dink." She said playfully. Just then, Seth came in.

"Hi, how are you doing?" He asked. Amanda smiled and tilted her head to look at him.

"Well, I'm having a baby. How are you doing?" She asked. Seth giggled and came over to the bed. He 'd her hand and looked at David.

"Why aren't you holding her hand?" Seth asked. David looked up at the clock and smiled.

"You'll see." He said. Seth frowned at him then all of a sudden he could feel bones crack in his hand as Amanda squeezed it with the strength of six men. He dropped to his knees and his eyes rolled back. She moaned with every breath she took. As did Seth. Her face turned red as the contraction pained her. When it was over and she let go of his hand. He rolled over into the fetal position on the floor holding his hand.

"Oh god Seth. I'm sorry." Amanda panted. Seth slowly stood up with help from Nancy and she looked at his hand.

"It's ok." Seth said. Nancy giggled and shook her head.

"Go to emergency and have them x-ray that hand." She said. Seth nodded and kissed Amanda on the cheek and said good luck before he left.

"Did I hurt him?" She asked. Nancy rubbed her arm and smiled.

"You may have broken a finger for him." Nancy said.

"Oh god. Is he ok?" She asked. David ran his hand through her hair and she looked at him.

"Don't worry. He'll be ok." David said. She nodded and closed her eyes. David giggled and his mom scowled at him. "What?" David asked.

"You could have warned him." She whispered. David and Amanda both laughed. Nancy spent the next four hours counting the minutes down between each contraction.

"How long has it been?" Amanda asked in a tired worn out voice.

"All together, about six or seven hours." Nancy said. She had gotten tired and David had found another chair for her. Alan would periodically poke his head in to see how things were going. It was 7:00 pm when the nurse came in.

"Ok, let's see how we're doing." She said. She checked Amanda's cervix and raised her eyebrows. "Have you had the urge to push yet?" She asked. Amanda nodded and the nurse smiled.

"Well, he's crowning so just wait till the doctor gets in here to catch him." She said and hurried out of the room. Nancy smiled and rubbed Amanda's arm again. Alan peeked his head in.

"Are we having a baby now?" He asked.

"As soon as the doctor gets here." Nancy said. David stared at Amanda's pale white face.

"Are you ok?" David asked. Amanda moaned and sat straight up again with another contraction. They had been coming one right after the other for quite some time. David winced and rubbed her back while she tried to breath. She fell back against the bed and looked at Nancy.

"It's coming." She panted. Nancy went to the foot of the bed and checked. She looked at the hallway and waved someone over. Seth came to the door.

"Go find any one in a hospital uniform right now." She said. Seth nodded and hurried away. "Ok, Amanda, hunny, don't push, ok. No matter what, don't push." Nancy said in an even tone. Amanda nodded and did her best to resist the urge to push. David looked at his mom.

"What's going on?" David asked. Nancy sighed and shook her head.

"She's going to have this baby on the fucking doctor's coffee break." Nancy said still checking the hall for a doctor. Soon, Doctor Crowley stepped into the room with two nurses and pulled a short stool to the end of the bed.

"Ok Amanda, are you ready to have a baby?" He asked. Amanda nodded and sat straight up with another contraction. "Ok good. Try to count to ten before you stop pushing." The doctor said. David rubbed her back and counted for her. She fell back against the bed with sweat flowing from her forehead.

"I hate you right now." She whispered to David.

"I know, I'm sorry." He said in a panicked voice.

"Ok, Let's do it again." Doctor Crowley said. Amanda sat herself up and pushed as hard as she could. David rubbed her back as he watched the muscles in her jaw clamp and grind. Her whole body shook while she pushed. When Nancy had counted to ten. Amanda fell back and panted. "Good job. You can rest for a second dear." Doctor Crowley said. She breathed heavy and wiped the sweat off her brow with the back of her hand. "Ok Whenever you're ready, I need to see two good ten second pushes ok?" The doctor said. Amanda nodded and seemed almost unable to sit up. David helped her and rubbed her back as Nancy counted. After six seconds, Amanda fell back on the bed and moaned.

"Come on babe. Ten seconds." David said quietly.

"I can't." Amanda said and closed her eyes. She sat back up and pushed again. This time she managed to do the whole ten seconds and Doctor Crowley let her have another rest.

"Well, we're almost there. One good push like that one and we'll have his head out, ok." He said. Amanda nodded and sat up to push again. The nurses in the room got some towels and things ready while Nancy counted to ten. When Amanda fell back on the bed, the Doctor looked at David and then at Nancy. "I need you guys to leave the room please." He said. David looked at him and shook his head.

"Why? I'm not leaving her to do this alone." David said. The Doctor sighed and looked at Nancy.

"Son, we are going to have to bring a bit more equipment in here than usual and we'll need the room." Doctor Crowley said. David looked at Amanda. She was breathing very quickly. She opened her eyes and looked at him.

"It's ok. I'll be ok. Please listen to the doctor." She said. David kissed her and looked at the doctor. One of the nurses came in with a few strange instruments and a few monitors. David walked around the bed and joined his mother.

"I can't leave." David said. Nancy hugged him with one arm and took him to the corner of the room.

"We'll stand here then son." David could see everything that was happening. The doctor put his hand on Amanda's stomach which seemed to move the baby around a little bit. Amanda moaned and the doctor told her to push. She did and the baby's head came out. David jumped and Nancy smiled. Amanda kept pushing and David could see the baby's shoulders. Amanda fell back on the bed and the shoulders went back inside. That's when a lot of blood poured from Amanda's vagina.

"Mom?" David said watching the blood pour out of her. The doctor looked at Nancy and she pulled David out of the room. A nurse closed the door behind them and David glared at her. "What are you doing? I have to be in there with her!" David yelled. Alan was beside him in a flash. Nancy shook and she started to cry. "Why would you pull me out of there?" David asked yelling at his mother. Alan put his arms around him and David fought him. Carman and Seth came over to them and Carman helped hold David.

"What's happening?" Seth asked Nancy.

"I'm not really sure. The baby was coming but there was too much blood. They asked us to leave." Nancy said through a panicked sob. Seth hugged her and stared at David. He stared at the door of the room Amanda was in. He could see the shadows of people setting up the equipment they had taken in to the room. He watched and shook in Alan and Carman's arms.

"Why can't I be in there with her?" David asked. Nancy went over to him and put her hands on his face.

"I promise to find out ok. You need to stay out here with Alan and Carman. Promise me you'll stay out here." Nancy said. David glared at her but nodded. Nancy knocked on the door. A young nurse came and opened the door. Nancy told them who she was and where she used to work and they let her in the room.

"Damn it! She can't just ask and come say something!" David yelled. Alan held him and David kicked Carman in the leg. Carman winced.

"Hey! Calm the fuck down. You're acting crazy. That's why you can't be in there right now. Your mom will find out and she'll let us know." Alan said. David slowly relaxed in Alan's arms. "Can I let you go?" Alan asked. David sighed and nodded. He paced back and forth waiting for his mother to come out of the room. Alan managed to convince him to sit down in a chair. He stared at the door. Carman and Alan sat on either side of him. David looked at Carman and sighed.

"I'm sorry I kicked you." He whispered.

"It's ok. I would have done the same thing." Carman said. They all sat silently waiting. Suddenly the door flew open and a nurse ran out of the room. David stood up and looked inside. Nancy and another nurse were blocking his view so he couldn't see. All the monitors where going off and making a lot of noise. The nurse who had run out of the room came running back with a white computer looking thing on a big cart. David watched her as she turned it to take it into the room. That's when he saw the paddles of the defibrillator . . .